NETANYAHU

~ A NOVEL ~

NETANYAHU

~ A NOVEL ~

#1 *NEW YORK TIMES* BESTSELLING AUTHOR

MIKE EVANS

P.O. BOX 30000, PHOENIX, AZ 85046

Netanyahu

Copyright 2016 by Time Worthy Books
P. O. Box 30000
Phoenix, AZ 85046

Design: Peter Gloege | LOOK Design Studio

Hardcover: 978-1-62961-119-8
Paperback: 978-1-62961-120-4
   Canada: 978-1-62961-121-1

This book is dedicated to

Benjamin Netanyahu.

In his office is a signet ring discovered
next to the Western Wall in Jerusalem.
It dates back about 2,800 years ago,
two hundred years following King David's
transformation of Jerusalem into
Israel's capital city. The ring bears the symbol
of a Jewish official; engraved on it
in Hebrew is his name: Netanyahu.
Netanyahu Ben-Yoash.

NETANYAHU

A COLD WIND HOWLED around the corners of the building and rumbled across the eaves but Ben-Zion Lurie paid it no attention. Seated at his desk, his head was bent over an ancient Torah scroll. Lurie's eyes were focused on the text, his mind on Jerusalem and the days of the Ancients when the words he read were first committed to paper more than two thousand years earlier.

As the wind continued to blow outside, a draft swept through the room. Lurie gathered his cloak tighter around his body and tucked his hands beneath the folds of the fabric, giving them the benefit of a moment's warmth before extracting them again to jot a note on the pad that lay in his lap or to wind the spindle and advance the scroll as he read.

It was the winter of 1878, in the city of Lodz, today a metropolitan area in Poland. Back then, it was part of the Russian Empire and situated in the northwestern section of a region known as the Pale of Settlement, a zone that stretched northward from Odessa at the Black Sea and spread to the west, reaching as far as the Prussian border. It was the only portion of the Russian Empire in which Jews could legally live as permanent residents and, as a result, was home to more than four million kinsmen. Ben-Zion Lurie served the Jews of Lodz as a rabbi at the Beth Jacob Synagogue.

About mid-morning, the sound of shuffling feet caught Lurie's attention and he looked up to see an elderly man standing in the doorway. His long white hair hung in strands from beneath his kippah and he had a full gray beard that reached to his chest. He was disheveled, and poorly kept, but Lurie recognized him at once as Judah Alkalai, the Rabbi of Semlin. One of the most influential rabbis in all of Judaism, Alkalai was a man of impeccable reputation and one of the earliest advocates for Zionism—the return of the Jews to their historic homeland in Palestine.

Known as a strong and persistent advocate of the Jewish cause, Lurie was struck that day by how frail Alkalai appeared. His eyes were sunk deep into their sockets and ringed by dark circles. The skin along his cheekbones seemed thin and tightly stretched. Still, he was a man who commanded the deepest respect and Lurie pushed himself up from his chair.

"Rabbi Alkalai. It is an honor to receive you." Alkalai did not reply but came through the doorway and walked with halting steps toward Lurie's desk. As he drew nearer, Lurie was all but certain the man must be dying.

Alkalai collapsed in a chair opposite the desk, folded his robe around his legs and gathered it over his torso, then looked up at Lurie. "You are the heir of the House of David."

Lurie nodded slowly, unsure where the conversation was going. Of all the Jewish families in the world, the House of Lurie was the one remaining family with an indisputable, uncontestable, unbroken line of descent from David, King of Israel, to the present, but theirs had been no easy life.

Cast out of Palestine, first by the Romans then by the Arabs, family members were scattered far and wide across Europe, but in each successive generation they gathered to designate one of their members as the child of the promise, the family heir, the one through whom the Davidic line would continue. The one who would ascend to David's throne as king.

Lurie recalled the family ceremony in which he had received that title. His father and brothers in the room with relatives from Spain, Germany, France, and Russia—most of them men he'd never seen before. The robe and scepter they gave him. The way they knelt when he stood and bowed their heads when he passed. It had been an exhilarating moment, but no one in the family expected the Davidic Kingdom would ever again become a political reality.

"You are the Anointed One," Alkalai continued. "The one through whom the Promise of God passes to subsequent generations."

Lurie smiled. "The title has been largely honorific. Important to us but it has little meaning or influence outside our family."

Alkalai seemed unfazed. "The things that are meaningless to man are often the most important to God."

"I agree," Lurie replied with a hint of impatience. "But how may I be of service to you?"

The faintest glimpse of a smile flickered through Alkalai's eyes. "It is I who should ask that of you."

"Has something happened?"

"The time of fulfillment is drawing near," Alkalai answered.

Lurie was puzzled. "If you mean the return of the Davidic Kingdom as a political reality, I think we are a long way from that."

"Not so far as you think."

"And how so?"

Alkalai seemed to ignore the question and adjusted his position in the chair. "Before long, your wife will give birth to a daughter. You must name your daughter Sarah. When she is of age she will meet a man named Nathaniel. They will marry. And after two years, they will have a son." He reached into his bag and took out a signet ring which he held between the fingers of his right hand. "You must give this to your grandson." Alkalai leaned forward, his hand outstretched, and offered the ring to Lurie. "The Promise will go to him."

Lurie took the ring and studied it a moment. "There seems to be something written here," he said, pointing to the shoulder of the ring. "A phrase of some kind, I think."

Alkalai nodded. "Can you read it?"

Lurie squinted. "It says, 'Netanyahu Ben-Yoash.'" He glanced over at Alkalai. "That's someone's name. Netanyahu. Son of Yoash."

"That ring was the official seal of your ancestor, King David."

Lurie arched an eyebrow as he read the inscription once more. "Netanyahu. 'Yahweh has given.'" He looked up at Alkalai again. "They used to tell us it was an official's name but my father said it was a reference to David."

"Could be either, I suppose. But I think it's more likely an inscription to the king."

"Why do you have it?"

"It was in another line of your family," Alkalai explained.

"Yes," Lurie nodded. "Jacob's line. My great-great-uncle or something like that. He died before I was born. There was a dispute about who should have it and so they kept it. Which is why there was no ring when I was named."

"Yes, but things have changed and Jacob's family members have been at a loss to know who should have the ring. They passed it to me for safekeeping."

Lurie thought again. "Jacob had a child by a woman he met. Before he was married. Last I heard, his descendants were doing well."

"And that was the origin of the dispute," Alkalai added. "But now—"

"You mean, a question of his legitimacy and whether he should be counted as a family member."

"Yes, but that no longer matters," Alkalai explained. "His last male descendant died two months ago." Alkalai pushed himself up from the chair and stood. "And the dispute died with him. Their line of the family has come to an end and the promise has passed to you without reservation. Give the ring to your grandson. He will take his place among the Netanyahus—men given to us by Yahweh."

Lurie stood as well. "My grandson will become king?"

"That is not for us to say. We only know that he will be the child of the promise."

Lurie gestured with the ring. "Then what is he to do with this?"

"When the time comes, he will know what to do."

"You are certain of this?"

Alkalai turned toward the door. "The ring follows the promise," he said over his shoulder. "No one can stop it. No one can take it where it does not want to go."

✦ ✦ ✦

Meanwhile, about that same time in Istanbul, five men gathered in a nondescript three-story house situated at the end of a narrow alley not far from the bazaar. Barakat, Abdullah, and Talal from the house of Hassan, Musa and Idris from the house of Hussein.

Known collectively as the Al-khulafā' Ar-rāshidūn—the Rightly Guided Caliphs, or by the shorter version, the Rashidun—they were an obscure, all-but-unknown group of designated male descendants of the Muslim prophet Muhammad, who for twelve hundred years ruled Islam, imposing order across all factional lines, governing Sunni and Shia alike, as well as many smaller sects, keeping inter-Islamic hostility to a minimum and directing the worldwide spread of Islam by all allowable means.

As Ibrahim al-Kazem entered the room that day he found the caliphs seated in overstuffed chairs arranged in a semicircle. An empty wooden straight-backed chair positioned in their midst awaited him.

In his public job, Ibrahim was a commodities broker and commercial facilitator who represented Arab businesses in Istanbul to European interests in Odessa, assisting them in conducting trade in both directions up and down the Black Sea. Working between the parties, Ibrahim connected Turk and Arab interests to non-Arab merchants, bankers, and shippers in Russia and other major countries. His services provided a vital link between those operating under Islamic law and those operating under Western law and gave him unique and far-reaching relationships with influential people in both regions. Because of those relationships, he had been recruited by the caliphs to use his business position and the access it afforded to represent Rashidun priorities, acting as their facilitator in exerting Muslim influence in the West, particularly in the Russian Empire.

"We continue to hear reports about the Jews," Barakat began. "Particularly those living in Russia."

"They say many things," Ibrahim replied. "But thus far they have done very little but talk."

"But the subject of that talk is our point." Abdullah noted. "Their increased talk of Jewish nationalism is quite troubling to us."

"The Russians will never let them establish a state of their own."

"Perhaps not in Europe," Musa noted. "But in Palestine the Russians are impotent to do anything." His eyes bore in on Ibrahim. "And that is our concern."

"Well, I don't think—"

Talal interrupted. "We hear of men like Yitzchak Reines and Yehuda Berlin. These are serious men, right?"

"Yes," Ibrahim answered. "They are serious men."

"And you know of these men?"

"Yes," Ibrahim said once more. "Of course."

"And you do not think we have good reason to be concerned?"

"Reason," Ibrahim shrugged, "but as many wish to stay where they are as want to leave. Successful men. Well established where they are. Content to indulge in the lifestyle their success affords."

Barakat spoke up. "You have helped us establish ties to the Romanov family."

Ibrahim nodded. "Ties with key members of the ruling family in the Russian Empire."

"We feel that now it is the time to reap some reward from those relationships."

"And what would you like for me to do?"

"Curb Jewish ambition," Barakat explained. "Before it becomes a problem."

"It already is a problem," Talal suggested.

"Before it gets out of control," Barakat added.

"We can't have them trekking back to Palestine." A frown wrinkled Musa's forehead as he spoke. "That would be far too dangerous. Worse even than the Christian crusaders who pillaged the homes of our ancestors. If the Jews return to Palestine, they will never leave. They will re-establish a Jewish political state and be a thorn in our side until the end of the age."

"And flaunt their Jewish practices," someone said.

"Desecrate the Holy Mount," Talal added.

"Our people are living there now," Barakat said, attempting to move the conversation forward. "But we have not enough people to exert control over the entire region. And the Sultans here in Istanbul are weak."

"Turks," someone grumbled. "We never should have trusted those non-Arab interlopers."

Barakat looked over at Ibrahim. "You have contacts with organizations loyal to the czar? Beyond members of the royal family?"

"Yes," Ibrahim replied. "Several. We have discussed this many times."

"And those organizations are prepared to increase their activities against the Jews?"

"Waiting for the opportunity."

"Good. We would like for you to give them that opportunity."

"Should I—"

Barakat cut him off. "We do not want to know the details. How you accomplish the goal will be up to you." He folded his hands in his lap and leaned forward. "But we very much want to see results. You understand us?"

Ibrahim nodded. "I understand."

NET∧NYAHU

A FEW WEEKS LATER, Zvi Mileikowsky walked with his wife, Liba, on a street in Kreva, a town located northwest of Minsk, in an area now known as Belarus. Then, it was part of the Pale of Settlement. The day was cold—but not freezing—and there was a hint of spring in the air, with a clear, cobalt blue sky overhead. It was a day that drew Zvi's mind toward the months ahead, when the weather would turn warm and plants would begin to grow again.

Zvi always noticed the weather; it was one of the things family members came to expect of him. A watchful eye toward the horizon in the morning and again at night. A note about the wind and a knack for sensing changes in seasons well ahead of the calendar date. Something many found quite odd for one trained and educated as a rabbi and serving the local synagogue—until they learned about the farm outside town where he grew wheat as the family's primary source of income. And then it all made sense. Farmers, by nature, are keen on the weather.

After a moment to scan the sky, Zvi turned his attention again to Liba, his young wife of twenty-something. She was pregnant with their first child and Zvi couldn't be prouder. As their eyes met that afternoon he flashed a boastful smile. "Our child," he beamed and glanced downward toward her belly.

"Shhh," she said with a twinkle in her eye. "We mustn't talk about it in public."

"Having a baby is nothing to be ashamed of."

"I'm not ashamed. I'm just a private person."

"And I am happy."

"You want a boy."

"I want a healthy child," he corrected. Then once again a grin spread over his face and he cut his eyes playfully in her direction. "But every man secretly hopes for a boy."

As they continued past the shops and stores, they came upon a group of men gathered in the lee of a hardware store. They stood just far enough back from the sidewalk as to not obstruct passersby, but close enough to hear and be heard. From the sound of their accent and the tone of their skin, Zvi was sure they were Ukrainian Russians. He studied them a moment, then looked away, his gaze falling on the sidewalk ahead of them as he squeezed Liba's hand tighter and picked up his pace.

From the corner of his eye, he saw the men leering at her. Whispering, pointing, and sneering in the lurid way gentiles seemed to reserve only for Jews. Then one of them—a young one with short hair and a black cap—shouted an anti-Semitic slur. The others laughed and one or two of them joined in.

Liba glanced up at Zvi, her eyes alert. "Are we about to have trouble?"

"I hope not." He gave her arm a tug forward. "Come on."

As Zvi spoke, he slipped his free hand into the pocket of his jacket and wrapped his fingers around the grip of a pistol. Liba noticed the movement of his arm and the bulge in his coat. Her eyes widened even more, this time on the verge of panic. "What do you have in your pocket?"

"Nothing."

"It's not nothing." She looked up at him once more and lowered her voice. "Is that a pistol?"

"Don't worry about it," he responded. "Just keep moving."

"You know that's illegal."

He didn't reply.

"They'll arrest you if they find it."

"They won't find it."

"This baby is not having a prison inmate for a father."

"This baby will have *me* for a father," Zvi assured. "Just keep moving."

Zvi didn't know the names of the men standing in the alley, but he had seen them around. Heard them talking. And he knew their kind. They all were members of the Holy Brigade, a band of Russians who claimed to be loyal to the Romanov monarchy, orthodoxy, and the Russian homeland. In reality, they were a group of thugs who were responsible for the latest rise of Jewish persecution. For the past two years their many units, located in towns and villages all across the Russian Empire, conducted pogroms in Jewish neighborhoods, burning homes, businesses, and synagogues. Slaughtering thousands in the process, much of it with the czar's approval. Some of it directly instigated by agencies of the Russian empirical government.

From the time the heckling started, Zvi and Liba had walked to the far corner of the hardware store. Behind them, the men in the alley no longer shouted but they continued to talk and though he couldn't distinguish individual voices, Zvi knew what they were saying. He'd heard them before and he was certain now they were chortling to themselves. "Pregnant Jews are a prize. Kill her now and we kill the child also. Stifle a generation before it's born. Get two for the effort of one. Plus the generations that would come from them both."

Liba glanced up at him again. "Nathan...what's going to happen?"

"Just keep walking," he insisted. "Don't look back. Don't make eye contact."

✦ ✦ ✦

Half an hour later, Zvi and Liba arrived at home and Zvi put her immediately to bed. "Rest! This day was too hard on you."

"I've had worse." The tone of Liba's voice was confident but Zvi noticed she prepared for bed just the same. He glanced at her, hesitating long enough to take in her form as she removed her coat, then her sweater, and unfastened the buttons of her dress. She glanced back at him over her shoulder and smiled. "I think you should leave the room now."

He smiled back. "I could help you."

"And then we'd be here all afternoon."

"It's a great way to warm up on a cold afternoon."

She chuckled. "Go on, now. I need to rest."

Zvi leaned forward and kissed her on the shoulder. "I love you," he whispered, then turned toward the door. "I'll come wake you in a few hours." As he stepped out to the hallway added, "Call for me if you need anything."

✦ ✦ ✦

Later that day Yevgeny Jabotinsky arrived at Liba and Zvi's house. Yevgeny, about Zvi's age, lived in Odessa, a city with the largest port on the Black Sea. He was a grain merchant and traveled through the Pale of Settlement buying grain for shipment. The town of Kreva was a long way north of the Black Sea, but competition in the grain business was fierce and Yevgeny was an aggressive buyer. Throughout the year, he traveled in a circuit up from Odessa, around to farmers in the region, and back to Odessa, buying grain during the harvest season, cultivating relationships the remainder of the time. It was a practice that made him one of the most successful grain merchants in the country.

But Yevgeny had another reason for maintaining a constant travel schedule. He was also instrumental in the organized Jewish resistance to Russian persecution. And he was a devotee of Leon Pinsker, a physician in Odessa who advocated for the Zionist cause—the notion that only in Palestine, in a land of their own and governed by themselves, could Jews find safety.

Inspired by what he learned from Pinsker, Yevgeny used his grain-buying circuit to spread both messages—resistance to persecution through the use of force and the return of Jews to their homeland in Palestine. He did that by slowly and carefully assembling groups of pro-Zionist men in the towns where he regularly purchased grain. At first they met to talk about Zionism, to review the latest ideas Yevgeny picked up from Pinsker's regular conferences in and around Odessa, and to discuss how to put his ideas into effect within Russian society. Gradually, under Yevgeny's careful tutelage, group meetings changed from mere discussion sessions to full-fledged resistance training exercises—following Yevgeny's belief that fighting back offered the only hope of immediate relief from the Empire's reign of organized anti-Jewish terror.

Yevgeny glanced around warily as he entered the house. "We need to talk," he whispered, his eyes darting from side to side. Checking, watching, noting.

"Keep your coat on," Zvi directed as he led the way through the house and onto the back stoop. When they were alone and the door to the house was closed, he said, "Okay, before you begin, let me say—I think trouble is coming."

Yevgeny glanced around nervously. "I know. That's why I came to see you."

"Liba and I were nearly accosted by a group of men earlier today."

"Where?"

"Here." Zvi pointed with his finger for emphasis.

Yevgeny's eyes widened. "At your house?"

"No. Here. In Kreva. By the hardware store."

"Did you recognize them?"

"I've seen them before. They're men from the Brigade."

Zvi nodded. "That makes sense."

"What do you mean?"

"As best I can determine, they're coming for us. Tonight probably."

"How many?"

"No one knows for sure. But it's the Holy Brigade, so it could be a mob."

"You got this from someone reliable?"

"Moishe Krasny."

Zvi arched an eyebrow. "Moishe told you?"

Yevgeny nodded. "He has a guy who's with them. On the inside."

"Okay," Zvi sighed and ran his fingers through his hair. "What should we do? Do we know where they will attack?"

"Here," Yevgeny gestured. "They're coming here. To your neighborhood."

"To our neighborhood."

"Yes. This is the night for your neighborhood."

Zvi had a quizzical look. "Why do they do that? One neighborhood at a time. Why? They could hit everywhere at once, but instead they attack one at a time."

Yevgeny shook his head. "The authorities are telling them it would be too obvious. If they attack everywhere at once, in a coordinated effort, everyone will know the government is behind it. Everyone knows that only the government could pull off something like that."

"Everyone already knows they're behind it."

"Yes, but if they hit everywhere at once, ministry officials won't be able to deny their involvement."

"Okay," Zvi decided. "We should get everyone together."

"At Yaakov Verlinsky's store?"

"Yeah. Tell them we'll meet at the usual time."

"Will that be early enough?"

"I think so. You can put out the word?"

"Yes. You want to go with me to tell them?"

Zvi shook his head. "No, I have something I have to do before then."

Yevgeny's expression softened and he had a knowing look. "Liba?"

"Yeah."

They turned to go back inside the house and Zvi said, "Tell Yaakov to bring his delivery wagon over here."

"Okay. When do you need him?"

"As soon as he can get here."

✦ ✦ ✦

When Yevgeny was gone, Zvi went to the bedroom to check on Liba and found her awake. She smiled at him from beneath the covers. "That was Yevgeny I heard?"

"Yes."

"What did he want?"

"Nothing good."

"Bad news?"

Zvi nodded.

"I can always tell by the look on your face."

"You need to go to the Navrotskyys."

"Why should I go there?"

"There could be trouble here."

She propped up on her elbows. "If there's going to be trouble, I don't want to leave you to face it alone."

Zvi shook his head. "You need to stay with the Navrotskyys."

"For how long?"

"I'm not sure. Maybe a few days."

"You won't be there?"

"No."

What's happening?"

"Better you don't know too many details. You should get ready. Yaakov is coming to take us there in his delivery wagon. I will ride with you. But we should get ready. He will be here in a few minutes." He reached under the bed, took out a satchel, and set it on a nearby chair. "Come on. Get moving."

✦   ✦   ✦

Half an hour later, Yaakov Verlinsky arrived with his horse-drawn delivery wagon. Zvi was in the front room watching out the window. As the wagon came to a stop, he picked up Liba's satchel and walked with her out to the street, then helped her up to the seat. When they were ready, Yaakov gave the reins a jiggle and the horse started forward at a slow, clopping pace.

From the neighborhood where Zvi and Liba lived, they made their way to the bridge on the south side of town that led over a ravine and into the Protestant section where Oleg and Marie Navrotskyy lived.

Oleg was a Lutheran minister, active in the meager Gentile effort to support Jewish resistance to the Empire's systematic persecution. He and Zvi had met at a Zionist rally two years earlier. A few months after that, Oleg invited Zvi to speak to his congregation about conditions in the Jewish neighborhood and about the Jewish effort to return to Palestine. They had been friends ever since.

When they arrived at the Navrotskyys' home, Yaakov brought the wagon to a stop at the curb out front. Zvi climbed down first, then helped Liba to the street. As he reached back for the satchel, Marie appeared on the front porch of the house. At first she stood motionless and looked out across the lawn toward them with a cautious, puzzled expression. Then Liba turned to face her, smiled, and tossed a friendly wave.

At once, Marie's face came alive with the look of surprise and happiness one senses at unexpectedly seeing a friend. In an instant, she hiked up the hem of her skirt, held it safely above her ankles, and hurried down the steps toward the street. Liba started toward her and they met in the middle and embraced as true friends do.

While they greeted each other, Zvi turned back to Yaakov. "This may take a few minutes. I'll see myself home."

"Are you sure?" Yaakov looked concerned. "It's a good long ways back to your street." He paused to glance around. "And I'm not too sure they'll like having us around."

"I'll be fine," Zvi replied, then turned toward the house and followed the ladies inside.

NETANYAHU

LATE THAT AFTERNOON, near dusk, members of the Holy Brigade in Kreva gathered at a warehouse on the eastern side of town. Among them were Pavel Orlov, Grigory Brusilov, Ivane Golovin, and Jovan Markov. Alexey Gagarin was their leader and as they gathered that evening he looked over at Golovin. "What do we have in the way of supplies?"

"Ten liters of kerosene," Golovin recounted. "Several dozen torches and the clubs. And a number of us have our pistols."

Markov spoke up. "We could use more of everything."

"We need rifles. They said we would have rifles, too," Golovin complained.

"We'll have to make do with what we have," Gagarin answered. "It is an honor merely to be asked to defend the Crown. Demanding more for the sake of making our job easier besmirches that honor."

"Well," Brusilov groused, "they gave us their word."

Gagarin ignored that last comment and continued. "In a little while, we will divide into groups of four or five, leave here in the usual staggered order, and go down there separately. Tonight we are meeting at St. Michael's Church as planned. Sit in ones and twos around the congregation. Make sure you don't all sit together," he cautioned. "We want this to appear spontaneous. Nikolai Essen, our contact to the regional interior ministry office will be there to deliver a speech about the Jews."

Orlov spoke up. "Any idea what he intends to say?"

"Or that he'll actually show up?" Golovin added. "Or will he be like the rifles they promised that never came through?"

"He'll be there," Gagarin assured. "And he'll deliver a speech outlining the trouble the Jews have caused us. Believe me. By the time he finishes, no one will have any doubt about where he stands on the issues."

"Is he going to mention the lost jobs? The lost business opportunities? The way the Jews steal all of that from us?"

"They're never satisfied," someone added.

"I'm sure he'll mention all of that," Gagarin said. "When he—"

"What about the threat they pose to our women and children?"

Gagarin looked frustrated. "Let's stay focused on what we—"

"And the threat to our safety with their mystical practices," another said, following on with the comments the others had made. "No telling what they do once they light those candles and begin their chants."

"They're an affront to God with their immoral lifestyle. No wonder they're hated by everyone. They eat young gentile babies. They killed the Christ. It's a wonder they haven't killed us all."

"And now they will pay for all of that," someone said confidently. "And then—"

"Listen," Gagarin commanded sharply, cutting off the discussion. "We need to concentrate on the task at hand. We need to make sure we're clear about what will happen tonight so we do everything necessary to get the crowd involved. So let's settle down right now and let's get organized." He paused to take a deep breath before continuing. "At some point in the speech, I will stand up and begin to shout, telling the audience that we must respond to what we have heard, put it into action, and insist we need to do it right away—this very night. That's your cue. When I do that, some of you—we've already talked about which ones—will stand up in response, shout something about your agreeing with me, and then start toward the door to go do it. I'll encourage others to follow. The rest of you will do that, one or two at a time, agreeing loudly with the call to action. That will be enough to create a vigilante atmosphere. From there, we can build a mob in the street."

"How many from the church will join us?" Orlov asked.

"I don't know, but enough will join us. We'll get the rest from the street as we go."

"What do we do with this stuff?" Brusilov asked, gesturing to a can of kerosene and a bundle of clubs. "We can't carry it inside the church with us."

"We'll hide it in the bushes near the front steps," Markov answered before Gagarin could reply.

"I've never been to this one," Brusilov said. "I don't know where the hiding places are located."

"Don't worry about it." Markov gave a reassuring wave of his hand. "I'll show you where."

✦ ✦ ✦

Early that evening, Gagarin and the men of the Holy Brigade left the warehouse and walked down the street to St. Michael's Orthodox Church. While Markov and Brusilov hid the kerosene and clubs in the bushes, the others entered the sanctuary and took their seats, scattering among the audience in ones and twos as they had been instructed. The crowd was already large and before long the room was packed. As the last seats filled, a door to the left of the chancel area opened and the priest entered followed by Nikolai Essen. Moments later, the service began.

As planned, Essen gave a passionate speech, full of vitriolic and bilious invective. Caring little for the truth and even less for accuracy, he spewed forth the most incendiary anti-Semitic rhetoric in a rant that lasted almost an hour. Finally he turned to a call for immediate action, challenging the audience to cast all care to the wind and jump into the fight. "Now is that time to save the lifestyle we know and love!" he shouted.

In response, Gagarin, long since nervous and ready to pounce, leapt to his feet. "Why not now?" he shouted in anger. "Why not do something about this now? We're here. The Jews live just down the street. All we have to do is march down there and put an end to this. Right now! Tonight!"

Other members of the Holy Brigade stood in response, agreeing with Gagarin and joining him in a call for action.

Finally, Brusilov jumped to his feet. "I'm going now!" he shouted. "Any of you going with me?" Without waiting for a response, he started toward the door. Some of the men from the Brigade rose to follow. "I'm with you," one of them said. "Me, too," another called. Then a member of the congregation stood as well and others joined them. After that, many more rose from their seats in the pews and started after them.

As the crowd poured out of the church building, some of Gagarin's men retrieved the clubs, torches, and kerosene hidden in the bushes. Others led the crowd to the street and then toward the Jewish neighborhood. Soon, torches were lit and the procession grew even larger as onlookers joined in. Two blocks later, they were a mob, chanting in unison while they walked, "Jews must die! Jews must die!"

A few minutes later, the group reached Kreva's Jewish neighborhood and one of the Brigade members tossed a torch through the front window of the first house on the block. Others picked up rocks and hurled them through the windows of the house across the street. Moments later, both were engulfed in flames.

The front door of the first house burst open and a man rushed out with a small child in his arms. His wife followed, another child trailing behind her. Men near the rear of the mob spotted them and set upon them with clubs, beating them about the abdomen and head until their bodies lay in a bloody heap.

By then, most of the mob was farther down the street, setting fire to house after house, clubbing the residents as they fled for safety. Screams of anguish and panicked shouts filled the air, but still the mob moved on, grinding its way down the street, cutting a swath of death and destruction as it went.

✦ ✦ ✦

Meanwhile, Zvi, Yevgeny, and the resistance group were gathered

NETANYAHU

at Yaakov Verlinsky's store. Seated on boxes and crates in the storeroom, they listened intently while once again Yevgeny exhorted them about the necessity of fighting back. "The only way to be safe is to fight," he said, returning to an oft-repeated phrase. "Russians don't understand anything else. If we fight, we live. If we cower, we die."

In the midst of his address, the door flew open and Levi Martov rushed in. "It's started," he blurted in an excited voice.

Yitzhak Yagoda stood. "Where?" he demanded. "Where are they?"

"Two blocks away." Martov leaned forward, gasping for breath. "A mob. They came from St. Michael's. Marched down the street, started burning houses and beating people."

Zvi's eyes were wide and alert. "That's not far from my house."

"Even closer to mine," another said.

They sat motionless, staring blankly at each other. Then someone raised the lid on a wooden shipping crate to reveal a collection of clubs and pistols. He lifted out a club and handed it over his shoulder. "Here. Take this. We have to go."

At once, the others in the room surged toward the crate, grabbing clubs and pistols and anything else they could use as a weapon. Zvi found a box of ax handles and took one for himself. Then Yevgeny turned toward the door and motioned for them to follow. "Let's go. If we hurry, maybe we can come up from behind and surprise them."

With Yevgeny in the lead, the men rushed from the store. Already, flames were visible, rising in the distance above the trees down the street. Without need of command or suggestion, they turned as a group and rushed in that direction and broke into a run.

In a matter of minutes they reached the first house in the neighborhood. By then it was little more than a pile of smoking rubble. Four bodies lay on the ground in front near the edge of the street, two of them obviously children, whose little broken and bloody bodies were all but unrecognizable. Zvi placed his finger between his teeth and bit down on it, choking back a cry of anguish. But Yevgeny hardly glanced in their direction and never missed a step. That meant Zvi couldn't pause, either, but had to keep running to stay up with the group.

The flames they'd seen from the store were two blocks ahead and in the glow of the fire they saw men wielding clubs, raising them overheard and striking downward in a way that would produce tremendous force. Seeing it added a sense of urgency to their steps and they quickened the pace, running flat out now in a race to stop the Brigade before anyone else died.

Two minutes later, they caught up with the Holy Brigade and fell upon them from behind, attacking with their own clubs and batons. Their sudden appearance caught the Brigade by surprise. Confused and disoriented, Gagarin's mob was instantly in disarray as Yevgeny and the men of the neighborhood struck with a viciousness they'd never known before.

As the melee continued, a gunshot rang out followed by another, and still another. At the sound of the third, the crowd parted and Zvi saw two men lying on the ground. Blood poured from wounds to their head and side. Around them, men paused to take note of their fallen comrades. But not Yevgeny. He continued to fight, wielding a club at all who came too close.

Eventually Zvi and the men of the neighborhood gained the upper hand and drove away the Holy Brigade. But when the fighting was over, they learned that more than fifty of their neighbors were dead. Hundreds more were injured.

Over the next several hours, calm returned to the streets of Kreva, and Zvi went home to check on his house. He feared the worst but was relieved to find only one of the front windows was broken but anti-Semitic slogans were painted on the door. Otherwise, nothing else appeared to be wrong or out of place.

Satisfied the exterior was passable, Zvi walked inside to change clothes. He returned shortly and began sweeping shards of broken glass from the floor of the front room. When the mess was cleaned up and the furniture placed back in its usual location, he took a seat by the window to rest and watched while a new morning slowly dawned.

✦ ✦ ✦

When the sun was fully up Zvi returned outside and continued to work on the house, doing his best to wipe away all traces of the violence so Liba wouldn't see it and worry. That afternoon, Yevgeny stopped by. "Looks like you came through without any major damage."

"Just the one window."

"You are blessed. On the next street over, six houses were destroyed. I guess we stopped them just in time."

"That would not have been possible without your help."

Yevgeny shrugged in response. "I just pointed out the problem. You and the others did the rest." He gestured toward the open window frame. "You have a piece of glass for it?"

"Yeah."

"Good." Yevgeny smiled. "I'll help you put it in place."

With Yevgeny supplying an extra pair of hands, Zvi fit the new piece of window glass into place and secured it with the trim of the frame. While they worked, they talked.

"Attacks like this happened all over the region last night," Yevgeny reported.

"Did many people die?"

"Hundreds, maybe even thousands."

"Did others fight back?"

"Most of them."

"How long will this go on?"

"No one knows. A number of people in Odessa are packing their belongings. Planning to leave."

"Where are they going?"

Yevgeny looked as if the answer were obvious. "Palestine. They're going to Palestine. That's our only choice."

"So, they're taking Pinsker and the others seriously about this."

"Yes," Yevgeny nodded with a sense of incredulity. "This has always been a serious affair. Did you think it was a game?"

"No. I'm interested in going. But I didn't know how others took it. Some would like to fight back and stay right here."

"They will die right here, too."

"Do you think this is true? Do you think that leaving is the only option?"

"Yes," Yevgeny said. "I know it is."

"Then why do you stay? Why not just take your family and go?"

"That is not my role. That is not my calling. I'll go. One day. But right now, my job is to help motivate others to leave."

"A few more attacks like we had last night and I think the entire region will be motivated for something."

"Well," Yevgeny sighed, "it needs to be for leaving. If the Russian army moves in to restore order, we'll be trapped. We can't possibly resist a force like that."

They worked in silence a while, then Yevgeny suggested, "You should come to Odessa sometime and listen to what Dr. Pinsker has to say. You can stay with us. We'll attend some of his meetings together."

"That sounds like a good idea."

"Come in the spring. Bring your family. We'll make a holiday out of it."

NETANYAHU

ACROSS TOWN, members of the Holy Brigade gathered at the home of Alexey Gagarin to discuss the previous night's activities and to regroup for the next operation. Gagarin looked around the room. "So tell me, how did the Jews get organized enough to stop us last night?"

Brusilov answered first. "They had more people."

"But their advantage was more than that. We've been out-numbered by them before and they've always collapsed into disarray as soon as the fighting started. This time, they got stronger the more we attacked."

"They seemed to know we were coming," Golovin offered.

"And they were better prepared," Markov added.

Brusilov spoke up again. "I think someone talked. I think that someone tipped the Jews off about what we were doing."

Gagarin surveyed the men once more. "Anyone hear anything about that? Anyone hear a rumor or suggestion of a rumor about an informant among us?" When no one responded, Gagarin said, "Well, if anyone hears anything about an informant, come to me with it immediately. And don't wait until our next meeting. Come find me right away." He paused a moment, then changed the subject, "Some of you were talking about a Jewish woman you saw on the street earlier. Anybody see her last night?" When no one responded to that request, Gagarin turned to Pavel Orlov. "You were talking about her. You found her attractive."

"What about her?"

"Did you find her last night?"

"No." Orlov shook his head. "I don't know who she is."

"Did you ask about her earlier? Before we went down there from the church?"

"Yes," Orlov replied. "But no one seemed to know where she lived."

"We should find her."

"Why?"

"I don't know," Gagarin shrugged. "But it seems important."

Markov spoke up. "Perhaps it's not her," he suggested. "Perhaps it's the child she's carrying."

Gagarin frowned as if puzzled but inwardly he was glad for the opportunity to change the subject. "What do you mean?"

"I don't know," Markov replied. "Maybe he's a threat to us, somehow."

"A baby? A threat?"

"No. Not the baby. But the adult the baby might become."

After the meeting ended, Gagarin received a note from Nikolai Essen summoning him to a meeting. The message gave little detail about the purpose or reason, but Gagarin was sure Essen wanted to discuss the riot.

✦ ✦ ✦

About mid-morning of the following day, Gagarin and Essen sat across from each other at a coffee shop in Minsk. Essen wanted a report on the attack and listened attentively while Gagarin described the fighting. When Gagarin finished, Essen spoke, "I heard something about a Jewish woman." He looked concerned. "You had your men out scavenging the neighborhood in search of a Jewish woman?"

Gagarin dismissed the question with an anguished look and a wave of his hand. "That was just us talking among ourselves. After the riot. Some of the men told me about seeing her earlier. The day before. With that rabbi. Mileikowsky. They saw them on the street in Kreva. So when we met after the riot, I asked about her. Whether they had seen her that night."

"Had they?"

"No."

"What about Fedor Gelfman? He's the one person I asked you to find."

"We didn't find him."

Essen looked perturbed. "That was the whole point of this operation."

"I know."

"These guys are plotting against the czar," Essen lamented. "They're serious. They want to kill him. Our point in all of this was to protect and defend the monarchy. Not to chase around looking for women, especially Jewish women, and certainly not to retreat from a fight like cowards."

Gagarin bristled at the suggestion they had acted in a cowardly manner but he kept his reaction to himself. "The Jews were much stronger than we expected. And much better organized."

"How did they get organized?"

"Yevgeny Jabotinsky," Gagarin said flatly. "He's the reason."

Essen frowned. "The grain merchant?"

Gagarin sighed, "Yes. And, as difficult as it is to accept, I think someone tipped them off about our plans."

Essen nodded. "We do, too. We checked."

"And?"

"You have a traitor."

"I find that difficult to—"

"No," Essen interrupted. "We're pretty sure you have one. And we think we know who it is."

Gagarin was attentive. "Who?"

"Pavel Orlov."

Gagarin frowned. "You have some evidence to back this up? He's a good man. If I confront him, I'll need to show some basis for the accusation."

"He talked."

"To whom?"

"I'm working on the name, but Pavel Orlov is the source of your trouble. And we don't want you to confront him."

Gagarin had a questioning look. "Why not? We can't let this pass."

"We don't want you to let it pass." Essen glanced across the table at Gagarin with a knowing look. "We want you to deal with him."

"Deal with him? You mean find out what happened?"

The look on Essen's face left little doubt what he meant. "No, I'm telling you what happened. Orlov talked. And I'm telling you—deal with him. Once and for all."

"What about Jabotinsky?"

Essen shook his head. "They'll take care of him in Odessa. At another level."

Gagarin looked puzzled. "You keep saying *they*."

Essen took a sip of coffee. "Don't worry about it. Just take care of Orlov."

✦ ✦ ✦

After the meeting, Essen traveled to Odessa and met with Ibrahim al-Kazem. They talked while seated on a bench just off the Potemkin Stairs, a long run of public stairs that lead up the hill from the coast toward the center of the city. Essen gazed out at the view of the sea. Both men avoided eye contact with each other. Ibrahim said, "I heard the Jews routed your men."

"We were outnumbered and outgunned."

"Outgunned?" Ibrahim sounded surprised. "They had guns?"

"Yes, and they knew we were coming."

"I am told you have an informant among your men."

"We're aware of that now and will take measures to put an end to it."

"The caliphs expect a better effort from you."

"We're doing as much as we can."

"Allowing the Jews to defeat you is not your best. That only emboldens them. We want to convince them that they can accomplish nothing together. Your debacle does quite the opposite. I understand from others that Jews in Kreva are talking of a permanent defensive organization."

Essen shrugged. "Doesn't surprise me. And they may have already done just that. They were well-organized when they attacked us."

"Soon they will be training and dreaming of achieving even more. We must end this now."

"Leadership," Essen intoned. "That is the key."

Ibrahim looked puzzled. "What about leadership? That is your responsibility."

Essen folded his arms across his chest. "Kill the Jewish leadership and the group will die."

"You know who their leaders are?"

Essen nodded slowly. "They were organized by Yevgeny Jabotinsky."

"He is the grain merchant from here in Odessa?"

Essen looked over at Ibrahim and for the first time that day their eyes met. "You have someone who can take care of him?"

Ibrahim smiled. "We do indeed."

Essen looked away. "Good. Eliminate him and much of this so-called Jewish organization will disappear."

✦ ✦ ✦

After talking to Essen, Ibrahim's first reaction was to report what he learned to the caliphs in Istanbul, but after thinking it over he decided that might not be the best course of action. If he told the caliphs what he knew about the attack in Kreva, they would only blame him for the failures and lack of progress.

Better to solve this on my own, he thought to himself.

Late that evening, he met with Vasily Denikin, a Russian operative who solved problems for anyone willing to pay the fee. After a brief and cryptic sketch of the situation and the goal—elimination of Yevgeny Jabotinsky—Denikin agreed to help. "I'll need several assistants."

"Hire anyone you like. Just don't tell me about it and don't tell them about me." Ibrahim took an envelope stuffed with cash from his jacket and handed it to Denikin. "This should be enough to get you started. Let me know when you need more."

Denikin picked up the envelope and slid it into his pocket. "I'm thinking this should be a subtle job."

"Subtle works as long as it gets the job done."

"How much time do we have?"

"Finish it sooner rather than later," Ibrahim isntructed. "But I don't want to know any more details. How you accomplish the goal is up to you. Just get it done."

"For a bonus."

"We already agreed on the amount of your fee."

"That's the standard charge for work done. You're asking for something more than the standard work."

"How much?"

"I don't know yet. But sooner will cost more."

Ibrahim's eyes darkened. "How much more?"

"I'll let you know the bonus amount when I see how difficult the task will be."

NETANYAHU

WHILE THE JEWS OF KREVA endured yet another attack, anti-Semitic violence swept across the Pale of Settlement from Odessa in the southeast to Lodz in the northwest. Small, random attacks at first, they steadily grew to organized nights of continual violence. Each night was worse than the one before.

Sensing the violence would not end soon, with mobs attacking neighborhoods closer and closer to Beth Jacob Synagogue, Lurie and his assistant, Emile Mayer, took measures to protect the synagogue's most precious items. Torah scrolls, always wrapped in their protective coverings, were placed in wooden boxes specially designed for each one. Then Lurie and Mayer carried them downstairs to the basement and placed them in a vault that was buried in the floor of a broom closet. Golden chalices, a basin for washing, and four yads—Torah pointers, used in reading the weekly text—were placed there, too.

When everything was inside, Mayer reached for the vault door to close it. Just then, Lurie remembered the ring he'd received from Judah Alkalai and grabbed hold of Mayer's forearm to stop him. "Wait, there's one more thing." Lurie turned toward the hallway. "I'll be back in a minute."

Lurie hurried upstairs to his study and made his way behind the desk. He opened the top drawer and checked the front corner, but the ring wasn't there. Frantically, he shuffled through the papers in the drawer and finally saw the ring hidden all the way in back. He reached through the clutter and carefully drew it out.

"That mustn't happen again," he whispered. He held the ring and stared at it, his eyes focused on the inscription. "You mustn't get away from me like that ever again," he repeated. "Never again."

A voice spoke to him from behind. "You talking to someone?"

Startled, Lurie whirled in that direction to see Mayer standing in the doorway. He forced a smile. "Oh, I just have one more thing for the vault." He held up the ring for Lurie to see. "We need something to put it in, a box or something. Before we put it with the other things."

"Come on," Mayer gestured toward the hallway. "I have something that will work."

Lurie followed Mayer back downstairs to a workroom and waited while Mayer shuffled through clutter on the workbench. After a five-minute search Mayer succeeded in locating a small wooden box and handed it to Lurie. "They made these one year for Hanukah. Put a dreidel in them for the kids. I have one at home that they gave to me."

The box was smaller than the width of Lurie's palm and when he closed his fingers around it, it all but disappeared. He stared at it as if gazing into the past. "You received one of these?"

"Yeah, I was about five years old."

"And the boxes have been here all this time?"

"Found some in that room under the steps on the other side of the building. I was looking for something else and came across them. Didn't have the dreidels in them. Just empty boxes. I've been using them for odds and ends." He pointed to the box in Lurie's hand. "That ring should fit nicely in it."

Lurie glanced at the box again and smiled. "This will be perfect." He set the box on a table that stood nearby and placed the ring inside. It fit, but with just enough room to spare to allow it to rattle when moved. "We need something to place inside it. Clean tissue paper or something to keep it from moving around."

Mayer turned once again to the workbench. "Well, there's this." He held up a cotton undershirt. "Brought this in the other day to use as a rag. Didn't really need it." He offered it to Lurie. "Rip off a piece and use that for now. We can always find something else later."

Lurie hesitated a moment, then set the box on the workbench, took the cloth from Mayer, and ripped it down the seam.

"Where'd the ring come from? I don't remember us having anything like that before."

"It's a very special ring." Lurie tore the cloth to a useable size and fit it into the box. When he was satisfied, he set the ring inside, nestling it into the fabric, then placed the lid on top. "A perfect home for it," he announced with a look of admiration. Then he turned toward the door. "Let's get these things locked away."

With Lurie in the lead, they made their way back to the vault. Mayer held the door open while Lurie put the ring box inside the chalice, then secured the chalice lid in place. "That should do it."

Mayer closed the vault door and gave the combination dial a spin, then twisted the handle to make sure it was locked.

✦ ✦ ✦

Two nights later, Lurie was awakened by the sound of someone pounding on the front door. Aniela, his wife, raised up on her elbows. "Who could that be at this hour?"

"I'll go see." Lurie rolled out of bed and pulled on his robe. "Stay here."

Lurie made his way out to the hall and over to the staircase. He paused there and looked out through a downstairs window in the front parlor, but saw no one. With halting steps, he placed one foot on the top step, trying not to make any noise, then slowly but quietly descended to the first floor.

The staircase came to an end with the bottom step opposite the front door. Narrow windows ran along either side and through them Lurie saw Emile Mayer standing on the porch. He opened the door and leaned out. "What's wrong?"

"The gangs attacked the neighborhood near the synagogue."

"When?"

"Just now."

"Have they reached the synagogue yet?"

"They're inside it now. Smashing windows, throwing things around."

"Has no one tried to stop them?"

"I don't know. I just heard about it a few minutes ago. Came straight over here to get you."

"Come inside." Lurie pushed open the door and stepped aside to let Mayer past, then pulled the door shut and pointed to a chair in the front parlor. "Have a seat in there while I put on some clothes."

✦ ✦ ✦

Even before they reached the synagogue, Lurie and Mayer saw flames rising above the treetops. Lurie came to an abrupt halt as he stared up at them.

"Is that from our building?" Mayer asked.

Lurie turned in his direction with a knowing look, then broke into a run.

They arrived to find the front of the synagogue engulfed in flames. Men, armed with rifles and clubs, stood out front warding off any who approached and shouting over and over, "Die Jews, die! Die Jews, die!"

Lurie stared at them, his eyes wide with a look of fear. "They're still here."

"Yeah," Mayer sighed.

"Usually, they're gone by the time the fire is noticeable. What does it mean?"

"I don't know. But I don't like it."

A crowd was gathered across the street, many of them members of the synagogue. Some stood silently watching; others were crying openly. Lurie scanned them for a familiar face and noticed Frances Roth near the curb. Tears streamed down her face and Lurie went over to her and put his arm around her shoulder. "It's okay," he soothed. "We can rebuild. It's only wood and concrete."

Frances looked up at him. "It's not that," she sobbed.

"Then what is it?"

"Eli Adler is inside."

Adler was a widower who came to the synagogue every day.

"They couldn't find any of the Torah scrolls or anything else of value," Frances explained. "But they found him and tied him to the podium. Then they whipped him with a belt, trying to make him tell them where the valuable items were kept. But he wouldn't talk. So then they set fire to the building and left him inside."

Lurie had a terrified look.

"We tried to get him out," Frances continued, "but they wouldn't let us in. And when we kept trying they beat us."

"That's why they're standing out there like that?"

She nodded her head. "They did it to block us from saving Eli."

Mayer, who was standing nearby, leaned closer. "Think we could still get him out?"

"I don't—" Lurie was interrupted by the sound of the roof crashing down to the sanctuary floor. Sparks rose in the night sky and beneath them, the men who surrounded the building roared with laughter.

✦ ✦ ✦

With the building apparently destroyed, gang members moved off into the night. Members of the synagogue remained across the street awhile longer, then slowly drifted away until only Lurie and Mayer remained.

"Think he's dead?' Mayer asked.

"If he was tied to the podium, I suspect he was dead before the roof caved in."

"And if not?"

"Maybe he found a safe place to hide."

"Think we could get in there and see?"

"Maybe." Lurie stepped from the sidewalk. "Only one way to find out."

Lurie led the way across the street and down the side of the synagogue to have a look.

Though the sanctuary, located in front, was totally destroyed, the

41

back portion of the building had somehow survived and was largely intact.

"Think it's safe to go inside?" Lurie asked as he scanned the walls and looked up at the roof.

"I don't know. Could be just one footstep from falling down."

"Well, maybe we should find out." A row of basement windows lined the wall from the charred remains to the back corner. Lurie chose one about midway down and moved toward it.

Mayer's eyes were wide open. "You're going inside?"

"Yeah." By then he was on one knee at a window. With a push of his hand, it opened and he leaned inside. "This is the kitchen."

"But maybe we should stay out of there until someone has a look around."

"Fire brigade won't be here until midmorning."

"What's the rush?"

"In a few hours, this place will be plundered by every junk dealer in town."

Lurie backed away from the window and turned around to face Mayer. "Nothing ventured, nothing gained." Then he slid feet first through the window and landed on a kitchen countertop.

From the window, Lurie picked his way through the darkness until he located a hallway that ran the length of the building. He followed it and soon came to the back wall of the building. There, he turned and made his way to the broom closet where the safe was located. Thankfully, it was not damaged at all by the fire.

Lurie moved aside the brooms and mops that cluttered the room, then dropped to one knee. Carefully, he entered the numbers, turning the dial first to the right, then to the left. When he'd entered them all, he held his breath and gave the handle a tug. With little effort, the handle unlocked the safe and Lurie lifted open the door. His heart raced as he retrieved the chalice and removed the lid. Then a broad smile spread across his face when he saw the ring box resting unharmed inside the golden chalice. "I will never let you out of my sight again," he whispered as he lifted out the box. "Never again."

6

NETANYAHU

A FEW DAYS AFTER the Brigade's attack on the neighborhood, Zvi brought Liba home. The first thing she noticed was how clean and neat the front room was. "They attacked our house?"

Zvi smiled at her. "How did you know?"

She smiled back at him. "This room hasn't been this clean in a long time."

"They broke out the window. I didn't want you to see the mess."

She leaned against his side and kissed him. "You're a good man, Zvi."

"I want to be."

She kissed him again then glanced around the room once more. "Did they damage anything else?"

"They painted one of their slogans on the door but I—"

"I thought it looked different."

"I used the same color as before."

"But it looked new and fresh. I wondered what happened."

They talked a while longer, then Zvi helped her to the bedroom and left her to unpack. After lunch, she took a nap and he walked outside. A neighbor, Uri Lembersky, was busy stacking firewood on his back porch. Zvi walked over to visit.

"I didn't notice any damage to your house," he said. "From the attack the other night."

"No. None at all." Uri gathered an armful of firewood and lugged it to the porch. "I see they got your window, though."

"Yeah. But that was still way less than what they did to some."

"I suppose." Uri brought another armful of wood to the porch, then set about adding it to the stack. "Did you hear the latest?"

"About what?"

"They found a man's body hanging from a tree in the park."

"I didn't hear that. Who was it?"

"Nobody seems to know his name. But they all say he's a Russian."

"Not one of us?"

"No."

Zvi was unconvinced. "Sure he wasn't Jewish?"

"I don't know," Uri shrugged. "They all say he's Russian."

"Hmm," Zvi mused. "Doesn't sound right to me."

"Why not?

"Well, for one thing, if he was Russian, we'd all be dead by now."

Uri looked up from the wood stack, a perplexed expression on his face. "What do you mean?"

"A Russian, swinging from a tree, in a town like Kreva—the authorities would never let an opportunity like that slip by unnoticed. Even if none of us did it, they'd accuse us of it immediately. Wipe out the entire neighborhood in retribution."

Uri returned to stacking firewood. "Well, that's what they're saying. He was a Russian."

✦ ✦ ✦

After checking on Liba, Zvi walked uptown and quietly asked around about the body. No one seemed to know much about it except for Levi Martov, the grocer.

"The dead man's name is Orlov. Pavel Orlov."

Zvi frowned. "Does that name mean anything to you?"

"No, never heard of him before. Have you?"

"Not at all."

A customer interrupted their conversation and Zvi stepped aside while Martov waited on her. A few minutes later, Martov was free to talk again. Zvi moved down the counter to where he stood. "Everybody says he was Russian. Anyone know that for sure?"

"Mordechai saw the body," Martov replied.

"How did he do that?"

"As a rabbi, he has connections. Not all the Russians in Kreva share the Holy Brigade's perspective. Mordechai wanted to see if the man was Jewish. To give him a proper burial."

"And they told him he wasn't?"

"Yes. And they let him see the body." Martov glanced at Zvi with a knowing look.

"You mean...he wasn't circumcised."

"No. He wasn't."

"Well, that's not conclusive. But I see your point."

"Why are you asking so many questions?"

"I'm trying to figure out why the Russians killed him."

"What makes you think the Russians did it?"

"If Orlov was Russian," Zvi answered, "that would mean the body hanging from that tree was a dead Russian. That's the kind of thing we Jews get blamed for all the time—whether it actually happened or not. Just another excuse to attack us which, in this instance, they would have done with a vengeance. But nothing has happened. That tells me the Russians must have killed him. Otherwise, we'd have been attacked by now."

Martov nodded. "So why would they kill him and leave the body for everyone to see?"

"Looks to me like they wanted to send a message."

"But what's the message?"

"I don't know."

"And maybe you don't know because the message wasn't for you."

Zvi arched an eyebrow in a look of realization. "Good point."

✦ ✦ ✦

A day or two later, Yevgeny returned to Kreva and came to Zvi's house. As usual, they walked out to the back porch to talk. After catching up on the latest news from Odessa, Zvi said, "Did you hear about the Russian they found hanging from a tree in the park?"

"Yes, Pavel Orlov."

"That's the name I heard. Sure he wasn't Jewish?"

"That much we're confident about. But here's something else." Yevgeny paused to let the moment sink in. "Orlov was the Brigade contact feeding information to Moishe. He's the reason we knew what they planned to do."

"So, Moishe met with him? In person?"

"Yes. Why?"

"The Russians must have found out what Orlov was doing. That's why they hanged him. And if they know that much, do they know Moishe was the person he told?"

"I don't know."

"Has Moishe thought about that?"

"You mean, that the Russians know who he is and might be coming after him?"

"Yeah."

"I don't know if he realizes that or not."

"Shouldn't we tell him? Maybe set up some of our people to guard his home?"

"If we do that, wouldn't we be acknowledging that the allegation is true?"

"Maybe."

"And wouldn't we be inviting them to attack us in retaliation?"

"Maybe. But we can't just ignore the problem."

"It's a tough—"

Zvi interrupted. "Couldn't we at least talk to him about taking his family away somewhere? To visit relatives somewhere else?"

"Yeah," Yevgeny conceded. "I suppose we should."

"Did Orlov know they were onto him?"

"I don't think so. He and Moishe met after the attack that night.

That was the last time Moishe saw him alive, but he said it seemed like business as usual."

"What did they talk about?"

Yevgeny glanced away.

Zvi pressed he question. "Yevgeny, what did they discuss?"

"The leader of the Brigade group that attacked us—a man named Alexey Gagarin—was asking about Liba."

Zvi frowned. "My Liba?"

"Yeah."

"He knows her by name?"

"No. He was asking about the pregnant lady they saw on the street the day before the attack. Orlov said it was Liba. They saw you with her by the hardware store. He didn't know her name. None of them did. They don't know your name, either. They just know you're Jewish. Do you remember seeing any of them?"

Zvi nodded. "I remember." But he didn't like the way the memory made him feel. He changed positions, leaning against the porch railing, "So they found out Orlov was talking to Moishe and they killed him?"

"Yeah."

"For telling Moishe about Liba?"

"I suspect it was for a lot of things. He and Moishe had been meeting regularly for quite a while."

"But he died because of that last conversation."

"I suppose."

Zvi ran his fingers through his hair. "I'm still wondering, though, why were they interested in Liba?"

"Ahh...you know," Yevgeny shrugged and glanced away. "Same old story."

"No," Zvi huffed. "I don't want to guess about this. She's my wife. She's carrying my son. I'm concerned about her safety. Why were they interested in her?"

"Come on, Zvi. You know what they say. We've heard it a thousand times..."

Zvi raised his voice. "Why were they interested in her?"

"Some of them think if they kill a pregnant lady they're killing the next generation before it's born. They call it getting two for the effort of one. Kill her. Kill the baby. It's just a lot of—"

"These people have no conscience," Zvi seethed. He glanced over at Yevgeny and caught the look in his eyes. "What?"

Yevgeny had a sheepish expression. "What do you mean?"

"What else is there?"

"Orlov said a little more," Yevgeny sighed.

"What?"

"He said this Gagarin guy seemed to think the child Liba's carrying might be special."

Zvi looked puzzled. "Special? How?"

"I don't know." Yevgeny shrugged once more. "And I don't think he knew. The child just seemed important to him. And to Orlov, though for the opposite reason."

Zvi's questioning look deepened. "Opposite reason."

"Gagarin wanted to kill the baby. Orlov wanted the child to live."

They were silent a moment, then Zvi said softly, "He died so Liba could live."

Yevgeny nodded his head slowly. "And so the baby could live."

NETANYAHU

MEANWHILE, IN LODZ, members of Beth Jacob Synagogue gathered at the home of Frances Roth to discuss whether to rebuild the synagogue's building or pursue other options. "We have to rebuild," Frances insisted. "We must have a synagogue for every ten people."

"Not *must*," Zino Deutsch corrected. "But *may*."

"It ought to be *must*," someone added.

"But it isn't," Deutsch responded. "Torah doesn't say we must organize ourselves into synagogues, or own buildings, or do any of those things. It only says we may and if we do, Torah tells us how. That's all."

Another spoke up. "It ought to say anytime persecutors destroy your building, you must rebuild it twice the original size."

"Yes," Shlomo Karelitz added. "And with twice the quality."

Deutsch listened with a growing sense of frustration. "Look, all I'm trying to say is, we don't *have* to go on as a synagogue. We don't *have* to continue as a congregation. Nothing in Torah says we must do any of that. We are under no obligation to replace that building."

Frances had a smile. "Why are you opposed to rebuilding?"

"I think we have to consider our own safety," Deutsch replied. "If we rebuild, we will only draw attention to ourselves. Attention we don't really need right now."

"You mean we should give in?"

"No. I actually think we should organize ourselves into fighting units and respond with force."

Men in the group chuckled at the suggestion. No one took Deutsch seriously on that point.

"Then why not rebuild as a way of showing our strength?" Karelitz asked.

"Maybe we should," Deutsch conceded. "But what about our children?"

"What about them?"

"They are the vulnerable ones, and it's our responsibility to make decisions that do not place them at risk."

"And you think rebuilding puts them at risk?"

"Not in the long term, but in the short term, yes." Deutsch nodded. "Rebuilding places them at greater risk than the risk they face right now."

"And fighting back? What about that? Doesn't that increase their risk?"

Hayyim Glick, who had been sitting quietly, listening to the others, finally spoke up. "What does it matter? If we rebuild, they will only tear it down again."

"If they tear it down," Karelitz replied gruffly, "we will rebuild again."

"Well," Frances sighed. "If we don't rebuild, what else could we do?"

"We can split into smaller groups," Deutsch suggested, "and meet in the houses of members."

"Most people would opt not to meet."

"The marginal ones would," Deutsch agreed with a nod. "But not the faithful."

The discussion continued for most of the afternoon as sentiment in the room wandered from one side of the argument to the other. Lurie listened but said nothing and sat to one side with a blank, unemotional expression.

Inside, however, an argument raged back and forth within his soul, roaming from side to side much like the group's debate. Inside he felt discouraged. Not the melancholy sense of sadness with no real reason, but rather a deep depression that expressed itself in the most cynical manner possible. Eating like a cancer through his spirit, it devoured core beliefs he'd held for years—many since childhood—and left him feeling hollow, purposeless, and wondering, not whether he could continue to function as rabbi, but whether he even wanted to. Or should he simply give in to the waves of despair that swept over him every day and... just disappear?

When the meeting concluded, Lurie went home. Aniela was in the front parlor when he arrived. She almost never sat there unless trouble was eminent or company was due to arrive and were running later than she thought they should be. Her presence caught Lurie off-guard. "You were waiting for me?"

"I've been worried lately."

"About what?"

"You."

"Why?"

"You haven't been yourself."

"It's alright."

"Something we need to talk about?"

"I don't think that would do any good. I'm going up to take a nap."

"How was the meeting? Was it a good meeting?"

"It went well. No one got into a fight."

Aniela said something in response, but Lurie didn't hear it clearly and was too tired to ask her to repeat herself. Instead, he plodded upstairs to the bedroom they shared, and collapsed fully clothed on the bed. He lay there in silence, his eyes wide open and staring up at the ceiling as scene after scene played over and over in his mind. Attacks he'd witnessed in other neighborhoods, one on the east side of town, another closer, and yet one more just a few blocks from the synagogue. The first ones were quite mild with only a few signs and not many marchers in the streets. He'd seen worse. Way worse. Houses on fire. Women screaming and crying. Little children hiding behind the folds of their dresses. Everyone watching the thugs—occasionally cheering them on—as they beat the men of the neighborhood senseless.

"We knew violence was happening around us," he muttered. "We prayed for safety. We prayed for God to keep us safe. To rescue our neighbors. To change the hearts of those behind the violence and hatred. We did all of that, but still they came for us. Still they destroyed the homes of our neighbors. Then they destroyed our homes. And finally our building—a house of worship and prayer. A house of education. A house of truth. Burned to the ground, with Eli Adler sacrificing his life."

Tears came to Lurie's eyes. "So if none of this affects any of that, then what's the point in continuing?" he whispered. "If our prayers make no difference, why take the time to pray? And why keep the ceremonial obligations? Why listen for God at all?"

After a while, Lurie rolled to a sitting position and swung his legs over the edge of the bed. He kicked off his shoes and slipped off his jacket, then loosened the top button of his shirt. As he looked for a place to hang his jacket, he caught sight of the ring box sitting on the dresser that stood nearby. Lurie retrieved the ring box, then lay back on the bed with his head propped against a pillow and lifted off the lid.

Inside he found the ring wrapped in a piece of cotton rag, just as had been done the day they placed the box in the vault. He pushed aside the cloth and gently held the ring with his fingertips. As he did, his eyes fell on the name inscribed along the ring's shoulder. "Netanyahu Ben-Yoash," Lurie said aloud. "Netanyahu—Yahweh has given."

Suddenly the words Judah Alkalai had said to him filled his mind. *You are the Anointed One. The one through whom the Promise of God passes to subsequent generations.*

And then the specific prophecy:

"Before long, your wife will give birth to a daughter. You must name your daughter Sarah. When she is of age she will meet a man named Nathaniel. They will marry. And after two years, they will have a son… the Promise will go to him."

Lurie's eyes shone with wonder as he studied the letters of the inscription, the scratches left on the ring by centuries of wear, and the smoothness of the inside surface. "Of all the generations that have held you," he whispered, "you have come to me." A ring of promise. A ring that once was on the finger of David, king of Israel.

He'd never thought of himself as a descendant of David. Not really. He knew it in his mind, but not in his heart. And certainly not as a birthright endowing him with the gifts of one given by Yahweh. Now, however, a renewed since of obligation swept over him.

"I have a duty to see that you reach your next destination," he said to the ring. "Which apparently is my grandson. A child who is not even alive yet."

A smile came to Lurie's face. He would have a grandson. As surely as he was lying on his bed, holding the ring, he would have a grandson. God would see that it happened. And then another thought came to him. One that left him strangely warm inside. *If God could give me a grandson, surely He could rebuild a building. Surely He could show a discouraged, depressed rabbi how to move forward.*

"Yes," he whispered with a smile. "I think he could."

8

NETANYAHU

IN THE SPRING of the following year, Yevgeny returned again to Kreva as he worked the grain-buying circuit. By then Liba had given birth to a son, Nathan, who was almost a year old. Yevgeny had a son by then, too—Ze'ev—a newborn. And in spite of his excitement over his growing family Yevgeny still was talking about going to Palestine. And about Leon Pinsker.

"Many people are talking about moving to Palestine and some individuals have gone there on their own. But the two major groups with enough support to actually create a lasting settlement are Bilu and Hovevei Zion. Hovevei Zion is Pinsker's organization," Yevgeny explained. "They are already establishing settlements there and making plans for more."

"How do they do that? Zvi wondered. "Just move in, find an open spot, and settle down?"

"Palestine is controlled by the sultans of Istanbul. Pinsker and his group have purchased land from them. They own the property and are recruiting people to move there and work it."

"Farming."

"Yes. Which is precisely what you are good at."

"Not really. I'm good at securing the property and hiring someone to do the work, but I don't really farm."

"But you know how to."

"Yes. I know how it's done." Zvi paused a moment, thinking about what a move to Palestine might mean for his family. "I've heard of Hovevei. Though I can't remember any details."

Yevgeny reached inside a satchel he was carrying and took out a copy of Pinsker's latest book *Auto-emancipation*. He handed the book to Zvi. "Here, read this."

Zvi leafed through the pages. "This will answer all of my questions?"

"Not all of them, but you should read it anyway. And you should hear Pinsker talk about it. Hear him in person, for yourself. Listen to him talk about his ideas."

"Is he coming this way any time soon?"

Yevgeny shrugged. "I don't know, but he's having a series of meetings in Odessa in a few months. You should come and hear what he has to say. Bring the family. Our wives should have met a long time ago. I'm sure they will get along well. Perhaps Ze'ev and Nathan would enjoy playing together."

Liba, who'd been busy at the counter on the opposite side of the room, laughed. "I don't think Ze'ev and Nathan could do much just yet. But your wife and I might enjoy each other's company."

"Good," Yevgeny said. "We'll plan on it." Then he looked over at Zvi. "I'll send you a letter with the dates for the meetings."

✦ ✦ ✦

Early that summer, Zvi and Liba traveled with Nathan by train to Odessa to visit Yevgeny's family. Liba and Yevgeny's wife, Chava, became immediate friends. Zvi and Yevgeny spent two days listening to Pinsker address a Zionist conference, then had a day alone with him to discuss his work in greater detail. Zvi came away from that experience thoroughly convinced that peace and freedom for the Jews lay in Palestine and that permanent freedom from persecution could only be achieved by the creation of their own Jewish state.

While there, Zvi noticed Yevgeny didn't look well and he mentioned it to Liba. "His color looks...gray."

Liba nodded. "He is sick. Chava says going to the conference with you is the most he's done in over a month."

"What's wrong with him?"

"They think he has cancer."

The next day, when Zvi and Liba were preparing to leave, Yevgeny called him aside and led him out to the backyard where they could speak in private. "I wanted to tell you about something. Yevgeny shoved his hands in his pockets and looked down at the ground. "I have been to the doctor. Several doctors, actually."

"You aren't feeling well?"

Yevgeny shook his head. "Doctors found some abnormal blood cells. They think its cancer."

"I'm sorry."

"Yeah," Yevgeny sighed. "Me, too." He looked over at Zvi and shrugged his shoulders. "That's their best guess, anyway. They aren't sure. I'm not sure. But whatever the problem, it's not good."

"Can they treat it?"

"Not here in Odessa. Doctors in Berlin have developed some new drugs and new procedures. We're thinking about going to see them."

"Anything I can do to help?"

"Not right now. But I won't be around to look after the group...or the wheat. I'll arrange for someone to take over your farm account, but you'll have to look after the men in the group."

"I won't be much of a substitute for you, but I'll do my best."

Yevgeny placed his hand on Zvi's shoulder. "I'm sure you'll do far better than I."

✦ ✦ ✦

Over the next two months, Yevgeny's physical condition worsened and when he finally arrived in Berlin, he was too weak to care for himself. He was seen by Dr. Otto Huppert, a specialist in the rapidly developing field of oncology. Dr. Huppert sent him that same day to Ernst Horn Hospital where he was promptly admitted and assigned to a room on the cancer ward. Maria Bothe, a nurse at the hospital, cared for Yevgeny's daily nursing needs.

Unbeknownst to Dr. Huppert or the hospital administration staff, the nurse was secretly a member of the Christian Socialist Workers' Party, an anti-Semitic German political organization with ties to similar organizations around the world. One of the groups to which it was allied was a network established by Ibrahim al-Kazem, a network bent on containing the rising sense of Jewish nationalism and on ultimately eliminating the entire race.

Two days after Yevgeny's arrival, Bothe was on her way to work aboard the trolley. As the car came to a stop near the hospital, she made her way to the exit and stepped down to the sidewalk. Moments later, she spotted a man waiting on the corner ahead of her. He wore a German army uniform and carried himself with dignity and distinction as he made his way toward her. They passed within inches of each other and as they did he calmly removed an envelope from the pocket of his jacket and slipped it to her. She took it from him without breaking stride and without saying a word.

Later that morning at the hospital, she stepped aside to a storeroom and opened the envelope. Inside she found a small vial that contained a liquid substance and a note that read simply, "Administer daily. Yevgeny Jabotinsky." She slipped the vial back into her pocket and tore up the note, then flushed the pieces down the toilet in the bathroom across the hall.

The liquid in the vial was thallium, known to accelerate the formation of cancerous tumors and lesions. For the next three weeks the nurse administered small doses of it to Yevgeny on a daily basis.

Dr. Huppert worked tirelessly to treat Yevgeny's condition, but in spite of his best efforts Yevgeny continued to deteriorate. Before the end of the month, he was dead.

Two days after Yevgeny passed away, Ibrahim received a telegram in Odessa. The message read simply, "Goal reached. Bonus due." Ibrahim smiled and took the time to read the note once more, savoring the success of a plan that finally worked. Then he unlocked the bottom drawer of his desk, took out a locked box, opened the lid, and grinned. *No more Yevgeny Jabotinsky. This will be the best money we've spent so far.*

✦ ✦ ✦

Word of Yevgeny's death spread quickly among farmers on his buying circuit in the Pale of Settlement. When it reached Kreva, the news struck Zvi hard. He and Yevgeny had become acquainted when Zvi decided to use him to market his wheat crop, but Yevgeny's big ideas about Jewish nationalism captured Zvi's attention at a level much deeper than business. They talked often. About the evils of the Russian Empire, the way Russian monarchists often spoke the correct words when they discussed the Jewish situation but always meant the opposite of the spoken meaning.

After their last visit, Zvi had expected Yevgeny would die, perhaps even soon, but not that soon. And it wasn't until he was gone that Zvi realized just how deep their relationship had become.

Still, the work they had started together was too important to ignore. Time continued to pass. Circumstances for the Jews of Russia seemed to change daily, most of it for the worse. So, reluctantly, Zvi gathered the core group of men who'd trained with Yevgeny—Yaakov Verlinsky, Levi Martov, Yitzhak Yagoda. They met in the back room at Verlinsky's store and began working methodically through Pinsker's book, *Auto-emancipation*.

NETANYAHU

AS TIME PASSED, the years following Yevgeny's death fell into the familiar rhythm of the seasons—planting, growing, harvesting, and long cold winters. Zvi concentrated on his family, the farming that provided most of their livelihood, and his duties as rabbi. Nathan grew older and was joined by a younger brother. More children followed and Zvi's family continued to grow.

From the time he could talk, Nathan was schooled at home, mostly by Liba, but he was a precocious child, capable of learning far more than she could teach him. Nathan had a voracious appetite for learning, but despite Zvi's efforts to add more content, Nathan soon outpaced most of what his father could offer. When he turned five he was registered with the cheder—a traditional Jewish elementary school that concentrated on the fundamental principles of Judaism and the Hebrew language. Classes were held at the synagogue in Kreva, located near their home and taught by the rabbi, Simeon Risikoff. Instruction there wasn't much better than Zvi could offer but with all day to devote to the task, Risikoff was able to pose enough of an academic challenge to keep Nathan interested.

In the year that Nathan turned ten, Rabbi Yehuda Berlin came to visit the synagogue. A genuine Talmudic scholar, Yehuda came from a family steeped in the study of Jewish law, faith, and tradition. His brilliant mind was complemented by the force of his spirit and tempered by the twinkle in his eye. The boys attending Risikoff's cheder classes were immediately taken by him.

Yehuda spent most of a day with the class, using that time to talk about Zionism—the notion that Jews have a unique identity among the peoples of the world, a unique role in history, and a unique location from which to pursue both: Palestine.

That night, he spoke to a gathering of adults at the synagogue, repeating some of what he said earlier but also talking about the growing effort to establish a Jewish homeland in Palestine. Yehuda was associated with Hovevei Zion, an organization created to promote the immigration of Eastern European Jews to Palestine. The group sponsored the establishment of Rishon LeZion, the first Jewish settlement in Palestine, and Yehuda had much to say about that work.

Nathan attended the meeting with his family and was enthralled by Yehuda's message. His call for a renewal of understanding of Jewish history and in the Hebrew language. His suggestion that only in their own state would Jews be truly safe and free. And his insistence that such a Jewish state could only be established in Palestine.

On the way home, Zvi and Liba talked about what they'd heard. "This is much like what Pinsker was talking about," Zvi said.

"Are you interested in doing that?"

"Doing what?"

"Moving to Palestine?"

"I don't know. That would be quite an arduous task."

"Yes," Liba nodded. "It would be very difficult. And I notice that not many of the people talking about going to Palestine are actually making the move themselves."

"Well, I suppose—"

"They seem to spend most of their time urging others to go, while they remain here."

"Which means?"

"They know the topic is popular. So they talk about it because they can draw a crowd," Liba clarified.

"I'm not sure Yehuda Berlin could make that move. He's quite old.

Most people moving to Palestine are going to farm. He wouldn't be able to do that."

"And that's another thing. Why do they go there to farm? Are they all farmers here? Now?"

"Farming is the most readily available way of making a living. None of the people we've heard speaking about Zionism could do that kind of work. Not Pinsker and certainly not Yehuda Berlin. Talking about it and urging others to make the move is the best they can do. Someone has to promote the idea."

Before Liba could respond, Nathan spoke up. "Who is Pinsker?"

"Leon Pinsker," Zvi explained.

"What does he do?"

"He's a doctor in Odessa. And another person who is speaking out on the same topic we heard this evening."

"I like Yehuda Berlin," Nathan said.

"He is an interesting person."

"What else does he do?" Nathan asked. "Does he farm, too, like you were talking about?"

"No," Zvi looked amused. "Yehuda Berlin teaches at a yeshiva in Volozhin."

"Where is that?"

"Not too far from here. About forty kilometers, I think."

✦ ✦ ✦

It was late when they arrived at home and Liba sent Nathan straight to bed. A few minutes later, Zvi came to Nathan's bedroom to tuck him in. He brought with him the copy of Pinsker's book, *Auto-emancipation*, which Yevgeny had given him.

He handed the book to Nathan. "Take a look at this."

Nathan held it gingerly and carefully turned back the front cover. His eyes scanned down the page quickly, then he glanced up at Zvi with a puzzled expression. "This is not written in Hebrew."

"No, this book is written in German."

"I've never seen anything written in German before."

"German is the language of serious scholarship," Zvi noted. "All the important books on serious topics are written in that language."

"I thought we were supposed to learn Russian. That's what Rabbi Risikoff says."

"Certainly," Zvi responded. "We learn the Russian language and literature in order to fit in with the Russians. To accommodate the demands of Russian life—as far as possible. But those who choose a scholar's path learn German for the academic world. In order to participate in the academic discussion of the topics that interest us."

"But Yehuda Berlin says that we shouldn't do that."

"I think he means we should never forget our true identity." Zvi smiled. "Our Jewish identity. But we live in a land filled with Russians, who have a long history of their own traditions, and languages, and practices. We can live and move among them without forgetting who we really are."

"That's a lot to do."

"Yes." Zvi chuckled. "Some days it seems like too much."

Nathan thought for a moment, "Could I learn to read German?"

"Certainly."

"I would like that."

They sat in silence while Nathan leafed through the pages of the book. Then Zvi said, "That book was given to me by our friend, Yevgeny Jabotinsky."

Nathan had a puzzled expression. "Who is he?"

"A friend from Odessa. He used to buy our wheat crop."

"I don't remember him."

"You were very young when he used to come around."

"He doesn't do that anymore?"

"No." Zvi shook his head. "He is dead now."

"Did that make you sad?"

Zvi pulled the covers up around Nathan's chin. "Did what make me sad?"

"That he died."

"Very much."

"That's strange. He used to be here, but now he is gone."

"It is one of the mysteries of life."

"Did he have children?"

"Yes. He had a son, Ze'ev. Ze'ev Jabotinsky."

"What does he do?"

"He's in school now, I think. He's about your age."

"What is he like?"

"I don't know. I only met him once. You were there, too, but you were both very small. Too young to remember much of anything, I think."

"Will we see him again?"

"I think there is a very good chance the two of you will meet." Zvi was ready to change the subject and pointed to the book. "Would you like for me to read that to you?"

Nathan nodded. "I want to hear what Leon Pinsker has to say." He handed the book back to his father and slid even lower beneath the cover as Zvi opened it and began to read.

For the next several months, Zvi and Nathan huddled over Pinsker's book while Zvi translated the text, line by line, from German to Russian. Gradually, Nathan picked up bits and pieces of the language and began to translate portions of the book for himself, using the vocabulary he remembered from hearing his father read. When Zvi became aware of Nathan's effort to learn the language, he devoted even more time to their study, explaining as much German grammar as he could.

Though moving at a slower pace than simply reading the book, they gradually made their way through it, translating, reading, and discussing both the language and Pinsker's ideas. And as they worked together, Nathan's command of the issues raised by Pinsker continued to develop and grow.

"Pinsker says we must not lose our Jewish identity," Nathan noted.

"Yes. He does."

"So does that mean that some people have lost their Jewish identity?"

"I'm afraid they have."

"Weren't we born Jewish?"

"Yes."

"Then how do we get the Jewish out of us?'

Zvi chuckled. "He doesn't mean it quite that literally."

"Then what does he mean?"

"He means, they have rejected the beliefs that have traditionally been common among Jews. The practices and beliefs that define us as Jews. Not the physical features of our bodies."

Nathan looked concerned. "They don't believe in God anymore?"

"Many of them do not."

"Why?"

"Persecution has that effect on some."

"Does it have that effect on you?"

"No."

"It doesn't on me, either," Nathan proclaimed.

"Don't think too poorly of them," Zvi cautioned. "Pinsker was in favor of assimilation until the pogroms of '71."

"He thought we should give up our Jewish identity?"

"For a while, yes. He did. He thought the only way to avoid the pogroms was by becoming genuinely Russian. That people would then leave us alone."

"What's a pogrom?"

"The Russian attacks on our neighborhoods."

"Oh."

"There was a bad one in 1871. After that, Pinsker realized Jews would never be seen as equals by Russians, no matter how much Russian culture we adopted. That's when he began looking for a homeland for us."

"Palestine?"

"At first he wanted a separate place in Russia, but quickly realized that would never work."

"Don't we all want to go back to Palestine?"

"Not everyone. Some would live anywhere as long as it's not here. And some don't want to live anywhere else, no matter what happens to them."

"If we moved to some other place, wouldn't that just be trading trouble here for trouble there?"

Zvi laughed. "Yes, it would." He tousled Nathan's hair playfully with his hand. "But in Palestine, we would be in the home of our ancestors. And if we controlled the country with our own government, we might be able to avoid the repeated attacks against us."

✦ ✦ ✦

Having finished Pinsker's book, Zvi and Nathan moved on to other texts written in German. Zvi did his best to teach his son to read and understand the language, but his command of German grammar was limited and before long he was unable to answer all of Nathan's questions. Not to be deterred, Nathan turned to Rabbi Risikoff for help.

At first Risikoff dismissed the request out of hand, but when Nathan explained how he'd come to be interested in German while reading Pinsker's book, Risikoff relented and agreed to tutor him. "But only at the end of the day, after class ends. The Russian authorities will not allow me to teach German during regular school hours."

"Why not?"

"They want us to learn Russian. Only Russian. Russian language, Russian literature, Russian history and culture. Russian music. All secular subjects must be Russian. They must be taught in Russian, about Russians, for Russians."

"This is what Pinsker talks about in his book."

Risikoff frowned. "What is?"

"Only learning Russian. They want us to give up being Jewish and become Russian."

Risikoff nodded. "Yes, and some of our people encourage others in that effort. Claiming that being a Jew is only a religious preference and not an ethnic one."

"Is that true?"

Risikoff thought for a moment, as if considering a well-worded answer, then looked down at Nathan. "What do you think?"

"I think they want us to be like them."

Risikoff's eyes narrowed. "They want us to be Christian. That is what they really want. They want us to be Christian."

"Would they leave us alone if we were?"

"No, they would not leave us alone. Many claim they would, but it is a lie. Even if we renounced Judaism completely and were baptized they would always suspect we were lying. That we were conforming only to escape the persecution."

"Then we should become more Jewish," Nathan declared.

The answer caught Risikoff by surprise. "Yes," he chuckled. "I suppose we should."

"Papa says German is the language of scholars."

"Many serious and important scholarly works have been written in German."

"I am a scholar. That is why I must learn German."

"Wouldn't you rather play outside with the others?"

"This is my play."

Risikoff and Nathan met in the afternoon every day after class was dismissed. Six lessons into their time together, however, Risikoff found his understanding of German stretched to the limit. To keep ahead of Nathan's constant questions he was forced to study grammar on his own, too. In the process, his intellectual curiosity took on new energy and he worked well into the night, studying and preparing for the next day's lesson.

Late one afternoon, Zvi returned to town from inspecting his wheat fields and stopped by the classroom to collect Nathan for the walk home. While Nathan gathered his things, Risikoff gestured for Zvi to step aside and led the way out to the hall.

"Is everything all right?" Zvi asked when they were alone.

"Yes, everything is wonderful. And that is just it. Nathan is a special student."

"Yes," Zvi agreed. "He is talented."

Risikoff wagged his finger for emphasis. "No, this is beyond mere talent."

Zvi frowned. "What are you saying?"

"I'm saying, Nathan is a student with a calling."

"He's hardly more than ten years old."

"And that is how I know," Risikoff insisted. "He is special. He needs to be in school somewhere else. Somewhere with teachers who can teach him more. Already at a young age he has mastered subjects most men don't learn in a lifetime of trying."

Zvi grinned. "Are you saying you have nothing more to teach him?"

"I'm saying, I stay up half the night just to keep ahead of him in these German lessons. He could learn more. Much more."

"But where could he go?"

Risikoff's eyes flashed with excitement. "To the school in Volozhin."

Zvi's expression turned serious. "Yehuda Berlin."

"Yes."

"Can Nathan get in that school? They only accept a few each year and they are very careful about the ones they select."

"He would have no trouble gaining admission on intellect, but his age might be a problem."

"Too young?"

"Yes. He is far younger than their minimum age. But if they would agree to interview him, I think they would understand that he needs to attend their classes. I doubt they've ever seen a young man this gifted."

"I don't know," Zvi sighed. "What if we apply and he is rejected?"

"Then we will have at least tried. We owe it to Nathan to try."

"I'll talk to him," Zvi resolved finally. "And to his mother. But I'm not sure how this is going to work out."

"If you and Liba agree to let him apply, I will do all I can to help," Risikoff added. "I know Yehuda Berlin and some of the others who teach there. I will contact them on Nathan's behalf."

Zvi nodded. "Let me talk to Liba first."

✦ ✦ ✦

At home that evening, Zvi and Liba discussed whether Nathan should attend class at the school in Volozhin and whether he should even apply for admission. Liba was proud of Nathan's accomplishments and of the way others recognized his abilities, but the notion of sending him away from home for school, on an extended basis, left her uneasy.

She sat quietly at the dinner table and hardly spoke a word, even after the meal was finished.

While she brooded, Zvi took Nathan out to the back porch. "Am I in trouble?" Nathan suddenly inquired.

"No, why do you ask?"

"You only take me out here when I'm in trouble."

A broad grin turned up the corners of Zvi's mouth. "I also come out here to talk in private."

"Oh. Is something wrong?"

"I talked to Rabbi Risikoff this afternoon. He thinks you need to attend a different school."

"Did I offend him?"

"Not at all. He likes you and enjoys teaching you. It's just, you've learned far more than he expected. He thinks you need to attend a school that presents you with more challenges and more opportunities."

"Where would I go?"

"To the yeshiva in Volozhin. You would learn from Rabbi Yehuda Berlin."

Nathan's eyes were bright with curiosity. "Yehuda Berlin?"

"Yes."

"Wow. We're moving there?"

"No. Not us. Just you."

"How would I get there? Would you take me? I don't know where it is."

"That's just it." Zvi knelt beside him. "You wouldn't travel back and forth each day. You would have to live down there."

"They would let me live at the school?"

"We have friends. I'm sure we could arrange a place for you to stay."

"That's why Mama is upset?"

"Yes. She's glad for you to learn all you can. And she wants you to follow whatever path takes you to your destiny. But the thought of you not being at home with us makes her sad."

"It makes me sad, too," Nathan said. "But it makes me excited to learn from Yehuda."

"The scholar's life," Zvi added.

"Would I become a rabbi like Yehuda and Rabbi Risikoff?"

"Only God knows what will happen to us. But this is the way rabbis begin."

Nathan reached over and put his arms around Zvi's neck. "I think that would be a wonderful life."

✦ ✦ ✦

Later that evening, after everyone else was in bed, Liba and Zvi talked. Liba still was not happy. "I know he is the oldest and he will leave home first, and he is smarter than many boys twice his age, but he is still just a boy. A small boy."

"But a boy with talent and calling," Zvi added.

"He'll be raised by someone else."

"He can come home for vacations and we can go there any time we choose."

"It won't be the same."

"I doubt it's going to be the same regardless of where he attends. Already he has gone further in learning than either of us."

"He is too young for this."

"He is young," Zvi acknowledged. "But if this is the path to his destiny, do we want to be the ones who get in the way?"

"If this is his destiny," Liba said reluctantly, "getting in the way would only harm him."

"Exactly."

"Will the school accept him?"

"I don't know. And it would take a committed effort on our part to give him even a chance."

"What do you mean?"

"If we apply, we'd have to be willing to let him attend. If we apply, and they accept him, and then we try to back out, I don't think they will allow him to attend later under any circumstance."

"I'll agree for him to apply," Liba sighed. "But I'm not sure about letting him attend."

"That's what I'm saying. If we apply and he is—"

"I'll not let a schoolmaster force a decision from me regarding my child's future." She looked over at Zvi. "And that includes you, Zvi Mileikowsky. Rabbi or not. I am Nathan's mother. If this is the right move for him, I will agree. If it is not, I won't."

During their afternoon German lesson the following day, Nathan brought up the subject of changing schools with Risikoff. "Papa wants me to attend the yeshiva at Volozhin."

"Yes, he and I talked about that yesterday."

"I cannot attend here any longer?"

"You, at such a young age, have mastered more of Torah than any of the men in Kreva. You were given this ability for a reason and that reason is the calling of your life. You must be faithful to it. No matter where your study and work takes you, no matter how much or little you understand of the things you encounter, you always must follow the calling. You understand much, but always remember—as between understanding and obedience, obedience is the more treasured attribute."

Nathan nodded his head. "Then the decision is no decision at all. Merely a choice between obeying or not."

"Precisely," Risikoff agreed.

"Do they have many students my age?"

"They have no students your age. You would be the youngest person in the class. Their minimum age is fifteen. You are far younger than that."

"And still I should apply?"

"Yes," Risikoff insisted. "I think you must."

"So, if this is the direction for my life, and I respond in obedience to it, and if they are obedient to the call upon their lives, they will have no choice but to accept me," Nathan declared.

"Yes."

"Then I have no choice but to apply for admission."

As he promised, Risikoff contacted Yehuda Berlin and the teachers he knew at Volozhin. On his recommendation, Yehuda agreed to interview Nathan and consider him for class at the yeshiva. The following week, Nathan and Zvi traveled to Volozhin for an interview where he spent most of the day alone with Yehuda.

A few days later, while attending class at home in Kreva, Rabbi Risikoff informed Nathan that Yehuda Berlin had agreed to accept him as a student. Nathan ran home that afternoon excited to share the good news with his mother and father, but as he entered the house he saw from the look on her face that Liba had been crying. Zvi, however, beamed with pride as he drew a letter from the pocket of his jacket. He opened the envelope and held the page for Nathan to see. "This is the official acceptance letter."

Nathan held it carefully with both hands and read each word, then read them all again just to make sure. When he finished, he handed the letter back to Zvi and looked over at his mother. "Isn't this good news, Mama?"

"Yes," Liba nodded, struggling to hold back the tears. "It is good news indeed."

Nathan stepped to her side, wrapped his arms around her waist, and pressed his face close, burying it against the folds of her dress. "Then why are you so sad?"

"Because you will be leaving us to attend school."

"But it's not that far away."

"I know, but you won't be here, with me."

Nathan looked up at her. "You want me to stay here with you?"

Liba ran her fingers through his hair. "I want you to go, and I want you to stay, too."

"Then it's like Samuel," Nathan smiled.

Liba's countenance changed. "Samuel?"

"In the writings. His mother prayed for a child, then when he was born she gave him up to the priests at a young age."

"Oh, Nathan," she sighed, and wrapped her arms around him in a hug.

NETANYAHU

NATHAN WAS GLAD to be at the school in Volozhin where he learned under the care and tutelage of Yehuda Berlin, but life and study at the school in Volozhin proved more difficult than Nathan had imagined. On top of which, he was homesick almost every day for the first three months. Even so, Nathan's circumstances were far better than many of his classmates.

Zvi had arranged for him to live at the home of Bezalel Cohen, a watchmaker and friend whom Zvi had known since childhood. Bezalel and his wife had no children and were more than glad to have Nathan in their home. Their doting attention created an atmosphere that gave Nathan the freedom and latitude to concentrate on his studies much the same as he could at home. Many of his classmates were not so well-situated.

Isaac Panigel, one of Nathan's first friends at the school, lived with a family that had six children. He slept on the bare floor every night and food was always scarce.

Raphael Kovo, another friend, roomed in a former tool shack that stood behind a farmer's barn eight miles out of town. His bed was the top of a former work bench and in rainy weather a small stream trickled across the floor. Raphael often came to school with muddy shoes and his clothes smelled faintly of livestock.

But with the Cohens providing an environment conducive to study at home and Yehuda challenging him intellectually at school, Nathan's daily life soon fell into a familiar rhythm of school, chores, study, and sleep. Before long, the homesickness faded and Nathan began to flourish. And as he did, ideas and concepts now came vividly to life for him.

On most days, class was conducted with the students divided by age groups with instruction more narrowly tailored to their respective capacities. However, when Yehuda lectured, the entire school assembled in the sanctuary where he addressed them as a single group. Those lectures were always oriented toward the older students, with the younger ones expected to keep up as best they could. For some, the primary challenge was remaining awake for the duration of the session. Nathan, however, was eager to hear what Yehuda had to say. He attended his first Yehuda lecture on a Thursday just four days after his initial school term began.

As the youngest student at the school, Nathan sat with the first class on a bench at the back of the classroom. A writing tablet rested on his knee and he held a pencil, eager to scribble down notes and thoughts that came to him while Yehuda spoke. He sat with his eyes focused on the door up front, waiting to see Yehuda the moment he entered, oblivious to the boys around him who restlessly squirmed and soon began to giggle.

After a few minutes there was a rustling up front and a moment later Yehuda appeared in the doorway. His hair was long and gray and hung in twisted payots from beneath a black kippah. A full, fluffy gray beard tumbled from his jaw and cascaded down the front of his rekel. There was an intensity about him that made the room at once silent and still, but very much alive with energy, and his eyes shone with a childlike curiosity Nathan could see even from a distance.

That morning, Yehuda chose for his topic the historic Davidic Kingdom of old. More specifically, the notion of a relationship between the promise of a kingdom to David, the extent to which that kingdom flourished in historic times, and the possibility of a relationship between the eternal promise to David and the awakening interest among Jews of the present day to return to Palestine and create a modern Jewish political state.

The topic was not entirely new to Nathan. Rabbi Risikoff had suggested it several times, but only as a possibility. Never as a basic assumption of truth. That day, as Yehuda explored the passages from *Samuel*—the geographic reach of the kingdom both in the beginning and at its height, and the question of whether the destruction of Jerusalem by the Romans actually meant the end of that kingdom—he left little doubt he thought the matter was more than a mere possibility. He had large maps, which he displayed on an easel up front and used them to illustrate his points. And he had intriguing insight into the ancient writings of David and his contemporaries.

From the moment the lecture began, Nathan's mind came alive in a way he'd never known before. Yehuda seemed to notice his reaction and before long it appeared to Nathan that the lecture were no lecture at all but a conversation between the two of them—one mind to the other.

Yehuda pointed to one of the maps, "This is the Davidic Kingdom of old. All of this is rightfully ours. Rightfully set aside for the Jews. Some will suggest that those living in the land today are descendants of the Canaanites. Those who make such arguments are wrong. They neither know the subject nor scripture. The Canaanites are long gone. As are the Philistines. The people living there now are Arabs. Descendants of Arabs who conquered the region after the Roman Empire began to collapse."

Nathan could have listened to Yehuda all day, but after two hours, the lecture came to a close and students filed from the sanctuary to resume their normal class schedule. Nathan, however, remained at his seat on the bench and watched as Yehuda shuffled through the crowd to the door.

Something deep inside awakened in him that day. The Davidic Kingdom—the promise to David that his house would never come to an end—along with the call for Jews to return to Palestine and establish a Jewish state as a way of avoiding persecution in Europe. It all made such sense. It seemed so...right. Why hadn't his father told him this? Zvi had studied Pinsker and he had heard all the early Zionists lecture on the topic of returning to Palestine. Yet in all of their discussions he had never heard any mention that God was at work keeping His promise to David. Why?

Lost in thought, Nathan failed to notice Yehuda had returned to the sanctuary and now stood at his side. That is, until Yehuda nudged him on the shoulder. "You enjoyed the lecture?"

Nathan was startled by the sound of his voice and immediately jumped to his feet. "Yes sir. Very much."

"Move over," Yehuda said as he took a seat.

Nathan stepped aside to give him room. Yehuda settled into place and tapped the space beside him with his finger. "Have a seat."

Nathan sat and Yehuda smiled over at him. "You have questions you wanted to ask?"

"Yes, sir."

"Many of your classmates simply stared out the window, lost in daydreams."

"I did not notice."

"I know. And you also didn't leave to return to class with everyone else."

"I'm sorry," Nathan said as he stood. "I will go now."

Yehuda stopped him with a hand to his shoulder. "Sit here a moment longer and tell me your questions."

"I have heard people discuss this topic before. Adults. Men of wisdom and learning. My own father studied the works of Pinsker and he attended lectures from many of the leading Zionists. He and I talked about these things often. Yet I never heard any mention that God was at work keeping His promise to David. Why?"

"That is a good question."

"It would provide so much symmetry to the argument. So much *rightness* to the call."

"You are very perceptive," Yehuda said softly.

"Do they not see it? Do they not relate this to the words of the *Tanakh*?"

"Not all of our fellow Jews are believers. Many of them don't believe in anything other than the improvement of their own circumstances. Many of those who think that way wish to remain right here, pursuing their own secular interests. So they want to become as Russian as possible, thinking that if they do they will simply melt into Russian society and the persecutions will come to an end. But we have many who support the cause of Zionism for whom *Tanakh* holds little sway. They think of it as merely a collection of writings about ancient Jewish religious customs and Jewish folkways." Yehuda smiled again at Nathan. "This is not the way your father sees it, is it?'

"No."

"I should think not. And it is not the way that I see it. Nor do you."

Nathan pointed to one of the maps still hanging from an easel in front. "Isn't that the Jewish state you talk about in your Zion lectures?"

"Yes, it is the political state to which we aspire in Palestine."

"And isn't all of Palestine rightfully ours, just as God said to David?"

Yehuda nodded. "A Jewish state stretching from the Mediterranean, across Palestine, beyond the Jordan, to the land allotted to Israel by God as the Promised Land."

"Then why don't we talk about it that way? Why don't we talk about it as God fulfilling his promise?"

"For us, passages from the *Tanakh* are the words of truth and from them we find our meaning and the meaning of life." Yehuda patted Nathan on the shoulder. "We must each find our way in life. I must find mine. You must find yours. And those we meet along the way, even those who help us on our journey, will not always agree with us. But we should not be discouraged or deterred by that." Yehuda stood. "But come. We must be off for the remainder of our day."

Not long after that, rumors reached the school at Volozhin about a Jewish journalist named Theodor Herzl and a book he'd recently written entitled *The Jewish State*. Supposedly, the book detailed not only the reasons why such a state was necessary but also posited ideas about how it could be made a reality. Most of what Nathan heard about it was mere rumor, but Herzl had connections to journalists and writers throughout much of the eastern hemisphere. Consequently, the book had received wide distribution and was being discussed among serious-minded people on all sides of the argument.

Yehuda mentioned Herzl's book in one of his lectures and when Nathan went home for a visit not long after that, he asked Zvi about it. "Not only that," Zvi replied. "I have a copy." He crossed the room to a shelf, took down the book, and handed it to Nathan. "I can get you one if you like." Nathan was glad to say yes.

Nathan spent much of that weekend reading Zvi's copy of Herzl's book and when his own copy arrived at Volozhin, he read it again from cover to cover. He was particularly captivated by Herzl's ideas and arguments about two things—the effect of the Diaspora on Jews, changing them from what they were into what they had become (effects of Ghetto life and constant persecution) and in escaping anti-Semitism.

After one of Yehuda's lectures, Nathan approached him and mentioned Herzl's book, then asked if there were any possibility Herzl would visit the school

"I don't think that would be possible," Yehuda answered. "But Leon Pinsker will be traveling this way soon. I am expecting him to stop by."

"Will he address the students?"

"I'll see if that can be arranged. You are familiar with his work?"

"I've read his book."

Yehuda smiled kindly. "I am not surprised."

The following month, Pinsker visited the yeshiva and talked to the students about his work through Hovevei Zion and the settlements they had established in Palestine. He had also attempted to establish a central organization, the Jewish World Conference, to coordinate and facilitate the activities of all the major Zionist organizations attempting to work in Palestine. The Conference established its headquarters in Germany, as opposed to a location within the Russian Empire, in order to gain freer access to a broader world audience.

Nathan remembered hearing much the same message, though not about a coordinating organization, when Pinsker had come to Kreva years before. Pinsker was older now and the years of advocacy with their constant travel under Spartan conditions had taken a toll on his body.

His mind was as sharp as ever, but his movements were labored. Still, Nathan listened to every word he said and when the lecture concluded he cornered Pinsker in the sanctuary to discuss more of what was happening in what had become a global Zionist movement.

✦ ✦ ✦

The following year, Herzl issued a worldwide call for a Zionist congress—a meeting of representatives from every Jewish entity, large or small, to be held in Basel, Switzerland. Notice of the announcement was published in major newspapers and periodicals in almost every country around the globe. Handbills and posters were disseminated from house to house and from shop window to shop window by eager volunteers in towns and villages everywhere.

Eventually, news of the proposed meeting reached Volozhin and when Nathan read of it, he was eager to attend. Most of the students were supportive of the Zionist cause but none of them were as intrigued as Nathan by the political maneuverings endemic to a successful and thriving movement. When the others grew tired of discussing the matter, Nathan once again turned to Yehuda.

They talked at length about Herzl, his enormous popularity, and the similarity of his ideas with those of Pinsker. "Pinsker's organization is already in Palestine, building settlements," Nathan noted. "He's traveling the world recruiting volunteers to live there and raising money to support them. And yet he is not nearly as popular as Herzl, who is spending his time wooing world leaders."

"Herzl is young," Yehuda replied. "He has the appearance of youth and vitality on his side. But I think that part of his plan will not be successful."

"Which part?"

"He wants to gain the sponsorship of a known country, as a way of giving the effort a sense of legitimacy."

"And you don't think that will work?"

"No." Yehuda shook his head. "I think in the end he will do it the way Pinsker is doing it. Send people to Palestine, build Jewish settlements, and establish a Jewish population there before anyone can stop us."

"So," Nathan mused, "these two men are headed for a confrontation?"

"I doubt it would be a *confrontation*. But it will be a decisive point."

"And wouldn't that be one of the first issues they would address at the meeting in Basel?"

"I don't know if it would be first, but I think the ultimate success of Herzl may depend on whether Pinsker will support this new organization."

"Pinsker *will* attend, won't he?"

Yehuda nodded. "He says he will."

Nathan grinned. "That is why I must be there. To see these men. To see for myself whether they will set aside their own personal ambition for the greater good."

"Well," Yehuda sighed. "It is certainly an important meeting. But there is one problem."

"What is that?"

Yehuda pointed to the notice. "The minimum age for participation is eighteen. You are too young."

Nathan thought for a moment, "Would they allow me to attend, even if I do not participate?"

"I do not know. How would you arrange for travel?"

"I'm not sure. But this congress is important. Momentum has built around the idea of a separate Jewish state. Pinsker has demonstrated it. There is strong interest among our people, even if we Zionists are a minority." Nathan rapped the announcement with his knuckle. "I want to be at this meeting. Would I be excused from class to do that?"

Yehuda nodded. "Yes, as long as you return and provide us with a report."

"That would be my pleasure."

On his next visit home, Nathan talked to Zvi about Herzl and the proposed meeting that would form a congress to organize the far-flung Zionist entities under a single organization. They talked about it for hours and then finally Nathan turned the conversation to his desire to travel to Basel for the meeting even if he couldn't officially participate.

To his surprise, he learned that Zvi had already thought of such a trip—of traveling to the meeting either as a delegate or as an observer, and of taking Nathan with him. "I'll make the arrangements. You concentrate on your studies."

NETANYAHU

IN ISTANBUL, the five Rashidun caliphs also learned of Herzl's call for a Jewish congress and summoned Ibrahim al-Kazem to appear before them to discuss the situation. As was his custom, Ibrahim responded without delay, taking the first ship available, and sailed for Istanbul. He arrived there within a matter of days of the caliphs' call and took his place before them—Barakat, Abdullah, and Talal from the house of Hassan—Musa and Idris from the house of Hussein.

Barakat led the meeting. "You are aware of this Theodor Herzl and his proclamation of a meeting to gather the leaders of all Jewish agencies and entities from everywhere through the world?"

"Yes," Ibrahim replied.

"Will it occur?" Barakat asked.

"I have no doubt the meeting will be held. Whether it will be well-attended is a matter yet to be seen, but there is widespread interest among the Jews, both Zionists and non-Zionists."

Talal spoke up. "Herzl is a man who can do this? A man who can compel others to meet as he wishes?"

"Herzl is enormously popular right now. As I'm sure you are aware, he is a journalist who wrote a book about creating a Jewish state in Palestine."

"We have heard of many such writings," Abdullah said. "What is the title of his?"

"*The Jewish State.*"

Musa bristled visibly. "Rather presumptuous title, seeing as how the land they wish to occupy is already occupied by others and has been for more than a thousand years."

"Nevertheless," Ibrahim continued, "the book is very popular. Many copies of it have been sold in all the major countries. That has provided him with two important things: Money and an entrée to men of power and influence. He has used the popularity to gain audiences with heads of state throughout Europe asking for help and for their approval of his ideas."

Idris had a knowing look. "He thinks their approval will lend legitimacy to his ideas and political ambitions."

Ibrahim nodded. "And at the same time, elevate him in the eyes of his followers."

"This is most troubling." Barakat's forehead wrinkled in a frown. "Already he has held such meetings with the Sultans."

"We should read this book," Idris suggested.

Ibrahim had a satisfied smile, "Well, because I knew the purpose for which you called me, I took the liberty of bringing you each a copy." While he passed around the books, he continued to talk. "Sources tell me that this meeting will be the first of what Herzl hopes will become an annual event to further Jewish causes and issues. And, that it will become a permanent body that exercises control over all Zionist organizations and their activities in promoting the development of a Jewish state."

"This man Herzl is a problem for us," Musa said. "I don't like him." He shook his head for emphasis. "Not at all."

Abdullah agreed. "If they are able to do this and marshal their efforts in a coordinated fashion, they could prove to be a most formidable force. Jews in England, Germany, and the United States control enormous fortunes. The Rothschilds alone could fund their entire effort."

Barakat looked over at Ibrahim. "What are our options?"

Before Ibrahim could respond, Musa interrupted. "We should engage them in a direct offensive. Identify their leaders and eliminate them without delay. Finish them before they even get started."

"A frontal attack now," Ibrahim argued, "would only enrage the Jews more and once they learned we were responsible, leaders in nations like England, France, and the United States would feel compelled to act in their support. We would become the objects of scorn."

Musa arched an eyebrow in a perturbed look. "You have a better idea?"

"One that will work," Abdullah added, glaring in Ibrahim's direction. "Thus far your ideas have not been successful."

"Not all Jews are in favor of the nationalist movement," Ibrahim ignored the snide remarks. "Many in other areas of Europe have a good life and want to keep it. They see the Zionists as disrupting their lifestyle."

"And how does this affect us," Barakat wondered, "or our desire to prevent them from organizing a global effort against us?"

"There appears to be a deep division among the Jews. Not merely between Zionist and ethnic Jews but among Jews in general. Among those wanting to resettle, some are willing to abandon life in Europe and move anywhere that offers them enough space to create their own political state and allows them to be left alone. Others want to settle only in Palestine. Secular European Jews don't care to resettle at all, but have money and are willing to pay for others to go. And, some don't want to move to Palestine, don't want others to go there either, and would like to stop the entire Zionist effort before it disrupts their existing business relationships."

"Money-loving Jews," Idris scoffed.

"Greedy," Musa noted.

Abdullah shook his head in disgust. "I knew their true nature would become evident to the world."

"So, what are you saying?" Barakat asked.

"I think it is better to let them meet," Ibrahim suggested. "Listen in on their discussions. Learn what they have to say. Observe them at this meeting and identify those in attendance. Then determine how we should respond. Their conversations could prove to be a very helpful source of information. And noting the key participants would allow us to target all of their leadership in a single strike. Right now, we know some of the players, but I suspect there are that many more whom we do not know."

Barakat was intrigued by the suggestion. "You can have someone at this meeting, on the inside, to provide us with information?"

"Certainly," Ibrahim answered smugly.

✦ ✦ ✦

After meeting with the caliphs, Ibrahim traveled to Odessa where he attempted to contact Gersh Podolsky, a wealthy Jewish shipping magnate. He and Podolsky worked together each year to facilitate the seasonal grain trade between merchants in Odessa and importers and forwarders in Istanbul—Podolsky coordinating Jewish interests in and around Odessa, Ibrahim working with his clients in Istanbul. As a result of their business together, the two had developed a deep and abiding understanding of the priorities that motivated their respective clients and associates. An understanding that had been mutually advantageous on many occasions in the past in steering Jewish and Muslim business leaders away from potentially destructive ethnic and religious conflict and back to their shared business interests. Ibrahim hoped to do the same yet again.

A response from Podolsky's office indicated that he was out of the country on business but gave no further details. A call to his home and an hour chatting up mutual friends at Podolsky's favorite steam bath told him Podolsky had traveled to Spain and was working his way back home with stops in several locations. Ibrahim tracked him down at the Hotel Veronese in Genoa and arranged to meet at Podolsky's next stop, which was in Athens, Greece.

Five days later, Ibrahim and Podolsky met for lunch in a suite at the Hotel Grande Bretagne in Athens. Located in the heart of the city, the hotel overlooked a bustling commercial center that attracted business-men from all over the world, which made it a perfect location for their meeting—far from the prying eyes they might encounter in Odessa and cloaked in the veneer of legitimate trade.

They sat across the table from each other and dined on baked fish. Podolsky wasted little time on small talk. "You went to considerable effort to find me. I assume you have something serious to discuss."

"Yes. We face a critical problem, Gersh. Perhaps more serious than any we've faced in the past."

Podolsky looked concerned. "What has happened?"

"My clients in Istanbul are not pleased with Herzl and his call for a Zionist congress."

"Oh," Podolsky sighed with a note of relief. "That." He rolled his eyes. "Many of us are equally as upset with him."

"This is not about Islam and Judaism, Gersh," Ibrahim cautioned. "This is not about a theological dispute. From all that we can learn, Herzl means to organize Jews from around the world and focus their efforts on establishing a Jewish state in Palestine."

"I understand your clients' concern, but I don't think any more will come of this than has come of their Zionist meetings in the past."

"Things *have* come of those prior meetings," Ibrahim countered. "At least two Jewish groups have purchased land from the Sultans and are establishing Jewish farming communities right now. Even as we speak." Ibrahim set down his fork and looked over at Podolsky. "Those prior Zionist meetings were not mere *meetings*. And I think this meeting will produce far more than any of the others."

"Herzl and his Zionists see nothing but trouble in Europe and are focused solely on leaving. They are mostly people who never took advantage of the opportunities made available to them."

"Well, however that may be, I think they are determined to do go," Ibrahim argued. "And there will be nothing but trouble from it. Trouble for them. Trouble for us. Trouble for you and your associates."

"I don't know Herzl. I just know what I read about him. I'm not sure I can—"

Ibrahim interrupted him. "Gersh, Arabs are not unsympathetic to the Jewish situation. We have been subjected to brutalities at the hands of the Europeans, too. Many of our people identify with the sentiment

Jews feel toward the land of their forefathers. After all, our forefathers are from that same land. But Herzl's effort to facilitate a mass return of Jews to Palestine, on an organized, broad front, will be seen by the authorities in Istanbul as a direct challenge to their sovereign rule over the region. An influx of immigrants as large as rumors suggest would be disruptive of everything." Ibrahim looked across the table at Podolsky. "And I mean everything. Not just disruptive to life in Palestine, but of our business arrangements. And you know what that would cost."

Podolsky turned to the coffee urn that sat nearby and filled his cup. "I assume you came to see me because you think there is still time to avert a disaster."

"Yes. But we would have to work together."

"We have worked together many times in the past on matters such as this," Podolsky observed. "I see no reason why we should not work together again."

Ibrahim nodded in agreement. "Good. I was thinking precisely the same thing."

"What did you have in mind?"

"As a point of beginning, I would like to know what happens at the congress."

Podolsky looked surprised. "You do not wish to prevent it from happening at all?"

"If my understanding is correct, this meeting has such broad support among the Jews that it would be impossible for us to do that."

"But I thought your point was to stop the meeting from happening."

"No. Our point is to stop the resettlement of Jews in Palestine. That's what we want to prevent."

"I see."

"But to respond properly to Herzl's effort, we need to know what happens at his meeting and to identify the key leaders.

"So you know whom to...persuade and whom to leave alone."

"Yes," Ibrahim acknowledged.

"That's a less aggressive approach than I had thought you might propose."

Ibrahim gave him a questioning look. "You were thinking...?"

"I thought you might suggest eliminating Herzl."

"That would only make him a martyr. And it would energize the Zionists in ways they could never achieve for themselves."

"So, your approach is to let the meeting go forward and learn what happens at the meeting from someone on the inside."

"Yes. Someone who can observe the discussions as they progress and determine who emerges as the instrumental leaders. Do you have someone who could help?"

"Yes," Podolsky replied. "I have just the person you need. Felix Shatunovsky."

✦ ✦ ✦

Born in Warsaw to Jewish parents, Shatunovsky left home at eighteen to attend Moscow University as a math student. During his first year of study, he became infatuated with Ivana Yakanova, a woman of Russian and Spanish descent who was five years his senior and a teaching assistant in the philosophy department.

A devotee of Karl Marx, Yakanova had long since rejected capitalism and eschewed all things religious. Shatunovsky, intoxicated by her affection and enchanted by her exotic looks, followed her lead, became a student of Marx philosophy, and set about rejecting the norms and values that had marked his earlier life. By the time their affair ended four years later, he was thoroughly secularized.

Having renounced all practices and beliefs arising from his Jewish heritage, he came to view Judaism as merely a religious moniker and not as an ethnic or political identity. So deep was the severance with his past that he no longer referred to himself as Jewish but as simply a Russian.

Ibrahim, of course, had known all of this long before he contacted Shatunovsky and was concerned about how such a non-Jewish Jew could help him infiltrate a thoroughly Jewish meeting. Podolsky assured him Shatunovsky was the man for the job and insisted Ibrahim meet with him. "Talk to him," he urged. "You'll see why I suggested him."

Reluctantly, Ibrahim went forward as planned and joined

Shatunovsky at a café near the Odessa waterfront. They took a table in back where they sipped coffee while they talked.

Ibrahim looked over at him. "I assume Podolsky told you what we are attempting to do?"

"Yes. He also told me you were unsure about whether I am the man for the job."

"I checked into your background."

"And?"

"You seem to have spent a lot of time and effort rejecting Judaism."

"You wish to convert me?"

"No, but we want to place someone in the meeting who can report in detail about what happens. That would seem to indicate we need someone with a convincingly Jewish identity."

"And you think I cannot remember what it was like to be a Jew?"

"I think anyone who knows you would be well aware of the extent to which you have rejected Judaism."

"I said I would help. I didn't say I would do it all myself."

"Is that what you propose? Enlisting a cadre of informants?"

"These Zionists represent everything I detest. Capitalism. Religious zealotry. Intellectual arrogance. I propose we do whatever is necessary to stop them. And I am not alone in this."

"You have operatives you can use?"

"We have contacts in every major Zionist organization now in existence. Whatever you want to know, we can get it."

"That sounds like a lot of people."

"We've been doing this kind of thing for a long time."

"Can you make something like that work?"

"Hasn't been a problem yet."

"How many people do you have?"

"There are as many of us as there are of them."

"How would we work out the details?"

"We'll keep it simple for everyone," Shatunovsky answered. "You tell me what you need, I'll get it for you. If you come to Basel, I'll update you daily on all that happens."

12

NETANYAHU

IN AUGUST, Nathan and Zvi traveled to Basel, Switzerland, for the First Zionist congress. They took a room at the Grand Hotel Les Trois Rois, an historic hotel on the banks of the Rhine River not far from the Municipal Auditorium where the First Zionist Congress was to meet. Nathan, having never traveled so far from home, scanned the lobby, doing his best to take in every detail, while Zvi checked them in at the front desk.

Once that was finished, they followed a porter as he carried their luggage to their room. After a moment to rest, they returned to the lobby to have a look around.

As they came from the elevator, Zvi noticed a man standing at the hotel bar across the way. Rather nondescript, he nevertheless looked familiar and Zvi had the feeling he should know his name. "I think I've seen him before."

Nathan glanced around. "Who?"

"That man by the bar." Zvi indicated with a nod in that direction.

Nathan turned to see for himself and found the man staring straight at him. A hint of recognition flashed through the man's eyes. But just as quickly as it appeared, he turned away and set his glass on the bar, then started toward the door.

"I don't recognize him," Nathan said. "But it's been a while since I spent much time in Kreva."

Zvi shook his head. "I don't think he's from Kreva. At least, not someone I've seen there recently."

"Then perhaps he's from Odessa," Nathan suggested.

"Maybe so." Zvi started across the lobby after the man, intending to catch up and introduce himself, but before he could reach him, the man pushed open the front door and stepped outside to the sidewalk. A horse-drawn hansom cab waited at the curb and without breaking stride he stepped inside, said something to the driver, and the cab started forward.

Zvi had the distinct impression the man recognized him, too. He stood there watching as the cab blended in with the evening traffic. "But why did he deliberately avoid me?" he whispered.

✦ ✦ ✦

The following morning, Zvi and Nathan made their way to the auditorium for the congress' first session. At seventeen, Nathan was still too young to officially participate, but Zvi convinced the registration clerk to let him enter.

As they loitered near the entrance to the meeting room, Zvi spotted Yevgeny Jabotinsky's son, Ze'ev. Only sixteen years of age, he was even younger than Nathan but seemed to have no difficulty working the crowd. Zvi walked over to him and introduced Nathan and himself, then reminded Jabotinsky he knew his father. "I sold my wheat crop to him."

Jabotinsky gave a faint smile. "He had many acquaintances on the grain-buying circuit."

"Yes," Zvi nodded. "But he was much more than merely a grain merchant working a merchant's route."

"What do you mean?"

"Your father used those trips to establish resistance groups all through the region. In every town and village where his clients lived he brought men together to study the works of Zionists like Pinsker and to hear reports of Zionist efforts in other areas. And later, he organized us to fight back against the Russian gangs when they attacked our neighborhoods."

Jabotinsky beamed with pride. "He used to say that was the only way we could have peace." A genuine smile spread over his face. "Fight back. Arm ourselves. Many of his friends thought he was crazy."

"He wasn't crazy. He was right."

"Any of those groups he organized still in existence?"

"Ours still meets. In Kreva."

"They're talking about using this meeting to form a worldwide Zionist organization. Using annual congresses to govern it with local affiliates throughout the world."

"I don't know how any of the other groups feel, but the men in ours would be ready to join," Zvi vowed. "We're not formally organized with officers, but we could be in a single meeting. What else are they discussing?"

"A Jewish state in Palestine."

"Everyone is settled on that location?"

"I don't think many want to consider any other place. I don't. Do you?"

"No, but the region is occupied already," Zvi added. "I think that could be a problem."

"Which is why we must control all of it."

Zvi frowned. "All of it?"

"The entire region. From Lebanon to Egypt and east beyond the Jordan River. All of the area once held by the Davidic Kingdom."

Zvi grinned. "That was your father's opinion, too."

Nathan stood by, listening as they talked, feeling inadequate to join the conversation and taken by how articulate Jabotinsky was. None of the students his age in the yeshiva at Volozhin could discuss any topic—Torah, tradition, or Zionism—with such a sense of confidence.

✦ ✦ ✦

After the opening session, attendees broke into several working groups: One to address the need for a permanent, continuing organization with global reach, giving all Jews everywhere a way to participate and annual congresses at which delegates would govern the work. Another to address the role of the various independent Zionist organizations that were already in existence and to devise a means of incorporating them into the overall work. Another to hammer out the congress' core goals that would guide it into the future. And still another to address the effort to obtain official government charters from sponsoring nations, legitimizing, facilitating, and encouraging the work. With one final group to address the practical aspects of large-scale immigration into Palestine.

Zvi and Nathan attended the immigration session which met in a room at the opposite end of the building from the main auditorium. The leader of the group was Chaim Weizmann, an academician, trained in chemistry, who lived in London.

Weizmann stood near the entrance to the room and handed out pamphlets as participants entered. Zvi and Nathan each took one and made their way to a pair of open seats halfway down the aisle. Nathan glanced over the pamphlet while they waited. "They must have organized this meeting rather well."

"What makes you think that?" Zvi asked.

"This pamphlet is well-written and printed. They didn't create it at the last minute."

"I'm sure they put a lot of effort into getting this together." Zvi glanced around the room. "Have you seen Jabotinsky?"

"Not since the end of the first session."

"Me neither. I wonder where he went."

"I don't know, but he seems like a guy who can handle himself."

Zvi chuckled. "He does, at that."

✦ ✦ ✦

In a little while, Weizmann entered and made his way onto the stage at the front of the room. A lectern stood there, positioned at the center, and Weizmann took his place behind it, then addressed the gathering.

Most of the allotted meeting time was devoted to Weizmann's argument in favor of immediate immigration to Palestine. "We need to go, and go now," he insisted. "We can't wait for a decree of permission from some government. Various leaders might be sympathetic to our effort. They might want to help. But official governmental approval and backing of our effort would be far too politically risky for any of them to attempt. We will never receive permission. Waiting for it is simply a waste of time. The only way to establish a Jewish state—in Palestine or anywhere else—is by establishing our presence there. No nation on earth will ever agree in advance to let us go there. But none, save the Arab nations, will mount the effort necessary to remove us, either."

✦ ✦ ✦

When the session ended, Zvi and Nathan walked out to the main hallway. Once again, Zvi caught sight of the man he'd seen earlier in the hotel lobby. "I still can't remember who he is or how I know him. But I'm certain I do."

While he and Nathan watched, Jabotinsky walked up to them. He noticed they were focused intently on someone or something across the room and glanced in that direction. At once, a knowing look came over him and he said in a derisive tone, "What's he doing here?"

Zvi glanced at Jabotinsky. "You know him?"

Jabotinsky nodded. "Yeah, I know him. He's Felix Shatunovsky. Gersh Podolsky's accountant."

"That's it!" Zvi exclaimed. His countenance brightened with a look of realization. "I knew I'd seen him somewhere. Gersh Podolsky's accountant." He nodded his head. "But what's he doing here? I didn't think he was one of us."

"He's not, and neither is Podolsky. They and that whole crowd think they're above the rest of us. Think of themselves as *fully assimilated.*"

"Jews with no Jewish identity," Nathan offered.

"That's what they think. But that's not how the Russians see them. They see them as Jews. And they will always see all of us that way. Assimilation is not the answer to our problems."

"They have no idea they are as vulnerable as the rest of us," Zvi added.

"When the day comes, and it will come, the czarists will try to kill us all," Jabotinsky added.

"I wonder which sessions he attended."

"I was in the session about how to use the existing Zionist organizations," Jabotinsky said. "He was in there for a while, then left."

Nathan spoke up. "He was in ours briefly, too."

Zvi leaned closer. "You sure about that? I didn't see him."

"Sat over by the wall. Took some notes. Collected one of the pamphlets. Then left."

"We need to find out what he's up to," Jabotinsky decided.

Zvi took his watch from his pocket and checked the time. "I think that will have to wait. It's time for the next session to begin."

"Maybe we should skip it," Jabotinsky suggested.

"I think we should stick to our schedule," Zvi argued. "We can see about Shatunovsky after that."

✦ ✦ ✦

After the final session of the day, Zvi and Nathan prepared to return to their hotel. Jabotinsky said goodnight, but Nathan noticed he lingered behind as they started toward the door.

"Does he have a place to stay?"

"I don't know." Zvi glanced over his shoulder in Jabotinsky's direction. "Mind if he stays with us?"

"No, it's fine with me."

With Nathan following close behind, Zvi turned back from the exit and made his way to where Jabotinsky was standing. For the first time, Jabotinsky appeared self-conscious. As if he knew what they were going to ask and didn't want to answer.

"Where are you staying tonight?" Zvi asked.

Jabotinsky glanced away. "I'll get a room around here somewhere."

Zvi pressed the matter. "You don't have a place to stay, do you?"

"Not really. I had just enough for a ticket up here. Being here seemed more important than my comfort. I'll find an empty chair somewhere and get some rest."

"Nonsense." Zvi draped an arm across Jabotinsky's shoulder. "You'll stay in the room with us."

Jabotinsky's eyes darted to Nathan, then back to Zvi. "Thanks, but I don't want to intrude. I'll be all right."

"You won't be intruding on anyone," Zvi insisted. "The two of us can sleep in the bed, and you're welcome to the large sofa in the room." He gave a tug on Jabotinsky's shoulder. "Come on. You're going with us." And they started toward the door.

After a short walk back to the hotel, they ate dinner in the main dining room, then stepped out to the lobby and started toward the elevator. As they reached it, Shatunovsky emerged from a hallway and made his way toward the door on the opposite side of the room.

A look of anger flashed over Jabotinsky. "I'm going to find out where he's going."

As Jabotinsky started after him, Nathan glanced at Zvi for permission. Zvi nodded in response and Nathan hurried after him.

✦　✦　✦

Nathan and Jabotinsky followed Shatunovsky from the hotel, trailing far enough behind to avoid being noticed but close enough not to lose sight of him. Three blocks later, he crossed the street toward a park. Nathan and Jabotinsky slowed their pace as he reached the other side, then darted through traffic and hurried after him, going as far as a statue of Guillaume Henri Dufour that stood at the park entrance. They paused at the base of the statue and scanned the park around them and the street behind, doing their best to make certain they were not headed into a trap. When it appeared no one had noticed them, they moved from behind the statue and continued in the direction Shatunovsky had gone.

Near the center of the park was a grassy meadow and in the midst of it a fountain. A neatly kept garden surrounded it and nearby was a park bench. Shatunovsky was seated there, his legs crossed, one arm draped along the back of the seat, his eyes darting around nervously in every direction.

Nathan and Jabotinsky stepped from the walkway and took a

position behind a large ornamental shrub. From there they watched and a moment later a second man approached the fountain from the opposite side of the park.

About Shatunovsky's height, the man was slender with a wiry frame, olive complexion, and dark hair. He was dressed in a well-tailored gray suit with a white shirt and black tie and he walked with a gait that conveyed an air of confidence that was missing from Shatunovsky.

"Arab," Jabotinsky muttered.

Nathan frowned. "What's he doing here? And why is Shatunovsky talking to him?"

"Why do you think?'

The Arab took a seat beside Shatunovsky and they talked for a moment, then the Arab handed him an envelope. Shatunovsky took it from him and slipped it effortlessly into a pocket of his jacket. A moment later, the Arab stood and started back in the direction from which he came. Shatunovsky remained on the bench until the Arab was out of sight, then pushed himself up to a standing position and moved back toward the park entrance. Nathan and Jabotinsky stepped around to the opposite side of the bushes as he approached then ducked out of sight to let him pass.

When Shatunovsky was gone, Jabotinsky started toward the street. "Come on. We better get back."

"You don't want to follow either of them?"

"No, we've seen enough. We have to tell your father."

✦ ✦ ✦

At the hotel that evening, Nathan and Jabotinsky told Zvi what they'd seen—Shatunovsky with a man of obvious Arab descent, their time together on the park bench, and the envelope the man handed him. Zvi was concerned but not overly so. He was, however, pleased to see his son and Jabotinsky becoming friends.

The following morning, they ate breakfast at the hotel, then returned to the auditorium for the congress' second session. When they arrived at the hall, Zvi located a congress official and told him about what transpired the day before.

Theodor Herzl presided over the session, which featured Yitzchak Reines as the morning keynote speaker. His address was both informative and entertaining and before long Nathan was engrossed in the message. So much so that he didn't notice Shatunovsky seated on the far side of the room until Jabotinsky jabbed him with an elbow to the ribs. He looked up, startled over the interruption, but mellowed when he saw three men escorting Shatunovsky from the room.

13

NETANYAHU

WHEN THE ZIONIST CONGRESS adjourned, Ibrahim departed Basel immediately for Istanbul to brief the caliphs. As they had many times before, they gathered in a nondescript three-story house situated at the end of a narrow alley not far from the bazaar.

"As you feared," Ibrahim began, "they have agreed to bring all existing Zionist organizations under a single entity."

"Those other organizations—the ones that already were in existence—they were agreeable to that?" Barakat asked.

"They agreed to it during the meeting," Ibrahim continued. "But I suspect many of them will think it over later and become reluctant to surrender their independence."

"Let us hope you are correct," Talal said.

"They intend to establish chapters in every nation that does not now have an existing entity. Within the year, they expect to be organized in every major community throughout the world."

Idris spoke up. "Perhaps we underestimated them."

"We should have been more aggressive," Musa added.

"What else did they do?" Barakat asked.

"They have also agreed to establish a bank to fund the creation of Jewish settlements and businesses in Palestine."

"They could probably do that," Barakat nodded. "Who did they place in charge of that?"

"Max Nordau and Moses Gaster were elected as vice presidents."

"Herzl did not insist on controlling it?" Abdullah wondered.

"No."

Musa shook his head with a look of disdain. "They are more deliberate about this than we expected."

Idris' eyes flashed with anger. "They are mounting a frontal attack on Turkish sovereignty."

"But will the Turks even notice it?" Musa asked.

"It's a frontal assault on Arabs," Talal added.

Abdullah rolled his eyes. "But will *they* notice either?"

Barakat turned the conversation back to the subject. "Who were the key people in attendance?"

"All the big names were there," Ibrahim answered. "Herzl, Pinsker, Reines, Weizmann. All the men you would expect. And a few we haven't noticed before." A leather satchel sat beside his chair. He opened it and took out a handful of papers. "I have a list for each of you." He rose from his seat to pass the copies around.

Barakat scanned the list of participants. "I see someone named Jabotinsky."

"He is the son of Yevgeny Jabotinsky," Ibrahim replied.

"Will he be a problem for us?"

"That remains to be seen."

"Does he suspect us of having something to do with his father's death?"

"If he does, he has not expressed it."

"He was at the conference alone?"

"He arrived on his own but he attended in the company of a man named Zvi Mileikowsky."

Barakat frowned. "Who is he? Do we know him?"

"He's a wheat farmer from Kreva and a friend of Jabotinsky's father."

Barakat looked again at the list. "I see Pinsker on here."

"Pinsker is old. He won't be around much longer. And I think he knows it."

"As are some of these others," Barakat noted. "Weizmann is on the list. He has been traveling throughout Europe promoting the congress."

"And he's been very effective with that effort."

Barakat paused a moment and glanced over the list once more. "I'm still concerned about this young one." He tapped the list with his finger. "Jabotinsky. His father was a thorn in our side. We should keep an eye on him."

"Yes," Ibrahim agreed. "We should, but he is not the key to success or failure of the Zionist cause."

"Who is?"

"Herzl," Ibrahim answered flatly.

Barakat nodded his head slowly. "For now, Herzl is the key. He's the reason this congress occurred."

"And the reason they saw this through to the end of the first session," Ibrahim added. "Most of us expected it to collapse before the first session."

"We could kill him," Musa suggested. "We could kill everyone on the list."

"We can't kill them all!" Barakat's voice had an edge to it and he did little to hide it.

Ruffled by the apparent rebuff, Musa pressed the issue. "Why not? We have men."

"Eliminating all of the capable leadership would mean killing over a hundred people."

"And that is a problem for you?" Musa's tone was mocking at first but quickly became even more severe than before. "Killing them would be an act of allegiance to Allah. You would limit your allegiance to Allah to only one hundred Jewish vermin? If it's one hundred one, you will sell out to the infidels?"

"It's not about allegiance to Allah. It's about avoiding unnecessary trouble that might destroy any chance we have of stopping them." Barakat cut his eyes in Musa's direction. "That would be the ultimate betrayal of Allah. To sell out his long-term plan for the sake of venting our frustration of the moment. All of the people we would kill are Jewish.

Many of them with international reputations. All of them with a wide array of influential relationships. If we killed a hundred people like that at once, everyone would know we did it."

Talal spoke up. "Everyone would conclude Arabs killed them. Certainly. But no one would know who actually did it. And they would never suspect us. They don't even know we exist."

"We could kill just one," Idris offered.

Talal nodded in agreement. "Herzl."

"Yes, and then—"

"We don't need to kill anyone," Barakat cut off the discussion. "We can do something less sensational but more devastating than creating Zionist martyrs. Which is what would happen if we start executing their leadership."

"Like what?" Talal asked.

"Divide them among themselves," Ibrahim interjected. "Let them cancel each other out."

Talal glared at him. "Another of your ill-conceived, poorly executed plans?"

Ibrahim ignored the comment and continued. "The Jewish community really isn't much of a community and any appearance of unity among them is only a thin veneer, at best. They are easily manipulated to believe rumors rather than facts and seem drawn toward the most unbelievable conspiracy theories."

Talal continued to stare at Ibrahim. "You haven't had much success with this kind of approach in the past."

Musa spoke up. "We should kill them all. Immediately."

They continued to discuss the issue of Jews immigrating to Palestine and of the need to stop them from doing so, but though they talked for two more hours the caliphs could not reach an agreement on how to do that. Finally, when it became obvious no one view would prevail, Barakat again asserted control over the proceedings. "We have discussed this issue all day and, though we agree that something must be done, no three of us can agree on what that something should be. Therefore, I propose that we charge Ibrahim with the goal of ending Jewish immigration to

Palestine and grant him the authority to do whatever he finds necessary, by whatever means necessary, to accomplish that goal." After one more round of discussion, the caliphs agreed and the meeting ended.

Ibrahim and Barakat lingered in the room while the others left. When they were alone, Barakat leaned back in his chair and looked him in the eye. "You realize both our lives are on the line now."

"Yes. I assumed as much."

"You have to end this immigration business and do it in a way that convinces them you were a success. Otherwise, the Assassins of Alamut will sever our heads from our bodies."

"I understand."

"I don't know how you will stop the Jews. I don't care how you do it. Do whatever it takes. Just make it happen."

"I will," Ibrahim assured.

✦ ✦ ✦

Late in the evening, Ibrahim boarded a ship from Istanbul and sailed up the Black Sea toward Odessa. On the way, he considered the options.

The caliphs charged him with stopping Jewish immigration to Palestine. That at first seemed like an expression of confidence in his ability and their authority to attack the Jewish problem in any way he pleased. But as the ship moved farther up the Black Sea away from Istanbul, he realized that blessing was also a curse. *If I fail, they will kill me.* And before long he came to think of the caliphs' decision as a final effort on their part to work with him. *It's this, or nothing more.* He had to find a way to stop the Jews from immigrating and he had to do it in a clever manner that drew as little attention as possible to the caliphs or to Arabs in general. That would not be easily accomplished.

All of the Jews with whom he worked were businessmen. None of them favored the creation of a Jewish state—not in Palestine or anywhere else. The religiously motivated ones were a different matter. They were the Zealots. A Jewish version of radical Arabs. Reason would not sway them.

Among the Jews, the two groups shared only a common ancestral past. The businessmen and the intellectuals—the so-called *enlightened Jews*—felt themselves superior to all, not merely to other Jews, and had little patience with the zealots' ethnic or religious enthusiasm. If he could devise a strategy to exploit the division between the businessmen and the religious zealots he might be able to accomplish the goal the caliphs sought. But to do that, he once again needed an informant.

In Odessa, Ibrahim contacted Podolsky and arranged to meet him at Podolsky's office. Later, they sat opposite each other across Podolsky's desk.

"I understand you encountered some difficulty in Basel with Shatunovsky."

"Only after Herzl and others from the congress became suspicious."

"Were you able to gain the information you wanted?"

"Yes. We learned enough."

"Were you able to attend any of the sessions?"

"No, I would have been too obvious."

"So, what did you think of the meeting? Think anything will come of it?"

"It was worse than we'd expected." Ibrahim looked grim. "We might have made a mistake by not taking the aggressive approach."

"Perhaps so."

"It would be in both our interests to see that this organization goes away, or at least that it becomes a non-factor."

"You think they will meet this way again?"

"They have committed to a meeting next year."

"And to the goal of creating a worldwide Zionist organization?"

"Yes."

"They actually agreed to that? To make the individual Zionist organizations subject to an international body?"

"You sound surprised."

"I was born a Jew," Podolsky explained. "I have been a Jew all my life. We are rife with factions. My own family has factions. And factions within factions."

"They were a factious bunch. Rather a collection of independent Zionist organizations than of one unified people. Smaller Zionist efforts scattered across Europe with no connection or relationship other than this congress. Followers of various spokesmen and rabbis."

Podolsky thought aloud, "It's a wonder they stayed together long enough to conclude their meeting agenda. The more temperate members of these groups can't stand the extremists except to goad them into making increasingly outlandish statements. And the extremists usually find it very difficult to avoid personal attacks on anyone who refuses to agree with their position."

"Sounds like they must stay perpetually angry with each other."

"They usually do." Podolsky leaned back in his chair. "Is there some reason you are interested in this?"

"I was wondering if there was a way to use these...issues to our advantage."

"Well," Podolsky mused, "something like that might work...as a way of frustrating their efforts."

"Without resorting to violence," Ibrahim added.

"You are averse to violence now?"

"It is disruptive."

"How well I know. Your pogroms have cost us millions of rubles."

"What is the single greatest issue?"

"They are rife with the usual petty attitudes and behaviors. The religious ones have differing views on the role of rabbis, or whether rabbis are even authorized. But the one issue that might work to frustrate them is the location of their Jewish state."

Ibrahim frowned. "There is a dispute about the location?"

"More than you realize."

"Some would actually go to another location? Where?"

"Many places."

"I assumed that was an issue on which they all were united."

"Not nearly as united as one might think." Podolsky pushed back from his desk and stood. "You need to meet some of my associates." He gestured for Ibrahim to follow. Ibrahim rose from his chair and they walked together toward the door. "I will contact you in a day or two and arrange a meeting with them."

Ibrahim was suspicious. "These are men you trust?"

"Yes. Of course. Some of them are men you already know. They will be able to help you better understand our situation and can offer you the help you will need."

✦ ✦ ✦

Three days later, Ibrahim returned to Podolsky's office where he found half a dozen men—Emile Gernsback, Gabriel Hersch, Hugo Mayer, Moses Cohn, Alexander Kandel, and Oskar Epstein—waiting for him. Ibrahim knew them all, though he had little association with Kandel.

After a moment to exchange a word of greeting, they gathered near the desk where seven chairs had been arranged. While the men took their seats, Podolsky made his way behind the desk. "As all of you know," he began, "Theodor Herzl's congress met in Basel, and it was far more successful than we thought it would be." Podolsky sat as he continued. "That success has been reported around the world and has incited the Zionists to an even greater effort to form their own state. Our contacts tell us they are organizing themselves like never before. We're here today to find a way to stop them."

Gernsback looked over at Ibrahim. "Perhaps you should increase your attacks on them. Show them the real price they will pay for their irrational decision." He flashed a nervous smile. "I am correct, aren't I? You are the primary sponsor of the pogroms, aren't you?"

Ibrahim was taken aback by the frank mention of his involvement but maintained a stoic expression. "The czar is the primary sponsor. But I am aware of Arab interests in addressing the Jewish problem."

Cohn spoke up. "Well, regardless of who sponsors the action, we need to do something. Nothing we've done so far has forced them to abandon their dream of statehood."

For the first time, Ibrahim noticed how much Podolsky and his associates sounded like the caliphs, but he kept his thoughts to himself,

"An increase in violence would vent your frustration but I think in the longer term it would be counterproductive."

Cohn had a troubled look. "How so?"

"Our experience has shown that an increase in violence only stokes their desire to leave. It does nothing to convince them to stay."

"We want them to leave," Mayer blurted. "We just don't want to be forced to join them."

"And we'd prefer they went somewhere other than Palestine."

Ibrahim was curious. "Why not Palestine?"

"We all do business with entities based in London," Epstein explained. "Officials there are squarely on the side of the Arabs and against the Zionist claims to the area. We'd prefer to keep them happy. Don't you want them to go somewhere else?"

"We share your preference for another location," Ibrahim concurred, "Already they are taking land from Arabs whose families have lived there for generations." This was not quite true—the land in Palestine occupied by non-Arab immigrants had been purchased from the sultans who controlled the region often at staggering cost—but he liked the way the men nodded their heads in agreement.

"Well, I don't care where they go," Kandel chimed in. "I would gladly unload them on anyone."

"But where else might they go, other than Palestine?"

Ibrahim had been waiting for this opening in the conversation. "We would be open to the possibility of helping them find such a location. Is there another place that would accommodate everyone's interests?"

"Maybe."

"Would they take it?"

"We could make it enticing enough. We'd get other nations to agree to support the idea. Give them a place, but not Palestine. A convenient place where the authorities want them to settle and no one objects."

"But where could they go," Ibrahim asked again, "other than Palestine?"

"India."

"Australia."

"Africa."

"Ahh. Africa might work."

"The British control most of the continent. Surely there must be a place there."

"We would need the help of the British government," Ibrahim noted.

"We have many friends in London."

"But we must be careful in how we approach them. No one else should know the idea came from us."

They all turned to Podolsky and Kandel asked, "How do we do that?"

"Adler," Podolsky answered.

They all nodded in agreement. "Adler is the one who can help us with this."

Ibrahim looked over at Podolsky. "Who is Adler?"

"Marcel Adler. A diamond broker in Belgium. He knows key officials in all of the major European governments and is well-versed in the political situation each of them faces. He would know which countries among the international powers might be amenable to such a plan and he would also know the right people to talk to."

Gernsback spoke up. "You can arrange a meeting with him?"

"Yes," Podolsky replied. "I will take care of it."

✦ ✦ ✦

As promised, Podolsky arranged for Ibrahim to meet with Marcel Adler at Adler's office in Antwerp, Belgium. Adler sat at his desk and listened while Ibrahim outlined the situation that confronted Jews in Europe. At first he seemed unemotional but after a moment he held up his hand for Ibrahim to stop. His eyes narrowed and there was a hint of anger in his voice. "I think as a Jew, conditions in Europe are something with which I am all too familiar."

Ibrahim shifted position awkwardly in the chair, his eyes darting to one side. "Yes, I suppose you are."

"And," Adler continued, "I find it rather...strange that you, an Arab, are the one talking to me about this."

Ibrahim forced a faint smile. "Yes...well, that is part of my role. Part of the service I provide."

Adler had a curious expression. "How so?"

"I have contacts among many people throughout Europe. People who are otherwise on opposite sides of the major political and social issues. I provide them the opportunity to conduct business across all lines while maintaining the public decorum required of their domestic position."

"You're a broker, correct?"

"Yes."

"And I understand from Podolsky that you represent certain interested parties in Istanbul. Parties whose concerns go far beyond mere business."

Something in Adler's posture, the look in his eyes, the casual way he laced his fingers together when he talked gave a subtle and intangible quality to the meeting that Ibrahim could not quite put his finger on, but it left him feeling Adler's line of questioning thus far had been forced and contrived, more a vetting to gauge his reaction than anything else. And he'd had enough. If Adler didn't want to help, if he wanted to amuse himself by attempting to provoke a particular reaction, or if Podolsky had simply misunderstood the nature of his intentions, then Ibrahim would find someone else to help with their Jewish problem. But he was finished with passively enduring one more question from Adler.

Ibrahim sat up straight in his chair and squared his shoulders. "I am Arab, true enough. But I am not a religious man, if that's what you mean." He looked Adler in the eye. "And I don't believe you are, either."

"So you work both sides," Adler deflected the comment with a sardonic smile.

"As do you."

A broad grin spread across Adler's face. "If you and I have a religion, I believe it is the religion of business and of our own self-interest."

Ibrahim smiled. "So it would seem."

"And Zionist activity in Europe and the Middle East interferes with our business. Perhaps even threatens to undo hundreds of years of work."

"Precisely! Businesses built on generations of effort could easily hang in the balance."

"We should do something about that, before it escalates into regional war."

"My colleagues in Istanbul and in Odessa do not want a war of any kind," Ibrahim added. "Regional or otherwise. Especially not one fought over the Zionist desire to immigrate to Palestine. It would be far too disruptive and they have other matters to address."

"I am glad to hear that," Adler added. "But I must say, Palestine is the historic homeland of the Jews—Zionist or otherwise."

"Not really," Ibrahim countered.

Adler arched an eyebrow. "How can you say that?"

"It's true, the Jews once lived there. But their original homeland was far to the east, in the Euphrates River valley."

Adler raised an eyebrow. "You would have them occupy Persia instead?"

"No, but if we are talking about native homeland, that is their native homeland."

"Trace things back far enough," Adler said, "and everyone's homeland was there."

"Precisely. Which is the reason why issues such as which group occupied which space first is irrelevant. The only issue that matters is who is there now. And Arabs have lived in Palestine for an uninterrupted span of more than a thousand years. It's not right to disrupt those who live there now, just because Jews are having a hard time of it elsewhere and want to return to a place where their ancestors once lived. A place, by the way, that almost no one of the current generation has even visited, much less lived in."

"You might be right, but you will never win that argument with the Zionists. We need to derail this effort without getting to that discussion."

"Which is why Podolsky wanted us to talk."

"What did you have in mind?"

"There are plenty of unsettled, unpopulated places in the world. My contacts in Odessa have suggested Africa might hold the greatest possibility. Not only the possibility of cooperation from the country that controls the land, but also from its appeal to Jews. They suggested you would know whom to approach about this."

Adler leaned back in his chair. "England," he stated flatly. "That's the country that can help you. In spite of recent changes, the United Kingdom remains a vast empire. It controls millions of square miles of territory. Much of it in Africa. Most of it unsettled by Europeans. All of it sparsely populated. I suspect much of it has been untouched by human hands. They also control areas of Asia and South America. They could provide you with a location in just about any region of the world."

"Think they would be interested in our proposal?"

Adler nodded. "If they can make money at it. And if they are approached properly."

"Good," Ibrahim smiled approvingly. "Whom in England do we need to talk to?"

"Joseph Chamberlain is the Colonial Secretary. He would be the man to see. His approval would be necessary and if he presented it to the prime minister it would be all but an accomplished fact."

"Do you know anyone who knows Chamberlain well enough to provide an introduction?"

"Yes."

"Who?"

"Me," Adler replied.

"You?"

"Yes. I know him quite well."

"Would you be willing to introduce me to him? Perhaps join me in making a presentation?"

"Certainly. I would be glad to participate, provided the eventual settlers gave me concessions for the minerals found there."

Ibrahim knew it would come down to money. It always did with men like Adler. "I'm sure an accommodation could be reached. When should we see him?"

"I'm scheduled for a series of meetings in London later this month,"

Adler noted. "Why not let me take it up with him in private first. Then bring you in for a second discussion."

Ibrahim didn't like that arrangement. He preferred handling all the details himself. But he also felt he had little choice but to go along. If Podolsky thought Adler was the key, they would have to do it Adler's way. "If you think that's the best approach," Ibrahim replied, concealing his true feelings behind an agreeable smile. "Then that is what we shall do."

14

NETANYAHU

LATER THAT MONTH, Adler traveled to London for a series of meetings with key diamond importers. When those meetings concluded, he met for a drink in Chamberlain's office. It was a meeting of old friends—they'd known each other since early in Chamberlain's political career—and they chatted amicably, catching up on each other's lives and on news of mutual acquaintances. Then Adler turned to the matter foremost on his mind.

"I have learned recently of a well-organized group of non-Zionist Jews who would like to explore the possibility of creating a Jewish state."

Chamberlain interrupted, "You know we can't agree to that now. Palestine is far too unstable for a change like that."

"These men aren't talking about Palestine."

"Oh? Where are they talking about?"

"Frankly," Adler continued, "I believe many of them are ready to accept any location if it means they can escape the difficulties they now face in Europe. Those living in Russia are particularly open to the idea." He, of course, did not know this for a fact, but knowing Chamberlain as he did, he knew he had to couch the proposal in a way that would appeal to both his sense of duty and his appreciation of the practical. Telling him the truth—that he'd been approached by an Arab on behalf of Jewish businessmen—would have been a difficult sell.

"Where did they have in mind?" Chamberlain asked. "What country?"

"They were hoping you British might suggest a location."

"Why us? Why not the French? Or the Dutch?"

"You are their first choice. They know the British Empire controls vast areas of unsettled land throughout the world. Since as Colonial Secretary, you are charged with responsibility for administering those holdings, they thought perhaps you would like some settlers."

Chamberlain smiled. "It's an intriguing proposal. And we have several projects underway that could be greatly assisted by European influence. The kind we'd get from Europeans living on the land."

Adler pressed the matter quickly. "You'll consider it then?"

"Yes, I will consider it."

Adler looked over at him. "These are serious men, Joseph, with serious intentions. If I tell them you're considering it, they'll expect a response from you."

"When do you return to Antwerp?"

"The end of the week."

"I'll discuss it with members of my staff and call you before you leave."

✦ ✦ ✦

As promised, Chamberlain discussed Adler's proposal with David Bonar, his deputy in charge of policy in Africa. Bonar was surprised to learn there was interest among Zionists in settling anywhere other than Palestine. "They've always been adamant about that location. That's how they got the Zionist moniker."

"We all thought that way," Chamberlain acknowledged, "but apparently that is not quite the case. And I, for one, am glad to hear of it. Re-settling them in a location other than Palestine will solve a major problem for us."

"Settling them elsewhere would solve *several* problems. No further unrest in the Middle East. Peace with the Arabs. And ridding them of the Jewish threat would, no doubt, allow us to gain unrestrained access to their oil supplies."

"Not to mention eliminating the European Jewish problem."

Bonar nodded. "If they will go in sufficient numbers. Do you think they will?"

"I've known Adler a long time. And since he came to me with this, I'm sure the details have all been worked out ahead of time. So, based on my conversation with him, I think they will."

"We could provide incentives."

"I suppose," Chamberlain acknowledged, "but let's work on offering them free land for now and see where things go from there."

"Very well," Bonar agreed. "But where shall we send them? That is the bigger question."

"I've been thinking about that." Chamberlain stood and made his way to a map that hung on the opposite wall. "We have a region recently transferred from the Uganda Protectorate to the East Africa Protectorate." He located it on the map and pointed. "It's in a very desirable location. Lord Delamere received it as a concession for areas he was forced to contribute to the Uganda railroad project. It's somewhat isolated, but a lovely region."

"You've been there?"

"Yes. Several times."

Bonar joined him at the map. "Show me the location again."

Chamberlain tapped the spot with his index finger. "Right there."

Bonar leaned closer for a better view. "It's definitely remote. Is it inhabited?"

"A small band of Maasai recently seized control of it from the Sirikwa, but they don't actually live there. As far as I know, no one has a settlement there."

"Could the Jews survive in a place like that?"

"There's plenty of fresh water and lots of game. So, if they could eat the native diet, survival would be highly likely." Chamberlain studied the map a moment longer, then turned back to his desk. "Select one or two of the staff to assist you and get started on the preliminary work."

"Very well."

"Generate a report on the feasibility of the site and let me have a preliminary result by the end of the week."

Bonar looked startled. "End of the week?"

"Time is somewhat of an issue. You can get me something by then?"

"Certainly sir. We'll get right on it."

"Keep this among your staff until you report back to me. We'll circulate this around the office eventually and gauge the internal reaction, but not right now."

"This would require the prime minister's approval."

"We'll worry about that later."

"Certainly."

Bonar started toward the door. Chamberlain called after him. "Remember, we don't want word of this to get beyond our department until we've had time to fully explore the ramifications."

"I'll make that clear to the staff."

✦ ✦ ✦

A few days later, Chamberlain phoned Adler at his hotel and arranged to see him that afternoon. They met at Chamberlain's office.

"We have reviewed your proposal," Chamberlain began, "and would like to suggest a potential site."

"Good. What did you have in mind?"

"Understand," Chamberlain cautioned, "this is a preliminary determination. We still have to follow our processes and procedures."

"I understand. So, what location are you considering?"

"We are considering offering your Jewish clients a tract in British East Africa. It was one of the locations you mentioned."

"Right," Adler acknowledged. "Did you have a specific location in mind?"

"We were thinking of a tract comprising some five thousand square miles."

"That would certainly give them plenty of room."

"The site is in an area known as Uasin Gishu. Temperate climate. Sits atop the Mau Escarpment. A higher elevation than most African locations. Very European in atmosphere. I should think they would flourish there."

"They would be free to govern themselves?"

"We haven't gotten that far in our workup, but I would anticipate them doing so. As an autonomous region, of course," he added. "They would govern their own day-to-day life, subject to the governor general."

"Sounds intriguing."

"Will they accept?"

"I'm not authorized to commit them, but I assume they would. Otherwise, I don't think I would have been approached to pursue the matter this far."

"We need you to find out for certain," Chamberlain cautioned. "I don't want to make the offer if they aren't going to accept."

"I think there's a good chance they will agree to that site. But there's a bit of a dilemma about who should accept."

Chamberlain frowned. "I'm not sure I understand. A group approached you and you aren't certain to whom we should make the formal offer?"

"Zionists aren't an organized group," Adler explained. "They come from every faction and party. Collectively, they have no spokesman."

Chamberlain crossed his arms. "I should think there would really be only one person who can speak for a large enough group to make this work."

"Herzl?"

Chamberlain nodded. "Herzl and his Zionist congress. Isn't he attempting to address the situation you outlined?"

"About Africa?"

"No. About organizing the Zionists as a separate group. Jews from all over the world of every kind and sort. Orthodox, liberal, atheist, humanist. All under one organization and able to speak with one voice. Work for one purpose."

Adler nodded. "That is right, but have you dealt with Herzl before?"

"We've met on several occasions," Chamberlain explained. "He strikes me as someone with whom we can do business."

"He's a very agreeable man," Adler conceded. "But Zionists represent only a small portion of the Jewish population. Getting his approval won't mean gaining the approval of a majority of Jews."

"We wouldn't need a majority of all Jews. Just those who call themselves Zionists. Herzl is someone with enough acceptance among that group to sell them on the idea."

"And this new congress he's putting together might be just the right vehicle for such an enterprise as this."

"Exactly." Chamberlain had a satisfied smile. "As I understand it, some in that group are already working to establish settlements in Palestine. They should have little trouble applying that experience to a similar effort in Africa."

✦ ✦ ✦

With his business in London complete, Adler returned to Antwerp where Ibrahim had been waiting. He was excited to hear the news of Chamberlain's enthusiastic response.

"But," Adler cautioned, "he will not make a formal offer until we have identified a group or leader who can accept his terms and sell the idea to a significant number of Jews. He thinks Herzl and the Zionist congress is the way to go."

"I think we can arrange that," Ibrahim assured.

In fact, he had no idea how to present the proposal to Herzl or place it before the Zionist congress, much less how to win its approval. That part of the scheme would be up to Podolsky. Ibrahim, as a Muslim, could do little more than what he'd already done.

The following morning, he boarded a train from Antwerp and began the trip back to Odessa. He arrived there two days later and met with Podolsky the following morning.

15

NETANYAHU

AFTER THE FIRST Zionist Congress adjourned, Nathan returned to the yeshiva in Volozhin. The day after his arrival, Yehuda took him aside to discuss all that happened in Basel. Yehuda was impressed by Nathan's observations and by his involvement, even though he was too young to vote. And he was especially taken with Nathan's efforts to discover and remove an informant from the sessions. "You should tell the students about this," he instructed when Nathan concluded his account. "They need to hear it from you."

"I've been talking to anyone who would listen."

"I was thinking more on the order of a formal address."

Nathan had a puzzled frown. "To my class?"

"To the entire student body."

Nathan sat in stunned silence for a moment as he let those words sink in. In the time that he had been at the yeshiva, no student had ever addressed the entire student body, and legend had it that none had done so in the history of the school. "That would be big," he uttered finally. His choice of words was awkward and his voice sounded weak, but right then he was feeling overwhelmed.

Yehuda smiled. "Not many get that privilege." He gave Nathan a reassuring pat on the shoulder. "But I think you can handle this." he stood to leave. "We'll do it next week. That will give you a few days to organize your thoughts."

Nathan stood as well. "I'm... not...sure I'm up to it," he stammered.

"You'll do fine. Just tell them what you told me. Begin at the beginning and follow the chronology of events. Let the account unfold on its own."

As Yehuda walked away, Nathan returned to his seat on the bench and thought about what had just transpired. Not only had no student ever addressed the entire school, other than Yehuda, few people had ever been allowed to deliver a lecture. In fact, he could think of only three who'd spoken to them since the time he'd first arrived, and all of those guest lecturers were key figures in the Zionist movement. To be counted among them was something Nathan had hoped for, but he'd expected that moment to come in the future, when he was an adult and had accomplished something worth talking about. Certainly not then, while still a student.

On Wednesday of the following week, Yehuda convened the student body in the sanctuary of the synagogue. Rather than sitting with his class, Nathan took a seat near the front and awaited his time to speak. His palms were damp, his heartrate had quickened, and his right foot bounced up and down from the energy coursing through his veins. He'd spent hours preparing his remarks and created a dozen pages of notes, but he'd noticed before that none of the previous speakers used notes or prepared remarks and so he chose to do the same. Now he wondered if he'd made a mistake.

When everyone was seated and quiet Yehuda stood before them and explained where Nathan had been, told them the topic of his presentation, then turned the meeting over to him and took a seat on the front row. Nathan rose from his seat, made his way to the podium, and began.

At first his presentation was much like an academic lecture, following a chronology of events from the time he and Zvi arrived on the train until the morning of the first session. He described the hotel and the magnificent beauty of the city, then mentioned all the people who were present, dropping names of key Zionist figures he'd observed that first day.

By then, he was no longer nervous. His heartrate slowed and the nervous energy he'd sensed earlier dissipated. As he moved on to recount events of the congress' first session, he quickly became absorbed in the moment. Before long, the lecture became a fiery speech in support of Zionism.

"The controlling aim of Zionism," he quoted from the resolution adopted by the congress, "is that of establishing for the Jewish people a publicly and legally assured home in Palestine. A geographic location where we are free from physical violence and have the ability to practice our religion without persecution."

He outlined each of the points adopted by the delegates, stressing the creation of a Jewish homeland in Palestine and the federation of all Zionist groups under the Zionist congress as a single unifying organizational umbrella.

"For more than a thousand years, our people have been the subject of derision and ridicule by Europeans who blame us for all their ills. Now, their contempt for us has festered into physical violence. They burn our homes, beat and murder our neighbors, and do it all with the tacit approval of the government. Often with the urging and assistance of the government. But at last, a leader has arisen among us with the power and ability to lead us out of the pestilence that besets us. To lead us out of Europe. And like Moses, take us to the Promised Land. The land of Israel. The place they now call Palestine."

When Nathan finished, the room was silent, the students motionless in their seats. Nathan glanced at the audience a moment, then stepped away from the podium and started toward his seat. All at once, the students leapt to their feet and burst into a boisterous round of applause. Nathan stopped a few feet from the podium and waited while the students continued to clap and shout. Finally, he acknowledged them with a tip of his head and a wave, then took his seat on the front row.

It was an impressive speech by any standard, but even more so coming from a student of Nathan's young age. And yet, he'd delivered it with the ease of one who'd spent his life immersed in the study of ideas and seasoned with a lifetime of public speaking.

Unlike their experience with all-school lectures in the past, the excitement that energized the students that day did not fade, but instead matured into firm resolve. A determination to "do something." To participate in what was now clearly a major liberation movement sweeping through not only the Zionists but all of Judaism. In the weeks that followed, older students expressed that commitment by forming a local Zionist student organization. Through it they intended to gain a legitimate voice in the Zionist debate and hoped to obtain recognition from the Zionist congress as an official youth organization.

✦ ✦ ✦

A few days after his eighteenth birthday, Nathan was studying alone in a room off the synagogue sanctuary. He was seated by the window, a book in his hand and a notepad in his lap when the door opened and Yehuda entered. The unexpected intrusion startled him and he leapt to his feet sending the notepad tumbling to the floor.

Yehuda gestured with a wave of his hand, and then pulled a chair over by the window. "Keep your seat. You are eighteen years old now."

Nathan nodded. "That is correct."

"And you are nearing the end of the usual course of study."

"I had hoped to continue here a little longer. It seems like there is so much more to learn."

"That is because you are becoming a scholar. You have become one who can teach himself."

Nathan was flattered by the comment and hardly knew what to say.

"Have you any idea what you would like to do next?"

"I would like to become a rabbi."

"A pulpit rabbi?"

"Perhaps in the future, but right now I would like to be one of the traveling rabbis."

Yehuda nodded thoughtfully. "A maggid mesharim."

"Yes. An itinerate preacher of uprightness."

"I think you will do well at that. And as a first step toward that goal, I think you should sit for the semikhah diploma."

"That would be a first step," Nathan reluctantly noted. The semikhah examination would be long and comprehensive and the thought of taking it left him feeling small and intimidated. "But isn't the traditional age of a rabbi set at twenty-two?"

"There is no legal stricture against ordination at a younger age," Yehuda replied. "All that is required is that you pass the examination."

"I don't know. This is rather a surprise to me. I'm not sure I can—"

"You have proved yourself to be unusually capable," Yehuda interrupted. "I see no point in delaying your progress merely to suit some arbitrary practice."

They talked a while longer, then Yehuda left and Nathan sat staring out the window, lost in thoughts of home, his childhood, the dreams he'd had back then and the way they'd grown and developed into the dream he had now.

A scholarly life had been his first real vision of his destiny—to spend the days at his desk with nothing but books, thoughts, and paper to write them on. That was a dream that rose from his childhood bedroom, with the security of his mother and father close by. Tied to those first ten years, it ran to the depths of his soul and abandoning it seemed like forsaking home all over again.

But the pursuit of that ideal led him to the yeshiva in Volozhin. Studying there, hearing lectures from the leading Zionist leaders of the day, and participating in the Zionist congress, awakened him to the world beyond and left him wanting to break free of academia and the small geographic space he'd known around Kreva and Volozhin.

Nathan stared out the window for a long while, wrestling with what to do, and then a smile spread across his face. *I don't have to choose.* As a maggid rabbi, he could have both, a life of study and a life of contemplation—study of Torah, of developments in the world, and lectures that explained the manner in which those events affected Jewish life and thought.

It was a rough thought. A ragged, indeterminate sketch of the life he saw opening before him. Time and experience would fill in the missing details, smooth out the rhythm, and no doubt grow in unexpected directions. But for now, it was enough.

And then the words of Rabbi Risikoff spoke to him when Nathan told Risikoff about his plan to apply to study at the yeshiva in Volozhin.

"You were given this ability for a reason and that reason is a calling on your life," Risikoff had said. "You must be faithful to it. No matter where your study and work take you, no matter how much or little you understand of the things you encounter. You always must follow the calling. You understand much, but always remember—as between understanding and obedience, obedience is the more treasured attribute."

As the memory of that day rose, a sense of peace swept over him. The conflict that just moments earlier had raged in his mind and in his soul suddenly evaporated. He felt renewed, fresh, and clear. His body felt lighter, as if a great weight had been lifted from his shoulders. And as he glanced around, everything looked different, and felt different. As though it, too, had been changed and transformed by Risikoff's words.

"I am standing at the doorway to my future," he whispered. "The doorway to the life I've wanted since childhood. The opportunity to pursue the calling on that life, even if it leads me to places and duties I never imagined before. My obligation is not to determine the future, but to remain faithful to the calling, to apply my ability as it opens up for me." And with that realization, the last vestiges of intimidation and fear he'd felt before evaporated.

Two weeks later, Nathan sat for the semikhah examination. The written portion took most of the morning. That afternoon, he met with Yehuda for the oral part. When they finished, Yehuda reached into the drawer of his desk and took out a diploma. Nathan could see it already had been signed and prepared.

Yehuda glanced over it, then handed it across the desk to Nathan. "You are now a semikhah rabbi, with all the obligations, duties, privileges and rights of that office." There was no elaborate ordination ceremony. Simply the document, a handshake, and Yehuda's kind smile.

✦ ✦ ✦

Not long after Nathan was ordained, news reached the yeshiva that Yitzchak Reines was scheduled to speak at the synagogue in Kreva the following month. Nathan contacted his parents and made arrangements to travel there for the event.

A legend among Zionist Jews, Reines was an orthodox rabbi from Lithuania and one of the first to call for a return of Jews to Palestine. In addition to public addresses on the subject he published books and numerous articles, many of which appeared decades before Herzl ever considered the issue. As his work developed, Reines' reputation spread, generating great demand for speaking engagements and lectures at synagogues throughout Europe. He accepted as many of those opportunities as possible and spent the remainder of his life traveling from town to town, exhorting Jews everywhere to remember their distinctive heritage and to return to the land of their ancestors. A true and authentic maggid mesharim—an itinerant preacher—he became the model of the rabbi Nathan wanted to become.

Nathan arrived in Kreva two days before Reines' lecture. He spent some of the extra time visiting with family and friends, but the day before the lecture was spent with his former mentor, Rabbi Risikoff.

They sat in the living room and over a cup of tea discussed Nathan's progress in school and the latest news of his classmates.

"I heard about the address you gave when you returned from the Zionist congress," Risikoff related. "You made quite an impression on many people."

Nathan chuckled. "I got a little excited." He shyly glanced down at the floor and took a sip from his cup of tea.

"That's nothing to be embarrassed about."

"I suppose."

"And you have received ordination, too."

"Yes."

"If I had known I would have come to stand with you."

"No one knew in advance. Not even I. Yehuda seemed to be moving me along rather quickly."

"Yes." Risikoff looked down at the cup in his hands. "He and Rabbi Reines have talked. I'm not sure what they are trying to develop."

"Think we'll find out while he is here?"

"Maybe. But whether we do or not, you have to follow your calling. You remember what I told you about that?"

Nathan smiled. "I was thinking of that just the other day."

"Any ideas about what to do next?"

"I don't know how one gets started at it, but I would like to work toward a life similar to the one Rabbi Reines has lived."

"The maggid mesharim—the itinerant preacher of righteousness." Nathan nodded in response. Risikoff continued. "That is a hard life."

"But a useful and needed one."

"This is true. And perhaps you will learn more about that this weekend while Rabbi Reines is here. Which reminds me—" Risikoff sat up straight and glanced at a clock on a table across the room. "It's almost time to meet him at the train station."

Nathan set his cup aside and stood. "Then I should be going."

"I would ask you to come with me but we already have a luncheon planned for him, and I have to—"

Nathan cut him off with a smile. "It's ok. I understand."

✦ ✦ ✦

Nathan attended Reines' lecture in Kreva with Zvi, the two arriving at the synagogue almost an hour before the scheduled presentation. Even so, they found the sanctuary already half full but managed to squeeze into an open space near the front. While they waited, Nathan glanced around, noting the people he recognized. "Not much has changed in here."

"Most of the people you knew before are still here now," his father explained. "You haven't been gone a lifetime yet."

"I know. But it seems so odd now."

"That's because you've grown. And I don't mean physically, though you've grown that way, too. But you see Torah in a different way now than you did back then."

Nathan gave Zvi a puzzled look. "How can you know that? We haven't talked about Torah much at all."

Zvi smiled. "You've been studying Torah, correct?"

"Yes."

"And there you have it," Zvi gestured. "Anyone who studies Torah, anyone who follows God's commandments, anyone who does those things we are expected to do cannot prevent himself from being changed by Torah. Change is one of His properties."

"I think—"

Just then, a door opened near the front of the room and Rabbi Risikoff entered. Behind him came an elderly man with a gray beard and long gray hair. His back was stooped, his shoulders drawn forward, and when he walked he lurched, stumbling ahead in a halting, uneven gait, seemingly with the threat of pitching forward face-down onto the floor.

Nathan's eyes followed Reines as he plodded his way across the room to a pew on the front row. As he and Risikoff took a seat, Nathan leaned over to Zvi. "He looks old," he whispered.

"He *is* old."

"He didn't look like that when he was at the school."

"When was that?"

"Last year. Maybe the year before."

A few minutes later, Rabbi Risikoff rose from his seat and moved to a lectern that stood in front. By then the room was filled to capacity with an overflow crowd standing along both side walls and across the back. They'd been talking among themselves while they waited, but as Risikoff reached the lectern a hush fell over the audience and when the room was still Risikoff led them in an invocation prayer. When the prayer concluded, he introduced Rabbi Reines.

Though Reines was older and feebler than the last time he visited Kreva, he still was the master of his own mind and a gifted public speaker. Nathan was mesmerized by his voice and sat with rapt attention throughout the evening, hanging on every word.

When Reines was finished, Zvi turned to leave but Nathan took him by the elbow. "Let's say hello."

Zvi was taken aback. "To Rabbi Reines?"

"Yes."

"We don't know him."

"We've seen him before. He was here, remember?"

"Yes. Of course I remember."

"And I spoke to him when he visited the school."

Zvi hesitated. "I don't know..."

"So, let's say hello," Nathan insisted.

"I'm afraid we might seem brash."

"He's not like that," Nathan assured. "Come on," and he guided Zvi toward the front. "We'll just say hello and then head home."

Reines was occupied talking to Dah Grün, one of the synagogue's staunchest supporters, but when they finished Reines looked over at Nathan and smiled. "You enjoyed the lecture?"

"Yes," Nathan replied as he shook Reines' hand. "I am Nathan Mileikowsky. We met at—"

"I remember you," Reines held up a hand. "You're one of Benjamin Yehuda's students."

"Yes, sir. I am."

"He spoke to me about you the other day. You recently received ordination."

"Yes."

Reines looked past him and reached out to shake hands with Zvi. "This is my father," Nathan explained hastily. "He lives here in Kreva."

They exchanged a word of greeting, then Reines turned back to Nathan. "So you are finished now at the yeshiva?"

"I have completed my semikhah studies."

"Rather young though, for ordination."

"Rabbi Yehuda invited me to apply."

"I suspect so," Reines nodded. "You are his best pupil."

Nathan changed the subject. "We heard your address at the Zionist congress in Basel."

"You should have come up afterward."

"No," Nathan replied with a nervous laugh. "There were too many important people for me."

Reines rested his hand on Nathan's shoulder. "And one day you will be one of them."

Rabbi Risikoff joined them. "We should go," he said to Reines.

"Yes," Reines responded.

"We have a dinner planned for this evening," Risikoff explained. "Otherwise, we could visit the rest of the night. I would love to hear more about what you saw at the congress in Switzerland."

"And I would be glad to tell you about it."

"Come around in the morning," Risikoff suggested. "To the house. We can talk then."

"Yes," Reines added, his eyes bright with interest. "Come early. You and I should talk."

Nathan's face was clouded in a puzzled expression. He had many questions to ask but decided not to raise them now. "Very well. I'll come over in the morning."

The following morning, Nathan arrived at Risikoff's home a little after seven. Risikoff greeted him at the door and led the way back to the kitchen. Reines was seated at the kitchen table, sipping a cup of coffee. Risikoff poured a cup for Nathan and the three sat together.

"From the look on your face last night, I'm sure you are wondering why I wanted to talk to you," Reines began.

"Yes," Nathan replied. "You caught my attention."

"As I mentioned earlier, Rabbi Yehuda talked to me about you when I visited the yeshiva. Later, he and I exchanged correspondence about you and I came to the conclusion that I would like for you to join me in my work spreading the call of Zion to our people and organizing support for settlements that we have already created in Palestine."

"That is why he wanted me to sit for my semikhah diploma?"

"That," Risikoff interjected, "and the fact that you were ready. Yehuda has great confidence in you. As do I and Rabbi Reines."

"I had hoped to have an itinerate life," Nathan said, "but I assumed it would come later. After more years of study."

"You are the brightest student in the yeshiva," Risikoff continued. "Yehuda says you're the smartest, most eloquent he's ever had."

"And that is a precious gift," Reines added. "Intelligence and eloquence. We need your voice. Zion needs your voice. Our fellow Jews need your voice."

"When would I begin?"

"We leave for Vilnius this afternoon. I am to speak there tonight."

Risikoff placed his hand on Nathan's arm and looked him in the eye. "This is an opportunity of a lifetime. You can't turn this down."

16

NETANYAHU

AS WITH EVERY OTHER major decision in his life, Nathan took Reines' offer to Zvi. They discussed it on the back porch and came to the same conclusion as Risikoff: This was an offer Nathan could not afford to turn away.

That afternoon, Nathan said goodbye to his mother and walked with Zvi down to the train station. Ten minutes later, Reines and Risikoff joined them on the platform by the tracks. Not long after that, the train arrived. Nathan said goodbye to Zvi and boarded with Reines.

The trip to Vilnius took only two hours. Reines slept most of the way and only awoke when the train slowed to enter the station yard.

They were met at the station by Julian Kalecki, head rabbi at the Great Synagogue where Reines was to speak that evening. Reines and Kalecki were old friends and were obviously glad to see each other. Their conversation seemed to pick up where they left off at their last visit—which Nathan was sure must have been quite some time ago—and soon they were engaged in a lively discussion of people and events about which Nathan had no way of knowing.

As they reached the end of the ramp and turned to start across the tracks, Reines seemed to remember that he wasn't traveling alone and wheeled around to Nathan who was carrying both their bags. Reines quickly introduced him to Kalecki, but after a polite exchange of only the most trivial matters, Reines and Kalecki returned again to their previous conversation. Nathan listened with amusement as they proceeded on inside the station and across the room to the Gelezinkelio Street exit where a cab awaited them.

The meeting at Vilnius was much like the one in Kreva, only larger. The Grand Synagogue could seat five thousand. The crowd that evening was not quite that large but most of the floor level was filled.

Afterwards, they returned to Kalecki's home for a late dinner. Nathan listened while Kalecki and Reines continued their discussion about old friends and events from their shared past. But as the night grew late, Reines' tired eyes grew even darker and his attention seemed to drift off the topic. Kalecki was gracious and did his best to keep Reines in the conversation. Even Nathan chimed in a few times to help, but finally Kalecki gave up and rose from his seat at the table to show them to their rooms.

The next morning, Reines and Nathan had breakfast with Kalecki. Reines was refreshed and alert and picked up again with the conversation of the previous evening without missing a beat.

When breakfast was finished, Kalecki, who had an appointment to keep, sent them off on their own in a taxi to the train station. As the taxi started up the street away from the house, Reines leaned toward Nathan. "I don't want you to think I brought you with me to carry my bags and listen to me trading stories with old friends."

"I don't mind."

"You are gracious and I appreciate it. However, my point in asking you to join me was much more critical. I have not been feeling well lately."

The news was unsettling to Nathan and sent his thoughts careening off in a hundred different directions. He'd never taken care of the sick and knew nothing of how to assist someone in an emergency. And what about train fare? And cab fare? Hotel charges and meals? Who would pay to get him back home if Reines was unable?

But there was no time for all of that now so Nathan pushed the thoughts aside and said with a look of concern, "I'm sorry. Do we need to find a doctor?"

Reines shook his head. "I'm seeing the best doctors already. They say they're doing for me all that can be done, but it's not doing much to help. I wanted you with me because I'm not sure I can make all of these appointments." He looked over at Nathan. "You may have to fill in for me, so pay attention. Take notes. Prepare a speech. And be ready to step in at any moment."

If the news of Reines' physical problems was unsettling, the thought of filling in for him at a speaking engagement was terrifying. "I... could never...fill in for you," he stammered. "No one could."

"You can't be me any more than I can be you. But you can complete the task. You can do the work. Yehuda Berlin thinks you will make a fine maggid rabbi." The old man smiled over at Nathan. "I do, too. I have every confidence in you."

Nathan took a deep breath and forced himself to remain calm. "I will do my best not to let you down."

"Do your best to follow the call upon your life," Reines responded. "And you will do well." He paused to clear his throat. "The other reason I wanted you with me is because I wanted you to meet my contacts. The people I know and who have invited me to give these lectures. They are all key figures in the Zionist movement, but many of them are unknown even to our own people. You will need them when I am gone."

For the next two weeks, Reines and Nathan traveled back and forth through the Pale of Settlement, holding meetings every night. Twice they passed near Kreva, once as they worked their way down to Odessa and another as they traveled back through the countryside.

Each day the routine was the same: Rise early in the morning, catch the first train of the day, move on to the next town, address a packed audience that night, then do the same thing the next day. Reines was obviously extremely tired and by the end of each day dark circles formed beneath his eyes, but every morning he seemed renewed and they pushed on to the next location.

As Reines suggested, Nathan listened carefully to each address and took notes in a notebook that doubled as a journal. Later, in his room after the event concluded, he would review the notes and incorporate them into an outline of his own speech. Each day he added more content and more ideas, taking the message deeper and deeper into the meaning that lay behind the publicly stated Zionist rationale.

At the same time, he continued to study Torah, exploring the depths of Zionist theology, of Zion, of the Davidic promise. At first, all he found was a sparse collection of thoughts, but as he read and re-read key sections of Torah, the second and third levels of meaning became clearer and new understanding energized his mind, body, and soul. Pages of the notebook quickly filled and soon additional pages were stuffed inside, their edges hanging out beyond the cover boards until at last he was forced to purchase a new one.

Finally, they arrived at Lodz where Reines was scheduled to speak the following evening at Beth Jacob synagogue. It was the end of a grueling two-week schedule and the first time since Nathan joined Reines that they had an afternoon and evening free. Nathan was looking forward to spending extra time working on the outline for his own address.

They were met at the train station by a short middle-aged man of slender build named Ben-Zion Lurie. Reines greeted him warmly as he did almost everyone they encountered, but he seemed especially warm toward Ben-Zion.

"Ben-zion," Reines explained for Nathan's benefit, "is head rabbi at Beth Jacob Synagogue. The place where I will be speaking tonight."

"Tomorrow night," Lurie corrected.

"That's right," Reines chuckled. "I'm so used to arriving the day of the event, I completely forgot the schedule. I don't get many days with extra time in them." He turned to Lurie and gestured with his right hand. "This is my assistant, Nathan Mileikowsky."

Lurie expected Reines to be traveling alone and was surprised to learn he had a companion, but he was also startled when he learned Nathan's name.

"Nathan? As in Nathaniel?"

Nathan smiled. "Yes, Nathaniel Mileikowsky."

The words of Judah Alkalai flooded Lurie's mind. His soul came alive and the skin on the back of his neck tingled. He stared into Nathan's eyes for a moment that was almost too long, before he blinked and smiled. "I am pleased to meet you. How long have you been with Rabbi Reines?"

"Just the past two weeks."

"Your family must miss you."

"I have been living away from home since I was ten. My parents are used to not having me around."

Reines was a few paces ahead of them now and glanced over his shoulder in their direction. "Nathan has been studying under Yehuda Berlin at Volozhin. He recently obtained his semikhah diploma."

Lurie seemed pleased by the news. "So, you have been in school all this time."

"Yes."

"Then you have no—"

"He's not married," Reines called with chuckle. "I know that's what you want to know. Nathan, you'll have to excuse him. Ben-Zion has only daughters. He's always on the lookout for proper gentlemen who will see to their well-being." He turned back to Nathan and added, "If you know what I mean."

"I was only trying to find out a little about him," Lurie explained. "I didn't realize you'd taken on a protégé."

"I'm getting old, Ben-zion," Reines explained. "What do you think about the rally? Will we draw a crowd?"

Lurie laughed. "I think we'll have a capacity crowd."

"Good."

"I suspect we'll have our largest audience thus far. Even more than Leon drew."

Reines dropped back to walk beside them and glanced over at Nathan. "He's talking about Leon Pinsker."

Lurie looked in Nathan's direction. "You knew Pinsker?"

"I met him a few times. My father is a serious student of his writings."

"We had him up here for a series of fundraisers, raising money for Hovevei Zion."

"You support that group?"

Lurie nodded. "Yes, I would have gone to Palestine with them a long time ago but I couldn't get away from the work here. There was always so much to do. And then Hovevei merged with the Zionist Organization and I bowed out."

"You were opposed to the congress?"

"No. I just didn't see the need for one more organization, one more layer of people stirring the pot. We need to get to work building settlements in Palestine." The tone of Lurie's voice changed and he pumped his fists to emphasis each phrase. "Encouraging our people to go there. Helping them to go there. We don't need more organizations and more meetings."

"Think you'll ever make it to Palestine?"

"I don't know," Lurie shrugged. "I may. Life there is still rather difficult and, as Yitzchak already said, I have daughters. I didn't think it right to subject them to those harsh conditions just because I wanted to go."

"I can understand that," Nathan conceded. "Though I'm not sure how safe it is here, either."

"You're right about that," Lurie concurred with a knowing look. "But that's no reason to stop our work. Someone will always oppose us."

"Good point."

"We've continued to pursue the work in Palestine and have organized several groups of settlers who made the move there. And who knows? Our daughters are older now. Perhaps we will make it there yet."

When they reached Lurie's home, they were met at the front door by his wife, Aniela. She greeted them warmly and ushered them inside.

Beyond the door, a broad hallway led through the center of the house. At the far end of it Nathan could see the doorway to a large kitchen. To the right of where he stood was a parlor and to the left a stairway rose toward the second floor. As Nathan glanced up, a young woman appeared on the landing above.

She had a petite frame with delicate features and curly auburn hair that fell almost to her shoulders. She wore a blue dress that came below her knee and when their eyes met she smiled down at him with a look that made his heart melt.

Lurie interrupted the moment to introduce Nathan to Aniela who acknowledged him politely but had little else to say. By the time he turned back to glance up the stairs again, the young woman he'd seen before was near the bottom step. Lurie stepped in her direction and smiled. "Sarah, this is Nathan."

"I'm pleased to meet you," Sarah said and she offered Nathan her hand.

Nathan grinned awkwardly as he took her hand in his and mumbled something in return. When he remembered the moment later he could recall the touch of her hand in his, the warm glow of his cheeks, and the scent of her perfume, but he could never remember what exactly he'd said in response.

In the background Nathan heard the others as they talked amicably among themselves, but the words they spoke barely made an impression on him. His eyes and all of his attention were focused on Sarah.

Sarah's attention was fixed on him as well and they stood there in silence, staring at each other without saying a word. As if each knew the thoughts of the other in a way that words could only cheapen, her hand was still in his, his fingers gently but firmly around hers, until finally she slipped it free and asked, "Did you have a pleasant trip?"

"Yes, a rather uneventful train ride."

"And your meetings have been well received?"

"Rabbi Reines is always well received."

"Not always," Reines spoke up. "Nathan has only recently joined me. He hasn't yet experienced the reaction of the non-Zionist Jews."

"Rather hard to imagine there could be any non-Zionist Jews," Lurie commented.

Lurie noticed the look in Sarah's eyes, the way they seemed brighter and more alive. He saw Nathan's cheeks were red and his eyes were still fixed on hers. Once again he thought of Judah Alkalai and the way he'd described this moment long before Sarah was born. *This is the moment.*

A man named Nathaniel has arrived and they will have a son. The words of Alkalai—the words of the Lord—are coming to pass.

A sense of elation welled up inside Lurie and he wanted to shout, but he stifled the thought and kept his joy to himself. The last thing Sarah and Nathan needed was a meddling parent trying to push them together. And if God had, indeed, spoken through Judah Alkalai, He was fully capable of fulfilling those words without help from anyone. So instead of celebrating openly, Lurie simply watched and marveled.

Aniela must have noticed, too, but she was not marveling. She knew nothing of Judah Alkalai's visit or the prophecy he'd given about Sarah. In all the years that had passed since Alkalai prophesied her birth, Lurie had told no one. All Aniela knew was what she saw—a young man—a stranger, no less—enraptured by her daughter. And she saw her daughter—soft, tender, and unused to the ways of men and the world—waiting to be plucked, sampled, and tossed aside.

The pleasant look on Aniela's face that earlier had greeted Nathan and Raines instantly turned to one of firm resolve. In a brusque turn of her body, she wheeled away from the others and stepped toward the hallway. "Sarah," she called in an imperative voice, "I need you in the kitchen." It wasn't a request, nor a belligerent command, but it was uttered in a tone that made it clear to all in the room that she expected obedience without delay.

Sarah smiled to Nathan once again and in a soft voice whispered, "I have to go."

"Certainly. Do you need me to help?"

Aniela spoke up. "We can handle it."

Sarah smiled once again, then turned to leave.

"Perhaps we can visit later?" Nathan suggested.

Sarah glanced back at him, "Perhaps." Then she started after her mother.

Nathan stood there, watching as the two of them made their way down the hall, his eyes following her every move. When they reached the kitchen doorway, Sarah glanced over her shoulder in his direction, as if she knew he was watching, and gave a wave. But before Nathan could respond, she entered the kitchen and was out of sight.

✦ ✦ ✦

The following morning, Reines came to breakfast looking tired and out of sorts. Still, he didn't complain and when Lurie came to the table Reines seemed to perk up. Afterward, however, he retired upstairs to rest rather than remain with the others as he often did at homes where they'd stayed before. Nathan took note of his change in routine, but wasn't overly concerned.

When the dishes were done and the kitchen cleaned, Nathan and Sarah walked into the parlor. He sat down at one end of the sofa, she at the other. They'd been there only a few minutes when Aniela joined them and took a seat in a chair that sat on the opposite side of the room near the window. She busied herself with needlepoint while they talked.

Conversation with Sarah was stilted at first, but the longer they talked the more they learned of each other and in a few minutes the words came easily for both. So easy, they didn't notice when Aniela left the room or when Lurie set the table for lunch. Only when Reines appeared at the bottom of the steps did Nathan realize they'd spent the entire morning together.

"They're ready for us," Reines announced.

Nathan gave him a puzzled look.

"For lunch." Reines had a knowing smile. "Time passes quickly, does it not?"

"Yes," Nathan replied, glancing over at Sarah. "Too quickly."

"Oh, my," she said in a frantic voice. "It's lunchtime." She pushed herself up from the sofa. "I had better see if I'm needed in the kitchen."

"Of course." Nathan stood. "I'm not sure about our schedule this afternoon, but could I walk you home from the lecture tonight?"

"I would like that very much," Sarah smiled and hurried from the room.

Nathan turned to Reines. "Are you feeling better?"

"Yes, but not as well as I would like."

"Do we need to reschedule the lecture?"

Reines shook his head. "No. There's no time to fit it in later and besides, it's too late to cancel now. We'll just have to muscle our way through it." He took Nathan by the arm and guided him toward the dining room. "But you should bring that outline you've been working on with you tonight. You just might need it."

After lunch, Nathan helped clear the dishes from the table. As he gathered the plates, Sarah leaned close and said, "Time for an afternoon walk?"

"There is nothing I would love more," Nathan smiled, "but I have to work on something."

"Oh." She looked disappointed.

"It's not that I don't want to, it's just...I need to do this."

"I understand."

"But tonight, after the lecture."

"I'm looking forward to it."

With the table cleared, Nathan retreated upstairs to his room. A desk sat in the corner and he spread his outline across the top, then took a seat and began working his way through it, arranging the random ideas into some semblance of order.

After what seemed like only a few minutes there was a light tap at the door. He answered from his chair and when the door opened it was Sarah. She carried a tray with a tea pot, two cups, a dish of sugar, and a small pitcher of cream. "I thought you might need a break."

Nathan pushed back from the desk and helped her with the tray. "What time is it?"

"Almost four."

"I didn't realize it was that late." He set the tray on the dresser top and Sarah poured the tea. With their cups filled, she took a seat at the desk while Nathan sat on the edge of the bed.

"What are you working on?" she asked.

"Just some notes."

"You think you might need them soon?"

"Well...I just thought—"

"I saw the way Rabbi Reines looked this morning," she interrupted.

"It was *that* obvious?"

"Everyone noticed. And he didn't look much better when he came down for lunch."

Nathan looked startled. "I wasn't aware. Perhaps I should check on him."

"Relax." Sarah rested her hand on his knee. "Mother looked in on him already. He's been napping in his room."

"All afternoon?"

"Yes."

"This could be worse than I thought."

"I'm sure it will be fine."

"I'm not so convinced."

They talked a few minutes longer, then Sarah collected the cups, picked up the tray, and returned downstairs. Nathan worked on the outline a while longer but by five his mind was tired. Besides which, it was time to dress for the lecture. Before doing so, however, he walked down the hall to Reines' room and found the door ajar. Through the opening, he saw Reines standing at a mirror, straightening the lapels of his jacket. *At least he's up and moving around.*

NETANYAHU

EARLY IN THE EVENING, Reines, Nathan, and Lurie rode together to Beth Jacob Synagogue for the scheduled lecture. They arrived an hour early, which gave Reines time to work the crowd and meet privately with several prominent synagogue leaders. He was relaxed, affable, and more like himself than Nathan had seen since they arrived.

When it was time for the service to begin, Nathan guided Reines through the crowd to three open seats down front. Lurie followed and the three sat together for a moment to collect their thoughts. Reines stared silently at the floor.

A few minutes later, a door to the right opened and a young rabbi appeared. Lurie leaned over to Reines, "He is my young semikhah."

"You are grooming him for big things?"

"He wants to continue in school. I'm trying to get him into one of the universities in Berlin."

"What is his name?"

"Giora Cohen."

Cohen made his way across the stage to the lectern and led the audience in reciting one of the Psalms, which they voiced in Hebrew. When the Psalm was finished, Cohen offered a prayer which was delivered in Russian. At the conclusion, he gestured to Lurie, then retreated to steps at the far side of the stage and made his way to a seat in the audience.

Lurie came to the lectern, took a slip of paper from the pocket of his jacket, placed it on the stand, and began his introduction of Reines. The first half was a long-winded recitation of Reines' credentials—schools attended, degrees attained, and positions held. The second half was an even longer recounting of their youth. By the time he finished and Reines got up to speak, Nathan was all but asleep.

Reines began his lecture slowly, as he always did, laying the historic background for the Jewish fascination with Palestine and their expulsion by the Romans. With that in place, he moved on to explore the religious aspects of the matter—the promises God had made regarding the people of Israel and their claims to the region.

The lecture was tightly structured, a necessity to accommodate Reines' careful pronouncements, each section building on the next, slowly leading the listener in a step by step journey through the Zionists' right—even the imperative—to settle again in the Land of Israel.

By then, Nathan had heard the lecture many times. The next section—the final one—would eviscerate the conflicting Arab claim, which erroneously suggested Palestinian Arabs were descendants of the former Canaanites and therefore inheritors of a prior right to the land. But just as he drew a breath to speak, a startled expression came over him and he clutched at his chest. A moment later, he leaned forward and rested his head on the lectern.

Nathan jumped from his seat and glanced in Lurie's direction. "Come on. We have to reach him before he collapses."

Nathan hurried up to the platform and across to the lectern. From his angle he could see Reines' face was white and large drops of sweat were beaded on his forehead. Nathan reached Reines from behind, and wrapped his arms around him. An instant later, the full weight of Reines' body fell against him.

"He's passed out," Lurie said. "Judging by the look of his face, I'd say he's had a heart attack."

"Where can we take him?"

But just as quickly as Reines had collapsed, he pushed himself away from Nathan's grasp and stood. With one arm dangling at his side, he took hold of Nathan's arm and stepped to the lectern. To those seated in the audience, Reines no doubt appeared almost normal. But Nathan felt him leaning against his shoulder to remain steady.

The audience clapped in response to Reines' apparently renewed ability but Reines gestured for silence and the noise quickly died away. When the room was quiet he shared, "I appreciate your show of support but I am afraid I will not be able to conclude this lecture. However, my traveling companion, Rabbi Nathan Mileikowsky, will finish for me and I am confident he will do an excellent job."

Reines slipped his arm free of Nathan and turned to leave the stage. Nathan stood there watching, unsure what to do next.

As Reines made his way toward the steps, Lurie and Giora Cohen met him and helped him down to the audience floor. They tried to usher him from the sanctuary but Reines resisted and, instead, turned toward the seat where he'd been sitting earlier that evening.

When Reines was in place, Nathan stepped up to the lectern and looked out at the crowd. Earlier, when he was following Reines through the lecture, Nathan knew exactly what he would talk about in each section. The delivery might be slightly different from lecture to lecture, but he knew the three sections, the three topics, and the arguments in support of each. Now, faced with delivering the last section on his own, Nathan's mind was blank.

He gripped the lectern with both hands, bowed his head as if in prayer, and stared down at his feet as he tried to think of what to say. As he had hoped, his mind was filled with the memory of Reines' voice, but it wasn't the lecture.

"I don't want you to think I brought you with me to carry my bags and listen to me swapping stories with old friends," Reines had said.

And suddenly, in his mind, Nathan was no longer standing at the lectern but sitting in the cab as they rode to the train station in Vilnius two weeks earlier.

"You can't be me any more than I can be you," Reines had said. "But you can complete the task. You can do the work. I have every confidence in you."

The memory of that conversation brought a smile to Nathan, and he let go of the lectern, lifted his head, and faced the audience.

"You have heard from Rabbi Reines about the ancient roots of our desire to return to Palestine." He had no idea from where those words came. They simply appeared and rolled from his lips like the sound of the water of a powerful river as it poured down a mountainside.

"And," Nathan continued, "he has carefully placed before you the promises God has made to us regarding the land of that region and how its destiny and ours are inextricably linked. Yet, as clearly and concisely as he has put this before you, there is yet one final issue we must address. And that is the nature of the competing claims to Palestine between us and the Arabs who occupy the region today.

"When confronted by the question of priority, Arabs now living in Palestine argue that they are the region's indigenous people. Descendants of the former Canaanites who occupied the region at the time our forefathers entered the land. And, therefore, so the Arabs say, they are the inheritors of a prior right to the land. One that predates our own. Nothing could be further from the truth."

For the next thirty minutes, Nathan took the audience step by step through the Arabs' erroneous claim to the land, picking it apart at every step, covering each of the points Reines would have made, but doing so in a distinctly different manner. One that was uniquely his own.

The audience sat with rapt attention, eyes fixed on him as they took in every word. As if the words he was giving them were not his own, but from beyond himself. Nathan, totally immersed in the logic of his address, hardly noticed as he moved from section to section, swept along by the wonder of the moment.

When he finished, the crowd leapt to their feet in a round of applause that seemed to continue far too long. Nathan, somewhat embarrassed by their response, could only manage a sheepish grin and an awkward wave as they continued to clap and shout.

At last, the enthusiasm of the audience waned and Nathan stepped down from the platform to the audience floor. He did his best to make his way towards Reines, but before he could get very far members of the audience who were seated down front surged forward to shake his hand and exchange a word with him. By the time Nathan reached the place where Reines had been sitting, Reines was gone. Nathan glanced around searching for him, but he was nowhere in sight. Instead, he saw Sarah standing in the aisle at the end of the row.

"They took him to the house," she explained as Nathan came toward her.

"I'm glad they didn't take you," he commented sincerely.

She gave him a playful smile. "I told you we could walk home together."

Nathan took her hand in his. "Yes, you did." He gestured to the aisle. "And we should get going."

✦ ✦ ✦

Nearly an hour later, Sarah and Nathan arrived at the house. As they came up the sidewalk toward the porch steps, Nathan caught sight of Aniela through a window by the door. "Oh, no," he sighed.

"What?"

Nathan gestured toward the door. "Your mother."

Sarah glanced in that direction. "You think we are in trouble?"

"I don't know what to think."

"She was very proud of you this evening."

"Really?"

"Yes," Sarah smiled. "Really."

As they came up to the porch, Aniela opened the door and gestured with a finger to her lips. "We must be quiet," she whispered.

Sarah's forehead was wrinkled with a frown. "What is it?"

"Rabbi Reines is already asleep."

"How is he?" Nathan asked.

"The doctor thinks he had a heart attack. Not a major one, but a heart attack nonetheless." Sarah pushed the door closed and ushered them into the kitchen. "We should talk back here, so we do not disturb him."

"He didn't look well tonight," Nathan said.

"No, he didn't."

"I should have brought him back here instead of trying to finish the lecture."

Aniela shook her head. "No. You did exactly what he wanted." A proud smile turned up the corners of her mouth. "And you did an excellent job. Everyone was impressed. Especially Rabbi Reines."

"When I saw he was having trouble, I had this sense of knowing what to do and I did it. But when he was off the platform and I was behind that lectern alone..."

"It was more than you expected."

"Much more. My mind was blank. What did the doctor say about travel?"

"Out of the question," Aniela replied. "He needs to rest for several weeks."

"We have lectures scheduled for at least a month and more requests arrive each day."

Aniela patted him on the shoulder. "You can discuss that with him in the morning. For now, he must sleep and you two must eat dinner."

Sarah reached for an apron. "I will help you."

"No, you two sit in the front room. I will call you when dinner is ready."

Sarah had a startled look. "You don't need help?"

"I was preparing meals long before you were born. Sit with Nathan and...talk about all those things young people discuss." Aniela pointed toward the door. "Go on. This will only a take a few minutes."

Nathan took Sarah by the hand and walked with her up the hall toward the front room. When they were a safe distance from the kitchen he leaned close and whispered. "What brought this on?"

"The way you took charge of the service, cared for Rabbi Reines, and finished the lecture. Yesterday, you were Rabbi Reines' protégé. But tonight she saw you for who you really are—warm, caring, loving. And very much capable of meeting the expectations your confidence creates."

✦ ✦ ✦

The next morning, Nathan sat with Reines while he ate breakfast in bed. Reines looked better than he had the night before, but not well by any means. Still, they had things to discuss and time did not permit the luxury of waiting for a better day.

"We need to talk about the upcoming lectures."

"Yes," Reines responded. "I've been thinking about that."

"We have two more days here on the schedule and then we're supposed to be in Warsaw. I don't see how we can do that. Shall I prepare a brief message for a telegram announcing cancellation of the lectures? Warsaw and the remaining ones on your calendar? Then we could follow up with a letter giving a more elaborate explanation of the circumstances."

Reines shook his head in disagreement. "No! Do not cancel them. Not a single date."

"But you can't possibly do those lectures," Nathan argued. "You need to rest here until you are able to travel back to Odessa and see your regular doctors."

"I'm not doing the lectures."

"Then who is?"

"You are." Reines pointed his fork in Nathan's direction.

Nathan's eyes were suddenly wide with surprise. "Me?"

"I heard what you said last night. Remember? I was there all the way to the end." Reines paused to take a bite. "You'll do just fine."

"I appreciate your support, but there's a big difference between stepping in at the last minute and doing the entire event from beginning to end."

"Yes," Reines agreed. "But it's not much of a difference. Just more of it."

Nathan agreed. "Yes, much more of it."

Reines put down his fork and wiped his mouth with a napkin, then looked over at Nathan. "You and I both know that you can deliver a lecture at least as well as anyone alive. Including me. You don't need me to teach you anything. All you need is experience. And that's what I'm offering you. A chance to obtain experience. Take my schedule.

Fill the meetings. And go on from there."

Nathan had a puzzled look. "Go on from there?"

"Make your own contacts. Build your own schedule."

Nathan looked over at him. "Are you sure I can do this?"

"Yes," Reines smiled confidently. "I'm quite certain of it."

For the next three days, Nathan spent each morning preparing an outline for a full lecture. Working from the notes he had taken at Reines' previous presentations and from his own ideas, he had little difficulty assembling a thorough argument for the Zionist cause.

Afternoons, however, were reserved for Sarah, most of which they spent walking along the streets of Lodz near the synagogue talking, gazing into each other's eyes, and dreaming of the future. Then all too soon their time together drew to a close.

On their last afternoon together they went for a long walk, stopped to wander through a shop, had tea at a quaint café, then slowly started toward home. "I have to leave tomorrow," Nathan reminded her as they strolled along a narrow lane.

"I know. When will you return?"

"I'm not certain just yet. Some of the lectures aren't quite as firmly set as I thought."

"Oh?"

"Rabbi Reines had them on his calendar but I have since learned they weren't firm commitments. I've contacted others to explain the situation and haven't heard back yet. I'm not sure what they'll do once they know he can't attend."

"Once people hear you, word will spread." She took his hand in hers. "They will want you because of you. Not because of him."

"I hope so."

She had a confident smile. "I know so."

They walked in silence a moment, then he looked over at her. "May I write to you?"

"I'll come find you if you don't," she warned coyly.

Nathan stopped and turned to face her, then pulled her close and kissed her gently.

✦ ✦ ✦

The following day, Nathan boarded a train at the station in Lodz and traveled to Warsaw. At the lecture that evening, he spoke to a crowd that filled half the seats in the synagogue sanctuary. The content of his message was solid, but his delivery was not as polished as he'd hoped it would be. The audience, however, received him warmly. For one thrown into the breach at the last moment, he decided, the experience was not unpleasant.

The following day he departed Warsaw for Bialystok, the next city on the schedule. The lecture went much better than the night before and his delivery continued to improve as he traveled through the Pale of Settlement, filling the remainder of Reines' lecture dates. Attendance improved as well, with crowds growing larger and more enthusiastic as news of Nathan's fresh and invigorating oratorical style spread.

As Nathan concluded Reines' original schedule, new requests arrived and before long he had a full schedule for most of the remainder of the year. However, there was a two-week gap between Reines' last event and the first date booked solely under his name. With two weeks to spare, he hurried back to Lodz to spend the time with Sarah.

Though they had not seen each other for the past several months and had communicated solely by mail, their relationship had continued to grow. By the time Nathan arrived back in Lodz, things between them were serious. Conversation during their long walks turned to talk of their future and that quickly gave way to a discussion of marriage. "But I need a way to support us," Nathan noted.

"You can make a living lecturing," Sarah suggested. "Wouldn't that provide enough?"

"Perhaps, but there's no guarantee how long these lectures will last and even if they continue into the foreseeable future, I would be gone too much."

A frown wrinkled Sarah's forehead. "Too much?"

"If we have children," Nathan explained, "I would be gone much of the time. You'd be home alone. Raising them by yourself. That would not be fair to you or to them."

A strange smile lifted the corners of Sarah's mouth and her eyes shone with a misty brilliance.

"Is something wrong?"

"No, something is very much right."

"What's that?"

She slipped both arms through his and rested her head on is shoulder. "Children," she whispered as they drifted down the street.

18

NETANYAHU

IN 1903, the Zionist Organization held its Sixth Congress. As with the others, the meeting was held in Basel, Switzerland. Nathan was elected as a delegate from Kreva. He stayed at the Grand Hotel Les Trois Rois, the same hotel where he and Zvi had stayed when they attended the First Congress.

After settling into his room, Nathan went downstairs and out for dinner. When he returned, he saw Ze'ev Jabotinsky in the hotel lobby. "Didn't know you were here," he said as they shook hands.

"I actually have my own room this time," Jabotinsky quipped, remembering their experience during the first congress when he slept on the couch in Nathan's room.

"That seems like a long time ago."

"Yes," Jabotinsky sighed. "A lot has happened. And we should talk about some of it. Are you staying here alone?"

"Yes."

"Good. Let's go up to your room and talk."

When they were alone, Jabotinsky revealed, "There's a rumor going around that Herzl plans to propose that all of our groups agree to settle in East Africa."

"Africa? Why?"

"Supposedly, Herzl has worked out a deal with the British for them to give us a large tract of land in Uganda."

"I thought we were going to Palestine."

"We are," Jabotinsky insisted. "And we're going with or without Herzl."

"Will the congress discuss this? Officially? Or is this one of those deals they do and tell us about later?"

"I think Herzl intends to report the offer to the congress and recommend we accept. If the others vote for it, some of us plan to walk out in protest. Are you with us?"

Nathan nodded. "I'm not going to Uganda. Palestine is our home."

On the first day of the conference, Nathan checked with several friends who were members of the executive committee. They confirmed the rumors about an Africa plan and Herzl's decision to present the plan to the congress. Throughout the day, additional details emerged and by the middle of the afternoon, delegates were abuzz with this latest news.

✦ ✦ ✦

Late that day, Herzl reported to the congress on his meeting with Colonial Secretary Chamberlain. "He, on behalf of the British government, has offered us a tract of land encompassing five-thousand square miles in the British colony of Uganda. This area would be subject to the sovereignty of the king, but it would function as an autonomous region under the Colonial Secretary's administration. I recommend the proposal to you and urge you to consider it with all haste in your delegation meetings. The matter will come up for a vote about this same time tomorrow."

While Herzl still was speaking, Jabotinsky rose from his chair and started toward the aisle. Following his lead, the Russian delegation left their seats and walked out of the meeting hall in protest. Nathan had been an admirer of Herzl since reading *The Jewish State*, but he was deeply opposed to creating a homeland anywhere other than Palestine. He also felt compelled by friendship to support Jabotinsky and as the others left their seats and started toward the exit, he rose and went with them.

Rather than leave the building and the congress entirely, the Russian delegation gathered in a conference room across the lobby from the ballroom where the congress met. A few minutes later, Herzl arrived.

"Look," he began. "I didn't pluck this idea from thin air. I didn't even come up with it on my own."

"Then tell us who did and we'll take our complaints to them," someone replied.

"In a language they'll understand," another voice added.

"A group of businessmen in Odessa—our people, but they were not Zionists— approached me about the matter. Asked if we had spoken with the British about granting us a colony site in exchange for release of our claims against property previously appropriated by them. So, that's what we did."

"But for most of us," someone argued, "the effort to return to Palestine, the movement to return to Zion, is our best shot at establishing a new nation there."

"This would be only a temporary measure," Herzl informed. "It was never meant to replace Palestine as the ultimate goal. The opportunity presented itself and I thought it was an idea at least worth exploring. And I hope that when you have reviewed this matter, you will agree to join me and those of your brethren who want to work within a traditional context rather than one of radical protest."

Jabotinsky made his way to the podium and shook hands with Herzl, then for the next fifteen minutes gave a rambling discourse on the many things Herzl had done for the Jews. When he was finished, the group gave a rousing round of applause. While they were clapping, Herzl started up the aisle toward the door. Those seated nearby reached out to shake his hand, to touch him on the arm or shoulder, and share a word of encouragement with him.

After Herzl was gone, Jabotinsky returned to the podium and said, simply, "I'm against this Uganda plan in every form. It might look like a short-term option, but if we don't make our stand in Palestine now, we'll never have the opportunity to establish a state there again. This is it. Our one and only opportunity. It's either Palestine now or Palestine never. Both sides of the river."

"So what should we do?" someone asked. "What do we say when we return to the meeting?"

"I propose that we form our own organization. Make our own plans for establishing a presence in Palestine. And let all the others sit here in the meeting hall talking about it. While they talk about going to Uganda, or anywhere else, we will return to our homeland. The land promised to our forefathers!"

The delegates were on their feet clapping once again and this time peppering the moment with catcalls. Shouts of, "Both sides of the river!" rang out from here and there across the room. Nearly everyone in the audience picked it up, chanting the phrase in unison over and over again.

Nathan, however, did not join them but sat quietly in back, watching and doing his best to process all that had transpired in the short time since they walked out of the meeting. Leaving the Zionist Organization now, so soon after it had been formed and over an issue like where to settle, might be a fatal blow to the organization. Perhaps even to the Zionist cause. And whether or not that was a possibility, he felt the decision to part with the group was one that should not be made in haste or in the emotion of the moment.

As the crowd finally quieted and returned to their seats, Nathan made his way toward the front of the room where Jabotinsky stood. He caught Jabotinsky's eye and indicated that he had a matter to raise.

"Yes, Rabbi Mileikowsky? You wish to be heard?"

Nathan stepped to the podium. "This is an important moment for all of us. But I think we should realize it is an important moment for Zionism and for all Jews everywhere—those who join us, and those who do not. Those who want to find a homeland, and those who wish to remain where they are. For all of us, this moment—the decisions we make right now, today, this very hour—will affect millions of Jews, some of whom do not even know the Zionist Organization even exists."

"Our hearts are in the right place. We want a land we can call our own and we will not be satisfied with anything other than the land of our fathers in Palestine." The audience responded with thunderous applause and shouts of support. Nathan called for quiet and continued. "I think we would be well served in this hour to consider also that Theodor Herzl's heart is in the right place. Millions of our fellow Jews face harsh conditions where they live and only want out of their current circumstance. For them, moving to Uganda and establishing a Jewish colony with British support might seem like an answer to generations of prayer. And if going there would save even one life, it would save an entire generation. An opportunity like that puts Theodor Herzl in a tough position. I think as our leader, attempting to do the best for us, he would be obligated to explore that African option, which apparently he has.

"In fact, we *are* in the same position as Herzl. For we have the same obligation as he. The obligation to consider what is best for all Jews and not simply what is best for us. Herzl only wants us to consider the Uganda option. I suggest we return to the meeting and work with the other delegations. We can always leave later, but this may be our only opportunity to work as a unified congress."

When Nathan finished, the delegation sat quietly, giving him not even so much as polite applause. But the look in their eyes told him they were moved by what he'd said. Even Jabotinsky, who sat gently stroking his chin.

Finally Jabotinsky rose from his chair. "We have a motion on the floor to return to the congressional meetings, work with the other delegations, and, for the time being, remain with the Zionist Organization, where we shall work with all our might to maintain our return to Palestine as the sole focus of that group. All in favor say, 'Aye.'"

The delegation gave a thunderous response and followed Jabotinsky out the door toward the meeting room.

For the next three days, the delegation from Russia, under Jabotinsky's leadership, worked to stymie the Uganda issue at every turn. In the end, they succeeded in delaying a final decision pending further consideration, appointing instead a commission to travel to Uganda and view the site. But Jabotinsky and many others remained skeptical of the effort and it would become the first evidence of a much deeper rift within the Zionist Organization.

When news of the latest Zionist congress proceedings reached Ibrahim, he went to work instigating new pogroms against Jews living within the Russian empire. From 1903 to 1906, wave after wave of attacks swept over the country in an attempt to influence the final decision regarding a Jewish colony in Uganda.

Nathan, still traveling from city to city lecturing in support of the Zionist message, missed most of the violence but incorporated accounts of it in his speeches as he moved through the region, lecturing with renewed passion and commitment about the need to leave Europe and relocate in Palestine.

19

NETANYAHU

IN BETWEEN LECTURES, Nathan would return to Lodz to see Sarah. On one of those visits, Lurie took him aside to his study. "I may have acted imprudently," he explained nervously, "but I have arranged for a man to pay you a visit."

"Who is it?"

"Yossi Metzger."

"I've heard of him."

"He's heard of you, too."

"Doesn't he trade in fabric, linen, that sort of thing?"

"Cotton and wool. He's a wholesaler and a broker."

"Do you have any idea what he wants to talk about?"

"He's not coming on behalf of his business. Yossi serves on the board of trustees for the Hebrew Gymnasium in Warsaw."

Nathan nodded thoughtfully. "Mordechai Krinsky's school?"

"Yes."

"I suppose they're interested in scheduling a lecture?"

Lurie moved closer. "Nathan, the school is interested in hiring you."

Nathan frowned. "For what?"

"Director," Lurie grinned. "They want to hire you as director of the school."

Nathan's eyes opened wide and he arched a brow. "Director of the school," he repeated.

"Yes."

News of such an opportunity caught Nathan off-guard. He stood there in the study a moment, staring blankly ahead before collapsing into a chair that sat just a few feet away. "I need to think about this," he said as he rubbed his forehead.

Hebrew Gymnasium was a co-educational school for Jewish children. Students ranged in age from primary through secondary classes. It wasn't the kind of academic position Nathan had thought about years ago when he wrestled with the notion of which path his life should follow—academic or traveling lecturer—but in Jewish circles the directorship of this particular school was a prestigious post.

Mordechai Krinsky was a rabbi who, like Herzl, spent much of his life in support of Jewish Enlightenment, educating Jewish students in the classic Western topics and teaching them how to assimilate into Russian culture. Gradually, however, the pogroms wore him down and he came to realize that, at least in Russia, assimilation would never happen. They would always be Jews and nothing more. Because of that, they could never escape the constant acts of humiliation, destruction, and death foisted upon them.

His abandonment of the Enlightenment approach sent shock waves through the Jewish community of Warsaw and made him an instant hero among those devoted to the Zionist cause. Stepping into an office once held by Krinsky was an acknowledgment that Nathan had moved one step closer to the inner circle of Judaism. But it was not without its own risk.

"Lot of guys like me have withered in a setting like that," Nathan pointed out. "Came to an academic job as dynamic orators, well-known scholars, and brilliant authors. Only to watch the fire in their bones—the thing about them that made them so *right* for the job—get quenched by a flood of administrative details and bureaucratic in-fighting."

"You could continue to lecture as your schedule allowed."

"But it wouldn't be the same as being on the road."

"No," Lurie agreed. "It wouldn't. And if you'd rather not talk to him, I will contact him immediately and let him—"

Nathan shook his head. "Don't contact him. I'll meet with him. Listen to what he has to say." He smiled over at Lurie. "And who knows? This may be just the sort of thing I need."

✦ ✦ ✦

Nathan came from the study and found Sarah in the kitchen washing dishes. He picked up a towel and began drying. "What were you talking about in there?" she asked.

"Ahh," Nathan shrugged. "You know. Weather. The usual stuff."

"I know my father. And he never talks about the weather. So, tell me. What were you talking about?"

"The Hebrew Gymnasium in Warsaw wants to talk to me."

"Whatever for?"

"Apparently they want to offer me a job."

"What kind of job?"

"Director."

Sarah's mouth fell open in a look of surprise. She dropped the cloth she'd been using in the sink and put her arms around his neck. "Does this mean what I think it means?"

"Let's not get too far ahead of ourselves."

"What do you mean?"

"I mean, they haven't offered me a job yet. I haven't even met with them."

"But you are tonight, right?"

"I'm meeting with one guy. Yossi Metzger. One of the school trustees. I'm sure there will be many more meetings before they finally make an offer."

"But this means you'd be home more."

"Yes," he nodded. "I would be home more. It would be a steady job with regular hours and regular income."

She squeezed his neck with her arms. "This is exactly what we've wanted. What we've prayed for."

"Yes," Nathan nodded.

"We could get married."

"Yes, but this is just one meeting out of many more to come. He's not making an offer today."

"I know, but still," she continued, hugging him tightly once more, "This is it. I know it is. This is the answer we've needed."

Late that afternoon, Yossi Metzger arrived. He and Nathan sat in the front parlor and talked. Hebrew Gymnasium was very much interested in Nathan. "In fact," Metzger explained, "when we found out you might be available, we didn't contact anyone else about this."

"I'm your only candidate?"

"Yes. You're our sole candidate. We want you. Not someone else."

Nathan was flattered by their interest, but insisted on visiting the school before discussing details of the job. Metzger agreed to arrange a tour.

A few days later, Nathan, Sarah, and Lurie took the train to Warsaw and visited the school. The buildings looked tired and in need of a fresh coat of paint, but the classrooms were filled to capacity with students, most of whom seemed eager to be there. When Metzger finally offered the job, Nathan accepted on the spot.

✦ ✦ ✦

A month later, Nathan and Sarah were married in a small ceremony in the Lurie home in Warsaw. Nathan's family joined them, then remained in Lodz a few days afterward to help Nathan and Sarah get settled in their new location.

Much to his surprise, Nathan found his position as school director far less demanding than he'd at first thought. If anything, the academic life—even if it wasn't at the university level—seemed to invigorate him in ways lecturing and traveling could not. For the first time in a long time he had the opportunity to gather his notes and ideas and consider arranging them into a book.

The following year, Sarah gave birth to their first son whom she named Benzion, after his grandfather. Lurie and Aniela were on hand for the event, though Lurie spent most of his time downstairs with Nathan while Aniela and the midwife delivered the baby.

A few minutes after the child was born, Nathan was invited upstairs for a look at his son. He stood at the crib and stared down at the young body, squirming beneath the blanket that covered him.

As Nathan stood there, watching, Lurie walked up alongside him and held out his hand. "Here. This is for Benzion. Keep it for him until he comes of age."

Nathan glanced down at Lurie's open palm and saw a ring. Lurie gestured once more. "Go on. Take it."

Nathan plucked the ring from Lurie's palm and studied it a moment. "There's an inscription on here."

"Yes, but we should talk about this downstairs."

"Netanyahu Ben—"

"Shhh," Lurie said. "We'll talk about it downstairs."

Just then, Sarah spoke up from her place in bed. "What are you two whispering about?"

"Just talking about our son," Nathan replied. "Isn't he wonderful?"

"Yes, he is. Which is why I don't want you two hovering over him just yet. For now, he needs to rest."

Nathan grinned. "Staking out your claim to him already?"

"Just a mother looking out for her son," she smiled.

✦ ✦ ✦

Nathan followed Lurie downstairs and out to the front porch. "Okay," Nathan said when they were alone. "What were you trying to tell me about the ring?"

"Take a look at it."

Nathan took the ring from his pocket and studied it once more. "Well, it says, 'Netanyahu Ben-Yoash. Netanyahu—that part is a name. Or, it could be a title. It means, 'Yahweh has given.'

"And the next part?"

"Ben-Yoash means simply 'Son of Yoash.' So the inscription could be read as 'Netanyahu who is the son of Yoash.' Or it could be read, 'The son of Yoash, who is the Netanyahu.'"

"That ring was the seal of a Hebrew official who served thousands of years ago under David."

Nathan's eyes widened in a look of surprise. "David as in King David from the Torah?"

"Yes."

"How did you get a ring like that?"

"It was given to me because I am a member of the house of Lurie. We are—"

"Direct descendants of David." Nathan finished the sentence.

"Yes, we are his direct descendants. Which means your son lying upstairs with his mother is a direct descendant also."

"And you have the king's seal."

"And the promise."

Nathan had a quizzical expression. "You are the heir of the promise to the House of David?"

"For my generation. And now, I am passing the ring to you to keep on behalf of your son. When he comes of age, you must give it to him. He will be the heir of the promise for *his* generation."

"But why are you giving this to me now?"

"A year or two before Sarah was born, a rabbi named Judah Alkalai visited me. He told me that Aniela would give birth to a daughter. Her name should be Sarah. And then he said that we would meet a man named Nathaniel whom Sarah would marry. You and Sarah would have a son and I should give him the ring. That son would be the child of promise for his generation, just as I am for mine." Lurie pointed to the ring. "Today, your son joins a long line of men who have served the Jewish cause. All of us Netanyahus—men given by Yahweh to serve His people."

"Does this mean he will become king of Israel?"

Lurie shrugged. "I do not know, but I know the promise given to David—your kingdom will never end—passes to little Benzion lying upstairs."

"And then what?"

"That will be for him to figure out. Each of us can only follow the light we have been given." Lurie gestured for emphasis with his index finger. "If you do that, *you* will never fail. If he does that, *he* will never fail."

Nathan looked down at the ring lying in the center of his palm. "You don't want to keep it and give it to him yourself, later, when he comes of age?"

"No. I'm not sure how much longer I will be here."

Nathan's eyes were instantly alert. "What do you mean?" His eyes narrowed in a look of concern. "Is something wrong?"

"Things are being...arranged. We may finally make the move to Palestine."

"Oh." The look on Nathan's face softened. "This is the first I've heard of it."

"Not many people know about this yet and we'd like to keep it that way."

"Does Sarah know?"

"I don't think so and it would be better if we just kept this between us. Things are a little up in the air right now and I don't want news of our plans to get ahead of us."

"You mean, no one at the synagogue knows about this?"

"Exactly."

Nathan looked down at the ring still resting on his palm. "And this?"

"I don't want it to get lost in the confusion of leaving." Lurie closed Nathan's hand around the ring. "I want to make sure my grandson has it. Which is why I'm giving it to you—for safekeeping until that day arrives."

NETANYAHU

GETTING TO PALESTINE took longer than Lurie had anticipated, but finally, two years after talking to Nathan and giving him the Netanyahu ring, details for the move fell into place. When all the arrangements were made, Lurie met with the synagogue council and told them of his plans.

"We've had enough of life in Russia," Lurie explained. "The attacks on our neighborhood have been more than we wish to bear. Aniela and I are ready to leave for Palestine."

Herman Zamenhof spoke up. "Do you have any recommendations as to who should take your place here?"

"One. I have but one recommendation."

"And who might that be?"

"My son-in-law," Lurie replied. "Nathan Mileikowsky."

"Have you talked to him about this?"

"Actually," Lurie said with an embarrassed smile. "No, I haven't."

"That might be the first thing to do," Yehiel Borowski suggested. "You talk to him, then we talk to him after that. So we know if he wants the position or not. There's no need for all of us to meet with him, if he doesn't want the position."

"Yehiel raises a good point," Zamenhof added. "We would be glad to talk with him about the position, but perhaps you should discuss the matter beforehand and find out if he is interested in the position."

"I will be glad to bring up the matter with him, as long as he does not get excluded merely for being my son-in-law."

"We know him." Zamenhof smiled. "I know him. But you'll have to trust us on this. See if he wants the position. Then we will meet with him."

✦ ✦ ✦

A few days later, Lurie traveled to Warsaw for a visit with Nathan and Sarah. Over lunch, he told them of their plans to leave Lodz and immigrate to Palestine. "We will live and work on a farm in Galilee. Near one of the settlements established by Hovevei Zion years ago."

"Good for you!" Nathan exclaimed. "You've wanted to do that for a long time."

"But can you do it?" Sarah asked.

"Yes. We've made all the arrangements, finally. Filed all the forms. Received all the permission certificates."

"I don't mean that. I mean, can you live the life. This sounds like a place that will take a lot of physical labor. Can you do that sort of thing all day, every day?"

"I'll do as much as I can." The tone in Lurie's voice indicated he sensed the anger in Sarah's. "I think they know what they are getting in me."

"I didn't mean to be offensive," Sarah apologized. "It's just that you're not a young man anymore and I didn't know if you could work like that all day."

"I'll be fine," Lurie muttered as he turned his attention to the food on his plate.

"That sounds exciting," Nathan interjected. "After all these years, everything is finally in place for you."

"Everything except one final issue."

"What is that?" Sarah asked.

"The most important one of all." Lurie glanced away seemingly unable to look at her or Nathan. "The issue of who shall lead the synagogue as chief rabbi when I am gone."

Nathan looked over at Sarah who merely shrugged in response. "Who are you considering for the position?"

Lurie looked Nathan in the eye and pointed. "You."

"Me?"

"You're a perfect fit for the job."

Nathan gave him a quizzical expression. "Are you saying I should apply?"

Lurie grinned. "I've already taken that step for you."

"You told them I wanted to be their rabbi?"

"They asked if I had anyone to recommend for the position. I told them I knew of only one person who could do it. And then I gave them your name."

"What did they think of that idea?"

"They were intrigued."

"That's all?" Sarah's voice reflected the exasperation she felt inside. "Just intrigued?"

Lurie focused on Nathan. "Enough so that they want to talk with you about the position."

"When?"

"Day after tomorrow." He quickly added, "If that's good for you."

Two days later, Lurie boarded the train for Lodz, accompanied by Nathan. After an all-day session with the synagogue council, Herman Zamenhof offered Nathan the position of chief rabbi. Nathan accepted immediately.

✦ ✦ ✦

In 1914, Russia entered World War One, opening an eastern front against the Central Powers and aligning itself with the United Kingdom, the United States, and other Allied Powers. Many Jews from Lodz saw this as a positive step for them and wanted to form their own unit to assist with Russian attempts to protect its own best interests. Nathan steadfastly refused to support efforts to form an independent fighting unit.

"The Russians are not our ally," he argued. "They are our oppressors and our persecutors. They will never have our best interests at heart. We must attend to our own best interests, rather than relying on some misguided, baseless belief that if we participate in the czar's war we will somehow gain his favor. Nothing could be further from the truth.

"Once the war is over, the pogroms will continue against us once more. State sponsored pogroms. Persecution instigated against us by the czar. The same czar some of you suggest we should now risk our lives to support and defend.

"Instead, we must put our energy, our hope, our confidence in our ability to affect our own circumstances and devote ourselves to the singular effort of immigrating to the land of our forefathers. The land promised by God to Moses and fulfilled by Joshua. A land ruled by David with a kingdom that shall never end. Let the Gentiles fight their own battles. We must return to our homeland."

The content of Nathan's lectures bordered on sedition—a call for open, physical rebellion against state policy—but with the war occupying most of the government's time and effort, Nathan continued unchallenged by the authorities.

Meanwhile, letters arrived regularly from Lurie and Aniela extolling the beauty and wonders of Palestine. "It's a land far more beautiful than any of us hoped," the letters read. "Not a lush, green European beauty, but a Palestinian beauty. A beauty beyond any that Europe could produce."

"From the way they describe it," Nathan commented, "Palestine sounds inviting."

"I'm certain it's an *adventurous* affair for them," Sarah replied.

"For them?"

"Not all adventures were meant to be shared by everyone."

"I thought you wanted to immigrate to Palestine."

"I like the idea of it. But as the mother of young children, I think life there would be far too challenging."

"Well, challenging or not," Nathan said, "I've been talking about Zion for a long time. We've been talking about it."

"And?"

"I'm tired of just talking."

"Many people have been inspired to immigrate by your words."

"And now it feels like we should be two of them. Two of those who actually make the move." Nathan looked her in the eye. "We can't just talk it. We have to do it."

They sat in silence for a moment, then Sarah spoke. "Write to Papa and ask him about jobs there."

Nathan's face lit up. "You'll agree to go?"

"I'll agree to consider it, but not without a means of supporting ourselves after we arrive there. And not without a place for our children."

Over the next five months, Nathan and Lurie exchanged correspondence regarding employment possibilities. Lurie did his best to find something for Nathan and after several opportunities failed to materialize, he found one he thought would be perfect.

"There is an opening for principal of the Vilkomitz School at Rosh Pina," Lurie's letter read. "The monthly pay is not very good, but you get a house and domestic help. And the Jewish Agency will add a small stipend for food."

"The Jewish Agency," Sarah repeated in a downcast tone.

"Yes," Nathan replied. "The Jewish Agency for Palestine. The Zionist Organization's…"

Sarah interrupted him. "I know what it is. I just mean, we'd be working through *them*."

"Not really."

"What do you mean?"

"I mean, we'd be way up in Galilee. They're in Jerusalem, I think."

Sarah held out her hand. "Let me see the letter." He handed it to her and she read it quickly. "Sounds charming," she noted with a hint of sarcasm.

"It would be rather remote, but beautiful I'm sure."

"How remote?"

"Rosh Pina is north of the Sea of Galilee."

"Well," Sarah sighed. "Write back and ask for the job announcement."

Nathan grinned. "You're thinking about saying yes."

"Let's see the details. Then we can decide."

A month later, a letter arrived from Lurie along with a copy of the official announcement from the Jewish Agency giving details about the job opening. Nathan responded immediately.

After a flurry of correspondence, the Agency offered Nathan the position in Rosh Pina. Sarah remained wary of the move but in the end refused to deny Nathan something he'd promoted and encouraged all his life.

NETANYAHU

WHILE NATHAN HAD MARRIED and pursued a career in teaching, his friend Jabotinsky turned to journalism, initially writing and reporting for newspapers in Odessa. His articles were sometimes provocative but well received and by the beginning of World War I he had established a reputation for thorough and persistent work.

Not long after Russia joined the war, Jabotinsky heard a rumor about Arab leaders in the Middle East who were quietly organizing Arab tribes in North Africa for a Jihad against all foreigners. Eager to learn whether the rumors were true, Jabotinsky, who by then was writing for *Russkiya Vedomosti*, Moscow's leading liberal newspaper, convinced his editor to send him on a fact-finding trip through North Africa. Jabotinsky traveled by ship to Tetouan and set out from there to travel by land all the way to Jerusalem.

The trip turned out to be more challenging than Jabotinsky first thought, but eventually he arrived in Alexandria, Egypt, where he discovered Jewish refugees from Palestine living in British camps. The Jews, he quickly learned, had been victims of Ottoman aggression and had been driven from their farms and homes by Arab gangs that were sponsored by Ottoman rulers and Turkish soldiers.

True to the principles instilled in him by his father—the belief that aggression against Jews could only be deterred by resisting and fighting back—Jabotinsky set aside his journalist responsibilities and began organizing the men of the camp into a resistance group with the intention of returning to Palestine and taking back their farms and homes. Few of them had any prior military experience, but Jabotinsky pressed on with drills in basic military tactics.

To bolster the group's chances of success, Jabotinsky sought the support of the British army and arranged a meeting with General Maxwell, the general officer commanding British troops in North Africa. Jabotinsky's offer to provide troops for an incursion into Palestine was declined but Maxwell offered to allow Jabotinsky and his men to serve as an auxiliary unit in the transportation corps.

"Sounds more glamorous than it really is. You'd be driving mules," Maxwell explained. "Or, more to the point, you would be *leading* a string of mules from a supply depot inland to where the fighting is."

Jabotinsky seemed especially put off by the offer and refused it on the spot. Not long thereafter, he left Alexandria for London, where he returned to his previous role as a reporter and continued to lobby the British government for a Jewish military unit to retake Palestine. His efforts were eventually successful and resulted in the formation of the Jewish Legion. The Legion saw action near the end of the Palestinian campaign and was present in Jerusalem when the British took charge of the capital.

At the war's end, Palestine came under the control of the British government. That control was formalized in the Mandate for Palestine issued by the League of Nations. The mandate authorized, among other things, the establishment of a Jewish Assembly of Representatives to help govern Jewish affairs in the Mandatory area. The Zionist Organization, through its Jewish Agency for Palestine, coordinated creation of the Assembly. The year Nathan and his family arrived in Palestine, elections were held for the first Jewish Assembly. Jabotinsky was elected to a seat and later that year was added to the Zionist Organization's executive council.

At first, things went well with the Assembly, but in 1923, a long-simmering dispute between the practical group—those who sought to work for the Zionist cause within the existing legal and diplomatic framework—and the revisionist group—those who sought Jewish control over all of Palestine, including the area of Transjordan—boiled over. That dispute took the form of a personal confrontation between Jabotinsky and Chaim Weizmann. It was, however, a much more complex matter.

Very early in his attempt to secure the creation of a Jewish state in Palestine, Theodor Herzl sought the sponsorship of a respected and influential nation. He viewed that sponsorship as essential in winning international acceptance of the Zionist cause. Consequently, his meetings with government officials and dignitaries were decidedly cordial in nature, a tone and quality that carried over to the Zionist Organization.

Almost from the beginning, Herzl's approach bothered Jabotinsky and he showed little restraint in making his views and opinions known to members of the press. He reserved his most incendiary remarks for those who sought to accommodate British policy and practice in Palestine—policies and practices which he saw as favoring Arabs and prejudicial against Jews. After repeated incidents, some of which strained relations between the Jewish Agency and the British government almost to the breaking point, members of the Zionist Organization executive committee asked Jabotinsky to either refrain from publicly criticizing policy or resign, so he resigned.

After resigning from the Zionist Organization, Jabotinsky formed a new group known as the Alliance of Revisionist-Zionists. Nathan, by then a committed Jabotinsky supporter, joined in that work.

As expected, in one of its first acts, the Revisionists demanded establishment of a Jewish state in Palestine. A state with control of land on both sides of the Jordan River. There followed, however, an unrestrained attack on British policy as Jabotinsky guided the organization toward policy positions consistent with his vitriolic denunciations. His outspoken criticism and his agitation of Jews against Arabs—calling on Jews to take up arms and force the Arabs to flee from Palestine—led the British to expel him. No longer welcome there, he relocated to England.

Jabotinsky's departure from Palestine left a void in the Revisionist organization's leadership. Nathan was one of those who stepped forward to fill the gap.

NETANYAHU

ABOUT THAT SAME TIME, Barakat gathered the Five Caliphs for a meeting in Istanbul. Ibrahim was noticeably absent, a point Talal was quick to raise.

"I thought it would be better to meet without him," Barakat explained.

Abdullah agreed. "And we should spare him no pain in discussing his work and...effectiveness."

"You mean his lack of effectiveness," Musa added.

Abdullah frowned. "I was attempting to speak of him politely."

"That is why he is not here," Barakat added. "So that we do not need to concern ourselves with speaking politely of him."

"He has failed," Idris proclaimed. "Utterly and completely failed. Nothing he has proposed or attempted has proven successful."

"There are more Jews in Palestine today than ever before," Talal noted. "And at the same time we have lost control of our entire kingdom to the British."

"Not all of it went to the British," Musa corrected. "The Turks and Greeks were all too glad to step in and carve out a chunk for themselves."

"And the French," Abdullah added. "Don't forget the French."

"I believe then," Barakat noted, "we are all in agreement that we have arrived at a point where Ibrahim is no longer useful to us."

All five nodded in agreement. "Which presents another difficult matter," Talal said.

"What is that?"

Barakat spoke up. "Ibrahim knows too much to simply dismiss him from service."

"He must be removed," Musa muttered.

"You mean eliminated."

"Yes," Barakat replied as the others nodded in agreement.

Barakat glanced around the group. "Where is he today?"

"Odessa," Idris replied.

"Very well," Barakat said in a resolute tone. "We shall send someone to deliver the message to him."

✦ ✦ ✦

No one needed to tell Ibrahim he was in trouble with the caliphs. He knew without being told. That knowing sense of dread was confirmed when Omar Nazrallah, a friend from Istanbul, told him the caliphs met without him.

"And you are certain they have met to discuss matters in my portfolio?"

"They discussed among themselves the situation with the Jews and then they brought in someone from outside."

"Outside?"

"Not a caliph."

"Do you know this person's name?"

"No. And none of my usual contacts know either."

"But they knew of the meetings?"

"Yes."

"Why did they meet without me?" Ibrahim demanded. "What was the reason?"

"They are not pleased with the lack of results you have obtained with the Jews." Omar looked away. "In spite of intricate plans and great effort,

Jews continue to stream to Palestine, unabated except for an occasional limitation imposed by the British. And even then the limitations do not come as a result of your plans and actions."

"The British only limit the Jews when they want access to our oil."

"I am certain you are correct," Omar agreed, "but the word has been given."

"They are sending someone for me?"

"Yes. This Thursday. They want you to meet him at the mosque."

"What do they want me to do?"

"Come for morning prayers, then walk out to the courtyard."

"And they will not visit this upon my family?" Ibrahim asked once more.

"As long as your family members take no action against them, the matter will remain a private affair."

✦ ✦ ✦

The following Thursday, Ibrahim made his way to Al-Salam mosque in Odessa. His heart rate quickened as he entered the main hall and joined the other men as they prepared for morning prayers. A quick survey of the room failed to detect anyone new or out of the ordinary. *Perhaps Allah has intervened,* he thought as he knelt on his prayer rug. *Maybe no one will come for me.*

Forty-five minutes later, the prayers were finished and the men filed from the room. Ibrahim lingered, surveying the men as they moved toward the door. Looking each man in the eye. Checking each face. But once again he saw no one who looked suspicious and when all of the men had gone, Ibrahim made his way to the courtyard. A bench was located there and he took a seat.

A few minutes later, he heard the gate behind him open and then Abdel Zewail moved quickly to his side. Zewail was about Ibrahim's height, but he was ten years younger and still had the look of youth about him. Ibrahim first saw him at morning prayers about six months earlier, and they had struck up a kind of friendship over coffee at a café a few blocks down the street.

"I love this place," Zewail observed in a soft voice as he took a seat next to Ibrahim.

Ibrahim nodded. "When I come in here, the city seems miles away. Life seems to all but disappear." He smiled at Zewail. "In here, there is only me and Allah."

Ibrahim was not surprised that Zewail was the one. It made perfect sense to send him. Zewail had a way about him that made you glad to see him, even when you knew he brought bad news for you. Even now, Ibrahim was glad to see him, though he suspected what Zewail's presence meant.

While they continued to talk, Ibrahim was certain he heard the gate open once more but when he failed to note the sound of footsteps approaching, he didn't bother to look around. Moments later, an arm came from behind and squeezed tight across his chest, pulling him backwards and pinning him against the intruder's legs. At the same time a hand with a carefully folded cloth was brought toward his face Zewail said, "Relax, my friend. Do not resist."

The man whose hand held the cloth pressed it tightly against his nose and mouth and Ibrahim smelled the unmistakable odor of chloroform. He tried at first to take only shallow breaths but after a few moments, his lungs cried out for air and he gasped deeply, sucking air through his nose and mouth. In the next moment, Ibrahim's body went limp and he collapsed. His eyes rolled up beneath his lids, then closed altogether.

✦ ✦ ✦

Three days later, Zewail appeared before the caliphs in Istanbul.

"I hope you bring us good news," Barakat said.

"I bring you news that Ibrahim is gone," Zewail replied.

"Good. There were no complications?"

"None."

"Very well. Now, tell us about the new efforts through which you propose to succeed where he failed."

"In the past," Zewail began, "your focus was on Jews residing in the

Russian Empire. Specifically that area known as the Pale of Settlement. It is the location of a large Jewish population and the czar, struggling to hold onto his empire in the face of far-reaching social changes, was all too glad to accommodate your interests. He saw it as a means of effecting Jewish assimilation. You saw it as an opportunity to force them towards a land of their own, albeit in a location other than Palestine. For the time, the focus on the Pale of Settlement was correct. The plans applied to the Jewish population, however, were far too nuanced to produce success."

"Too nuanced?" Talal asked.

"You sought to drive the Jews out of the Pale of Settlement because you knew the czar would not interfere with your efforts. But driving them out of Russia, without awakening in them a long-lost affection for their ancestral land, would have been well-nigh impossible."

"You don't think Russia is the correct location to effect a solution to the Jewish problem?"

"No. I do not."

"Then what location do you suggest?"

"Central and Southern Europe. Germany in particular. But also France, Austria, and perhaps Italy. Anti-Semitism is on the rise in those areas. Post-war Germany is the most fertile location for the kind of result you wish to produce. Treaties that ended the Great War have left the German economy devastated, her population humiliated, and the entire country looking for someone to blame."

"And you think the Jews, as a group, are that entity?" Musa asked.

"Most definitely."

"And how do you propose to deal with them?"

"The only effective method to prevent them from returning in large numbers to Palestine is to deal with them."

"You mean, eliminate them."

"In large numbers."

"How would we to that?" Abdullah had a skeptical look. "That would mean the deaths of millions."

"Germany," Zewail answered. "Under the right kind of leadership, Germany could do this for you."

"But do they have that kind of leadership available?" Barakat asked.

"Yes," Zewail replied. "I believe they do."

"And does this person have a name?"

"Adolf Hitler. Nazi Party spokesman."

For the next hour, they discussed Hitler, the political movement coalescing around him, and how that movement might be convinced to assist the Arab cause in Palestine by eliminating the Jewish problem. It was a full, frank, and—at times—alarmingly gruesome discussion. Still, it seemed to the caliphs to be the only means available in preventing a mass exodus of the Jews from Europe and ultimate immigration to Palestine.

As the discussion wound to a close, Barakat looked over at Zewail. "You should return to Germany at once."

"Yes," Zewail replied. "I plan to leave day after tomorrow."

"Good. Make contact with this Hitler. Learn whether there is a way that we may assist each other."

"Yes." Zewail nodded. "I shall do my best."

"We need you to make this happen." Barakat urged. "Give him our assurance that we will do all within our power to help."

✦ ✦ ✦

Two days later, Zewail departed Istanbul from the Sirkeci station and traveled across Europe aboard the Orient Express. When he reached Paris, he transferred to a train bound for Munich. Otto Dietrich, one of Ibrahim's contacts and a man known to several of the caliphs, met him at the station. "I trust all is well in the East," Dietrich commented as they walked along the platform by the tracks.

Zewail looked over at Dietrich. "Now that the Allies have their boot on our back."

Dietrich gave him a wry smile.

"But perhaps the young Turks will save us," Zewail continued sarcastically. "Does Germany have any saviors?"

"Yes, indeed, and we shall meet some of them. But first, let me say, as much as I look forward to working with you, I shall miss my friend Ibrahim al-Kazem. Did you know him?"

Zewail's eyes darted away. "I met him once. It was a brief meeting. We didn't really talk about much of substance."

"I see. Well, he will be missed. But your reputation goes before you, too. Many of our people have heard of you and they're looking forward to meeting you."

"Whom do we see first?" Zewail asked.

"Max Amann," Dietrich replied.

"Never heard of him."

"He's a young man. Not a lot of political experience. But he has worked hard organizing opposition to the German aristocracy and has ties to a number of paramilitary units. I think you will find him indispensable in your efforts to find ways in which we can work to solve our mutual problems."

That evening, Zewail and Dietrich met with Amann following a rally for his Freikorp paramilitary unit known as Steel Helmet. He was a tall man, well over six feet, with blonde hair and blue eyes. The perfect example of what was being touted as the *master race.*

Zewail and Amann hit it off from the beginning and talked well into the night about the broad changes that were sweeping across Europe. "The last of the great monarchies are finally being forced to abdicate their corrupt lifestyles and cede power back to the people."

"And the people are rising up to force them to do that," Amann agreed. "We are no longer afraid to stand up for ourselves. Very soon, the German monarchy will be gone and in its place we shall install a new government that represents *our* best interests, not the interests of the royal family."

It was a splendid conversation—one that had Zewail thinking of moving to Germany and joining the cause. Until he remembered that he, an Arab, was categorically excluded from the German master race and would be relegated to the lowest ranks of their society. *Right along with the Jew and Gypsies.* Still, politics made for strange alliances and if the Germans were willing to support the Arab cause in the Middle East, then perhaps Arabs could support the German cause in Central Europe.

The following week, Zewail, Dietrich, and Amann met with leaders from key paramilitary units, all of them stocked with embittered veterans of the Great War who felt humiliated by the decision to surrender and infuriated by the terms of the peace. Now, they were prepared to do whatever was necessary to right those wrongs and free Germany from the oppression of its centuries-old monarchy.

The final group they met with was Storm Troop, an affiliate of the Nationalist Socialist German Workers Party, better known as the Nazi Party. Storm Troop was led by Hans Ulrich Klintzsch. Like Amann, he was young, blonde, and strikingly handsome. However, unlike Amann, he was not given to long-winded conversation. He was polite and cordial, but his answers to Zewail's questions were exact, precise, and to the point. He was also orderly and disciplined.

Fifteen minutes into their conversation Klintzsch glanced at his watch. "I'm afraid that is all the time I have for you today. I have another meeting to attend. Perhaps we can take this up later."

"Yes," Zewail replied. "Perhaps we shall."

The two men shook hands, then Klintzsch turned aside and made his way toward the door. Zewail stared after him as he reached the doorway and disappeared into the corridor outside the room. "Interesting young man."

"Yes. One of our best. And one of Hitler's favorites."

Zewail turned to Amann. "They all seem genuinely taken by Hitler."

"Yes. They are. And he is with them as well."

"A mutual admiration."

"One born of mutual misery, I suppose. The war wiped out many of our brightest and most capable young men. Destroyed our economy. Then the peace robbed us of what little remained."

"Reparations?"

"The Allies not only defeated us, they wanted us to repay them for the cost of doing so."

"That would be humiliating."

Amann nodded. "It was."

"Any possibility I could spend a few minutes with Hitler?"

"We'll see him tomorrow tonight."

"Oh." Zewail's eyes were wide with a look of surprise. "Dinner?" he asked with a hopeful tone.

"No. I am afraid not. He's speaking at a party rally in Munich. We'll attend the rally so you can hear him speak, then meet with him afterwards.You'll come away with a deeper understanding of him than you could ever get simply by talking to him face-to-face."

✦ ✦ ✦

The following evening, Amann and Zewail arrived at Hofbräuhaus, a beer hall not far from where they had met with Klintzsch. A crowd filled the street out front but Amann paid them no attention as he guided Zewail to the door and they squeezed their way inside.

The crowd that filled the main portion of the hall was loud and boisterous, but still Amann kept going, making his way to a stairwell and they threaded their way to the top.

On the second floor, a corridor ran across the front of the building with doors that opened into a large meeting room. Like the space downstairs, that room was filled beyond capacity. Guards manned the entrance, but when they saw Amann approaching they redoubled their effort at crowd control and made a way for Amann and Zewail.

Inside the meeting room, Zewail followed Amann to the fourth row from the front.

"I wouldn't miss this for anything," Amann quipped.

A few minutes later, Rudolf Hess strode to the podium and looked out over the audience. Amann expected a long, rambling introduction. Instead, all he heard from Hess were three words: "The Führer speaks!"

As Hitler rose from his seat, the crowd stood and shouted its support—one side of the room saying, "Heil Hitler! Heil Hitler!" The other side shouting in response, "Deutschland erwache! Deutschland erwache!"

Hitler moved slowly to the podium, making no attempt to dampen the crowd's enthusiasm but rather seeming to enjoy it. Finally, when several minutes passed and the din had not slackened at all, he raised one hand ever so slightly. Almost instantly, noise in the room evaporated and a sudden stillness took its place as the audience returned to their seats. When they were ready, Hitler took a deep breath and began.

For the next ten minutes, Hitler delivered a brutal diatribe against the German monarchy, first attacking its economic policies as nothing less than a means of enslaving the German people, then its social policies, blaming the monarchy for allowing the inferior races to pollute the historic German race.

Then he turned to the hope offered by the National Socialist German Workers Party, calling it, "The remnant of Germany's best who formed the old guard leadership of the Party have given birth to the next generation. A generation of pure, unadulterated Germans, bred from the heartiest stock, trained by our most brilliant and capable warriors, and now ready to guide the party into a future filled with promise and victory!"

The crowd which had been hanging on every word suddenly leapt to their feet, shouting again, "Heil Hitler! Heil Hitler!"

Their loudest cheers, however, were reserved for the final section of the speech when Hitler moved toward his closing remarks. "The challenges this new generation of leaders face are not imagined challenges, as some suppose. We are not speaking of fairy tales or childish legends. No. The horrors that await us are more real than ever before. The dire economic conditions brought upon the German people have also been brought upon the world, making this not only a German problem but a global one. Yet while the world wrings its hands and frets over economic data, blindly attempting to divine some statistical cause of their misery, we Germans see clearly to the heart of the matter. We see as no one else can, that the dire consequences we face were brought on by the greed of one race. The lasciviousness of one race. The devious duplicity of one race. The race that steals our jobs, destroys our businesses, and threatens the lives of our children. The Jews have done this to us!"

The crowd roared with approval, but Hitler kept going. "Jews perform no useful work, provide no useful service, supply no useful product. Yet they control more of the world's wealth than any other single race. Hoarding for themselves gold and silver they did not accumulate by work or ingenuity. Instead, they stole it from hardworking Germans!

"Many of you seated here this evening have lost your jobs to their obsession. They have devoured your jobs, your children's jobs, and, as it were, they have devoured your children themselves, all in the name of riches.

"The United States may stand by and watch, the British may allow it to happen again and again, but here in Germany, we are doing something to stop it. And we will do more. All across the Motherland, men just like you are organizing themselves, arming themselves, training themselves, for the day very soon when we will rise up and banish the filthy Jews from our land!"

It was a rousing speech and when it was over Zewail glanced around expecting to see the audience rushing out to take up the fight right then and there. They didn't, but from the comments of those seated around him, Zewail was certain there would come a time when they would.

Zewail waited with Amann while the crowd pushed toward the exits. Once the rush had dissipated, they made their way downstairs to the first floor, then continued down one more flight into the basement where a casino was located. "We will get a table back there." Amann pointed to the far side of the room. They threaded their way past gambling tables and found an open table in the corner. Zewail took a seat while Amann stood to watch. "I talked to Hess. He said this is what we should do."

"Hess?" Zewail frowned. "Rudolf Hess?"

"Yes. He's the one you contact if you want to reach Hitler."

In a few minutes Hitler entered the casino. Everyone in the room turned to face him and greeted him with salutes and loud applause. He smiled and nodded as he made his way slowly across the room. Zewail stood, too, and joined the others in clapping, but his eyes were glued to Hitler's every move, every gesture, every expression on his face.

After what seemed like a long time, Hitler finally drew near the table where Amann and Zewail waited. Amann, suddenly nervous and awkward, introduced them to each other and gestured toward the chairs. "Perhaps you would like to sit?"

Hitler settled into a chair opposite Zewail, crossed his legs at the knee, and waited while Zewail did the same. Amann, sensing they wished to speak in private, stepped away leaving Hitler and Zewail to talk alone.

"So, tell me," Hitler began, going straight to the point of their meeting. "Why are the caliphs of Istanbul interested in the Workers Party of Germany?"

"They are looking for a way to prevent Jews from immigrating to Palestine and thought you might have some ideas about how to accomplish that."

"That is very easy to accomplish," Hitler averred. He had a business-like expressing as he spoke. "Very easy indeed."

"Oh?" Zewail responded with a hint of skepticism. "How so?"

Hitler stared across the table, his eyes focused on Zewail as if he were looking straight through him. "We kill them all," he vowed in a low, matter-of-fact tone.

"Yes," Zewail smiled. "I suppose that would solve it."

"If they are dead, they will not be of any trouble to you or anyone else."

"Yes, but I don't think—"

"You Arabs have been trying silly plans and schemes to influence them." Hitler's eyes now turned away and his voice seemed to come from somewhere outside himself. "Jews are like dogs. They cannot be trained without the application of force. In fact, many of them cannot be trained at all. Merely used up and disposed of like so many farm animals. That is what we intend to do when we come to power." His gaze returned to Zewail. "And we *will* come to power."

"Yes." Zewail nodded. "The caliphs are certain you will, which is why they wanted to approach you now."

Hitler's face was stoic and unmoved except for his eyes which were as intense as any Zewail had ever seen. "If you can help us here," he added. "We can help you there."

"You want our support for your effort in Europe?" Zewail asked.

"The more we kill here, the less you will have there."

Zewail smiled. At last he'd found someone who made sense of it all—someone with supporters willing to take decisive action to impose their understanding on the situation.

"And how would you want them to show their support for you?"

"The caliphs have three things that we need," Hitler outlined. "The first two are men and oil. The third is access to markets outside of Europe. Give us those three things and when we complete the resurrection of Germany to her former glory, we will turn our attention to Palestine and together exterminate the Jews once and for all."

NETANYAHU

ZEWAIL RETURNED to Istanbul and reported to the caliphs about his meeting with Hitler and other officials from the Workers Party. They were glad to hear of his warm reception and agreed to help Hitler. "In fact," Barakat said. "We have already prepared a gift for you to take to him." He lifted a suitcase from beside his chair and handed it to Zewail.

Zewail grasped it by the handle and paused to check the locks, wondering if he should ask to see the contents. If he asked, the caliphs might take it as an insult, but if he didn't and the contents were not as everyone supposed, his contacts in Germany might shoot him. After a moment, he glanced over at Barakat and gestured with a nod to the case. "May I?"

"By all means," Barakat urged. "Assure yourself."

Zewail popped the latches on the suitcase and raised the lid. Inside he found the case was packed with cash. Most was in British Pound notes that were strapped and neatly stacked in place.

"We know Hitler didn't specifically request cash, but we thought it would be a good gesture," Barakat explained.

"One we could deliver promptly," Musa said.

"I agree," Zewail replied. "It is a good idea. International currency is difficult for them to obtain right now. But shouldn't we talk to someone first? Make some arrangements? Discuss what we expect in return?"

"We don't expect anything in return," Abdullah answered. "This is our gift. A show of good intentions. That is all."

"The details have already been addressed," Barakat explained. "You should go at once."

Zewail was taken aback to learn that they arranged the details of his trip through someone else, but he knew better than to ask how they did it or why. Instead, he departed for Berlin that afternoon carrying the suitcase stuffed with cash.

✦ ✦ ✦

Not long after Zewail delivered the suitcase, ranking members from the National Socialist German Workers Party arrived in Istanbul. The caliphs received them graciously, treating them to a lavish banquet.

The following day, they turned their attention to the details of a cooperative arrangement between the Party and the caliphs. By the end of the day, the caliphs had agreed to supply Germany with large quantities of oil, assuming the Workers Party was successful in getting Hitler elected. In return, the Germans agreed to supply arms, munitions, and explosives to Arabs in Palestine and to send military instructors there to train Arab fighters in the latest infantry tactics. The talks were cordial, straightforward, and brief.

When the Germans were gone, the caliphs summoned Zewail. He responded promptly.

"As you know," Barakat began, "the Germans have agreed to supply our friends in Palestine with arms, munitions, and training."

"You struck a good bargain," Zewail said.

Barakat accepted the compliment with a smile. "We will need someone to take charge of that relationship—to organize the Arabs of Palestine and get the equipment distributed to them."

"You will need someone experienced in logistics."

"Precisely. We were wondering if you had a preference for that. Someone you have dealt with in the past."

Without hesitation Zewail answered, "On the Arab side, you

should work through Haj Amin al-Husseini, the Mufti of Jerusalem."

"Excellent choice." Musa smiled. "We are good friends with him."

"Surely you know this man," Abdullah said. "But have you worked with him in the past?"

"Yes, I know him. But I have not worked with him in the manner I think you are contemplating now."

"Good," Barakat agreed in an attempt to move the conversation along. "Go to Jerusalem, meet with Husseini and work out the details through him."

✦ ✦ ✦

Arranging travel from Istanbul to Jerusalem took more effort than Zewail thought possible, but five days after meeting with the caliphs, he departed for Jerusalem. A short ride from the airport brought him to the King David Hotel. He settled into a room, then went downstairs to the lobby where he found a public telephone. He placed a call to Fawzi al Qawuqji, a Lebanese Druze who once had been an officer in the Turkish army but now served as one of Husseini's most trusted advisors. Qawuqji was expecting him and had already arranged a meeting for Zewail with Husseini that afternoon.

An hour later, Zewail left the hotel and took a taxi to a coffee shop located a few blocks from Temple Mount. He was met at the entrance by a young man dressed in a tan business suit with a white dress shirt that was open at the collar. The young man seemed to recognize Zewail at once and escorted him to a room in back. "We wait here," his escort instructed.

Twenty minutes later, a door to the alleyway out back opened and Husseini entered, accompanied by Qawuqji. After proper introductions, Qawuqji and the first young man glanced furtively around the room one last time, then excused themselves. When the door closed behind them, Husseini looked over at Zewail, "I understand you have made some new friends in Europe. Will this be a long-term arrangement or only for a short while?"

"That remains to be seen. Right now, they are interested in oil."

"Of which the caliphs control plenty."

"The caliphs have agreed to sell oil to Germany at a very favorable rate in exchange for weapons, ammunition, and instructors."

"What kind of instructors?"

"Instructors who can advise your men on the tactics of a modern army on a modern battlefield."

"We have Arab tactics. They have served us well all these years. Why should we abandon them now?"

"The world has changed. Battlefields have changed. Wars are no longer fought on horseback or with swords. We need to adapt to the times."

"After we kill all the Jews, we will make everyone else adapt to us."

"Perhaps so, but for now we need to at least consider using the tactics of proven, twentieth century armies."

"These advisers will come to Palestine?"

"Yes, they will be assigned to your men."

"I am glad for this apparent show of support, but I am skeptical of German promises, especially Germans who are members of the Nazi party."

Zewail nodded in agreement. "Nazis can be deceitful and they are not offering us assistance out of a commitment to our cause, but from an attempt to pursue their own best interests. They need oil. But perhaps we can use that to our advantage."

"You mean, ride the tiger while sitting in a place on his back from which he cannot reach us with his jaws?"

"Something like that. Our future, the future of our people, the future of the entire Muslim world is on the line. We cannot afford to turn away a helping hand, even if it comes with a clinched fist."

"Very well," Husseini said. "How shall we coordinate our work with these advisers and the distribution of the arms? I suppose the caliphs want to control this from Istanbul."

"Actually, we were hoping you could handle it on this end. Get the arms to the best people. Inform the proper local leaders about the military instructors. Prepare them to receive weapons and training. Will you do that?"

"Certainly."

✦ ✦ ✦

When Zewail was gone, Qawuqji returned to the room. He listened attentively as Husseini told him of the caliphs' plan for working with the Germans. "I don't like the Germans," he declared when Husseini finished.

"I know," Husseini nodded. "None of us do. Not even the caliphs. But we need arms and munitions. The Germans are willing to supply those, plus trainers to show us their battlefield tactics."

"We have our own tactics. Adapted over many centuries for use in the desert." He raised both hands in a gesture of frustration. "What can the Germans teach us?"

"I don't know, but perhaps we should let them show us their tactics and deliver their arms to us. Then we can decide whether to use them."

"They will want something from us."

"The caliphs are paying them in oil."

"No." Qawuqji shook his head. "After we have driven the Jews into the sea, the Germans will want something more."

"When the Jews are gone we will deal with the Germans, if they remain to be dealt with."

"We should kill them all."

"A goal many have suggested," Husseini noted. "But for now, we must concentrate on the Jews living here in Palestine."

Qawuqji fell silent for a moment, then with a look of resignation glanced over at Husseini. "What do you need from me?"

"We must select the ablest of the tribal leaders—"

"Warlords."

"We must select them and bring them to Jerusalem when the trainers arrive."

Qawuqji's eyes flashed with energy once more. "How do we know this is not a trap?"

A frown wrinkled Husseini's brow. "A trap?"

"A dozen tribal leaders, the ablest and best, all in one room. With as many Germans. Suppose they are of the same opinion as we—kill them all—we would be easy targets."

"We will take care of that," Husseini reassured. "For now, help me determine the best of our leaders."

"The men we select will have as many questions as I. Some even more."

"I am sure they will, but we need to focus on selecting the leaders with whom we shall deal. We can answer their questions when they raise them."

Once more a look of resignation settled over Qawuqji. "As you wish," he sighed. "But I do not like it."

Developing the list of tribal leaders did not take long. Most of them were readily obvious even without asking. Among them were Hafez al-Turabi, Hatim al-Ta'i, Rifa'a Zaghlul, and Abel Rawahah. Husseini summoned them to Jerusalem and outlined the proposal from the caliphs to cooperate with the Germans in exchange for German arms and instructors.

After explaining the proposal, Husseini invited their responses. He was genuinely interested in what they thought of the plan, but careful to stop short of implying that the warlords had any option other than to participate.

"If the Germans follow through," Zaghlul noted when Husseini finished his presentation, "if they send arms and munitions as they have indicated. And if they send trainers to instruct us on their battlefield tactics, then we will have what we've wanted from the British but never received—the support of a nation that understands our problem, is willing, and that is capable of, providing us with the means to eliminate that problem."

"Then we can solve the Jew problem once and for all," Turabi agreed. "I'm not sure what we can do about the British."

"The only solution to our situation in Palestine is to kill them all," Rawahah stated flatly. "The Jews and the British."

"And anyone else who stands in the way of absolute Arab control of Palestine," al-Ta'i added. "This has been our home for almost two thousand years."

Others shouted from the back of the room. "Jerusalem is a holy city. Allah demands that we defend it."

"The prophet Muhammad commands it in the Koran. We must follow his teaching and use every means possible, even if it means cooperating with German infidels."

"So long as they can help us, we shall receive their assistance. But we shall fight all who attempt to take this land from us, even to the death of the last man."

"And that includes the Germans if necessary," Zaghlul stressed.

NETANYAHU

MEANWHILE, Nathan continued to work as principal of the Vilkomitz School at Rosh Pina. At the same time, he maintained a full and busy schedule lecturing in locations throughout Palestine and beyond, encouraging those already in the settlements to hold fast and urging those outside Palestine to join the cause.

On one of his lecture trips through Europe he was approached by Levi Klein, an associate head of the Jewish National Fund, with an offer to work for the fund, raising money to support settlements and real estate development in Palestine. Having attended the Zionist congress since the beginning, Nathan was well aware of the Fund's work in purchasing farmland for settlements and developing areas in Tel Aviv, Jerusalem, and Haifa.

"The pay is better and you can live in Jerusalem," Klein pointed out. "In fact, we would hope that you *would* live in Jerusalem, both for the convenience of travel and to safeguard your family while you are away."

When Nathan returned to Rosh Pina, he told Sarah about Klein's offer. She was ready to move on the spot. Nathan wrote to Klein that evening accepting his offer.

Leaving his position at the school took several months; existing obligations had to be fulfilled and a temporary successor appointed. They also had to locate housing in Jerusalem and arrange for the transportation of their household belongings, but by the end of the spring semester of 1924, Nathan, Sarah, and their children were settled in Jerusalem, and Nathan was busy arranging his first schedule of presentations on behalf of the Fund.

That first trip took Nathan through France, Germany, and England, where he witnessed the growing hostility toward Jews that would ultimately culminate in the horrors of the Holocaust during World War II. To his amazement, most Jews living in Europe seemed to ignore the threat, choosing instead to concentrate on the routine of their daily lives, focusing their attention on business affairs and maintaining a proper outward appearance. However, they were generous and though few of them were interested in moving to Palestine, they readily supported the efforts of others who wanted to live there, which made Nathan's trip an enormous fundraising success.

Spurred on by the response he received in Europe, Nathan next journeyed to the United States. Arriving in New York in the fall, he conducted meetings in and around the city, then continued westward with stops in Cleveland, Detroit, Indianapolis, and Chicago. At each location he was warmly received by audiences that had heard of the ill winds gathering in Europe and were eager to finally have a means of taking constructive action against it.

However, like the Jews in Europe, most were not interested in personally relocating to Palestine. When Nathan asked about it, Judah Cohen, one of his hosts, told him, "The United States offers security from external threat and freedom from organized, government-sponsored harassment, like they face in most of Europe. To put it more bluntly, most have it easy here and are not willing to give up the lifestyle America affords."

Nathan looked perplexed. "But they contribute with genuine enthusiasm."

"They agree that for those living under oppressive regimes, relocating is the best option. The *only* option for some. And they probably feel more than a little guilt that they have experienced some of the better things in life while their relatives and acquaintances in Europe experience much of the evil. So," Cohen shrugged, "they buy a little relief from the guilt by giving money to the Fund."

As he continued westward, Nathan found time on the train to read. He familiarized himself with American Jewish newspapers and periodicals, and also with major newspapers like *The New York Times,* Cleveland *Plain Dealer,* Chicago *Sun,* and the Milwaukee *Journal.*

Somewhere between one paper's home city and the next stop on his schedule, Nathan remembered the desire he'd had as a young man to write. He'd wanted to produce scholarly work, but traveling for the Fund gave him little time for original research. Still, he had plenty to say about the need for establishing Jewish settlements in Palestine and the need of all Jews everywhere to reclaim a sense of identity and belonging that was rooted in an awareness of their historic past, rather than one defined for them by Gentiles in Europe or the United States. Articles on those ideas and topics could be produced without academic support.

So, as he proceeded west from Chicago, he decided to give written expression to those ideals and began crafting a series of articles for Jewish publications. As he put pen to paper, the writing took on a fresh, strident voice, a marked departure from articles he'd written in the past. Rather than polishing these articles or attempting to sculpt the language into a more refined voice, he let the words flow and as he did he found they came straight from the heart, with passion and force he'd never known before.

In keeping with the tone of those articles, and in a nod to reclaiming his own historic identity, he avoided use of his traditional family name in the byline and instead signed them as Nathan Netanyahu—the name taken from the ring he'd been entrusted with by Lurie years before.

✦ ✦ ✦

While Nathan crisscrossed the globe on behalf of the Jewish National Fund, Benzion, his eldest son, continued to grow and mature in the rough and tumble world of Palestine. After completing his secondary education, he enrolled at the David Yellin Teacher's Seminary. From there he was accepted into a graduate program at Hebrew University. He shared Nathan's love for the academic life but with Nathan gone more often than he was at home, Benzion charted his academic career largely on his own understanding. It proved to be a career without much regard for the religious training his father had experienced.

Those times that he *was* home, Nathan was more distant and combative than ever. Benzion struggled to make sense of it—the caring, loving father he'd known as a child now changed to a touchy, ill-tempered authoritarian—but understanding it proved impossible. Instead, he found ways to avoid being home as much as possible when Nathan was in town. It was an easy task to accomplish, really. Classes occupied most of Benzion's day and when he wasn't in class there was always studying to do in the library. He spent many long evening hours there, reading, researching, and writing. Most nights he worked until the building closed, arriving home after everyone else was asleep.

The time Benzion spent away from his father lessened the number of angry confrontations, but still took a toll on their relationship. And by the time they realized what had happened, neither of them knew how to find their way back to the easy, warm rapport they'd known when Benzion was a young boy. That did not stop them from trying and they continued to make an effort toward each other—an episodic, disjointed, effort, but an effort nonetheless.

✦ ✦ ✦

In 1935, as Nathan prepared to leave on yet one more fundraising trip, Benzion arrived home earlier than usual. Nathan called him aside and led the way to the study. Nathan seemed in a better mood than usual—softer, more reflective—but after the history they'd had together, Benzion kept a wary eye on his father, expecting to see the back of his hand at any moment.

When they were alone, Nathan closed the door behind them, then turned to Benzion with a look of genuine concern. "I know things have been difficult with us these past few years," he began. "It's just that things in the world are changing rapidly. Forces—evil forces—are aligning against us. More evil than anything we ever faced before. In just a few years, we could see a horrible manifestation of that evil sweep through Europe, engulfing everything in its path."

Benzion was puzzled. "I'm not sure I understand what you're talking about."

"Europe is only one maniacal leader away from exterminating the Jews."

"Actually exterminating us?"

"Many have wanted to do that for a long time," Nathan explained, "but respectable people spoke against it. Now those otherwise respectable people, many of them decent Gentile Christians, have fallen silent. Leaving no one to oppose those who blame us for everything they think is wrong with their lives, even for the conditions they themselves imposed on our people." He reached out and placed a hand on Benzion's shoulder. His eyes were full and his voice almost breaking. "I...I just wanted you to know that I realize how difficult I've been..." He paused on the verge of apologizing, then turned away, moved behind his desk, and took a seat. "I have something I want to give you."

Benzion found a chair nearby. "I didn't expect a gift." He couldn't remember the last time his father had given him a present.

Nathan opened the top drawer of the desk and took out a small wooden box. He set it on the desktop, rested one hand on the box as if protecting it, and looked over at Benzion. "About two years before your mother was born, your grandfather Lurie was in his study at the synagogue in Lodz."

"I remember that room," Benzion recalled. "It had the wonderful smell of books."

"Yes," Nathan agreed. "It did indeed." He paused a moment to gather his thoughts before continuing. "While he was working there in the study, a visitor arrived at his door. The man's name was Judah Alkalai."

"The Rabbi of Semlin."

"One of the most influential rabbis of his day."

"Did you know him?"

"I think I saw him once, maybe. I'm not sure. I have a memory of what he looked like but I've seen pictures of him many times since then and I wonder sometimes if my memory of him has become confused with the pictures."

"Interesting man."

"Alkalai told your grandfather that his wife would give birth to a girl. That the girl would be born about two years from then and they should name her Sarah. Then he said, sometime after that, when Sarah was older and of marriageable age, a man would visit them. That man would be named Nathaniel and he would become Sarah's husband."

Benzion raised an eyebrow in a skeptical expression. "And Saba Lurie believed it?"

"Yes." Nathan replied matter of factly. "Why wouldn't he? Alkalai spoke the word of prophecy and it came to pass. That has always been the ultimate proof—both of the word given and of his authority to deliver it."

"You don't think Gran just made it up?"

A scowl darkened Nathan's eyes and wrinkled his forehead. "Don't say such a thing. Your grandfather wouldn't do that and you know it."

"I know" Benzion shrugged. "It's just that it sounds too...correct. So correct it sounds contrived."

"Your grandfather had no reason to lie to me. Your mother and I were already married when he told me. In fact, he didn't tell me about Judah Alkalai's visit until the night you were born."

"And why did he tell you about it then?"

"Because." Nathan tapped the wooden box with his index finger. "He wanted to give me this to hold for you."

"This box?" Benzion asked, gesturing to it.

"Yes."

"What's inside it?"

"As you know, the Luries are descendants of David."

"As I've been reminded many times."

"What you don't know is that with each generation one child is selected as the child of promise, the one who inherits the promise from God that David's kingdom would never end. That inheritance was signified by a ring that was passed from one generation to the next.

Your grandfather had it during his lifetime." Nathan handed the box to Benzion. "Then he gave it to me to give to you."

Benzion opened the box to find a ring inside.

"This ring goes all the way back to the reign of David," Nathan explained. "And it has been passed to the child of promise in each generation." He looked over at Benzion. "You are that child for your generation."

Benzion chuckled. "Does this mean I will be king?"

"I do not know. No one knows."

"Then what should I do with it?"

"Keep it. Stay alert. Remain faithful to the call upon your life."

"And?"

"And then you will always know what to do."

"You know I don't believe in this stuff."

Nathan leaned back in his chair. "Don't start with me, Benzion. It's been a pleasant evening. Let's just leave it at that."

✦ ✦ ✦

With box in hand, Benzion went upstairs to his room and sat on the edge of the bed. Slowly, he lifted the box lid and gazed inside. The ring was nestled safely in the folds of purple velvet that lined the box—the cotton cloth from the used shirt long since replaced. After a moment, Benzion reached to lift it out, then hesitated and drew back his hand.

David was king of Israel almost three thousand years ago. Could this ring really be that old? And who was this David anyway? Were the stories about him real? He wondered. *Or were they merely myths and legends created after the fact to bolster the ancient accounts of Israel's history?*

Those questions and more swirled through Benzion's mind as he continued to stare at the ring until finally he pushed all thought aside and carefully lifted the ring from the box. He held it, turning it slowly from side to side, reading the inscription as he did.

"Netanyahu Ben-Yoash," he said aloud. "Netanyahu—Yahweh has given. And he is the son of Yoash."

The ring certainly looked old. Definitely not like anything produced by jewelers and smiths of the modern era. For one thing, the surface of the shoulders was smooth, suggesting the ring had been created by pouring molten gold into a mold. When it had cooled, the ring would have been worked into the correct size by tapping the surface with a small hammer. Hammer marks were visible along the edge of one side. Only then was the inscription added.

Along the top of the ring was an image of a man holding a staff in one hand and a scepter in the other. *Staff and scepter,* Benzion pondered, *A depiction of royalty, no doubt. And this was his signet ring. A ring he had given to Yoash symbolizing the delegation of authority to him.*

The image had been added by first carving it into an oval shaped ivory setting which was fitted into a similarly shaped opening that, in turn, had been carved by hand into the flat surface at the top of the ring. The setting was held in place by four delicate tabs created from droplets of molten gold that had been added after the ring was finished.

Benzion turned the ring from side to side, studying its features, marveling at the craftsmanship and wondering how it had survived all these years.

If I really am a descendant of David, he thought, and if this really is a signet ring from the time of his reign, this would make me next in line for the throne.

Like many who would live through the Holocaust years, Benzion came to question whether God existed at all. When he arrived with his family at Rosh Pina he entered a life that was surrounded by fellow Jews who came to Palestine to work on the farms. They came to assert their ethnic right to settle in the land of their ancestors, but they did so as an expression of enthusiastic devotion to liberal, labor-oriented, political action—not unlike the rise of liberal politics in other regions of the world. For them, returning to Palestine was a political act, not an expression of faith in God.

By the time he entered high school, Benzion found himself trapped. On the one hand, the traditional theological expressions of God he'd learned and studied prior to the Holocaust were deeply engrained. God is all powerful, all knowing, all present, all good. An understanding of God with which all monotheistic religions agreed. Yet standing opposite those traditional concepts were the equally powerful and starkly real events of the Holocaust. Atrocities that strained human understanding to the breaking point. By the time he entered college Benzion had concluded that whatever else God might be, He couldn't be a god who possessed the qualities at the center of pre-Holocaust theology.

Yet, here he was, holding an artifact from the past that connected him directly, personally, by birth, to the most revered king in all of Jewish history. And not merely a ring but a ring that conveyed his authority.

"David's signet ring," he whispered. But as soon as he said those words, a harshly cynical attitude rose up in him.

His grandfather and someone from every generation before him had received the Davidic promise—that David's kingdom would have no end—but none of them had seen that promise fulfilled in *their* lifetime. They lived in the hope of it, died in the hope of it, and passed that hope to the next generation, but not one of them lived to see a new, actual, Davidic Kingdom take its place among the nations of the world.

Still, the ring was intriguing and the more he concentrated on it the more it seemed to draw him away from his cynical attitude. Away from skepticism. Away from the comfortable, secular, agnostic view he'd held since high school toward faith and a sense of mystery and wonder he'd never entertained.

Is this the time? he asked himself. *Is the Zionist movement a rising army that will take back the land of Israel? Is God bringing to pass the fulfillment of His promises?*

Finally, Benzion slipped the ring onto his finger. "Maybe it has magical powers," he muttered sarcastically. "Maybe the one who wears it has the power to make the impossible happen." The ring, however, was easily two sizes too big. He twirled it around his finger once or twice, then slipped it off. "Maybe it will fit on my thumb." The ring went snuggly onto his thumb but Benzion grimaced at the sight. "That doesn't look very royal."

Frustrated, he returned the ring to its place inside the box and set it on the dresser, then lay back on the bed and stared up at the ceiling. His father had said, "If you remain true to the calling upon your life, you will know what to do." But what *was* the calling upon his life? Was he even called to anything? Besides, he wasn't even sure that God existed. And with that his thoughts left the ring, the box, and the House of David and returned once again to the problem that had troubled him most of his life—does God exist and if so, what is He really like?

✦ ✦ ✦

Several months later, Nathan returned from another fundraising trip. He looked unusually tired with bags under his eyes, and when he walked he seemed to gasp for breath. At night when he lay down to rest he coughed uncontrollably.

Benzion noticed his father's appearance but thought little of it. He'd always returned from his trips physically spent from trying to accomplish as much as humanly possible. Years before, it had seemed not to slow him much. He'd take a long, hot bath, then sleep late the following morning. After that, he was back at his desk studying and working the telephone to set up his next assignment.

This time, however, things were different. He spent most of the first night propped in a chair in the front room, a pillow behind his head and a blanket over his legs. The following morning, as the sun crested the hills to the east, he failed to stir and showed no interest in moving from the chair until midmorning. Even then he took only a few sips of tea and bites of toast. And most noticeable of all, he smiled more than he spoke and when he did speak it was in a soft, low voice. Everyone sensed something was wrong.

After lunch, Nathan shuffled to the study, steadying himself with a hand against the furniture or the wall until he reached his desk and dropped onto the chair behind it. He spent a while sorting through mail that had arrived while he was gone, but by mid-afternoon he was back in the chair in the front room, a pillow behind his head and a blanket over his legs. That's when Sarah called Dr. Sisselman.

After examining Nathan, Sisselman took Sarah aside, "I'm all but certain he has pneumonia. If he were in the office I could do a more thorough examination but I think that would only confirm what I suspect now."

"Can you treat it?"

"That depends on whether it's viral or bacterial. With bacterial pneumonia, maybe. If it's caused by a virus, there isn't much we can do except treat the symptoms—alleviate the coughing, that sort of thing, and hope he pulls out of it. We need to get him to the hospital."

"Benzion can drive him in the car."

"I'll arrange for an ambulance to come and get him," Sisselman decided. "I think that would be best. They'll come for him in a few hours. I'll need that much time to get to the hospital and arrange for a bed."

It was late afternoon before the ambulance arrived and by then Nathan's condition had worsened, with periods of lucidity and then incoherence. He improved somewhat when he reached the hospital and began receiving oxygen, but late that night he sat up in bed with a look of panic in his eyes. He clutched his chest and gasped for breath, then fell back on his pillow. Moments later, Sisselman examined him for the last time, then looked over at Sarah and shook his head. "I'm sorry. Nathan is gone."

NETANYAHU

IN KEEPING WITH Jewish tradition and religious law, Nathan's funeral was held the next day. Rabbi Abraham Isaac Kook presided and less than twenty-four hours after he died, Nathan's body was lowered into a grave at the Mount of Olives Cemetery.

Benzion stood near Sarah, the dutiful son supporting his mother, as the body slowly slipped from view. He took note that the service was ending and was aware the crowd that had joined them was drifting away, but Benzion continued to stare straight ahead as though seeing into a world that was far away. And indeed, he was.

In his mind he was back in Lodz, a time in his life when his father had been his hero. A man who always had time to listen—no matter how tedious his questions might be—and who always had an answer. He'd been warm and loving and Benzion remembered walking from the house to the synagogue, his small hand enveloped by his father's seemingly huge paw.

But then they had moved to Palestine.

Almost from the day they left Lodz, Nathan began to sink into an angry, disgruntled state of mind. Things that never bothered him now drew a cross answer or a harsh response. And then those responses became physical. A shake of the shoulders, a slap on the cheek.

Even after they made the trek across Palestine and arrived at Rosh Pina, his mood refused to lift. When he began traveling for the Jewish

National Fund, he often seemed in a good mood before he left, but when he returned would fall into the same angry, disgruntled disposition.

Maybe he should have stayed on the road. Maybe that was my father's calling. He seemed to enjoy it far more than being at home. "Some people are not suited for a domestic life," Benzion whispered.

"Are you okay?" a voice asked.

Startled, Benzion jerked his head around to find Celia Segal, a class-mate from Hebrew University, standing next to him. "Are you okay?" she repeated.

"Yes, I think so."

"It was all so sudden. I know you must be devastated."

"It was quite unexpected," Benzion responded. "I had so many questions I wanted to ask him."

Celia slipped an arm beneath his and pulled him close. "He was a good man. He did his best. Maybe he was just worn out."

"Oh, he was that alright. After this last trip, his body was spent."

The family was already back at the car and Benzion's younger brother waved for him to join them. Benzion and Celia walked in that direction. "Do you have a ride home?" he asked.

She glanced around as if searching. "I think they left without me."

"Well, if you don't mind riding with all of us to the house," Benzion offered. "I'll get you home from there."

✦ ✦ ✦

A few days after Nathan's funeral, Benzion returned to class at Hebrew University where his study and research had narrowed from the broader topic of Jewish history to specific aspects of the Jewish story that would be examined in depth. That interest led him to concentrate on the history of Jews in Spain, particularly their reaction to the Spanish Inquisition. It was, at last, a topic that fully engaged his mind, but not all of his professors were content with that decision and his progress on the topic was not encouraged.

To help defray the expense of his education, Benzion worked as editor of a Revisionist Zionism newspaper known as *Ha-yarden*. He enjoyed piecing words together on a page, making them fit within a constrained space while still conveying a message to readers. Several of his articles, however, pushed the limits of British tolerance and resulted in a warning. Rather than back down, Benzion pushed even harder. Not long after that, the British Mandatory Authority shut down the newspaper.

Benzion was proud of what he'd done—standing up to defiant, arrogant British officials. When he walked the streets of Jerusalem people called to him from the doors and windows of their shops and apartments, congratulating him on his courageous stand. But it wasn't long until Benzion realized that his defiant gesture had cost him dearly.

The meager salary he'd earned from the paper made a big difference in covering the cost of school. If he wanted to continue his studies he needed to find a source of income to replace the one the British took away. He dusted off his resume, made sure it was up to date, and sent it out to the friends and influential leaders he'd come to know through his work on the paper.

A few days later, Benzion's friend, Abba Ahimer, approached him about working with Scopus Publishing. "Right now, we're trying to publish the works of Max Nordau and Israel Zangwill," Ahimer explained.

"I've read both," Benzion said. "Difficult to find their books now. Especially Zangwill."

"That's because his original publisher didn't print very many of their books in the first place, which is why Scopus is pursuing this project."

"No one pays much attention to men like Zangwill anymore. Certainly not the people who are here," Benzion added. "There was a time when men measured themselves by the books they read." He glanced at Ahimer. "Maybe that's why we find the Zionist Organization so difficult to control. They don't read enough."

"Well, to change that, we'd need some of those obscure titles to explain how we came to be here in Palestine. And to do that, we need as many available in Hebrew as possible. Which is what we're trying to do. Bring those older books back into print."

Benzion stood gazing out a window. Hands behind his back. "That's a sobering thought. We've been here less than a generation and yet the point of our coming might well be lost to the generation that follows us."

"So, you'll at least meet with them?" Ahimer asked. "Talk to them about working with us at Scopus?"

Benzion smiled. "Yes, I would be pleased to talk with them."

Two days later, Benzion joined Martin Tishbee, a senior editor with Scopus, for coffee. Tishbee outlined the company's work and what they hoped to accomplish through it. When he finished, he offered Benzion the job of working under him as an associate editor.

The offer appealed to Benzion on at least two levels. First, he was genuinely interested in preserving the history and writings of modern Zionism. Almost all the earliest founders of the movement were dead and although many had written numerous articles, treatises, and books on the topic, those writings were out of print and fast disappearing from library collections.

Of more immediate importance, the job came with a salary that was three times what he had made while working for the newspaper. Benzion accepted immediately.

While working at Scopus, Benzion published several articles about his ideas on Zionism, the way forward for Jews in Palestine, and his critique of Zionist policy in general. As he worked on those articles he was reminded of his father and all that had happened since their late-night sessions when he was a boy in Kreva. The thought of it touched him deeply and he decided to honor Nathan by adopting the name Netanyahu for the byline—the same byline Nathan had used on his articles. It was a practice that many who immigrated to Palestine had adopted—changing their Polish or Russian or German names for something more Hebraic.

By the time he finished a third article he decided to use the name not merely as a byline for publishing purposes, but as his own last name. Henceforth he was known exclusively as Benzion Netanyahu.

✦ ✦ ✦

As much as he enjoyed the work at Scopus, Benzion remained committed to pursuing a doctoral degree. While he worked at his editing job he continued studying at Hebrew University, hoping to complete a master's degree program as the next step toward an academic career. By then he was certain his life's work—the calling upon his life, to use his father's terms—lay in scholarship, academia, teaching, and writing.

To that end, he focused his study purposefully on the history of Jews in Spain. Not far into that effort he became suspicious that the prevailing scholarly understanding of the Jewish experience in Spain during the Inquisition was wrong.

Modern scholarship had concluded that Jews in Spain during the time of the Inquisition had outwardly converted to Christianity in order to avoid persecution, but inwardly and secretly remained religiously Jewish. Benzion took the opposite tack, proposing instead that Jews in Spain did in fact genuinely convert to Christianity in an experience much like that of the Jews in Russia who abandoned their Jewish beliefs and traditions in an attempt to become fully assimilated into Russian culture. They did this, Benzion argued, not to escape persecution but as a means of moving beyond their historic past toward full and complete racial acceptance and social integration.

Benzion wrote about the topic for a class in European history taught by Haim Zariski, one of Hebrew University's best-known professors. For Benzion, it was a way of satisfying a class assignment while also clarifying his thoughts regarding an idea he hoped would form the central concept of a doctoral dissertation. A week after turning in the paper, Zariski called him to his office to discuss the matter.

"Interesting paper, Mr. Netanyahu."

"Thank you," Benzion replied.

"You do realize no one in the scholarly community agrees with you, don't you?"

"Yes," Benzion shrugged. "I suppose I do."

"And I admire your courage," Zariski offered, "but I think you should consider whether this is the correct institution for you."

Benzion was stunned. "You think I should go somewhere else over the content of one paper?"

"It's not just this paper." Zariski picked up the pages from his desk and flipped through them. "You write well. The manuscript has a polished feel, as if you weighed every word carefully. And your logic holds all the way through."

"Then what could possibly be the problem with it?"

Zariski dropped the paper back onto the desktop and looked over at Benzion. "Most of us are put off by the fact that you always take the contrarian position. As if your thoughts on a subject are the only ones with any validity."

"Is that such a bad thing? Shouldn't a scholar agree with his own opinions? Shouldn't he sell out to them? Shouldn't he be ready to defend them at all costs?"

Zariski scooted closer to the desk, rested his forearms there, and lowered his voice. "Frankly, Benzion, no one here wants to support work that suggests there is something wrong with our Jewish past—religious or otherwise."

"I didn't—"

"The thought that Jews faced with persecution would give up one set of beliefs and adopt another is very...insulting. Especially in light of what we endured and continue to endure in Europe—the pogroms in Russia that even you witnessed as a young boy. Surely you can see this."

"I am a scholar," Benzion argued. "A scholar-in-training for certain, but a scholar nonetheless. I follow the research. Where it leads me is where I go. The conclusions I have reached are all based on a thorough review of source documents."

Zariski was unmoved. "When you enrolled here, you indicated you were interested in pursuing a PhD. Is that still your plan?"

"Yes."

"And this," he gestured to the paper, "would be the focus of your work?"

"Yes."

"Then I think you should decide now, before this goes any further. Either choose a different topic, or choose a different school."

Benzion could not believe it. How could they be this upset over a single paper? How could there be this much opposition to him? Most of the faculty was made up of people he only met when he started class. They didn't know him. He didn't know them.

"Professor, you have been teaching us to follow the facts. They are like a trail, you said. Follow the facts and they will take you to the heart of the matter. I did that. I followed the facts. And they led me to the ideas articulated in that paper. Now you are asking me to ignore all of that and choose a topic that is in agreement with the faculty's opinion? In agreement with *your* opinion?" Benzion stared at Zariski a moment, their eyes focused on each other. "I think you should ask who among us really has a problem facing the truth."

"What do you mean by that?"

"I mean, everyone wants to blame someone else for the manner in which we've been treated over the past two centuries, but no one wants to look inward at how we might have contributed to that misery. Is that the scholar's job? To prepare arguments that promote the prevailing view of who treated us the worst, or do the hard work of getting at the truth?"

"You should be careful with that line of reasoning. It will get you nowhere at all among us."

"We each must be faithful to the calling upon our life, you and I. This document," Benzion paused, leaned over the desk, and tapped the paper he'd submitted for emphasis, "This document and the ideas it contains represents my calling and my topic. The history of the Jews in Spain during the time of the Inquisition, developed along the lines of reasoning that paper provides, is the core of the thesis upon which I intend to work."

Zariski sighed. "You are as stubborn as your father."

26

NETANYAHU

IN A FEW MONTHS, German weapons, ammunition, and explosives arrived in Istanbul. Zewail oversaw the unloading process and had the items stored in a warehouse that was guarded day and night.

Over the next several months, the weapons and ammunition were transported from Turkey through Syria into Palestine and arrived at Jerusalem where Husseini took charge of them. Once again, he gathered the tribal leaders and reviewed the terms of the plan.

When he was finished, Hafez al-Turabi spoke up. "How soon should we expect to see the distribution of these arms to our men?"

"They will be distributed when the German trainers arrive."

"And if they do not arrive?"

Qawuqji, Husseini's assistant spoke up. "The Germans will arrive, I assure you. But if they do not, we will proceed without them."

Abel Rawahah was seated on the far side of the room. "Our men would benefit from having the equipment now," he said, "in order to familiarize themselves with its operation."

"I have considered the matter," Husseini replied, "and think we should wait."

"Where are these weapons being kept?" Rifa'a Zaghlul asked.

"In a safe place."

"Shouldn't we be allowed to inspect them?"

Husseini glared at him. "You think I am not telling you the truth?"

"I think our people will have questions," Zaghlul replied, "and it would be better for us if we had firsthand answers. From our own knowledge, rather than asking them to rely on the word of someone else whom they have never met."

Husseini stood. "I have given you your firsthand answer. The weapons and ammunition have arrived. They will be distributed when the German trainers arrive."

With that, Husseini turned toward the door and Qawuqji followed him. When they were a safe distance down the hall, he looked over at Husseini. "That's not what we told them before."

"I know," Husseini agreed.

"We were supposed to give them the weapons and a small amount of the ammunition now."

"I decided not to do that."

"Why?"

Husseini came to a halt and turned toward Qawuqji. "It occurred to me that every time we've given them weapons, a noticeable number are traded into public hands."

"Some of their men need the weapons for that very purpose," Qawuqji argued. "To trade for money with which they can buy food."

"And do you not think the British soldiers will notice?"

"What do we care if they notice? We serve *our* people, not the British."

"These weapons are not antiques. They are some of the most recent. Fully automatic. When the British see them, they will know where they came from and they will know that we have established a relationship with another foreign country. One that is fast becoming an enemy of the United Kingdom."

"But we cannot fight them without these men. We should go back in there and—"

"No," Husseini snapped. "Not this time. This time, the weapons and *all* the ammunition will be used for killing the Jews. And when we are finished with them, we will deal with the British."

✦ ✦ ✦

Not long after that, the German instructors arrived in Jerusalem to train local Arab leaders in tactics designed to introduce them to modern warfare practices. Husseini received the German instructors with open arms, but he eschewed the traditional welcoming banquet often given in honor of guests and instead quietly slipped the Germans into Jerusalem, dressing them in traditional Muslim attire, and whisked them to a remote camp south of Beersheba.

The next day the instructors went to work expanding the effectiveness of traditional Arab hit-and-run tactics. The first change they proposed was an increase in the number of men in the attack groups.

"Using a larger force," they explained, "will multiply the effectiveness of each raid, changing your lightning attacks from merely hit-and-miss harassment of the enemy to obliteration of him."

After training local Arab leaders, each of the Germans was assigned to a specific Arab gang to observe and assist in the adoption of the new practices. When they'd worked together for several months, Husseini called for a general strike in Jerusalem and Tel Aviv. In response to that call, Arabs stopped working and took to the streets.

With the disruption as a cover, German instructors disguised as Arabs led the units with which they'd been training on sporadic raids against Jewish targets—Jewish workers traveling from Jerusalem to Tel Aviv at night, Jewish newspapers and businesses in Jerusalem, Tel Aviv, and Haifa, and synagogues both large and small.

At first, the British looked the other way, but as the violence continued and even expanded they were forced to address the situation. As was their usual practice, they offered the Arabs concessions in the form of sanctions against the Jews—limits on the times when Jews could access the wall at Temple Mount, tightening of the number of Jews allowed to immigrate each year, and the like—and the use of force against Jewish groups that fought back when Arabs raided their homes.

In spite of the uneven British response, most in the Jewish Agency were glad to see the trouble brought to an end. Benzion, however, thought quite the opposite and he said so at the Agency's public meeting not long after the attacks stopped. "This is the worst possible outcome," he suggested.

David Ben-Gurion, head of the Jewish Agency and chairman of the meeting, responded with an indulgent smile. This wasn't the first time he'd encountered Benzion. "How is that so?"

"The British approach has empowered Arabs to do even worse to us than before."

"But how?" asked Golda Meir, a member of the Jewish Agency executive committee. "How does the British response send that kind of message?"

"The Arabs started this trouble," Benzion explained. "They were the aggressors. And what did the British do? They rewarded them with favorable concessions, then used force against us, pushing us bodily from the street when we demonstrate, beating our people, shooting some, and arresting those who dared to defend themselves against Arab attacks. We get beaten and arrested, while the Arabs get most of what they demanded with a little arm twisting over the rest." He looked over at Golda. "That is how they conveyed their message. A rod to the Jews, a pat on the back for the Arabs."

"What does it matter?" someone asked. "Peace has been restored. Now we can get on with our work."

"It's not so much what they did," Benzion grumbled. "Like I said, it's more about what the British *didn't* do. The British response came in the form of a reprimand for the Arabs and a beating for the Jews. The Arabs started the conflict and are aware that the British know it as well. The British response tells the Arabs that the British are on their side and it empowers the Arabs to engage in even greater violence against us."

Ben-Gurion chuckled. "This is the same kind of thinking your father brought to the issues we faced when he was alive."

"And he was usually right," Benzion argued.

"He was much of the time," Ben-Gurion conceded. "And he did a lot to help by raising money for the Fund. But he wasn't the easiest person to get along with either."

Golda spoke up. "I think we ought to let the matter drop for now."

"Okay," Ben-Gurion cut off further discussion. "Anything else we need to address tonight?" He glanced around the room and when no one responded said, "Great. We're adjourned."

✦ ✦ ✦

Over the next three years, Arab uprisings shifted from populated areas around Jerusalem and along the coast, to rural areas farther inland. Using tactics learned from their German instructors, the attacks grew increasingly violent, forcing the British at last to respond with force against the Arab gangs. Arabs, who previously understood the British, sided with them against the Jews, felt betrayed and, for the first time, responded with attacks on British military units.

British authorities and members of the Jewish Agency seemed surprised, but not Benzion. "This is what I predicted would happen," he reminded any who would listen. "This is how the Arabs are. It's their nature. If the British look the other way when the Arabs attack our villages, or if the British mete out light punishment to Arabs while punishing us with a heavy hand, the Arabs always will take it as authorization from the British to do violence against our people. And that's precisely what's happened with these increased attacks."

Although Arab violence in rural areas of Palestine forced the British to respond, their troops already were spread thin keeping peace in the more populated areas. As a result, they had no option but to cooperate with Jewish paramilitary organizations. That, in turn, necessitated a more cooperative relationship with the Jewish Agency which organized and subsidized the paramilitary groups defending Jewish settlements. Working together, they devised a strategy of using the Jewish units as regional response teams. This proved especially successful in rural areas of the Galilee and the Negev.

Freed from British harassment by the newly cooperative arrangement, Jewish intelligence officers identified Husseini as the person controlling most of the local Arab groups. They passed that information to the British, including photographs and written reports.

Two days later, British troops under the command of Major Nevil

Simpson tracked Husseini to his residence in Jerusalem. With the house surrounded by an overwhelming military force, Simpson and a team of twenty men barged through the front entrance and made their way upstairs to Husseini's bedroom where they found him preparing for his afternoon bath.

"I don't think you'll have time for a bath today," Simpson shouted as he and his men entered the room.

Simpson's voice startled Husseini and he turned quickly toward the door. At first his eyes were wide with surprise but when he saw it was Simpson he relaxed. "I thought we had an understanding that you wouldn't do this again."

"That was then," Simpson reminded.

"Have you forgotten that things didn't go so well for you last time? Which, by the way, was the reason you agreed it would be the *last time*?"

"That was before I had this." Simpson held out his hand and one of the men standing with him gave him a folder.

"Papers," Husseini scoffed. "You Infidels are all the same. You put your trust in papers."

"And you?"

"Relationships, major. Relationships. When I send a message to London about this intrusion, you'll have plenty of time to think about that. You'll be posted to some forgotten billet in one of your long-lost colonies."

A table stood nearby and Simpson stepped toward it. "When London sees this," he lifted a folder, removed a photograph and pointed it toward Husseini, "you'll be the one in trouble." With a flick of his wrist he dropped it onto the tabletop. The picture showed Husseini with three German officers, all of whom sported Nazi armbands.

Husseini glanced in that direction. "That means nothing," he replied dismissively.

Simpson then removed a second photograph and laid it on the table. This one showed stacks of wooden shipping crates bearing German labels. One of the crates was open showing automatic weapons and ammunition inside.

"And what does this have to do with me?" Husseini asked.

Simpson produced yet a third photograph. This one showed Husseini standing to one side, watching while a dozen Arab men unloaded the crates from a truck. "We became suspicious after we captured some of these weapons during recent battles."

"I see," Husseini scowled. "And the Jews gave you these photographs?"

"You have only two options. Either leave Palestine or go to prison."

"Nonsense." Husseini turned toward the tub. "It would take weeks to conclude my business here and prepare to leave. I will give you my answer day after tomorrow."

Simpson nodded to his men and four of them rushed Husseini. They lifted him from the tub by the arms and legs and started toward the door. Simpson took a robe from the bed and tossed it in Husseini's direction. "You'll need this. Your ship sails in an hour."

NETANYAHU

WITH HUSSEINI IN EXILE and unavailable to provide day-to-day leadership for Arabs in Palestine, Zewail was directed to fill his role. To do that, Zewail divided his time between Jerusalem—directing what had now become a full-scale Arab uprising—and Berlin, where he maintained a strong relationship with Hitler and members of the Nazi Party, which was by then the de facto government-in-waiting. This proved to be a very successful arrangement that kept arms and armaments flowing regularly from German munitions factories to Arabs fighting in Palestine. It also put Zewail in a position to build new relationships that offered potential for even greater accomplishments in the future. Much of that aspect of his work centered upon parties. Germans, he learned, loved to celebrate—particularly when the party involved copious amounts of liquor and an array of lovely women.

While on one of his regular visits to Berlin, Zewail attended just such a party where, as the evening grew late and after innumerable rounds of Jägermeister, he overheard Hans Forester, one of Adolf Hitler's closest aides, talking about a special weapon. Zewail was acquainted with Forester and lingered nearby hoping to learn more. "A special weapon?" he asked finally.

"Zewail." Forester feigned surprise, "I didn't realize you were here. How are things in the Middle East?'

"Things there are rather warm," Zewail quipped. "What's this about a special weapon?"

"I assure you, it was nothing. Just the dreams of underfunded physicists," Forester chuckled.

"You can imagine how incomprehensible that might be to us normal folk," one of the others joked.

Zewail looked over at Forester. "To be *nothing* you were pretty excited about it when you were talking to them just now," he needled. "I doubt it could have gone from something to nothing that quickly."

Forester glanced at the group with a knowing look and a roll of his eyes. "I'll be back in a moment," then he guided Zewail toward the door and into the hall. "Don't press me like that in public ever again," Forester ordered when they were out of the room.

"Do you want me to leave now?"

"No. But I would prefer it if we discussed these things in private."

"So it's true. You *do* have a special weapon in the works."

"It's in development, as are many other weapons. That's all I know. It's just a research project to keep the academics happy."

"But this one is different from all the others."

Forester looked away. "Yes," he sighed. "This one is different."

"How so?"

"If we succeed in developing this one, we could wipe out entire cities with just one bomb."

Zewail frowned. "An entire city?"

"London, gone in an instant. Loss of life and property totally on the Brits, where it belongs, by the way. Not a single loss of German life from the attack."

"Except for some poor German soul who happened to be in London that day."

"Yes," Forester admitted. "There is that."

"And Germany has people working on such a project right now?"

"As I said, we have *researchers* working on it."

Zewail suppressed a grin. "And they don't count as people."

The remark caught Forester off-guard. "How much have you had to drink tonight?"

"A lot less than the others in that room," Zewail pointed through the doorway.

Forester glanced in that direction and chuckled. "They have consumed a lot tonight. More so than usual, I think."

Zewail turned back to the topic at hand. "So where are these researchers working?"

"Heidelberg University has part of the project. Georg-August University in Gottingen has some of it. It's divided among a dozen different places. Keeping the most people happy with the least overall cost." Forester looked over at Zewail. "Why are you asking all these questions?"

"I have heard rumors of such a weapon and wondered if it were possible."

"It is very much possible," Forester assured. "In theory, it is absolutely possible."

"If we had such a weapon at our disposal," Zewail mused, "we could end our troubles with the Jews in a single day."

"Yes. Well, a weapon like that could end a lot of things." Forester gave Zewail a pat on the shoulder. "I must get back to the party before I'm missed."

"Who is in charge of the program?"

Forester looked away once more. "I don't know."

"Nonsense," Zewail insisted. "Someone is always in charge."

"Talk to Werner Riehl," Forester sighed. "He's head of the physics department at Heidelberg University. But don't mention my name."

✦ ✦ ✦

As Zewail had expanded his working relationships beyond the Black Sea to Europe, Asia, and beyond, he'd heard reports about Germany re-arming for war and of how they'd begun that effort from the day they signed the treaty ending the Great War. Most of the armament stories involved standard military measures, though supposedly on a scale much larger than anyone expected. Soldiers filling units that had gone idle since the war before the last Great War, the further adoption and adaptation of motorized vehicles for military use, and the advent of air power beyond anything previously conceived.

Yet, behind Germany's moves toward acquisition of conventional arms and armaments lay other rumors—deeper, darker rumors—of a capability that *was* beyond the reach of Germany's neighbors—rumors of just such a weapon as Zewail overheard Hans Forester discussing that night at the party. Only now he had a name to go with it—Werner Riehl.

The next morning, Zewail walked up the street from his hotel to the Berlin State Library where he spent the remainder of the day researching Riehl's background. There were few newspaper stories about him, but he was a prolific writer and had authored many scholarly essays on the topic of nuclear structure and the untapped energy that lay in that unseen world. The things Zewail read—of exponentially explosive energy from even a single atom—revealed details about Riehl's academic career and convinced Zewail that this was the kind of thing—properly weaponized—that could be used to once again unify Muslims into a single people. *If we could find a way to escape the clutches of dogmatic religious purity,* he thought, *a weapon made this way could free us from all outside influence—Jewish and Gentile alike.*

Late that afternoon, Zewail left the library and walked back toward the hotel. As he made his way in that direction he considered what he should do next. The logical thing would be to telephone Riehl and arrange to meet him for lunch, but they had not been introduced and a call like that could be easily refused. *I should just show up,* Zewail concluded, *and if he turns me away I will have only lost a train ride and a day.*

Early the next morning, Zewail took a taxi to the station and caught the next train to Heidelberg. He arrived there by mid-morning and made his way to the university. He found Riehl in his office and, in spite of Forester's insistence that he not be mentioned by name, Zewail did not hesitate to mention him as a shared acquaintance.

"How do you know Hans?" Riehl asked.

"I represent important clients in the East. Hans and I have been working to put my clients' resources to work for Germany's benefit."

"Oil."

"Yes. But from what I've been reading, you might be working with something that could make oil obsolete."

"And how would your clients feel about that?"

"They would not object in the least, as long as their objectives are met."

"And how does this concern me?"

"You are in charge of a research program that has the government's ear. But your government has other interests that will threaten to subsume your project."

"That's already happening."

"Oh? I thought yours was still first on their list."

"It was until now."

"And now?"

"Planning for next year and beyond has shifted toward conventional matters. Our program still has a lot of fundamental questions to answer. At the rate we're going, payoff from our project wouldn't come for another ten years. The only way to shorten that time is to spend more money. Many in our government think that would be an issue for the next generation and are not interested in approving greater expenditures at the expense of conventional arms."

"And there you have it," Zewail smiled. "Our interests intersect before our very eyes."

"Your clients would want access to our research, I assume."

"Yes," Zewail acknowledged. "And eventually, technicians to assist them."

"The money wouldn't be difficult to protect, but access to the research would require approval at the highest level."

"I think I can solve that."

"That would be most appreciated." Riehl glanced at his watch, then hastily added, "I have a class in ten minutes. Shall we meet for lunch to discuss this further?"

"Certainly."

"Good. I'll meet you back here around noon. We'll walk from here. It's not far."

✦ ✦ ✦

As planned, Zewail met Riehl and they walked to a café located a few blocks from the University campus. While they ate, they discussed special weapons theory—the term among German physicists for the underlying principles of weaponized fission reactions. The conversation was academic in nature—not much more than one would hear in a college lecture—but Riehl seemed to enjoy talking about it, so Zewail let him talk.

"All of that is beside the point now. The project has been purposely underfunded." He sighed. "And that is that."

Ahh, Zewail suppressed a smile. This was what he'd been listening for—a point of entry. It is a problem in need of a solution. "Underfunded?"

"The government's way of telling us the program is no longer useful to them."

Zewail had a puzzled look. "What about it would not be useful?"

"The ultimate results of the program would be *very* useful to them. But they don't think it will produce anything for use in the field before they achieve their military objectives and the continent stabilizes under their control."

"Why not simply end it? Why not just shut down the program?"

"Ahh, the classic bureaucratic conundrum. No one wants to fund the program, but no one wants to be the one who ended it, only to later realize they let the greatest scientific achievement of the century slip away."

Zewail arched an eyebrow. "And this really would be an historic scientific achievement?"

"Beyond anything you could imagine. It's true, the hope of ultimate success lies some distance into the future. The scientific theory behind it is complicated, but success, when it comes, will give the holder of the technology the ability to produce a weapon of leverage that far outstrips anything attainable through the use of conventional means."

"Leverage," Zewail repeated. "You mean, the threat of great destruction?"

"I mean," Riehl answered ominously, "the threat of annihilation. Actually using it would unleash a horror the likes of which the human race has never witnessed."

"And working on a project like that doesn't trouble you?"

"From my perspective, and from that of my colleagues, we are scientists. As such, we are obligated to explore the areas of our expertise and to continue with the research as long as we are able. And as long as that work does not meet with the objections of our superiors." Riehl reached for his water glass and took a sip. "So, how would you see the interests of your clients progressing from here?"

"With your permission, I would like to present our discussion and your situation to them to see if they will agree to some specific form of...participation."

Riehl's eyes brightened with interest. "Money?"

"Yes. Then if their terms seem helpful to you, I will take this to the next level."

Riehl looked puzzled. "The next level?"

"Of government approval."

"Your government?"

"No." Zewail shook his head. "My clients require no government approval. I mean, approval on your end. Once you and I come to an agreement, I'll take it up through the ranks of your government and keep you out of the bureaucratic process as much as possible."

"Excellent," Riehl smiled. "That is a good idea."

✦ ✦ ✦

A few months later, after the expected election of Adolf Hitler as chancellor, the Nazi Party took control of the German government. From its position atop the governing apparatus, the party slowly tightened its grip on German society and paved the way for Hitler to rule with absolute authority.

In Istanbul, the caliphs viewed Hitler's meteoric rise as a sign that he was a leader of divinely ordained destiny. They were confident that their support would produce the kind of cooperative relationship they had sought for a long time with rulers in the West. To that end, they did as Zewail suggested and began moving cash into Riehl's special weapon's program—some of it money that had been given to Arab leaders by the British government as part of the British effort to bring peace to Palestine.

28

NETANYAHU

IN GERMANY, the old order—royal families with ancestral ties to the ancient European city-states of old—noted Hitler's rise to power only as an example of proletarian politics in its crassest form—a common laborer taking advantage of his fellow laborers by manipulating an electoral system that would surely right itself in short order. Rather than form a forceful, effective political opposition, they stood by and watched with amusement expecting to see Hitler and his cronies, drunk on the wine of elected office, stumble through the first year, stagger partway into the second, and collapse before summer. Surely, they mused, power would naturally restore everyone to their rightful places—Hitler to his laborer's job and the House of Hapsburg to its position as the only proper governing class of anyone, free or servile.

Hitler, however, seemed hardly to notice the royals and the few times he *did* notice them gave them little more than a dismissive wave with the back of his hand. "Let then play their silly parlor games," he said dryly. "By the time they awaken from their delusions of grandeur, only the delusions will remain and the grandeur will be ours."

Moving incrementally at first, the Nazi Party slowly but systematically marginalized moderate members of the German civil service, replacing them with administrative clerks whose allegiance was only to Hitler. At the same time, they enacted changes in the law that steadily reduced the royal family's government subsidies and privileges—effectively consigning them to political irrelevancy—even as it tightened its grip on the everyday lives of ordinary German citizens. Identity cards, ominously noting the holder's race to the third generation, were provided for every person claiming German citizenship. Travel—domestic and international—required prior approval. Physicians were forced to make their records available to government auditors. Church membership rolls were carefully monitored as were Sunday sermons and gossip among attendees. No detail escaped the scrutiny of government agents.

But in the darker, more sinister corners of the Nazi Party, special units known as Dirlewanger Brigades—so named in honor of their commander, Oskar Dirlewanger, one of the most brutal and sadistic leaders in the Nazi movement—were on the move, rounding up the country's elderly, infirm, and insane. Ruthless and unmerciful in fulfilling their mission, troops of the Dirlewanger Brigades dispatched their duties with speed, efficiency, and discretion, emptying the nation's state-operated institutions and summarily executing them, all with little or no public objection.

Emboldened by their success and energized by the lack of public reaction, the Brigades stepped out of the shadows the following year and roamed the streets and highways, openly searching for any who appeared to meet their selection criteria, making sport of the entire grisly affair, often leaving the dead bodies on the street where they fell.

With the initial cleansing completed, the Nazis turned their attention to others thought to taint the purity of Germany's supposed Aryan race—groups that included Africans, gays, and Gypsies, to name a few. And when those had been dispatched, it wasn't long before Hitler's attention turned the Brigades to Europe's largest ethnic population—the Jews.

As with their approach to the elderly and infirm, the Nazis avoided immediate, wholesale implementation of their policies, opting instead to apply them incrementally. At first, Jews were prohibited from filling certain professional occupations, then they were prohibited from *all* professional occupations. They were excluded from studying in the universities and trade schools, then prohibited from filling faculty positions or working in the skilled trades. At the same time, political rhetoric singled out the Jewish race as the source of Germany's economic woes. Leader after leader denounced the Jews as leeches on the Germany economy, sapping wealth and soaking up jobs that would otherwise be filled by "more deserving" and "better qualified" Germans. As one might expect, public sentiment rose against the Jews and in response they were forced to abandon their homes and move into state-administered ghettos, ostensibly for their "safety."

When the ghettos were filled, the Brigades began transporting Jews by rail to a place designated only as "the East," a vague but supposedly idyllic location where achievement would be limited only by one's ability. Where green meadows and rolling hills awaited them, with pleasant skies to greet them in the morning and peaceful sunsets to see them off to bed at night.

It wasn't long before news of what "the East" really meant drifted back to those still in Germany. There were no rolling hills, green meadows, or blue skies. No boundless or limitless potential. Only death camps operating under a gray cloud of human smoke and ash, where the lives of their loved ones were ended in death factories that operated with the speed and efficiency of a modern industrial process. And all of it for one single purpose—the total and complete extermination of the Jews.

As news of the true nature of Nazi policy drifted back to the West, it also spread to other portions of the globe, eventually reaching the villages and towns of Palestine. Benzion learned of it when he attended a dinner party at the home of Martin and Tova Nussbaum, a couple who'd only recently arrived in Tel Aviv from Bern, Switzerland. In the course of conversation that evening, Martin mentioned the extent to which conditions among Jews and other minorities had deteriorated in Europe. "Even Switzerland is not immune from it," he added.

Benzion was surprised, but not altogether caught off-guard. "The Swiss government supports this kind of thing?"

"The Swiss government has no official policy of persecuting Jews,"

Martin explained. "But they have not hesitated to confiscate Jewish property when the Nazis demand it."

The bankers, Benzion thought. That part made perfect sense. "Always the money first," he said. "And everything else after that."

"It's not quite as physically devastating as the German purges," Tova added. "But just as troubling."

"Ethnic cleansing," someone commented.

"Ethnic cleansing," Benzion repeated with a nod. "Makes it sound so...antiseptic when we give it a title like that."

"That's what they are doing," Martin said. "Cleansing Germany and the occupied territories of Jews and others they feel taint their Germanic bloodlines."

"But it's not ethnic cleansing," Benzion insisted, "They are murdering our kinsmen. That is what they are doing. Assigning it a clinical label like cleansing removes it one step away from us."

"Though it does make it easier for us all to handle," someone commented. "Especially when you consider how little direct influence we have over their policies."

"But that is all they need," Benzion explained. "One step short of personal and all you have is the impersonal. The other. An atrocity becomes a thing we can talk about with the detachment of a physician or scientist."

Tova frowned. "You think they do that on purpose? Could they really be that subtle?"

"I think they do that by design. And when we adopt impersonal labels to describe their conduct, we join them in their madness."

"We join them? How so?"

"If we talk about what's happening in a personal sense—murder, slaughter, dismemberment—we confront the moral reprehension implicit in their conduct," Benzion clarified. "It meets us head-on in all its revoltingly disgusting horror. And we are faced with the unavoidable realization that we must act—even if it seems our actions will produce little visible effect. But if we address their conduct with the titles and labels of a social scientist—genocide, ethnic cleansing, purges—we give ourselves the liberty and license of discussing it as an academic exercise. Something to be pondered, considered, weighed, evaluated. But never with the corresponding personal demand that we act against it."

"How easily they divorce all of that from the faces of their victims."

"And reduce the whole thing to something resembling the amorality of a business transaction."

"They tell our people that they are being transported to the East," Martin offered. "As if it's an honor."

"Do any of them actually reach the East?" someone asked, as if the hollowness of the lie was somehow a problem in and of itself.

"The first trains reached Krakow," Tova said.

"And now?"

"The most recent ones," Martin enlightened, "didn't get past the Polish border before the killing started."

"In the train cars?"

"These aren't exactly passenger coaches," Tova explained.

"Then what are they?"

Martin stared down at the floor. "Cattle cars," he uttered softly.

The room fell silent a moment as the thought of it sank in. Humans shuttled and shunted to the slaughter like farm animals. Humans reduced to nothing but human meat. Surely not.

"And the bodies?" another asked.

"They were removed from the rail cars," Martin continued. "Loaded onto trucks and hauled away."

"Germans touched the dead bodies?"

"Don't be ridiculous. They forced some of the prisoners to remove them," Tova said.

"And our people participated?'

"You can't imagine the coercive stress something like that can exert."

"They did it to survive, I'm sure."

"But they didn't survive," Martin added thoughtfully.

"What happened to them?"

"Once the trucks were unloaded at the burial pits, the guards shot the laborers."

"Only way to insure secrecy."

"Where were they buried?"

"Auschwitz," Tova replied.

"The ones that were buried," Martin added.

"Some weren't buried?"

"Many were left lying right where they fell."

"You think there are other locations where this happens?" someone asked. "Besides Auschwitz?"

"I'm certain there are many."

"This is a widespread operation."

"The Jewish population in Europe before the war was in excess of six million," Benzion noted. "How many do you think they've killed?"

"Millions."

Most were surprised. "Millions?"

"And they are simply buried in mass graves?"

Martin bowed his head. "Some are buried. Some are simply left where they were killed."

"But many are cremated," Tova said. "Not all by any means, but many are. They have ovens at Auschwitz. They operate night and day."

"Crematoria," Benzion noted. "Burning factories."

Martin nodded. "The operation there is a veritable assembly line."

"We have reports," Tova explained, "of rooms with tables where jewelers sort the diamonds confiscated from the prisoners. And others that sort and weigh the silver."

"Silver?"

"From dental fillings."

"They extract the fillings?"

"They extract the teeth. Jewelers remove the fillings later."

"Do they use something to lessen the pain? They don't just yank out the teeth, do they?"

Martin seemed dismayed and when Tova didn't step in to explain

Benzion added quietly, "These are teeth taken from the bodies of the deceased. After they are dead, I'm sure." He glanced at Tova as if to make certain he was correct.

"Crews move among the bodies and remove the teeth that have fillings," she acknowledged.

A terrified look swept over the faces of those in the room.

Benzion looked puzzled. "I'm curious. How do you know all of this about what goes on there?"

"We have connections on the inside," Martin offered. "They tell us some of it."

Tova excused herself from the room and returned with a letter. "Read this," she handed the letter to Benzion. "I think it will give you an idea of what they are doing." Benzion scanned the letter while Tova continued. "The person who wrote that was my cousin."

Benzion glanced over at her. "Was?"

"He died not long after that letter was written."

"How did the letter get out of the camp?"

"A Catholic priest visits the camp on a regular basis. My cousin gave it to him and asked him to send it to us."

Benzion started over again, reading the letter more carefully this time. As he did, a worried look clouded his face. "Are you okay?" Tova asked.

"Yes." Benzion quickly corrected himself. "No. I'm not okay. None of us is okay. And faced with this kind of official policy from the German government, none of us should ever feel okay again. I see violence. Violence, persecution, obliteration. Against Jews in every region of Europe...and beyond." He handed the letter back to Tova. "I see the future here," he added solemnly.

"Surely not a future like that, though," someone said.

"A future exactly like this at the hands of the Arabs, perhaps the Germans. Maybe even the British."

"The British?"

"Unless we find a way to prevail," Benzion continued, "even the British could turn against us. They have already shown that they cannot be relied upon to take our best interests to heart. We must do that for ourselves."

✦ ✦ ✦

As he walked home from the dinner that evening, Benzion thought about the news he'd heard from Martin and Tova and their report of how similar conditions were spreading to all European countries, not just Germany. He'd seen this before in the way British policy toward the Jews of Palestine empowered and emboldened the Arabs to engage in still greater violence. And how that violence spread like a disease beyond Palestine to the surrounding countries.

"I am sure," he mumbled to himself, "that all of this—evil here in Palestine delivered at the hands of the Arabs and evil in Europe delivered at the hands of the Nazis—is merely a form of the same thing. To be sure, Jews in Germany are at the leading edge of the surge, facing all but certain annihilation, but the evil is one and the same in both places."

Unlike many who attended that dinner, Benzion left feeling compelled to do something. To act. To no longer stand by and merely think but to put those thoughts to work. And as he thought about the issues an image of Ze'ev Jabotinsky appeared. He remembered how they'd worked together to confront Herzl, and almost every other delegation that attended the Sixth Zionist Congress, over the plan to settle for the establishment of a Jewish colony in Uganda rather than pressing forward with resettlement in their historic homeland of Palestine.

Those were heady times—two brash teenagers banding together against so many learned minds and men of reputation. And they'd done it. They'd stood their ground, rolled back the vote, and fought the issue all the way to the end. And here they were in Palestine as a result. Well... at least *he* was in Palestine. Jabotinsky, after that unfortunate business with the British mandatory authorities was in...London.

A smile spread over Benzion's face at the thought of that. They wouldn't allow Jabotinsky to live in Palestine but had no objection to his residing in London. "If only I could talk to him now," he whispered. "We could figure out what to—"

Suddenly, a knowing look came over his face. That was the answer. They really *could* talk. Face to face. London wasn't that far away. Only a couple of short flights with maybe a layover or two. But he could go there and meet with Jabotinsky, talk the matter through, formulate a plan. In spite of the apparent hopelessness of the situation and the suggestion that nothing they might do could ever actually make a difference, they could find a way to make it work, just like they did in the past.

✦ ✦ ✦

The following day Benzion sent Jabotinsky a telegram asking to meet with him. A few weeks later, after a flurry of correspondence and last-minute scrounging for money to cover the expense, Benzion departed Tel Aviv for Paris where he laid over one night before continuing on to London. He arrived at mid-morning the following day to find Jabotinsky waiting for him at the airport.

Catching up with each other personally took little effort and after a brief stop at Jabotinsky's apartment in the Spitalfields neighborhood of London's East End, they walked down the street to a café for lunch.

"Jews in Europe are in trouble," Benzion began when they finally reached the topic of his visit.

"Serious trouble," Jabotinsky acknowledged.

"We need to do something about it."

"You have some ideas of what we could do?"

"Well," Benzion sighed, "we could raise money, find a way to get our people out, document their personal experiences with newspaper articles to spread the latest news...I don't know." He glanced away with a look of frustration. "It seems like such an enormously unsolvable problem."

"That's what the Nazis want us to think." Jabotinsky added.

"I think the problem extends beyond just the Nazis."

"Most assuredly," Jabotinsky nodded. "We face opposition from typical, ordinary Europeans. Good Frenchmen and Germans who might otherwise do the right thing are being swept into an anti-Semitic storm of the most virulent kind."

Benzion gestured to the crowd in the café. "And I'm sure you've seen it right here in London."

Jabotinsky nodded. "Even here, we are not free to do all that we might."

Benzion looked over at him. "Then perhaps we should find another place from which to work."

"Any suggestions?"

"I think you should consider relocating your entire operation to the United States. You'd be working right there in the closest proximity to your financial support. And while the United States has its own anti-Semitic problems, no one would stop you from doing your work."

Jabotinsky reached for his water glass, took a drink, and swallowed. "Actually, I've thought of this for some time, to be honest. Would you be interested in joining me there?"

Benzion glanced down at his plate. "That would be fun, wouldn't it?" Their eyes met. "Like old times."

"I'm serious," Jabotinsky insisted. Come to New York. Join me there as my secretary. My assistant." When Benzion did not immediately reply, Jabotinsky repeated himself. "I'm serious, Benzion."

"I know."

"Then what's the problem? You aren't married. You have no family obligations to tie you to Palestine. Come to New York. Help me complete the work. Our work. The work of our fathers."

"It's not quite that simple."

"Oh?"

"I have my research—"

"The history of Jews in Spain?"

"It's a topic I'm really interested in pursuing."

"I know, but that is a matter of history. This right here —Jews in Europe and Palestine—is a matter of the future. We're talking about the lives of generations," Jabotinsky insisted. "And it's not an idea in the abstract. This is a matter of real life and death. Perhaps the life and death of our entire race."

"I know," Benzion insisted.

"Will you at least consider it?"

"Certainly. I certainly will."

✦ ✦ ✦

Though enticing—and perhaps for that very reason—Jabotinsky's offer brought Benzion once again face-to-face with the familiar dilemma between academia and activism and the admonition of his father to be faithful to the call upon his life. For Nathan, that calling had been a matter of religion—a calling to the rabbinical life in service to others through the synagogue—albeit one he held with an antagonistic inclination away from work with *others* toward scholarly research and the solitude of a writer's life.

For Benzion the calling was something less spiritual—more akin to a personal preference. Activism on behalf of Jews in Europe and Palestine was as antagonistic to that personal interest as it had been for his father. He would much rather spend his time in a library or in his study immersed in academic research. But he saw that Jews in Europe faced a horrible end and there seemed to be so few interested enough to do something about it.

After an extended stay with Jabotinsky in London and many long hours spent discussing the future of Palestine, their own futures, and the offer which Jabotinsky continued to insist he accept, Benzion returned to Palestine determined to pursue an academic degree first, before turning to Jabotinsky's offer.

Though work on his dissertation consumed most of his time, Benzion did not completely ignore the matters he and Jabotinsky had discussed, or the horrific news he'd learned from Martin and Tova Nussbaum regarding the circumstances Jews currently faced in Nazi Germany. While he worked on several academically oriented articles directed toward his dissertation, he also created a series of easily accessible articles that provided personal accounts of German Jews who were murdered in the death camps. Many of those articles appeared in regional Jewish newspapers and in magazines marketed to readers in select countries in the West, most notably the United States.

Benzion's continued presence and study at the University did not go unnoticed, particularly by Haim Zariski who'd been the one to confront him with the faculty's displeasure over the direction of his study and what they saw as his disruptive personality. However, the popularity of Benzion's articles regarding the condition of Jews in Europe, together with the grades he'd achieved for coursework, made it difficult for the faculty to take corrective action against him. They were not, however, prevented from showing their opinion in other ways and over the following months Benzion found himself increasingly isolated from them.

Rather than hindering his work, Benzion found the isolation liberating. Freed of the need for faculty approval, which he now knew he would never attain, he found himself drawn further and further from their intellectual world as well. Theirs was the world of labor-oriented liberalism and its practical view of a Jewish future in Palestine—build the nation others let us build now and expand incrementally over time—a vision that stood in stark contrast to the Revisionist Zionist view which Benzion and Jabotinsky embraced.

As his personal and academic isolation increased, Benzion found himself drawn deeper and deeper into the older Netanyahu identity he earlier adopted, seeing it now as a model through which to fashion the remainder of his life. A man called by Yahweh to a special work.

All day he devoted himself to research and writing but at night, when the lingering sense of isolation melded into loneliness, he retreated to his room, took the Netanyahu ring from its box, and lay upon his bed, pondering the significance of it for himself, for the political events forming around him, and the dark future that seemed about to burst open before them all.

Benzion's accounts of Jewish persecution at the hands of Nazis were widely read and though the details were revolting, the articles were readily received by readers far and wide. The scholarly articles, however, addressed a much narrower audience and for a time met with nothing more personal than a pre-printed rejection letter.

One of them, however, was published by the *Journal of European History and Religion*, a journal of serious historic scholarship produced

some businesses, and improving sanitation of public places. All fro
church partners, and therefore all Compassion center activities, are
until March 31.

You may notice a lack of letters in the coming months, as children v
at the Compassion centers to write or send their letters. Please res
that our staff in Ecuador is working hard to provide support whereve
possible. While the program activities cannot happen in groups at t
churches, staff will continue to keep in touch with the children and a
health issues as they are able. The main goal during the program
suspension is to keep the children safe and protected.

**Can I ask you to join us in praying for the people of Ecuador?
Particularly, will you pray for:**

- Protection from the virus for all children registered with Cor
  Ecuador and their families.
- Health and safety for all Compassion staff, frontline church
  child development center volunteers in Ecuador.
- God's provision for people who are unable to work during tl
  of quarantine in Ecuador.

Thank you for the love and support you've shown to this beautiful c
pray that God will bless you abundantly as you continue to minister
children in poverty.

Your brother in Christ,

at the University of Paris. The text of Benzion's work was published in its entirety, along with a review that gave a scathing rebuke of the work and called into question Benzion's intellectual ability to succeed as an academician. When news of that reaction reached Hebrew University in Jerusalem, the faculty at last had the ammunition they needed to force him out.

Pressed by the reaction at the University, Benzion accepted Jabotinsky's offer to work in New York. He resigned from his work with Scopus Press in Jerusalem, gathered his papers and notes, and departed for New York where Jabotinsky put him to work raising money for the evacuation of Jews from Europe.

NETANYAHU

WHEN HE ARRIVED in New York, Benzion moved in with Jabotinsky in his one-bedroom apartment but by the end of the second week they both realized he needed his own place. A friend and supporter of Revisionist Zionism helped him locate a studio apartment in Manhattan's Lower East Side—a working class neighborhood that lay just above Canal Street between the Bowery and the East River. A decidedly Jewish neighborhood, many of the sights, sounds, and especially the aromas, were similar to those Benzion had encountered every day in Jerusalem and helped him settle in quickly.

Not long after arriving in New York, a friend suggested he might enjoy lunch at Katz' Delicatessen on Houston Street, a location not too far from his apartment and more or less on the way to Jabotinsky's office. A few days later, Benzion decided to give the suggestion a try and mentioned it to Jabotinsky.

"Come on," Jabotinsky said eagerly. "I'll go with you."

"You've been there before?"

"Yeah. A little expensive but you must have their corned beef."

Benzion opened the office door to step out to the hallway. "What's their pastrami like?"

"You can't even imagine." Jabotinsky followed Benzion out and closed the door behind them. "But don't get it if you go there with a girl."

"Why?"

"The spices set your taste buds dancing but the last time I had it I smelled like pastrami for three days."

Fifteen minutes later they were seated at a table near the far back corner of the deli. Jabotinsky faced toward the front of the building. Benzion sat across from him with his back to the room.

Benzion glanced around. "Interesting place," he observed.

"Yeah, and if you sit back here you can see anyone who comes in before they see you."

"Already people here you *don't* want to see?" Benzion quipped.

Jabotinsky grinned. "Doesn't take me long. No matter where I am."

"You seem different from before, though. When you were in Jerusalem, when we were at the Zionist congresses. You don't seem quite as tense as you were then."

"I hadn't really thought about it, but dealing with Americans is a lot easier than dealing with the British."

"And we don't have Arabs riding around on horseback trying to kill us. At least not yet."

"But, I'm plenty worried," Jabotinsky added. "And every day I get more worried than I was the day before."

"About the work here?"

"About our people in Europe, dying in the camps. We—" Jabotinsky stopped in midsentence, his eyes focused over Benzion's shoulder toward the door. "That looks like someone you know."

Benzion turned. "It is." He looked surprised. "I didn't know she was here."

Standing near the door was Celia Segal, whom Benzion hadn't seen since his father's funeral. She graduated from the University that year and moved to England to study law, eventually gaining admission at Gray's Inn, one of four Inns of Court through which barristers in England were permitted to practice before the court. He hadn't seen her since but a mutual friend who lived in Jerusalem occasionally mentioned her.

"Wonder what she's doing here?"

"Looks like she's having lunch." Jabotinsky gestured with a nod as they watched her take a seat at a table near the counter. "You should go say hello. Girl like that won't be sitting alone for long."

Benzion hesitated. "I heard she was married."

"Go find out," Jabotinsky urged.

"Yeah." Benzion rose from his seat and walked toward the front. A moment later, he slipped into a chair across the table from her. "Hello, Celia," he said quietly.

Her eyes lit up and her cheeks glowed. "Benzion," she said with surprise. "What are you doing here?"

"I'm living here now. What about you?"

"I live here, too."

"Last I heard, you were in London."

"I was."

"Someone said you were studying law."

"For a while."

Benzion could see from the look in her eyes that there was more to the story, but she seemed reluctant to talk. "So, you're a lawyer now?"

"No. But I work for a law firm. How about you? What brings you here?"

"I'm working with Ze'ev Jabotinsky."

"Really."

"Yeah. He's back there." Benzion gestured with a nod. "At a table near the corner."

Celia glanced over her shoulder, gave Jabotinsky a smile, then turned back to Benzion. "Is this a temporary assignment, or are you here permanently?"

"I don't know how long I'll be here. But it's not temporary. I'll be here a while."

"Good. We should get together."

Benzion had a playful smile. "What about dinner tonight?"

She smiled shyly. "That would be great."

✦ ✦ ✦

That evening, Benzion met Celia at Delmonico's, a steak restaurant in lower Manhattan. It was expensive, but it was also the only other restaurant he knew and he wanted the evening to be special. He liked Celia and enjoyed spending time with her.

As they ate and talked, Celia slowly opened up about her life since leaving Palestine. "I saw you at the funeral, but after that I didn't see you much and then you were gone. I got busy finishing classes." She looked away. "And busy with Noah."

"Noah Ben Tovim?"

"Yes. That summer, I went to London with him. We left right after graduation." She glanced at him. "You never liked him much, did you?"

"It wasn't that I didn't like him, I just didn't like him with you."

Celia seemed pleasantly surprised by the comment. "Why?"

"You had things you wanted to do with your life and I didn't think you would be able to do them with him."

"Yeah, well," she sighed. "You were right about that."

They ate in silence a moment, then Benzion prompted, "So, you went to London with Noah. He was in school?"

"Yes. He was in school and I read law. Supposedly, the plan was that we would stay there long enough for him to finish his degree and for me to gain admission to the bar, then we would decide about whether to return home or go somewhere else."

"But things changed."

"He had an offer to teach in California, so we came here to America. He took a position at the University of California in Berkley and I went to work at a law firm out there."

"As a lawyer?"

"No." She shook her head. "I read at Gray's Inn in London but I wasn't there long enough to enter private practice. And practicing law in California is completely different from London. So, I took a job as a secretary at a firm there in Berkley."

"He was teaching in Berkley?"

"Yes. The Berkley campus. He's still there."

"But you're here."

"Things didn't work out for us, Benzion. He wasn't mean. He didn't treat me poorly. It just wasn't what I wanted."

"So you came to New York."

"He found a way we could get divorced in Florida, so we did that, then I came here."

"Aren't your parents back in Minnesota?"

"Mother lives there. In Minneapolis. And a couple of my sisters are there. Dad died a few months ago."

"I'm sorry. I didn't know that."

"You knew they left Petah Tikva."

"Yes. I knew they came back to the US. He wasn't in good health then, was he?"

"No. Life in Palestine was hard for him. He wasn't used to that much physical labor and the climate proved to be much too different from what he'd experienced here."

"I'm sorry you lost him."

"Thanks." She paused to take a sip of water. "After he died, Mili Fehr got in touch with me. She lives here. Do you remember her?"

"Yes. But I didn't realize she was here, too."

"Actually she's been here several years."

"I knew she wasn't in Jerusalem anymore but I thought she went to Paris."

"She wanted to. And she talked about moving there all the time. But she ended up coming here instead. When she found out I was in the US and about what I was going through, she offered to let me room with her." She smiled over at him. "But enough about me. What about you?"

They talked through dinner, then spent the evening wandering the streets of Manhattan. Conversation came easy for them and when they'd caught each other up on their lives they talked about politics, Palestine, and the ideas that seemed to propel them forward into a future that was both frighteningly uncertain and filled with promise. For Benzion, it was the most wonderful evening of his life.

✦ ✦ ✦

Over the next few months, Benzion's life in New York settled into a rhythm. He spent his days working with Jabotinsky and the New Zionist Organization to promote the rescue of Jews from Europe and the establishment of a Zionist state in Palestine. His evenings, however, were spent with Celia.

It was a challenging life with much to be done simply in the one area of defining New Zionism's vision for a Jewish state, an area that had gone lacking in detail. Added to that was the organization's underlying work of gathering and distributing the latest news about atrocities in Europe, lobbying influential Americans to shape policy in favor of admitting as many Jewish refugees as possible to the United States, and raising money to pay for it all. But with all that, Benzion made time for Celia every night, even if it was only take-out dinner from a restaurant up the street eaten together at his office desk, or a phone call from some distant city where he'd gone for a fundraiser.

But just as Benzion was getting a handle on his relationship with Celia, and on New Zionism's efforts in America, Jabotinsky suffered a heart attack and died. In an instant, Benzion went from protégé to interim director of the entire organization. And by the end of that first year he took the directorship as a permanent position.

In the days that followed Jabotinsky's death and his own rise to the top of the organization, a noticeable number of friends tried to convince Benzion that it was time to disband the organization. Aaron Hartman, head of the International Garment Workers Union and one of Jabotinsky's primary financial supporters, was particularly forceful on the matter.

"This is the perfect opportunity to close the organization," Hartman argued.

Benzion was astounded. "What are you talking about?" A frown wrinkled his forehead. "We can't close the organization."

"Yes," Hartman replied. "We can. And if we do it now, we can bow out gracefully. Jabotinsky had his say. We all helped him take a run at it, but Ben-Gurion and the others hold the dominant view and if we persist in forming an opposition we'll look like nothing more than disgruntled losers."

"I'm sorry, Aaron," Benzion said with the hint of a caustic tone in his voice. "I didn't realize we were in a contest."

"Yes, you did. That's why you've been unable to shake free of this struggle about a Zionist future in Palestine. You're as competitive as any of them and you more than anyone else have realized we have no future at all in Europe. Only death and destruction await us there." Hartman looked over at him. "Now tell me I'm wrong."

"But why close the organization?"

"This dream—of a Jewish state controlling all the land once held by the Davidic Kingdom—is a myth. It can't happen. It won't happen. The British have already carved out a huge part of it for the Hashemite kingdom in Transjordan. Do you think they're going to walk off and leave it to us now?"

Benzion was shocked by Hartman's words and strident tone and struggled to make sense of it all. "Why are you talking to me like this?" His frown deepened. "Why are you telling me this? You have been one of our strongest supporters."

"Jabotinsky was my friend. Just as he was yours. You gave up an academic career to come here. I sent him a check. I did it because he was my friend and I hoped he could help our people in Europe. But as for this business with his vision of a Jewish state, they will never let us have the entire region and it's a great distraction to continue to try. Perhaps deadly, even."

"They?"

"The British." Hartman gestured with his free hand in frustration. "The Americans. The French. Pick a country. They won't allow it. And the Arabs in the region aren't going to sit around and watch while we take over the whole place either."

"No. You're right about that." Benzion's voice still held a hint of sarcasm. "They aren't sitting around watching now, either. They're attacking our settlements at every turn. But we can handle their threats. The Arabs won't be a military challenge to us."

"I'm not talking about roving bands of Arab thugs. I'm talking about organized, legitimate countries with well-equipped armies. Egypt, continually armed and supplied by the British already, won't sit idly by while we take over. Transjordan, which has proved to be the friendliest of all the neighboring countries, won't either. Even the Turks, who aren't Arab at all, would join the fight against us."

"Did you tell Jabotinsky any of this?"

Hartman nodded. "From the beginning. From the day he arrived and started talking about the New Zionist Organization of America. And it did not do one bit of good."

"He never mentioned any of this to me."

"We had long arguments about it. All the time. I talked to him about this the night before he died." Hartman paused a moment before softening his tone. "Look, trying to gain control of the entire region will ultimately fail. We'll never gather the kind of international support we'd need for an expansion like that. It's too much."

"We wouldn't know that for sure unless we tried," Benzion countered.

"Maybe," Hartman shrugged. "But what's more likely is that we try really hard and end up with just enough support to stop anyone from doing anything, and not enough to actually create a state the nations of the world would support or recognize."

"I don't think—"

"Listen to me," Hartman insisted, cutting him off. "If we press forward with this effort of his, we may gain enough support to stop current efforts, but not enough to implement an alternative. Surely you can see that's the risk we run. And that would cost all of us the dream of having any of the region for a homeland." He looked Benzion in the eye. "You have to end this. You can continue working on behalf of Jews in Europe if you want to. I'll help you do that. I'll help you establish an underground route to smuggle them out. I'll lobby Washington to raise the limit on the number of Jews they allow into this country and to put pressure on the British to allow more to enter Palestine. But you have to stop this nonsense about controlling all of the traditional land on both sides of the Jordan River."

✦ ✦ ✦

That evening, Benzion went for his customary walk with Celia and told her of his conversation with Hartman. "He really thinks we should quit," Benzion kept saying. "He really thinks that's the thing to do."

"I know."

He looked over at her. "You know?"

"He's not the only one who feels that way. Others feel the same."

"Others? How do you know what they're saying?"

"I've heard them talking after some of your meetings."

Benzion looked over at her. "Do *you* feel that way?"

"Most of the people I've heard talk about the subject talk about the risk. That opposing each other and fighting among ourselves runs the risk of giving an excuse to good people who might otherwise help us. And, in the end, prevent us from doing anything to form a Jewish state." She slipped her arm in his and rested her head on his shoulder.

"Do you think that's true?"

"I think that's the risk, but I don't know if it would happen that way or not. And I don't know what I would do if I were in your shoes. But I know this, I will support you in any decision you make." She leaned even closer and kissed him on the lips. "Whatever you say, that's what we'll do."

That last sentence struck him deep in his heart and made him jump inside. *Whatever you say, that is what we'll do.* It seemed like more than a response to their conversation. As if she were hinting at a deeper yes she wanted to give, to a deeper question he'd wanted to ask almost from the day he first saw her after arriving in New York. But not just yet. Not now with so much work competing for his attention. Instead of saying more, he tucked her arm inside his and squeezed her close.

"When I used to ask my father what to do, he told me I should be true to the calling on my life."

"And what is that?"

"I'm not sure," Benzion answered with a hint of ironic laughter. "I used to think it was to the scholar's life. The life of an academician. Teaching. Writing."

"But now...

"I don't know."

"The Zionist Organization—Ben-Gurion and the Jewish Committee in Tel Aviv—are way ahead of you in terms of funding and influence."

"I know. You've been keeping up with this?"

"It's a topic you've given yourself to and one that brought us together. Of course I've been keeping up with it."

Celia's comment left him feeling warm and accepted, as if he had found not merely a companion but his soulmate. Still, he hesitated to push that part of their relationship too much, preferring to allow it to unfold on its own, in its own time. "Ben-Gurion and the others have insinuated themselves into a wide range of issues and organizations." Benzion added, finally. "Creating the illusion that they are a government in waiting. *The* government in waiting."

"And that's okay, I suppose. If that's what the people want. But I'm not sure they've had much of an opportunity to express their choice. Many of them probably don't realize exactly what's going on. Can you work with Ben-Gurion?"

"I think I could work with him," Benzion answered. "All of them. Ben-Gurion, Golda Meir, the Committee. But I don't think many of them could work with me."

"Well, then," she sighed, "I think the place for you to begin is with the question of calling. You don't have to decide about the organization. In fact, I doubt you can make the decision of whether to close it or not solely on your own. It might not be the dominant voice of Jewish Palestine, but it's still a rather large organization with a number of committed members. They might have a say in what happens to the New Zionist Organization. And I don't even know if you should ask them about it. Certainly not right now. The only question you can decide now is whether *you* want to be involved with it. You came here to work with

Jabotinsky. But he's gone now. No one would blame you if you bowed out and went back home."

"I know. But that would seem like an excuse to me. Not a reason."

Celia gently placed another kiss on his cheek, "Well, I'll be glad to talk to you about it as long as you like."

✦ ✦ ✦

At home that night, Benzion opened the top drawer of the dresser. In the back corner, he felt past rows of neatly folded socks and a stack of handkerchiefs until he touched the small wooden box that held the Netanyahu ring. He slowly drew it forward until it rested on the palm of his free hand. With the box in hand, he sat back on the bed, lifted the lid, and studied the ring that rested inside.

A ring made of gold from the time of David. The king's signet ring. An object of immense historic significance, it should have been placed in a museum a long time ago, but there it was in a wooden box hidden in his dresser drawer. As if the ring had a mind of its own, a will of its own...even a spirit of its own. Must be what brought it down through the ages from hand to hand through his mother's side of the family until it rested with him. Sometimes, when he allowed himself to focus solely on just that one fact, it was almost more than he could comprehend.

After a moment, he lifted the ring from the box, and once again attempted to fit it onto the fourth finger of his right hand. The ring, however, was still much too large and when he slid it past the first knuckle it spun around his finger as it had before. *But no matter,* he thought to himself. *I have it with me. That's the important thing.*

"The ring and all it brings with it," he said aloud as he, for one of the few times in his life, allowed himself to be swept up in the mystical, religious significance of the moment.

"I am heir to the house of David," he continued. "David, the once and future king of Israel. And I am heir to his throne, if this is the time of its fulfillment—or so the story goes. But I can't tell people I'm David's heir. And I can't tell them my calling in life is to reestablish his rule over all the territory Israel once held. I haven't told anyone about *that*. I'm not even sure I can tell Celia about it or the family, for that matter." He continued to stare at the ring, slowly turning it from side to side. "Celia would think I'm crazy if she heard me talking like this." He grinned. "Crazy, but I don't think she'd be put off by it."

Benzion sat up with his legs dangling over the edge of the bed. "Still, I have a calling and a mission. I will not be deterred from fulfilling it. When I heard about what was happening in Europe, I felt compelled to act and I acted and those actions brought me here."

In an instant, images of the things he'd heard that night at Martin and Tova's house flashed through his mind. Vivid, horrific images and with them came the same sense of knowing he'd experienced that evening. Powerful, and demanding an immediate response. Maybe a prophetic insight—if there still is such a thing—but knowing just the same. And if he'd had nothing other than that, he would have felt compelled to act, regardless of how he saw the broader call upon his life.

He stood. "And so, I will continue this work and see where it leads." He returned the ring to the box, closed the lid, and placed it in the drawer. "And if I am mistaken, I think I will find my way to where I belong anyway. The ring found me when I wasn't looking for it. If I am the one to witness the fulfillment of its promises, the ring will surely be able to accomplish that. And if not, it will find the next person, just as it found me."

✦ ✦ ✦

In spite of calls to disband the New Zionist Organization, Benzion continued to promote the Revisionist cause of establishing a Jewish state in Palestine and freeing Jews from Europe. The work was enthralling but all of it took money, which meant most of his time was spent arranging and attending fundraisers. One of those fundraising trips took him to Philadelphia where he met for lunch with Aaron Jastrow, a lawyer who was helping with the effort.

"I suppose you're getting lots of calls to close the organization?" Jastrow inquired.

Benzion arched an eyebrow in a look of surprise. "How would you know that?"

"I hear most of what our people are talking about, one way or another."

"Do you think they're right?"

"Right, on this topic, is difficult to say. Arabs in Palestine aren't descendants of the ancient Philistines. We were there a long time before them but our ancestors left and they occupied the land with force. So, our return is disruptive and will continue to be. I don't think Jabotinsky was totally right. But neither is Ben-Gurion."

"The Arabs won't even accept a middle ground."

"I know," Jastrow sighed. "I used to think we might be able to work together—Jews and Arabs—but I don't think that's going to be possible. And I often wondered what Jabotinsky and Ben-Gurion might have been able to accomplish if *they* had worked together, but then I realized that one was just as stubborn as the other. So, I chose the one who was my closer friend. I think you did, too."

"He was a good friend, and I never seem to have very many of those."

"I think it comes with the territory. No one on any side of the issues we face in Palestine is ever going to be satisfied."

Benzion had more to say on that topic—much more—but he wasn't there to talk politics and did his best to turn the conversation toward the topic at hand. "I never realized how much of Jabotinsky's time went toward raising money."

"In the United States," Jastrow explained, "everything is about money. That sounds crass, but that's the way it works. Money is power. Money gets things done. And not just for this cause. Every cause is that way. I have a guy right now who's trying to get me on the board at Dropsie College. I'm a lawyer by training, not a scholar, but they want me because they think I have contacts with people who might support their school."

"And you do," Benzion acknowledged, hoping to test Jastrow and give him a means to get out of their fundraising effort if he really wanted to. Better for him to go now than later.

"Yes. I have many contacts who open many doors. But right now, I'm committed to our work. Jews in Europe need us and I intend to help them."

They ate in silence a moment, then merely to continue conversation Benzion said, "I've never heard of Dropsie. Or, if I did, I never thought much about it."

"Interesting place, actually. It's the only school in the country that focuses solely on the research and study of Jewish Civilization. That's all they do."

"Where is it located?"

"Here in Philadelphia. You might be interested in contacting them. I heard you left a research program at Hebrew University to come work for Jabotinsky."

Benzion nodded. "I did. But education is just like all the other things we want to do. It's expensive and it takes time."

"It would take time. But not money. Not at this school."

Benzion looked puzzled. "What do you mean?"

"Dropsie has a huge endowment. That's part of the reason I'm not interested in working with them. They don't really need the money and the Germans mean to kill anyone we can't rescue."

"Yes, but having an endowment doesn't always mean the money from it gets spent on the right things. That's why Jabotinsky wanted to avoid endowing the New Zionist Organization."

"Dropsie applies most of its income toward its students. They don't charge tuition. If you are accepted, you can attend free of charge."

The comment stunned Benzion—as if the dream of a lifetime was being offered to him right there over lunch—but rather than commenting further he turned to the details of the coming meetings they'd planned and got down to business. But for the remainder of the evening he felt a tingle in his spirit as he thought of how he could do both—attend Dropsie and operate the New Zionist Organization.

✦ ✦ ✦

By the time he boarded the train for the return trip to New York, Benzion had decided to keep his ideas about attending Dropsie to himself. Instead, he made an initial inquiry to the school by letter. In the exchange of correspondence that followed he learned that all of his prior work at Hebrew University would transfer and apply toward the award of a PhD.

A few days later, he returned by train to Philadelphia for an interview with Dropsie's dean, followed by introductions to key faculty members. He found the school's major professors were enthusiastic about his interest in studying the history of Jews living in Spain at the time of the Inquisition and equally enthusiastic about the possibility of having him as their student.

That evening, as he once again rode the train to New York, he thought about the opportunity that had opened up to him. The chance to study a subject he loved with the help of professors who appreciated his work, a source of income that would support him while he did that, and the opportunity to shape the New Zionist Organization with some of his own ideas. Not to repudiate Jabotinsky or his views, but to shape the direction in line with the apparent interest of members in putting additional emphasis on rescuing Jews from Nazi Germany—a cause that had been foremost on his mind since the dinner party at Martin and Tova Nussbaum's home.

Only one thing remained—a serious conversation with Celia about the direction their relationship might take—and that worried him the most. Not that she'd indicated anything over the previous year that made him doubt what her answer would be. But, still, it was time. And he had to ask her. And wagering everything on a single question made him nervous.

NETANYAHU

AS WAR IN EUROPE CONTINUED, the United States proved to be a formidable foe against Germany and the Axis Powers. By 1943, the caliphs' previous confidence in a German victory began to wane. Several of them sensed a complete German defeat by Allied forces and lamented doing so much to support the Nazis. After lengthy private discussions among themselves, they recalled Zewail to Istanbul to discuss how they might distance themselves from Germany and prepare for a postwar Palestine without German assistance.

"I agree," Zewail said after hearing Barakat's analysis of Germany's war prospects. "Unless Hitler does something totally unexpected and unpredictable, the Allies will win the war. But, a total withdrawal of our support right now would be seen by Hitler and the Germans as an act of betrayal and it would be interpreted as a sign of weakness. Hitler deplores any kind of human weakness and he would almost certainly find a way to strike back at us."

"I doubt he could reach us even if he wanted to," Idris interjected. "There is another aspect of this that we should consider before we completely withdraw our support from the Germans,"

"Which is?" Barakat asked.

"The special program you've been supporting." Zewail answered. "The bomb."

"It's much more than a bomb," Zewail stressed.

For the next several minutes Zewail told the caliphs the latest news about Germany's work on a nuclear bomb, once again describing in detail the kind of power it would unleash and the potential that power had to change the entire region.

Musa was skeptical. "If it works."

"Yes," Barakat looked over at Zewail. "Do you still think this idea of theirs will work?"

"Yes. It will work."

"When?"

"That is a question everyone is asking. Even Hitler."

"He has doubts?"

"Not about the science of the program," Zewail replied. "But about how quickly it will produce something useable on the battlefield."

"If he's skeptical maybe we should be, too," Musa opined.

Barakat caught Zewail's eye. "We have heard of this bomb from other sources who think it will not work."

"Well," Zewail commented, "I'm not an expert but the people I've talked to assure me that a bomb of this kind is possible and that it will work."

"You have actually met with these people?"

"Yes."

"People who actually work on the program?"

"I've talked with some of the scientists," Zewail explained. "These are people whom I actually know and with whom I have actually interacted."

Musa spoke up. "They allow you to wander around and talk to their people?"

"The project has been broken into separate pieces and parceled out to several research facilities, private institutes, and universities. The research is done right there on campus."

Abdullah spoke up. "This is the program to which you diverted our money, when we held back last time from sending it to the German army."

"Yes," Zewail replied.

"And you gave it to—

"Heidelberg University."

"And we told you to do that."

"Yes," Zewail confirmed.

"But this latest amount, you gave them that without our permission?"

"Without your explicit order," Zewail nodded. "The most recent gift was money designated for private organizations, that's all. You gave me no names, no contacts, and told me to figure out where it should go. Since you made no designation as to whom it should be given, I assumed that I was free to choose. So, I chose to add it to the research project at Heidelberg University, since you were already supporting it anyway."

Barakat brought the conversation back to the original subject. "Earlier you were explaining to us why we should not simply withdraw our support for Germany."

"Yes." Zewail sighed with relief. "I was saying, with the war now turning decidedly against the Germans, this would be a good time to get some of those scientists out of Germany and resettle them here so they can work on this bomb project for us."

"I am not sure we want to do that," Abdullah countered.

"Yes," Barakat added. "We are not a military organization. We don't know about these things except what you and others tell us and based on that, I don't think I can support bringing their scientists here. Not under our sponsorship."

"This is much bigger than simply a bomb," Zewail explained. "This is about a totally new source of energy."

"We have oil," Abdullah said pointedly.

"Nuclear energy is the energy of the future," Zewail replied.

"I thought oil was the answer to everyone's problem."

"It is for now, but not for the future."

Talal appeared intrigued. "How would we do that? How would we get them out and put them to work here without anyone noticing? We are in Istanbul, not in the desert. The Turkish government would find out about these scientists and I think they would find out rather quickly."

"We will hide them," Zewail responded.

Barakat frowned. "How?"

"And where?" another added.

Zewail grinned. "In plain sight. We will hide them right here, in plain sight, before the Turks' very eyes."

"What do you mean?"

"We place them at a research institution, put them to work, and no one will pay them any attention."

"But we have no connections that would permit us to do that."

Zewail grinned. "We can create our own," he countered.

The suggestion struck a chord with the caliphs and for the next two hours they discussed how they might make it happen.

✦ ✦ ✦

When Zewail returned to Germany he brought additional money for the German nuclear program. With financial support as leverage, he continued to have access to researchers and scientists working on the government's special projects, particularly at Heidelberg University. He used that access to choose program participants who might agree with the caliphs' assessment that the war was going badly for Germany and who might thus be interested in continuing their research work elsewhere.

By the end of his first week Zewail had identified five researchers from the program who seemed to be the most likely prospects. The first of those was Leo Auerbach, a young man from Bavaria who received his PhD from Leipzig University where he'd studied under Werner Heisenberg. After carefully watching him for several days, Zewail invited Auerbach for coffee. They met at a shop not far from the school.

After polite conversation about family, friends, and life before the war, Zewail turned the conversation to the future. "Any thought about what you'll do after the war?"

"I suppose I'll continue teaching," Auerbach replied, his eyes glancing quickly around the room.

"And the research?"

"That would be interesting but it would depend on funding so we'll see." He looked over at Zewail with a wan smile. "And I guess what any of us will do after the war will depend on what the Allies think of us."

Zewail feigned a look of surprise. "The Allies?"

Auerbach leaned forward and lowered his voice. "You know as well as I that this is all coming to an end. The war. The Nazi socialist programs. The whole thing. The others talk and laugh and act as if everything is fine, but I know the war is going badly for Germany." He pointed with his index finger. "You know it, too."

"Does that bother you?"

"It doesn't bother me that the war is coming to an end. No one in their right mind wants war. The real problem is what happens afterward and no one can answer that question. But I know what I see when I look around. We are fortunate here to have escaped the destruction. Most of our cities have been decimated by the bombers. And news is spreading about what really goes on in the camps with all those people. I think most of us knew, we just didn't want to know. That part bothers me." He took a sip of coffee and shook his head slowly. "This isn't going to end well for anyone associated with the Nazis."

"Including you?"

Auerbach looked away. "I am not a party member."

"But you are working on a government-sponsored program."

"And that's the part that troubles me most. Our program is not exclusively funded by the government but they have control over the final product. As you know, though, we've received funding for the program from outside sources."

"Was that part of the plan? To get outside donors to contribute so you could say you weren't exclusively government sponsored?"

"I don't know what they thought in the beginning, but now that everything seems to be falling apart, that's how they're presenting it." Auerbach smiled over at Zewail. "Why else did you think Werner Riehl was willing to accept your assistance?"

"He didn't seem all that interested in it at the time."

"That's only because he had to make sure you really were who you said you were. He had to check your background."

Every word from Auerbach's lips confirmed Zewail's assessment of him as a candidate for their project in Istanbul, but still he forced a frown and feigned an indignant response. "He checked my background?"

"Of course. He could not afford the risk of dealing with the wrong person."

"And you think he wanted the money to show the program wasn't a Nazi program?"

"I'm sure he wanted the money to help pay for the work. Riehl is a professor and a dedicated scientist. The work always comes first for him. But I know he's glad he took it now because it came from an outside source."

"What does he think of the Nazis?"

"At first, when all of this began with Hitler and the party, Riehl didn't care about the Nazis or their policies or their programs. Like I said, he's a professor. Professors conduct research. Governments these days like to spend money that way. He knew how the system worked."

"And now?"

A wry smile appeared on Auerbach's face. "Now he's as worried as the rest of us."

"Worried?"

"About how the Allies will treat us after they win the war."

"Because of the research?"

"Nuclear physics has many peaceful applications. Helpful applications. A country could solve all its energy issues simply by substituting nuclear energy for wood in the firebox, so to speak. Properly applied, ships could travel limitless distances with it. But that is not what we were working on and anyone who knows anything about physics would see that from even a cursory reading of the memos in our files."

"Do you like the work?"

Auerbach glanced sharply at Zewail. "Physics?"

"Yes."

"I love physics. It's the most precise language known to man. An elegant language for understanding an elegant world." He took a sip of coffee and set the cup on a saucer. "Sometimes I think God must be a physicist."

"Would you have any interest in moving to another part of the world and continuing your work there?"

"I would leave today," Auerbach replied, "if I thought they would not come after me."

"They?"

"The Nazis. The government."

Zewail glanced around cautiously and lowered his voice. "I could help you do that if you wanted to."

Auerbach's eyes opened wide in a startled expression. "Excuse me?" he said, and for a moment Zewail thought he had made a terrible mistake. But there was no turning back now so he said once more, "I could help you."

"Help me?"

Zewail's heart pounded against his chest as he struggled to push aside the fear that he'd walked into a trap. "Yes, I know people who can help."

"Help me leave?"

"Yes. And help you continue your research."

Auerbach sat silently staring into space for a moment. "Where would I go?" he asked finally.

Zewail's heart still raced and his palms were damp with perspiration. In his mind he saw Nazi soldiers rushing into the café, surrounding their table, and dragging him from the room, but he pushed those thoughts aside and managed to whisper, "Ever been to Istanbul?"

"When would we do this?"

"As soon as possible." Zewail paused to take another sip of coffee. "Are you in?"

"I'm in."

Over the next three days Zewail approached Hans Bothe, Herbert Gerling, Emile Kerner, and Helmuth Neumann with the same offer. All five readily accepted his help.

✦ ✦ ✦

The following month, Zewail and the six scientists arrived in Istanbul. Zewail housed them in an apartment on the eastern side of the city, then reported to the caliphs.

"Everything is well?" Barakat asked.

"Yes."

"How many came with you?"

"Six," Zewail replied.

"How were you able to get them out of Germany?"

"You don't want to know the details."

"You are certain these are genuine scientists? Not just a bunch of lab assistants?"

"These are the real thing."

Barakat looked him in the eye. "They must not be discovered."

"I understand."

NETANYAHU

BY 1944, Benzion was enrolled at Dropsie University and immersed in research toward his PhD. He was also deeply involved in the New Zionist Organization's work, having taken the director's job left vacant by Jabotinsky's death.

As a doctoral student, Benzion spent two days each week at the school in Philadelphia, attending class or in the library where the school's growing collection of primary resources proved invaluable to his work. The other days were spent either at the New Zionist office in New York or on the road raising money and promoting the organization's work of rescuing European Jews from the Nazis. And, as always, when he traveled he used the time on trains and in the air to collect his thoughts and to write.

By any measure, the year would have been busy enough with that alone but in the United States the year 1944 was a presidential election year. A year that provided issue-oriented groups their best opportunity for gathering support for their cause from candidates and incumbents alike. Taking advantage of that opportunity, however, required an intense, personal, one-on-one effort. The kind of effort that required a constant presence in Washington, DC. With all the changes in the agency after Jabotinsky's death, the only person left to do that was Benzion himself.

As with most immigrants, Jews arriving in America from Europe in the nineteenth and early twentieth century tended to be politically liberal. Many were at the forefront of the labor movement in Europe and naturally gravitated toward the Democratic Party when they arrived in the United States. The Party was glad for the support as it continued to cobble together a coalition based on grassroots involvement rather than rich donor support.

Over time, however, the Democratic Party's coalition matured. As it did, party officials and candidates came to take Jewish support for granted. As a result, candidates and party officials grew less and less responsive to Jewish needs and concerns. Benzion saw this for himself when he tried to meet with President Roosevelt to discuss the conditions Jews faced in the German concentration camps in Europe and the intransigent positions maintained by the British in mandatory Palestine.

In an effort to get the president's ear, Aaron Hartman, head of the International Garment Workers Union, arranged an introduction for Benzion with vice president Henry Wallace. More than merely the vice president, Wallace was personal friends with Roosevelt and enjoyed quick and easy access to him.

They met in Wallace's office in Washington, DC, where they were joined by William Hassett, the president's appointments secretary.

"He won't see you," Hassett announced after listening to Benzion outline the subjects he wanted to discuss.

"Why not?"

"We're still at war. We need our Allies in order to finish the job."

"I realize that, but our people are dying in the German camps. We could get them out but the British won't allow them to emigrate to Palestine which leaves them nowhere to go."

"I assure you," Hassett emphasized, "The president is well aware of the situation Jews face in Europe and Palestine, but he's not going to press the British regarding their policy in Palestine, or the creation of a Jewish State."

"Or increased immigration quotas," Wallace added.

"So," Benzion said, "let me see if I understand what you're telling me.

The head of an influential Jewish organization has asked to speak with the president about issues both agree are important, but the president refuses to see this Jewish official. Yet, it's an election year and, his refusal notwithstanding, the president expects to receive the full support of the Jewish organization on Election Day." Benzion glanced around at them. "Is that about where we are?"

"You don't have to get testy," Hassett chided.

"Oh? And why not?"

"The president is a busy man," Hassett responded. "He can't—"

"You said he refused to see me because he wants to keep the British happy. That has nothing to do with how busy he is."

Wallace looked over at him. "We all know there's only so much he can do about the people in the German camps."

"And we all know he hasn't done anything about them," Benzion replied. "And we all know the supposed reason he doesn't raise these issues with the British is because the president has been told that Churchill is an anti-Semitic racist."

"I don't have to sit here and listen to this," Hassett said.

"No, you don't," Benzion replied. "And you'll understand why we'll be listening to the Republican candidate, too."

Hassett stormed from the room, and when he was gone Wallace turned to Benzion. "We both know you aren't going to convince many of your members to vote Republican."

"I don't know why not. What good has it done them to vote for the Democrats?"

Frustrated, Benzion boarded the train that afternoon for the trip back to New York. To relax, he took a seat by the window and read that day's edition of the *Washington Post*. Before they reached Baltimore, an article on the second page caught his eye. It told the story of John Ray Lewis, a delegate to the Democratic convention from Roxbury, Vermont. Lewis had attended every convention since 1876 when the party nominated Samuel Tilden to run against Rutherford B. Hayes and hoped to live long enough to see the election of 1976. "That would make an even hundred years," he told the reporter. "I came in on the nation's centennial birthday. I'd like to go out on one, too."

The article went on to note that for the 1944 cycle, both parties were holding their nominating conventions in Chicago and both would use Chicago Stadium, the city's premier indoor arena. This wouldn't be the first time both parties met in the same city but it remained a rare event due to the space necessary to accommodate the number of people attending such a gathering. Republicans were to meet in the Windy City in June. The Democrats were set to arrive in July.

Benzion laid the paper aside and thought about that. Both nominating conventions, in the same city, one month apart. As he gazed out the window, he thought about what he'd said in the meeting with Wallace and Hassett. He was right when he said Roosevelt wasn't interested in talking to him about Jewish policy because he had already decided he had the Jewish support anyway. That much was true. And talking to him offered the president no upside while exposing him to the possibility of offending the British. If Roosevelt had needed the Jewish vote, he would have been glad to meet with the head of almost any Jewish organization. But he'd seen from previous elections that the Jewish voter wasn't going anywhere on Election Day except to the polls to vote for the Democrats. That's the way it had always been.

A knowing smile crept over Benzion's face. "We've made things too easy for him," he said to himself. "Perhaps now is a good time to see what we can do about changing that."

Benzion was right. Jewish leadership in America had bent over backwards to show their support for Roosevelt. Stephen Wise, an ordained rabbi and co-chair of the American Zionist Emergency Council, was friends with Roosevelt and visited him on a regular basis, but rather than using that friendship to impress upon Roosevelt the severity of the moment, he instead did everything possible to avoid even the hint of controversy. That might have been good for Rabbi Wise, but it did nothing to advance the cause of Zionism and did nothing to help those facing death at the hands of the Nazis.

By the time Benzion reached New York, he had decided it was time to look beyond the Democratic Party for political support. He began spreading the word around New York, Washington, and Philadelphia, that Jews in America were disgruntled with Roosevelt over his failure to respond decisively to news of Germany's systematic murder of European Jews who were being held in the concentration camps. In speeches and elsewhere, he talked about the growing sense of frustration among Jews over Roosevelt's failure to increase US immigration quotas for those fleeing Europe and applying for admission to the United States as refugees. And he talked of the anger many felt over Roosevelt's refusal to raise with Churchill the UK's failure to keep its word regarding the Balfour Declaration. Finally, in an attempt to show the seriousness of the situation, he let it be known that Jews might consider listening to the Republican candidates a little more closely. Perhaps the Republicans would be interested in helping the Jewish cause.

To back up that threat, Benzion began meeting with as many influential Republicans as possible. Always making sure to announce the meetings to reporters with press releases and reporting on them in Jewish publications. Among those with whom he met were Clare Boothe Luce, a member of Congress from Connecticut, former President Herbert Hoover, Alf Landon, and Robert Taft, a US Senator from Ohio.

As the Republican Party gathered for its nominating convention in Chicago that summer, Benzion traveled there and spent the week lobbying key party members. With Senator Taft's help, he attended meetings of the Resolutions Committee and participated in the drafting of a party platform provision calling on the British government to increase the number of Jews allowed to enter Palestine and a statement announcing the party's support for a Jewish State in Palestine. On its own accord, the committee added a sentence condemning Roosevelt for failing to insist the British enforce the Balfour declaration—a declaration he previously only pretended to support.

When the full party gathered, the resolution was adopted by acclamation and the Republican Party became the first American political party to declare its support for the establishment of a Jewish state in Palestine. News of the measure reached reporters the day before floor sessions began. With little time to spare, reporters interviewed Benzion who was all too glad to share his views on the matter. He told them, "We are excited to see the Republican Party take such a courageous stance on behalf of Jews here in the United States and around the world."

News of the Republican Party's support for a Jewish state reached the headlines of major newspapers across the nation. Its criticism of Roosevelt, however, offended many traditional American Jews and they wasted little time in bringing their complaints to Benzion.

"I think the truth is more important than politics," Benzion stated. "I told the truth, others played politics." Rabbi Wise knew the comment was directed at him but could do little in response.

A few weeks before the Democrat Party convention, Benzion prepared articles for publication in several regional Jewish newspapers, noting that since the Republican Convention, Congresswoman Clare Boothe Luce and Senator Robert Taft had been working New York Jewish neighborhoods on behalf of the Party ticket. It was true, both had been in New York where they spoke to large crowds at synagogues and Jewish Centers throughout the city on behalf of the Republican candidates. In addition, Governor Dewey and Governor Bricker, the party's nominees for president and vice president, had appeared at several fundraisers held by influential and wealthy Jews in Manhattan.

The news articles quoted two Republican precinct captains as suggesting that a substantial number of Jewish votes, perhaps fifty thousand or more, appeared to be up for grabs among Jews who were dissatisfied with Roosevelt's response to the crisis in Europe. The article went on to note that most of those votes were located in and around the city of New York which, the article suggested, had the potential for tipping the results in favor of the Republican slate in the general election that fall.

For added emphasis, Benzion and the New Zionist Organization purchased full page ads in *The New York Times* criticizing British policy toward Jews in Palestine. Other advertisements brought equally harsh accusations against the United States for failing to address the Jewish refugee crisis in Europe. Many established Jewish leaders in the US were offended by the advertisements but Benzion paid them little attention.

With the Republican Party now taking the lead on Jewish statehood, the Democrats had little choice but to follow. When the Party adopted a platform that pledged support for a Jewish state in Palestine and called on the British to raise their immigrant quotas for Jews attempting to return to Palestine, Rabbi Wise did his best to make the most of it with reporters. But everyone knew the Republicans had the issue first.

The internal politics of the matter aside, the 1944 election was an important moment for Jews and for the Democratic Party. For the Party, it marked the first of many political steps away from domination by conservative southern delegates. For Jews, it was the beginning of bilateral support for their dream of a political state in Palestine—support that began with the work of one outmanned, out-staffed lobbyist and continues to this day.

✦ ✦ ✦

As expected, Roosevelt won the 1944 presidential election and entered his fourth term in office with Harry S Truman as vice president. For Roosevelt, this was but a continuation of the work he'd begun twelve years earlier. For Truman, who was largely unknown outside his home state of Missouri, it brought a new and unexpected turn in his political career. Never a member of the Party's inner circle, he was unaware of many of the details behind the president's public decisions and programs and now that he was in office, many of Roosevelt's closest advisers worked harder than ever to keep it that way.

In Europe, the Allied army was in the midst of its final push into Germany and though much of the fighting was fierce and difficult, everyone knew the war in Europe, for all practical purposes, was over. Fighting in Asia and the Pacific would continue through the summer with major battles yet to be fought in the Philippine Islands, Okinawa, Iwo Jima, and China. The outcome there, however, seemed equally as determined, with only the body count up for discussion. Most anticipated the casualty count would be high.

At home, with the war nearing its end, Roosevelt turned his attention to the creation of a worldwide organization that would provide a means for settling disputes without the need for another global war.

Dubbed the United Nations, the new international body would serve as a successor to the largely ineffective League of Nations. Its founding session was scheduled to convene that April in San Francisco, apparently with only a few details left to address.

In Palestine, both the Jewish Agency, representing the World Zionist Organization, and various dissident groups aligned with the New Zionist Organization, viewed the creation of the United Nations as a promising step forward in the drive for Jewish statehood. From the earliest talks among Allied nations both groups had launched an effort to promote the UN and to nudge the new body toward their respective positions on the matter of Palestine. Zionist advocates David Ben-Gurion, Golda Meir, Abba Eban, and others associated with the Jewish Agency did their best to convince the public to accept the new organization. The New Zionist Organization did likewise but, with limited resources, relying primarily on Benzion's efforts at personal diplomacy and activism.

Behind the scenes, out of the public eye, they worked even harder to make sure the UN was firmly committed to the establishment of a Jewish state in Palestine. At every meeting, large or small, every gathering, formal or informal, the World Zionist Organization had a representative present to make sure the Jewish perspective on the matter was presented in its full and proper context.

Though he was outmanned and out-financed, Benzion did his best to promote the New Zionist view through speeches at public events and face-to-face meetings with people of influence and notoriety. To that he added op-ed articles in prominent newspapers and magazines and, when money allowed, supplemented those with paid advertisements.

All seemed to be going well until that April. Benzion was at the New Zionist office in Manhattan, preparing for a fundraising trip to the Midwest when Elena Morgenthau, his secretary, appeared at the door. She looked stricken. "News reports on the radio are saying President Roosevelt has died."

"Is it true?"

"I assume so." There was a hint of frustration in her voice. "They're saying he's dead on the radio."

"I know, but who's saying it?" Benzion asked. "Just a reporter or someone from the White House?"

"I don't know." Her voice was sharper. "Come out here and listen for yourself."

Almost begrudgingly, Benzion followed Elena to the reception area, but already his mind was on the work that remained to be done that day and as he neared the center of the room he thought of turning back to his office. While he was still thinking, Elena—who was ten paces ahead—reached the radio that sat on a table behind her desk and gave the volume knob a twist.

"Just minutes ago," a reporter announced, "the president's spokesman, Steve Early, announced that President Roosevelt had been resting at his home in Warm Springs, Georgia, when he suffered a massive cerebral hemorrhage. He died within a matter of hours. Mrs. Roosevelt is on her way to Georgia to accompany the body back to Washington.

"Well," Benzion sighed, "that changes everything."

The radio continued to give details about the president's death but Benzion ignored them and returned to his desk. With Roosevelt gone, the White House contacts he'd spent months developing seemed in doubt as the machinery of government paused while Truman was sworn into office as president.

Truman was a good man, better than most people knew and far more capable than Roosevelt's inner circle thought, but he would need weeks to get his administration together. During that time, most of his energy would be directed toward addressing the immediate issues of his new job, many of them issues that Roosevelt had handled on his own.

No doubt Truman would want his own appointees, both in the White House staff and the Cabinet. That meant Benzion would need to develop new contacts throughout the executive branch and, in effect, start over again in an effort to reach people of power and influence in the administration.

When he reached his desk, Benzion collapsed in his chair, leaned back all the way, and stared up at the ceiling, frustrated by the enormity of the work that lay ahead. But as he sat there in silence, his mind turned to a meeting with Robert Taft the year before, when he was trying to persuade the Republican Party to support the creation of a Jewish state. He'd felt equally as frustrated before that meeting, but the discussion with Taft went much better than he'd hoped and, with Taft's help, the Party came around to supporting their position.

After a moment to gather his thoughts, Benzion leaned forward and took a clean legal pad from the desk drawer. He laid the pad on the desk and slowly began making notes of people to contact for help in reaching the Truman administration.

✦ ✦ ✦

At the time of Roosevelt's death, one of the most important pending items was the creation of the United Nations. The UN's founding session was scheduled to occur in San Francisco just two weeks after Truman took office. Washington insiders were certain the session would be postponed. Much to their chagrin, Truman insisted the assembly be held as planned and traveled to California to attend the first day's events.

Though most of the details regarding establishment of the UN had been agreed upon in advance by the major powers, the founding session in San Francisco included a much wider group, in the end totaling fifty-one countries. Reaching an agreement with the larger group proved more contentious than expected and negotiations continued until October. The UN's first working assembly wasn't held until the following January.

In the meantime, representatives from the United States and United Kingdom formed the Anglo-American Committee of Inquiry. Created at the request of the British, the committee was tasked with exploring ways to solve the Palestinian question without the assistance of an international body. After a deliberative session in Lausanne, Switzerland, the committee issued a report which recommended that the region be maintained as a single political entity but governed in a manner that permitted neither group—Jew nor Arab—dominance.

Shortly after the report was issued, the British asked for US help in implementing the plan—a task estimated by the US War Department to require some three hundred thousand US troops. President Truman declined to assist at that level. Thereafter, the British announced their intention to quit the Mandate and referred the matter to the UN.

For Benzion and others in the Zionist movement, the British announcement came as good news. However, Jews living in Palestine, particularly David Ben-Gurion and others at the Jewish Agency, found it unsettling. If the British intended to withdraw from Palestine, a Jewish government had to be ready to take charge the moment they departed—both as a matter of safety and as a way of showing the world that a Jewish state was a viable option.

With the British wanting out of Mandatory Palestine, the UN appointed the United Nations Special Committee on Palestine (UNSCOP) to determine what to do next. UNSCOP studied the matter and issued a report that proposed a two-state solution, dividing Palestine along the lines of occupation as they existed on the ground. Atop those political divisions, UNSCOP proposed to overlay a single unified economy. Jerusalem would become an international city administered by the UN.

David Ben-Gurion, as executive director of the Jewish Agency, accepted the proposal immediately. Arabs rejected the proposal out of hand and demanded exclusive control of the entire region.

Benzion and the New Zionist Organization were adamantly opposed to the plan and wasted little time in saying so. They insisted instead on a single-state solution that placed the entire region exclusively under Jewish control.

"I am not opposed to the formation of a Jewish state in Palestine," Benzion told reporters. "That has been my work and the work of my family for many years. I am simply opposed to this particular plan. Jews cannot be safe in Palestine unless they control the entire region. Arabs are confrontational by nature. That is the way they were in the past and they have shown themselves to be that way on many occasions in the present."

In support of his position, Benzion pointed to the recent history of the region—how the Arabs were offered their own state on multiple occasions and each time chose war instead of peace. "They cannot live otherwise," he insisted. "It is their nature. Which is why we must be in full control of the entire region."

In the days that followed, Benzion made frequent trips to Washington in attempts to convince congressmen and senators that the UNSCOP approach would lead to permanent conflict between Arabs and Jews. To his dismay, he found overwhelming support for the creation of a Jewish state, but a polite refusal to give that state exclusive control over the entire region.

When his effort to sway Congress proved futile, Benzion took his ideas about Palestine to members of the Truman administration. With the help of Aaron Hartman, he obtained an appointment with John Steelman, President Truman's chief of staff, but little came of it.

In the end, Benzion and the New Zionists failed to stop the UN's two-state solution. The UNSCOP plan, with the unified economy omitted, was adopted. Shortly thereafter, the British government announced that it would withdraw from Palestine on midnight May 14, 1948. Arabs living in Palestine responded by taking up arms and once again plunging the region into war.

NETANYAHU

AT MIDNIGHT, May 14, 1948, at a gathering in Tel Aviv, David Ben-Gurion issued a declaration of independence on behalf of a new Jewish state in Palestine. A state to be known to the world as the state of Israel. In New York, Benzion, like many others around the world, listened to the proceedings on the radio.

Not long after Israel announced its independence, President Truman issued a statement recognizing Israel's sovereignty as a member of the family of nations. Other countries quickly followed.

With the declaration of Israel's independence, the Arab-Israeli conflict that began as a civil war in November of the prior year now became a war for Israel's independence. This time, however, Arabs living in Palestine were joined by trained troops from Jordan, Egypt, Syria, and Iraq.

As the war of independence began, Israel mobilized all able-bodied men and women living in Palestine to fill the ranks of the Israel Defense Force. A few months later, many Jews living in the United States traveled to Israel to join the fighting as volunteers. Those volunteers also organized an effort to obtain arms and munitions from the United States, including a dozen World War II bombers. Pilots from the US trained Israelis to fly the bombers as well as fighter aircraft purchased from Yugoslavia. Fighting continued through the year and finally came to an end in the summer of 1949 with Israel entering separate armistice agreements with Egypt, Jordan, and Syria.

✦ ✦ ✦

That year was a banner year for Benzion, too. After years of study, he completed the requirements for a PhD and was awarded the degree by Dropsie University. With degree in hand, he eschewed other opportunities and remained at Dropsie to continue his research into details surrounding the Spanish Inquisition. While doing that, he also taught several courses.

Celia, whom he'd married earlier, gave birth to their first child, a boy whom they named Jonathan, a name reminiscent of Benzion's father, Nathan Mileikowsky and his hero, John Henry Patterson, a British officer who helped form the Jewish Legion which fought to liberate Palestine during World War I. Benzion was enthralled with his son and thought of the Netanyahu ring, wondering if his son would be the one to rule a Jewish state.

Inspired by the birth of his son and the family connection to the ancient King David, Benzion decided they should return to the newly formed Israel. Even though Ben-Gurion and others who did not share his views held the major government offices, he was convinced he could work to promote the New Zionist view of Israel from Jerusalem or Tel Aviv just as well as he could from New York.

By the time Benzion and Celia returned with their son to Israel, the war of independence was over and the issue of Israel's statehood was settled. Over the next two years, Benzion tried his hand at politics, but lost each time. In between elections, he applied for teaching positions at Hebrew University and several other schools, but his applications failed to raise so much as a polite acknowledgment.

After yet another frustrated Knesset election, he and Celia joined a group of friends for coffee at a Tel Aviv café. Benzion was disappointed and it didn't take long before the conversation was dominated by his grousing.

"You know," Tova Nussbaum said, after listening to another of Benzion's complaints, "your side lost the argument."

Benzion's forehead wrinkled in a frown. "My side?"

"Yes. The Zionist Organization, David Ben-Gurion, they won. Their argument prevailed. Your side did not."

"And," Martin added carefully. "You weren't here for the war of independence. You didn't participate in the fighting."

"Why should that matter?"

"Others opposed Ben-Gurion," Martin tried to explain, "but when the fighting started, they put aside the arguing, took up arms, and were right in the middle of the greatest battles."

"Even Martin." Tova slipped an arm in his. "It wasn't much of a fight by American standards but it was scary for those of us who were here."

"Most of those who fought found a place to fit in after the fighting ended," Martin continued. "It might be a somewhat limited place, in the government, or in one of the schools, or the IDF, but they were given a place to participate just the same."

"A job," Tova added. "A way to make a living."

"Even though politically they were opposed to Ben-Gurion," Martin continued. "They still found a place."

"I worked for the state of Israel," Benzion argued. "I lobbied congressmen and senators. Ambassadors...former American presidents... and every other person of influence I could find."

"That's right." Martin nodded his head. "You lobbied all of those people—in America."

"And you were lobbying *against* Ben-Gurion's plans," Tova added. "And against the direction being promoted by the Jewish Agency."

"And not just that," Martin added. "You were promoting Jabotinsky's plans."

"That shouldn't matter," Benzion countered. "I was there. They were here. It shouldn't matter. We are all Jews. We are all on the side of Israel." His shoulders slumped. "Just a different view of what Israel should be, that's all."

"But it does matter," Tova commented.

They sat in silence a moment, then Martin spoke softly. "I think you have made too many political enemies here. I like you and it hurts to say it, but I think you ought to consider somewhere else."

"That's what they told me before I went to New York," Benzion responded. He paused to take a sip of coffee and sat staring blankly for a while. "Where would I go?" he asked finally. "If not here, then where?"

"Europe," Tova offered.

"Or back to America," Martin interjected. "I know it seems harsh and cruel, but I don't think the people in decision making roles here want to deal with you, Benzion. The Jewish Agency, the Knesset. They're controlled by people who were here for the war. Most of them are Ben-Gurion loyalists."

"Or at least Labour supporters," Tova commented.

"And they all remember," Martin added. "They remember who was here and who wasn't. You are one of the ones who wasn't here."

They continued to talk but already Benzion could feel the weight of what they were saying settling on his shoulders. He hadn't meant to alienate those who disagreed with him. He just wanted to make a point. To have his say. Wasn't that what independence was about?

And he did try to participate. Not during the fighting, but they were fighting for a different kind of Israel. The one *they* wanted. Not the one *he* thought they should have. Theirs was a small, practicable version. He had a much bigger vision of a Jewish state and he would work for it as long as he had the slightest hope that it might yet be formed.

Yes, he had been in America, as were many others, but he wasn't hiding. He was doing his best to help. But now that all of that was over, he'd returned. He'd come back to Palestine and attempted to participate in the new state by standing for election to the Knesset and looking for a place to serve.

In the meantime he'd pursued job openings for teaching positions at Hebrew University and other places. He was qualified. Over-qualified, actually. More education and teaching experience than many of those he'd seen lecturing to classes. Ben-Gurion and the Jewish Agency found jobs for them. Found jobs for thousands of immigrants who showed up unannounced after the war, wanting to live in the new State of Israel. None of them were around to fight for independence. That didn't hinder them finding a place. They weren't denied a position or told to live somewhere else because they weren't there from the beginning.

And if we're counting who came to Palestine earliest, Benzion thought, *I had been there before any of them. My father helped form the organization that sponsored the Jewish Agency. He was there when they did it and turned back the dissidents when they wanted to bolt over the Uganda proposal. Didn't all of that count for something? Didn't it matter?*

Not long before sundown, Benzion and Celia started home. Celia had been quiet all afternoon and as they walked together he asked, "What do you think about what they said?"

"I guess I can see their point. We weren't here for the fighting."

"I'm forty years old. And I've never held a rifle in my hands, much less been trained how to use it."

"I know."

"I was in America lobbying for the kind of Israel I thought we should have. Golda Meir was there raising money for an army to fight for the kind of Israel *she* thought we should have. No one suggested she should be excluded now because she wasn't at the front using the weapons she helped procure." Celia slipped her arm in his and leaned against his shoulder. Benzion continued, "They found a place for Menachem Begin. He was head of Irgun. One of the most radical resistance groups in the whole country."

"I know. It doesn't seem at all fair."

"But you think they're right?"

"I think they have a realistic view of how things are. Not how things ought to be, but how they really are."

"But I want to live in Israel." Benzion's voice broke. "I just want to live here and raise our family here."

"I know you do. And I do too. I just don't see how we're going to do that."

"Why can't they understand?" Benzion muttered. "I'm not against *them.* I'm just in favor of a different approach."

A few months later, Benzion was given a single class to teach at Hebrew University, but as his friends had suggested, he wouldn't get any further in a teaching career than the one class. The university, he learned, was controlled by members of Ben-Gurion's party. They made sure their members filled the available slots first.

Not only that, Benzion's academic work, which always ran counter to the generally accepted theory on Jews and the Inquisition, was now seen in a post-Holocaust light. The notion that Jews in the fifteenth century responded to persecution by genuinely converting to Christianity in an attempt to assimilate into popular culture was seen by some as suggesting Jews of the twentieth century should have abandoned their Jewishness and assimilated into German culture. That view ran counter to the prevailing post-war perspective of Holocaust survivors, who tended to see any critical examination of their response to Nazism as suggesting that they, the victims, were responsible for their own persecution.

Between the two—his academic research on the Jews in Spain and his political views regarding the new Jewish state—Benzion felt out of step with everyone. Frustrated, angry, and dejected he groped for more than a job, but for a vision of himself and his life that could carry him into the future.

The dream of a future in an Israel that covered the territory once held under King David now seemed just that—a dream and nothing more. And the Netanyahu ring was just a trinket in the top drawer of his dresser.

✦ ✦ ✦

Finally, Joseph Klausner, one of Benzion's few friends in Israeli academia, recommended him for a position as an editor of *Encyclopedia Hebraica*—a first-of-its-kind project to create an encyclopedia of general, Jewish, and Israeli topics. The multivolume work was written in Hebrew and began with a projected sixteen volumes which the publishers anticipated would be finished in four or five years. The work quickly grew to an overwhelming task with no end in sight.

Not long after Benzion went to work on the encyclopedia, Klausner died. Shortly after his death, Benzion was promoted to editor-in-chief. He still longed for an academic life in a university setting, but consigned himself to the reality that such a life would never happen in Israel. Instead of brooding about it, he settled into the work as editor-in-chief and did his best to produce thoroughly-researched, well-written volumes.

✦ ✦ ✦

In 1957, Benzion and Celia attended a concert in Tel Aviv. During intermission they ran into Uri Riskin, a graduate of Dropsie who had been a student there with Benzion. Uri, who had only just arrived from the United States, had plenty of news to share and mentioned a professor from Dropsie who recently retired.

"They're looking for someone to fill his position," Uri revealed. "You might be just what they need."

"Did you apply?" Benzion asked.

Uri shrugged and laughed. "No, they only gave me a degree to get rid of me. They wouldn't let me anywhere near the classroom now."

All through the second half of the concert Benzion's mind was on the conversation he'd had with Uri and on the potential position at Dropsie. The school wasn't his first choice as a place to settle down for a career but he'd had a good experience there as a student. And no one else was offering him the kind of academic career he really wanted. But he would need to get the details from Dropsie and he couldn't do anything without talking to Celia first.

As they drove home later that evening, Benzion looked over at Celia, "What do you think about that position at Dropsie?"

"I think you're going to write them and ask about it."

Benzion smiled. She always knew his mind. "But what do you think about it?"

"I suppose that depends on what kind of offer they make." She turned to look at him. "We're doing well right here where we are."

"I know," Benzion sighed. "But I've wanted to teach for a long time."

"You should wait to say anything about this until after we hear from the school," she cautioned. "We don't even know if the position is still open."

When they reached home that evening, Benzion wrote a letter to the school and asked about the position. The next morning, he mailed it on his way to the office. A few weeks later, Dropsie's academic dean responded with an application package.

Several months and numerous rounds of correspondence later, Benzion was offered a teaching position at Dropsie. After discussing the matter with Celia, he decided to accept the school's offer.

By then Benzion and Celia had three sons, Johnathan, their oldest, followed by Benjamin, who was three years younger, and Iddo, who was born in 1952. The two older boys were well along in school—Jonathan was already in high school, Benjamin was in middle school. They enjoyed close, established friendships, and were thoroughly devoted to life in Israel. For Benjamin, Israel was all he'd ever known. For Jonathan the following school year would be his senior year.

Yet despite that, a few days after accepting the job at Dropsie, Benzion announced to them that the family was moving back to the United States. The news came as a shock to the two older Netanyahu boys. Neither wanted to leave Israel.

✦ ✦ ✦

In his final weeks in Israel, Benjamin spent long hours with his best friend, Oded Geller, plotting ways to avoid moving away.

"What if you stayed with us?" Geller suggested.

"What do you mean?" Benzion asked with a puzzled look. "Spend the night tonight?"

"No. Well, yes. But I was talking about when your parents move to the United States. What if you stayed with us and finished high school here?"

"Do you think your parents would go for it?"

"I'm sure they would. You spend most of your time with us as it is."

That afternoon, Benjamin approached Benzion with Geller's suggestion that he could live with him and his family for the upcoming school term.

"No," Benzion said. "We will move to the US as a family."

"But I've gone to school here all my life. All of my friends are here."

"You're too young to live away from us. We're not dividing the family with some here and others there."

Jonathan had a similar idea, but when he saw the answer Benjamin received he decided to keep quiet. Being minors, they were forced to move with the family.

The family settled in Wyncote, Pennsylvania, a suburb of Philadelphia, and the boys enrolled in school there. Uprooted and forced to live on the opposite side of the Atlantic from the place they considered home, the two older brothers—Jonathan and Benjamin—became very close. Both wanted to go back home to Israel, at least for a summertime visit, and spent much of their time after school talking about how to do that. Benzion, still hurt and aggravated over the way things hadn't worked out for him in Israel, showed no interest in helping his sons return, even if only for a visit.

Jonathan was old enough to work and held a variety of jobs after school and on weekends. He saved his money through the school year and after graduation, announced his plans for the future. "I'm going back to Israel and join the IDF."

Celia didn't like the idea and thought he should remain in the United States. "You have dual citizenship," she pointed out. "You were born here. You have the option of obtaining permanent US citizenship."

"I know. But I want to do this. I *have* to do this."

Benzion, however, was proud of his son's independence and fully supportive of his decision to return to Israel. "I expect great things from you," he said as Jonathan prepared to leave. "Perhaps you will succeed where I have failed." He stood with his hands on Jonathan's shoulders and stared at him a moment, thinking of the Netanyahu ring. He considered giving it to him right then, but just as he started to speak, Celia entered the room. Jonathan turned to look in her direction. Benzion caught his eye once more and said, "Come downstairs to the study when you are finished up here."

✦ ✦ ✦

An hour later, Jonathan came to Benzion's study and took a seat near the desk. When the door was closed and they were alone, Benzion continued, "I know moving here wasn't easy for you, and maybe we should have considered a way for you and Benjamin to remain in Jerusalem." He paused as if thinking. "Maybe not for Benjamin, but at least for you. To let you spend your last year of school there, with friends."

"It's okay, Dad," Jonathan assured. "I adjusted. Things worked out."

"And now you're ready to go back."

Jonathan smiled. "Yes, sir."

"Have everything packed?"

"Most of it. A few more clothes to wash."

"I have something I want to give you."

"Oh," Jonathan said with surprise. "I didn't expect a going-away gift."

Benzion opened the top drawer of the desk and took out the box that held the Netanyahu ring. He set it on the desktop and looked over at Jonathan. "You remember hearing about how members of your grandmother's family are direct descendants of David."

"Yes, sir. You've told us that many times."

"Yes. I have. But that's not all of the story. About two years before your grandmother was born, your great grandfather Lurie was in his study at the synagogue in Lodz. While he was there, a visitor appeared at his door. The man's name was Judah Alkalai."

"The Rabbi of Semlin," Jonathan noted.

"Yes. Perhaps the most influential rabbi of his day."

"Did you know Alkalai?"

Benzion shook his head. "No. He died long before I was born. Alkalai told your great grandfather that his wife would give birth to a girl. That the girl would be born about two years from then and they should name her Sarah."

"Our grandmother."

"Yes." Benzion nodded. "Alkalai told him that when Sarah was of marriageable age, a man would visit them. That man would be named Nathaniel and he would become Sarah's husband."

"Wow," Jonathan sat up straight in the chair. "You didn't tell us that part. That's exactly what happened."

"And as we've already mentioned, you're grandmother's family, the Luries, are descendants of David."

Now Jonathan's mind whirred. *The Luries. David. The promise recorded in the scrolls that David's kingdom would never end. Was that what my father wants to see me about?*

Benzion continued. "In each generation one child is selected as the child of promise, the one who inherits the promise from God that David's kingdom would never end."

Jonathan leaned forward, elbows propped on his knees, and lowered his voice. "Dad, I don't know where this is going, but I can't go back to Israel and announce that I am king of the country."

"I know," Benzion smiled. "But let me finish. That right of Davidic inheritance was signified by a ring that was passed from one generation to the next. Your great grandfather Lurie had it during his lifetime, then he gave it to my father to hold for me. And now I'm giving it to you." Benzion picked up the box from the desktop and thrust it toward Jonathan.

Jonathan reached over the desk, took the box with both hands, and slid back into his chair. He rested the box on the top of his thigh and stared at it, taking time to study its features and its burnished finish. When he did not immediately look inside, Benzion became impatient. "Go ahead," he insisted. "Open it and have a look."

Jonathan did as he was told and raised the lid to look inside. Benzion grinned at the expression on his face. "Impressive in its simplicity."

"Yes, sir."

"There's an inscription on it. Can you read it?"

"Not really."

"Then I'll tell you what it says. It says 'Netanyahu Ben-Yoash.

Netanyahu—Yahweh has given.' And 'Ben-Yoash he is the son of Yoash.'"

Jonathan knew about the Netanyahu name. He was a child when they changed their name. Benzion told him often about the meaning of it and why he'd chosen it for their family, but Yoash was a word he'd never heard.

"What does Yoash mean?"

"That is someone's name," Benzion explained. "He was an official at the time David was king. That ring is David's signet ring. It was used to seal documents with the king's authority. Used properly, it was the same as if David sealed the document himself. He was bound by every agreement his agent made that was sealed with an imprint of that ring."

Jonathan glanced in Benzion's direction. "This ring goes all the way back to the reign of David?"

"All the way back to David," Benzion nodded. "And in the Lurie family it has passed to the child of promise in each generation. You are that child for your generation."

"What should I do with it?"

"Keep it. Stay alert. Remain faithful to the call upon your life."

"And?"

"And then you will always know what to do."

"Ok, but I'm leaving for Israel to join the IDF. I can't take this with me into training or keep it in a footlocker." He glanced at the ring. "This is too valuable to be treated like that."

"I understand. But take it with you for now. You have a few days before you go. See what happens between now and then. You can decide then about what to do with it."

✦ ✦ ✦

Box in hand, Jonathan went upstairs to his room and took a seat at his desk near the bedroom window. He placed the box on the desktop, then opened it and gazed inside. The ring was nestled safely in the folds of purple velvet that lined the box, but even so, it looked magnificent. So simple, yet regal. Worn smooth along the shoulders that held the setting, yet holding the setting firmly in place. Strength and vulnerability in perfect balance.

After studying it a moment longer, he carefully lifted the ring from its place and rested it on the palm of his hand. As he sat there admiring it, Benjamin entered the room and stood behind him. "What's that?" he pointed.

"A signet ring. From the time David was king of Israel."

"That was two thousand years ago."

"Almost three thousand. You think this ring could really be that old?"

"I don't know. Where'd you get it?"

"Dad gave it to me. It's been passed through our family from one generation to the next. And now it has come to me."

Benjamin had a sinking feeling inside. "Not just from one generation to the next. But from one child of promise to the next. That means you are the child of promise for our generation."

Jonathan cocked his head to one side. "You knew about that?"

"I overheard him talking to Mom about it a couple of times."

Jonathan held the ring, turning it slowly from side to side, reading the inscription as he did. "Netanyahu Ben-Yoash," he read aloud. "Netanyahu—Yahweh has given. And Yoash—he is the son of Yoash."

Along the top of the ring was an image of a man holding a staff in one hand and a scepter in the other. "Staff and scepter. A depiction of royalty," Benjamin enlightened. "This was David's signet ring alright."

"Yes." Jonathan nodded. "And he gave it to Yoash symbolizing the delegation of authority to him."

Jonathan continued studying the ring's features, marveling at the craftsmanship and wondering how it had survived all these years. *If I really am a descendant of David,* he thought, *and if this really is a signet ring from the time of his reign, this would make me next in line for the throne. If that is my destiny, only God could bring something like that to pass.*

"Think it will fit?" Jonathan asked.

When Benjamin did not respond, Jonathan cocked his head and

repeated himself. "Think the ring will fit one of my fingers?" When there still was no response, he turned around and checked the room; there was no one in sight.

Finally, Jonathan grasped the ring and slipped it onto his finger. The ring went on easily but it was much too big for his finger. Disappointed, he slipped it off, returned it to the box, and tucked it into the inside pocket of a suitcase that lay open on his bed.

✦ ✦ ✦

Benjamin often noticed the affection his father had for Jonathan and longed for the same affirmation, but never quite received it. Still, he did his best to gain his father's approval and followed Jonathan's example—when he was old enough to work he got a job, saved his money, and paid for his own flights back to Israel for summer vacation. Even with that, Benzion was not supportive, to the point of telling Benjamin he would have to get himself to the airport for the flights. Not to be outdone, Benjamin arranged for a taxi to take him.

Throughout his remaining years of high school, Benjamin spent the summers visiting friends in Israel. He stayed with Oded Geller and for a few months each year things were just as they had been before. During the daytime, he solidified old friendships and at night he and Oded laid in bed discussing the future, making plans, and dreaming of life as adults.

On one of those days that first summer, he noticed an old acquaintance from school—a girl named Miriam Weizmann. Known to everyone in their class as Micki, she was just a young girl the year Benjamin left for America. Now, as they were both entering high school, she looked different to him. They spent time with the same group of friends that summer and before long he learned she was interested in politics, almost as much as he. They spent long hours discussing the issues of the day, often over coffee at a local cafe, and as the summer months passed, they enjoyed movies together.

One evening late that August, as Oded and Benjamin lay awake, talking, Oded asked, "You like Micki?"

"Yeah," Benjamin said after a moment. "I do like her. She's a lot of fun and she knows a lot about politics. Why do you ask?"

"No real reason. It's just that some of the guys noticed."

"Yeah? What do they say?"

"Ahh, you know, the usual stuff. Some of them think it'll just be a summer romance."

"Last a few months and then fade away?"

"Something like that."

"I don't know if it'll last. I just know I like her and enjoy being with her. And I think she likes being with me."

A few weeks later, with summer coming to an end and school back in Pennsylvania about to begin, Benjamin arranged for a bus ride to the airport. Oded rode with him and they said goodbye at the gate.

33

NETANYAHU

BY 1960, several of the caliphs Zewail had known and worked for in the past had died and younger men had been selected to take their places. The younger members were equally as committed to the Muslim faith as were the older caliphs but they were dissatisfied with the caliphs' prior inability to control affairs in Iraq and Iran.

In Iraq, a coup d'état removed the monarchy from power and placed a succession of generals in control of the country. Now, a younger general, Saddam Hussein, was accruing power to himself. Positioning himself for the next change of leadership.

The caliphs, watching from a distance, thought Hussein was a capable leader, but worried that his recent efforts to obtain arms from the United States would move the country much too close to the US. "Infidels," they asserted, "must not defile our soil *or* our minds. It is our responsibility to make certain that rule is never broken."

In Iran, things appeared even worse. With Shah Pahlavi forced to rely on US support to maintain his hold on the office, he was little more than an American puppet. The younger caliphs were adamant that this situation must change. Not only that, the shah and those holding the upper tier of political appointments were seen by the younger caliphs as corrupt. "If the infidels must not be permitted to corrupt us," the younger caliphs argued, "then we must not allow ourselves to tolerate corruption among our own people. Corruption of a true believer is even more tragic than the intrusion of infidels. We expect the infidels to be ruled by greed and avarice, but *we* must strive for a higher standard. A standard that gives glory to Allah."

The younger caliphs were also dissatisfied with Zewail's work in general and Palestine in particular. "He has been ineffective in Palestine," they said. "Arabs are better armed than before, that much is true, but Jews still live in the land and now they have declared their independence. And even worse, nations of the world are lining up to support them."

Reluctantly, the older caliphs conceded the point and Barakat, still the senior caliph, assigned Musa to handle Zewail's removal. When the decision was announced, Waheed Jannati, one of the younger ones, insisted that a younger caliph be allowed to participate. "How will we know what to do when you are gone if we don't learn while you are here?"

Sensing that the real reason was a lack of trust, Barakat and the older caliphs argued against the inclusion of anyone else. "We have always handled this with one caliph alone," Barakat stated.

"It is indeed a matter of trust," Talal added.

"And," Barakat explained, "a way of insulating the rest of us from knowledge of the acts necessary to effect the order."

"Our request does not arise from a lack of trust," Jannati responded. "But from a desire to learn the ways of the caliphs."

The argument continued for almost an hour when finally the older caliphs relented and appointed Jannati to assist in the matter. "Since you argued for the privilege," Barakat ruled, "you will be the one to experience it."

✦ ✦ ✦

A few weeks later, Zewail was at home in a fourth-floor apartment in Odessa. Samad Harawi, watching from a building across the street, saw him there sitting in a chair near a lamp, reading. Harawi backed away from the window in his apartment, obscuring himself in the shadows, and reached inside his robe for a .45 automatic that was secured in a shoulder holster. He checked to make sure the pistol was loaded, then returned it to the holster. He glanced out the window to check once more and saw Zewail now with his head slumped forward, asleep in the chair.

Harawi made his way quickly downstairs, crossed the street to Zewail's building, and made his way up to the fourth floor. With a quick count of the doors from the end of the building, he located the one to Zewail's apartment. He stood in front of it for a moment, gathering his thoughts about what must happen next, then grasped the door knob lightly, and carefully turned it. To his surprise, the door was unlocked. He quietly pushed it open, then stepped gingerly inside.

A glance down the hall told him the chair where Zewail had been seated was empty. Before he could let go of the knob, Zewail suddenly appeared in the doorway at the far end of the hall. He held an automatic pistol.

Zewail and Harawi stared at each other a moment, then Zewail lowered his pistol, looked over at Harawi and calmly asked, "Would you care for some tea?"

For a moment, Harawi stared at Zewail with a puzzled look, but after a moment he lowered his pistol. "Yes, of course. I would love some tea."

Zewail entered the kitchen, filled a kettle from a shelf by the stove and put on the water, then took down a sugar bowl and tea pot. He held a box of loose tea and spooned some into the bottom of the teapot.

Harawi entered the kitchen and came up behind Zewail. "I assume you know why I'm here."

"Certainly. Either you were sent by the caliphs to relieve me of my duties or you are a senseless pawn in the hands of—" He paused a moment and looked up with a sense of realization. "—any one of several dozen groups we've offended over the years."

Zewail concentrated on preparing the tea as Harawi moved closer, took the pistol from its holster, and placed the end of the barrel against the back of Zewail's head. "I am sorry it has to end this way."

Zewail set aside the box of tea and braced himself with both hands propped against the edge of the countertop. "Tell them it was an honor to serve them."

"Certainly." Harawi then squeezed the trigger and fired a single shot. Zewail's body slumped lifelessly to the floor. Harawi nudged Zewail onto his back, then fired two more shots into the body just to make sure.

✦ ✦ ✦

Two days later, Harawi arrived in Istanbul and appeared before the caliphs. "You were successful?" Barakat asked.

"Yes. Zewail has been relieved of his duties."

"Very well. You were briefed on our current situation?"

"Yes."

"We are concerned about moves toward closer relations to the US in Iraq and Iran," Talal explained. "What are your thoughts on that?"

"There is a cleric in Iran named Ruhollah Khomeini," Harawi replied. "He teaches a highly politicized version of Islam, applying it not only to daily life, but to the government and political affairs."

"Sharia law," someone noted.

Harawi nodded. "He has been an outspoken critic of the shah and the shah's government and has a large following in Markazi province, in northwestern Iran. Most of his followers are young people. Under thirty years of age. I think there is growing unrest among Iranian youth with the presence of Americans on Muslim soil. If we work through Khomeini and the existing younger anti-American groups, I think we might be able to remove the shah and put the country in truly Muslim hands."

"This would be good," Talal acknowledged. "I understand he has developed a structure of government that conforms to Sharia and our oldest traditions."

"I have heard the same thing. But he has moved slowly in creating a movement to make his ideas the law in Iran."

Talal smiled. "Perhaps we can nudge that forward."

"We have heard of him," Barakat noted. "But have never held any consultations with him. Perhaps we should do that now."

"I would be glad to arrange that," Harawi offered.

"Very good," Barakat nodded. "We would be glad to entertain him and consider his thoughts on the subject."

34

NET∧NYAHU

IN MAY 1967, Benjamin completed the required coursework to graduate from high school. On the final day of classes, and after finishing his examinations, he announced to his parents his intention to skip the graduation ceremony, return to Israel, and, like his brother, join IDF.

As with Jonathan, his mother tried to talk him out of it. "You can remain here in America. You don't have to return. You can remain here, become a US citizen, and avoid being forced to serve in IDF."

"But I don't want to be a US citizen and I don't want to avoid the IDF," Benjamin replied. "I am Jewish and I am an Israeli. Israel will always be my home."

"Great," she said. "So are your father and I. We are Jews and Israelis. But you don't have to do it that way. If you become a US citizen you can return to Israel any time you like and live there as long as you like without the service obligation. Many US citizens live there, but they live there as US citizens."

"I don't want to live there as a US citizen," Benjamin insisted. "I want to live there as an Israeli."

Though his mother was outspoken in her objections, his father voiced neither support nor opposition to the decision. "He's a man now," Benzion said. "He can do what he thinks he must do." But unlike the response to Jonathan, there was no open show of pleasure with Benjamin's decision.

Later that month, Benjamin arranged for a taxi ride to the airport, boarded an airliner, and returned to Israel. When he arrived there, he went straight to Micki's house for an emotional reunion with her. After seeing her, though, he decided not to volunteer early but to wait until he was called in the draft for IDF service. In the meantime, he spent the nights with the Gellers as had been his earlier custom and spent the days with Micki.

Two months later, the notice arrived from the IDF informing Benjamin that he was required to give three years of service. Benjamin reported at the induction center as ordered with his friend, Oded Geller who had been called up as well.

They completed basic training in a few months and, like Jonathan, volunteered for IDF Special Forces. Service in that unit required additional training, which they finished in time to see limited action near the end of the 1967 Six Day War.

When the fighting ended, Benjamin remained on active duty but his peacetime assignments did not require him to live on base. He moved from the barracks to an apartment in Jerusalem that he shared with Jonathan. Living there allowed him greater freedom to spend his spare time with Micki. They didn't have much time together, but he saw her as often as possible. And even with that limited time, their relationship grew deeper and more serious every day.

The following year, 1968, Benjamin's unit took part in the Battle of Karameh during a confrontation with forces from the Palestinian Liberation Organization (PLO) and the Jordanian army. The confrontation was known as the War of Attrition and consisted of a series of raids on PLO training camps in an attempt to lessen cross-border guerrilla attacks by the PLO.

In December of that year, Benjamin participated in Operation Gift, a raid on the Beirut Airport. The attack was in response to an attack by forces from the Popular Front for the Liberation of Palestine on an

Israeli El Al Airliner several days earlier. Benjamin and members of his unit destroyed twelve airliners that were parked on the tarmac at the airport.

In 1972, Benjamin was selected as part of a sixteen member special operations unit that participated in Operation Isotope, the rescue of passengers from a Sabena Airlines plane that had been hijacked by four members of a Palestinian terrorist group known as the Black September Organization. During that rescue, Benjamin was wounded in the arm when a hijacker's pistol discharged.

Later that same year, Benjamin's and Geller's initial term of IDF service came to an end. They were both offered the option of renewing for another term but by then, Jonathan had re-enlisted with every intention of making a career in the IDF. With Jonathan finding success in military service, Benjamin decided to step out of his older brother's shadow and pursue a career elsewhere.

As he thought about the options he might have outside of the IDF, he quickly narrowed the list to two primary areas, business and architecture. Those were the two areas that appealed to him most and about which he could speak openly around his father. Secretly he harbored an unstated interest in politics. *That* interest he kept to himself for fear it might conflict with Jonathan's plans. And, more to the point, for fear it might conflict with their *father's* plans for Jonathan's future.

Finally, after weighing all the options carefully, and much to everyone's surprise, Benjamin applied for admission to Massachusetts Institute of Technology—MIT—in Boston. Most people who knew him well thought that once he returned to Israel after completing high school in America, he would never live anywhere but Israel. His decision to study again in America caught them off-guard.

To no one's surprise, however, Benjamin was accepted into MIT's architectural program for the term that would begin the following fall. He was not naturally the most stellar student, but had graduated fourth in his high school class by studying harder and longer and by paying greater attention to detail than his fellow classmates. In light of that accomplishment and the success they'd witnessed from his naturally competitive personality, his friends already knew that when he applied himself to a task, he almost always achieved it. No one doubted for a moment that if he applied to MIT, even with its high academic standards, he would be accepted. And no one doubted that if accepted, he would graduate near the top of his class.

Oded Geller, however, wanted to work as a journalist in radio, television, or newspaper and chose to remain in Israel to pursue that dream. Benjamin tried to persuade him to come to America and study journalism there, but Oded chose Hebrew University instead. "We live in Israel," he explained. "I should learn how to communicate with Israelis."

Meanwhile, at Benjamin's prompting, Micki agreed to join him in studying abroad. She already held a bachelor's degree in chemistry, which she attained with excellent grades, so she applied to a PhD program at Brandeis University. She was accepted in that program with ease.

In Boston, Benjamin and Micki settled into a small apartment which they rented while both of them attended school. Several months later, they were married in a service held on the lawn at the home of Benjamin's uncle in Westchester, New York.

Life together was hectic for Benjamin and Micki but Benjamin couldn't have been happier. He was at last settled in a life with his childhood sweetheart and engrossed in work toward a degree he planned to finish in two years, rather than four. Life couldn't have been better.

Later that year, however, Benjamin's idyllic life was interrupted when he was recalled by the IDF for service during the Yom Kippur War. He traveled to Israel as quickly as possible but even with that he arrived only in time for a brief period of service related to the war. During those months, however, he took part in dangerous and critical raids along the Suez Canal and deep into Syrian territory.

When his obligation to the IDF for the Yom Kippur War was complete, Benjamin returned to Micki in Boston and took up his studies once more. This time, he applied himself even more diligently and finished his degree in architecture in only three years. Immediately after receiving that degree, he enrolled in a master's program at MIT's Sloan School of Management.

35

NET∧NYAHU

BY 1973, Iraq had endured multiple coup d'états that produced successive changes in power before moving into a less turbulent era as elections brought the Ba'ath party into office. Ahmed Hassan al-Bakr, was elected as Iraq's first Ba'ath president and, from the top down, daily life for Iraqis moved toward a more normal routine.

Not long after coming to power, however, Iraqi intelligence sources reported rumors of a supposed surreptitious nuclear research program operating in neighboring Turkey. A check of available information led Iraqi analysts to conclude the program was sponsored by a tightknit group of Turks who wanted al-Bakr removed from office.

In response, al-Bakr decided Iraq should develop its own nuclear program and began quietly asking for help from officials in France and Russia—known nuclear powers. At the same time, he contacted officials in North Korea, which was rumored to have its own nuclear program.

Not long after that, news of al-Bakr's efforts reached Harawi, who moved immediately to limit exposure of the program in Turkey. But rather than deny the program's existence, he traveled to Baghdad where he met with al-Bakr and explained that although the program he'd discovered was in Turkey, it was not a Turkish government program. "The people involved with this program are our people," he explained.

Al-Bark looked puzzled. "Our people?"

"Yes. Our fellow Muslims." Harawi gave al-Bakr a knowing look. "You understand?"

Al-Bakr thought for a moment longer, then a look of realization broke over his face. "Oh," he replied. "You mean the Five Caliphs."

"Yes."

"Well, in that case, I want to meet with them."

Harawi sighed heavily and slowly shook his head. "No," he said with a disapproving expression. "I don't think you want to do that."

"I insist," al-Bakr responded.

Harawi hesitated, then shrugged his shoulders. "Very well. If you insist, I will arrange it."

Al-Bakr smiled. "Good, I shall look forward to our discussion."

✦ ✦ ✦

A few weeks later, al-Bakr appeared before the caliphs in Istanbul and explained his situation. "We understand the position in which you find yourself," Barakat replied when al-Bakr concluded his remarks. "And we are sympathetic to the strain that places on you. However, we are not comfortable with supporting a nuclear program in your country."

Al-Bakr frowned. "I was not aware you felt that way."

"Have you considered Saddam Hussein and his connection to the military encroachment on your civilian government?"

"Yes," Al-Bakr nodded. "Others have pointed this out to me and I have reviewed the actions he has taken over the past twelve months. Some of them bear closer scrutiny. But there is one variable that has been overlooked in this matter."

"What is that?"

"Hussein and I are friends. We were friends before now and we have been allies since we both came into decision-making positions."

Barakat looked a bit skeptical. "It has been my experience that one's friendship in these circumstances only affects the manner in which one is removed from office. When a friend makes the move against you, you get to keep your head. If someone else makes the move," he shrugged, "the head becomes expendable."

"I agree," Jannati added. "Ally or not. Friend or not. When the end comes, friendship will only offer you a graceful exit. That is all. And the end of your time in office is coming quickly."

"I beg to differ," al-Bakr replied. "Hussein and I have known each other as friend and ally in far more difficult circumstances than these."

"Well," Jannati continued, "regardless of that, we have seen for ourselves that Hussein is steadily neutralizing you and steadily gathering more power to himself. Soon, you will be out of office altogether and he will have full control of the government."

"The legislature would never allow such a thing."

"The legislature will never stop him." Talal jumped into the conversation for the first time.

Jannati nodded. "They won't even try."

"These are but a few of our concerns with Hussein," Barakat continued, his tone indicating that the session was coming to an end. "Regardless of your personal position, we cannot support you in this matter. Not with the threat of Hussein hanging over you. If you—"

"I assure you," al-Bakr interrupted. "There is no threat from Saddam Hussein."

A hush fell over the room as all five caliphs braced themselves. An interruption of a caliph was a grave show of disrespect.

Barakat looked away and cleared his throat. "Still," he repeated, obviously troubled by the offense, "that is our decision. If you want our support, you must deal with Hussein and take measures to insure your hold on power. We will not support a program that places such powerful technology in Hussein's hands."

With that, Barakat rose from his chair. He glanced over at Harawi with a knowing look and turned to speak with the others. Harawi took the cue from Barakat and placed his hand on al-Bakr's shoulder. He smiled politely but firmly. "The session is over."

"I had other things to say," al-Bakr protested.

"You have said quite enough for now." Harawi gestured toward the door. "Come," he rose to his feet. "I will show you out."

When al-Bakr was gone, Harawi returned to the room and took his place before the caliphs for further discussion. In a change of protocol, Jannati spoke first. "We have considered your suggestions regarding Khomeini, and are interested in pursuing that relationship."

"Very well," Harawi replied.

"We understand he is living in Paris."

"Yes. He has been exiled from Iran by the shah."

"And that is most troubling," Talal noted.

"That and the shah's relationship with the United States," Barakat added.

Talal shook his head. "It is a sacrilege for a Muslim leader to choose the infidels over his own people."

Jannati spoke up once more. "You are in a position to address this matter now?"

"Yes," Harawi answered. "Shall I leave at once?"

"We would like that very much."

"Then I shall be off."

As Harawi stood to leave Barakat spoke up one last time. "And you will discuss with al-Bakr the proper way to handle himself before us?"

"That shall be the first thing on my list."

✦ ✦ ✦

That evening, Harawi departed Istanbul for Paris where he contacted a friend who, two days later, arranged for him to meet with Ruhollah Moosavi Khomeini, an Iranian Islamic scholar who just a few years later would become an Ayatollah, one of the highest ranks achievable in Islam, return to Iran, and lead a revolution that brought changes to life in every continent on earth. The day Harawi met with him, however, he was an outcast, an exiled dissident living in a small, one-bedroom apartment in Paris and subsisting on gifts provided by his friends and followers.

After appropriate introductions had been made, the two men sat down to talk alone. Harawi outlined the plans that he and the Five Caliphs wished to pursue in order to move the nuclear program out of Turkey and into an appropriate Muslim country.

"We think Iran would be the perfect place for it."

Khomeini had a troubled look. "The caliphs would deliver a full-scale nuclear program to the shah? He already gets what he wants from the United States. They have funded reactors and nuclear power plants in several locations."

"We would never entrust such a program to the shah, but the United States will cease its support of Iran when the shah is removed."

"And who is to remove him?"

Harawi smiled slyly. "You."

A smile broke over Khomeini's face. "The caliphs want to place me over Iran?"

"They want you to lead a revolution to create a truly Islamic state. A state with a government built upon Sharia law, ethos, and philosophy."

"The caliphs will support me in this effort?"

"Yes, they are asking you to do this."

"To replace the shah."

"Yes. You already have a connection with university students in Iran. They want you to build upon those relationships."

Khomeini turned toward a window on the wall at the far side of the room. He stared out at the city for a moment, as if thinking. Then finally he asked, "Why are the Five Caliphs suddenly interested in Iran?"

"They have developed their nuclear program with the assistance of German scientists whom they secretly removed from Germany at the close of World War II."

"So I have heard."

"This is a program established for one purpose. To help spread the message of Islam throughout the world. And to create nations that can serve as sponsors for Islam, to sustain it and support it in attaining the goal of world domination."

Khomeini glanced at Harawi. "This is a military program."

"Yes. At first the program was small and easy to conceal." Harawi continued. "It could be placed almost anywhere. Now, it has grown and has moved into a phase in which it needs state support to continue toward the goal."

"And what is the goal of this program?"

"To produce nuclear weapons."

"For the spread of Islam."

"For the spread of an Islamic revolution built upon your concepts of how in Islam, state and religion are one and the same. You have gained a reputation from your involvement with dissident Iranian youth. Particularly the connection you've made with university students."

Khomeini thoughtfully nodded. "Yes, they are an interesting group. And like you, they approached me. Not the other way around."

"They are wise."

"We shall see."

They discussed the matter further and, as the afternoon wore on, came to an agreement. Khomeini would cooperate with the caliphs and issue recorded messages prepared for Iranian youth. The particular topics would be of his selection, but would fit within an explanation of how the true teachings of Islam and of the prophet Mohamad had been corrupted by the shah and his agents, how the Koran demanded that they purge the nation of such erroneous teachings and rid it of all false teachers.

"And how do you propose to deliver these messages to Iran?" Khomeini asked.

"You have established a means of getting them into the country. They would like for you to continue in that same manner, but at a greater frequency."

"And after they are taken into the country, they are to be distributed among university students in Tehran?"

"Yes."

"Will the Iranian generals side with us in removing the shah?"

"They are as frustrated with him as you," Harawi assured. "They are willing to do whatever we suggest, so long as the shah is removed from power."

"He will have to leave the country," Khomeini insisted.

"Yes," Harawi nodded. "He must."

✦ ✦ ✦

Against the caliphs' explicit instructions and prohibitions, al-Bakr proceeded with efforts to develop Iraq's own nuclear program. A meeting with representatives from both Russia and France produced expressions of interest in the project, but no written commitments of assistance. The caliphs learned of the meeting from the Russian representative who was at the meeting.

At the same time, members of Turkish intelligence became increasingly suspicious of the research institute created as a cover for the caliphs' nuclear program. In response to rumors, Turk agents questioned scientists working at the institute, apparently without knowing their true identities. That activity set the caliphs' nerves on edge.

And, as if not to be outdone by the Turks, American agents increased their presence in Istanbul and other key Turkish cities, though the Americans seemed to have no clue who or what the Turks were investigating. The caliphs, however, were suspicious that the CIA was attempting to infiltrate their nuclear program.

Because of increased intelligence activity in Turkey, the safety and security of the program now became a top priority with the caliphs. They wanted to move the nuclear program out of Turkey immediately and began scouting the region for a stable location. Iran, their optimal choice of sites, was still months, if not years, away from removing the shah and establishing the nation envisioned by Khomeini—a nation in which political power was based on *his* application and interpretation of Islamic law.

A village outside Baghdad, selected earlier for a different plan, was attractive to them but with al-Bakr refusing to follow their directions, the caliphs remained reluctant to pursue that option and needed an alternative to Iraq, at least as a temporary location.

After circulating the issue among themselves through notes and private meetings, the caliphs met formally to discuss the matter. When their discussion had reached its end, Ja'far al-Kadhim, one of the younger caliphs, said what seemed obvious. "There's always Iraq."

Barakat frowned. "What do you mean?"

Kadhim continued. "We don't have to work around Saddam Hussein or al-Bakr. We can use them."

"What does that mean?" Musa asked.

"As of now, we don't have an alternative site for the program, right?"

"Correct."

"And time is now of the essence."

Barakat spoke with an authoritative tone. "Time is most certainly of the essence. We must get the program and our scientists out of Turkey. Before their existence is publicly disclosed."

"So," Kadhim continued, "isn't Iraq—even under Saddam Hussein, and even with al-Bakr—a better alternative than waiting for revolution to change the government in Iran?"

Talal spoke for the first time. "But in Iraq a change of leadership would be necessary for us to have the best circumstance in which to operate. Saddam is not yet in power."

"Actually," Jannati interjected, "Saddam is not that far from having absolute power."

Barakat looked over at Harawi. "Is that correct? Is Saddam Hussein in control of Iraq?"

"He does not yet have total control," Harawi replied, "but removing al-Bakr would not be difficult."

"Easier than what you are doing in Iran?"

Harawi confirmed, "Yes, much easier than Iran."

"And you can do this?"

"Move al-Bakr out and Saddam Hussein in? Certainly," Harawi had no clue how to remove one and install the other, but the last man who held his job came to a painful and unacceptable end over issues just like this. He wasn't giving anyone an excuse to do that to him. "Shall I talk to Hussein?"

"That would be good," Barakat said. "That would be very good."

36

NETANYAHU

MEANWHILE, GIDEON NEYMAN, a supervisor in Mossad's intelligence analysis and assessment section, assembled a team of analysts in a workroom on the sixth floor of the Mossad headquarters building in Tel Aviv. Fashioned from the renovated space of three offices, the workroom covered a quarter of the floor. Oversized desks were arranged in a semicircle near the middle of the room, each equipped with a computer terminal and keyboard that provided direct access to a mainframe computer on the fifth floor.

"Okay," Neyman announced as he made his way past the desks to the front of the room. "Over the past several weeks, our operatives working in Iraq have noticed the presence of what appears to be Russian and French technicians working on the campus of Baghdad University. Agents obtained pictures of these teams and the building where they work and passed the film to us. Our job is to determine who the men are that comprise the teams and why they are there." Neyman glanced around the room with a smile. "So, open your envelopes and get to work. I'll check back with you in a little while and we can talk more then."

Moshe Goldstein, the newest member of the team, spoke up. "That's it? That's all the direction we get?"

Everyone in the room burst into laughter. Mili Dohan shook her head. "That's what they all say the first time."

Goldstein looked embarrassed and then smiled nervously, "I'm just used to a little more direction."

"That's all you get for now," Neyman called back as he turned toward the door. "We'll talk in a little while." And with that he left the room.

When Neyman had gone, the assessment experts spread the photographs on their desks and went to work, scanning them with a handheld loupe to magnify the images. Behind them, analysts worked at three light boxes doing the same thing. The room fell silent for a while, but gradually conversation returned as details from the photographs emerged and the assessment section migrated to the analysts' workstations.

"Anybody got any idea what this building is used for?" Moshe Goldstein asked.

"Looks like a classroom," someone offered. "Not sure which subject, but it looks like a classroom. The windows. The doors. Very utilitarian in function."

Someone spoke up. "What are they teaching?"

"And why are they using Russian and French instructors? Why not American?"

"Or just British?"

"Iraq has a good relationship with all four."

"Maybe the Russians and French gave them a better price on whatever it is they're doing."

"You think price is involved?"

"I don't think they came to Iraq for free."

"But back to the earlier question—why Russian and French? Why invite those two?"

"And look here," Alona Ginzburg pointed to a photograph on her desk. "That guy on the left is a Russian. The guy on the right is French."

Someone leaned over Ginzburg's shoulder. "They're taking a smoke break together."

"Yeah, but look at the smile on his face," she pointed. "And the expression on this one's face. Those two men know each other."

"They've have been working together a while."

"What do the Russians and French have that no one else has?"

"Or maybe that no one else is *willing* to sell to Iraq."

"What would someone not want to sell to Iraq?"

Daniel Dushinsky spoke up. "Well, there's always the obvious."

"Which is...?"

"Nuclear technology."

The room was suddenly silent as they considered the idea for a moment. "Russia and France are two countries that are more than willing to export nuclear technology," someone offered.

"And they've discussed this with Iraq before."

"France tried to underbid the Americans in providing an instructional reactor for the University of Tehran in Iran."

They continued talking as more details emerged from the photographs, were weighed and sifted, then set aside for later consideration. An hour into the process, Neyman returned and the team members began working toward a preliminary assessment of information provided from the photographs. That information was then reduced to writing in a document that raised troubling questions about Russian and French cooperation in Iraq. Particularly disturbing was the suggestion that the presence of technicians seen in the photographs might indicate that Russia and France were providing Iraq with nuclear power plant technology.

The report was passed up the chain of command and eventually reached the desk of Baruch Gutmann, the director of Mossad. He reviewed the report with Amos Megged, Mossad's supervisor of clandestine operations. Together, the two decided to send additional operatives into Iraq to find out what the Iraqi government was doing at the Baghdad University site and at other key locations across the country.

"We have just one problem," Megged noted.

"What's that?"

"With the reassignment of personnel to operations along the Golan Heights and the Sinai, we're stretched pretty thin. We discussed this when we made those assignments."

"I remember. Any ideas about who we could use?" A photograph lay on Gutmann's desk and he tapped it with a pen as he talked. "I think we should have a better look at what's going on in Iraq, but to do that we need more people on the ground there."

"If we only want surveillance," Megged offered, "we could probably take some personnel from IDF Special Forces. They could get in, observe a while, take pictures, and get out. So, that might be an option."

Gutmann's eyes brightened. "That's a good idea."

"Think they would agree to loan us a few?"

"How many do you think it would take?"

"Not that many. Twenty at most. We don't want to invade the place. Just get some people in there. Take a few pictures. Get them out."

"Then we should find out what IDF says about it."

"You want me to ask them?"

"No, I'll find out."

✦ ✦ ✦

As promised, Gutmann met with Major General Yehuda Cohen, the IDF chief of staff, to discuss the proposed joint IDF-Mossad operation in Iraq. Cohen agreed to the request for IDF personnel and passed the project to Yakir Warshel, IDF's chief of operations.

Warshel met with Reshef Livio, Mossad operations director, to establish criteria for use in determining which IDF personnel to use in the surveillance operation, now code named Operation Ezra. Using that selection criteria, they sorted through personnel files looking for soldiers with training and experience specifically suited for the project. Very quickly it became obvious that most of the IDF personnel who met the projects requirements were Special Forces members who had been trained for service in special missions units—ad hoc, lightly armed, quick-strike units assembled as needed to address specific threats. Jonathan Netanyahu was among those approached for the Iraq assignment.

After graduating from high school in Pennsylvania, Jonathan served the mandatory three years active duty in the IDF, and when that obligation was satisfied, he went back to the United States and attended Harvard. He excelled in the study of math and philosophy, and briefly considered a career in that direction, but his love of Israel never left him and at the end of the first academic year he departed Harvard for Israel where he rejoined the IDF. This time, he volunteered for Special Forces and was assigned to Sayeret Matkal, a recon unit trained to gather intelligence deep behind enemy lines.

Not long after joining, Jonathan was recruited for Operation Crate 3, a clandestine maneuver planned for deep inside Syria with the goal of capturing senior Syrian military officers for trade in exchange for captured Israeli pilots. The success of that operation led to his selection for Operation Spring of Youth, a joint Mossad-IDF mission to assassinate the leadership of Black September, a Fatah splinter group.

Jonathan's superior intellect, training, and experience made him an obvious choice to lead Operation Ezra's Special Missions unit. Warshel and Livio approached him first, disclosing only the barest of details in case he turned them down. They needn't have worried. Jonathan would have accepted the assignment blind if they'd asked him.

After securing Jonathan to lead the unit, Livio and Warshel met with him to review the pool of potential personnel to complete the remainder of the unit. They spent the day poring over service files and conducting interviews before choosing six other IDF soldiers to join the unit. Five of them Jonathan knew from prior assignments. A sixth, Naor Berger, Jonathan had never seen before, but Berger had received force recon training with the US Marines at its Camp Pendleton base in California. None of the others, including Jonathan, had been given that kind of training. Jonathan thought he might be particularly useful.

Once they had the team in place, Livio met with Jonathan to discuss the details. They talked late into the night before Livio said, "Don't try to brief your men with this much information. Just stick to the basics. Make it as easy as possible."

"Okay," Jonathan agreed. "What should I tell them?"

"Not much now. We have two agents operating at the university already. They'll contact you when you get there."

"Yes, sir."

"They'll take you to a safe house. Those of you who remain in Baghdad will work from that house. The others will go right on to their assignment. You won't know their location, but if you need to contact them you can do so through the agents already in-country."

"Sounds good," Jonathan nodded.

"All we want you and your men to do," Livio continued, "is observe, photograph, and make notes about what you see."

"Yes, sir."

"Get in. Recon the university. See what you can find. Take pictures. Take notes. Then get out and report back to us."

"Right."

"And by all means, avoid hostile contact at all costs," Livio cautioned.

"Right."

"No fights in a bar over a girl."

"Understood," Jonathan grinned.

"That said," Livio concluded, "if things fall apart, we have a special pickup location at the south end of the soccer field." He pointed to a map. "Right there."

"Okay."

Livio looked over at him. "Do your best to avoid using it."

"Yes, sir."

In spite of the simplicity of their mission, Jonathan spent most of the following week conducting exercises with his men to refresh their use of basic recon techniques and tactics. They did that at a training course located on the far side of Hatzor Airbase.

Early Thursday morning, Jonathan and his team departed Tel Aviv, transited through Jordan, and entered Iraq from the west. Three days later, they reached Baghdad and made contact with two Mossad agents already working in the country. They spent a day reviewing their plans one more time, then four of Jonathan's men left Baghdad to recon locations north of the city, near Mosul and Erbil. Two other team members remained with Jonathan in Baghdad.

Dressed as college students, Jonathan and two men from the unit walked onto campus the next day. They did their best to fit in and worked their way to the building where the Russians and French were previously seen. While the other two men went inside, Jonathan took a seat on a bench out front and, using a Minox camera, snapped pictures of those entering and exiting the building.

An hour later, the two men emerged from the building. One took up a position on the far side of the building, the other man came to the near side. With them for backup, Jonathan moved from the bench and wandered around back.

There was nothing noticeable there but he saw a construction crew at work across the street. Jonathan made his way to the site and snapped pictures as quickly as possible. As he did that, he made mental notes of what he saw—a foundation under construction, concrete reinforced with steel bars, wooden shipping crates to one side.

✦ ✦ ✦

Jonathan and the two men working with him took turns trolling through the construction site, taking pictures as they went. At night, rather than risk trouble, they stayed at the safe house and reviewed their plans for the following day.

A week later, they'd exposed all the film they brought with them and made arrangements to leave. With the help of the two in-country agents, Jonathan and the men who worked with him were reunited with the other four who had gone to different locations. They all spent the night at the Baghdad safe house, then early the next morning began the journey back to Israel and Hatzor Airbase.

When they arrived at Hatzor, the film for the pictures they took in Iraq was dispatched to Mossad headquarters where it was processed and individual images on the film were printed. Late in the afternoon, the prints and negatives arrived at Gideon Neyman's workroom on the sixth floor.

As with the earlier photographs, Neyman's analysts worked methodically through the pictures while members of the assessment team watched over their shoulders.

Daniel Dushinsky pointed to pictures of the building. "That is a classroom."

"What makes you so sure?" Harel Shwartz asked.

"Standard windows on every floor," Dushinsky pointed to the picture. "Air conditioners on top of the building."

"Nothing so big about that, is there?"

"They don't have a central chiller system. Look at the other photographs." Alona Ginzburg turned to a table and picked up a stack of pictures. "Look through these." She handed the stack to Shwartz. "All of the known classroom buildings on the site look just like this one we're looking at now. They all have their own AC units."

"It's a classroom." Dushinsky said. He reached over Shwartz's shoulder and tapped the picture in Shwartz's hand. "Students with books. Notebooks. Entering the building."

"What about the site in back?"

Rami Damari handed a photograph over his shoulder. "Somebody needs to check on this one."

"What about it?"

"Take a look at the wooden crates. Check the numbers on them."

Mili Dohan took the photograph to her desk near the center of the room, where she hoped to examine it without being interrupted by the others. Using a loupe to magnify the image, she worked her way across the photograph, beginning in the lower right corner of the picture. Alona Ginzburg joined her. "What do you see?"

Rather than bothering her, the sound of Ginzburg's voice was actually welcome. Dohan pointed to the picture and handed the loupe to Ginzburg. "Numbers. There's a crate near the corner of the picture. Check out the numbers on it."

"Yeah." Ginzburg held the loupe over the image. "Write these down."

"Okay. Read it out. I'll write it down."

"One nine six five three. LD. Zero, two, zero.

"What's it mean?"

"LD is the airline designator. Lufthansa. The zero, two, zero after it are for Lufthansa Cargo. That's one of the numbers stenciled on the crate."

"What about the other one?"

"Looks like a manufacturer's mark. Something to keep track of the crate's contents in the warehouse."

"What is it?"

"ASZ32873TRN and N-25004."

"Anything else? What about the paper stapled to the edge?"

"LFPG on the top one. There's more underneath it but I can't read it."

"Now we just need to decipher the numbers and letters."

"Well, we know about the Lufthansa designations. They shipped this on a Lufthansa Cargo plane."

"And the routing tag?"

"Assuming that's what it is—and I'm pretty sure it is—then LFPG is Charles de Gaulle airport in Paris. That's the International Air Transport Association's designator."

"That still leaves the other ones. ASZ32873TRN and N-25004."

Ginzburg took a seat in a nearby chair. "Let me see it on the page." Dohan handed her the notepad where she'd written the number. Ginzburg studied it a moment, trying to think of what it might mean.

A few minutes later, Moshe Goldstein moved behind Ginzburg. He looked over her shoulder at the pad. "That's an N-type certification number. Did that come from one of these photographs?"

Dohan handed him the photograph she'd been examining, then offered him a loupe. "Have a look. The numbers are from a crate in the lower right corner of the picture."

Goldstein scanned the corner of the picture with the loupe. "Yeah. That's an ASME N-Type certification. American Society of Mechanical Engineers."

"So," Ginzburg said. "Whatever is in that crate has been certified for use in a nuclear power plant."

"In America?"

"Yes. But that doesn't mean it came from America. It just means that the standard that was applied was one developed by ASME."

"So, the contents of the crate meet ASME standards."

"Yes. But it doesn't mean the project has approval of anyone,"

Goldstein explained. "It just means the parts in that crate meet ASME standards. European manufacturers routinely use that standard because it is accepted by most other countries in Europe."

"And it means that whatever they're building has something to do with a nuclear power plant," Ginzburg added.

"Yeah," Goldstein acknowledged. "It doesn't mean that they're building a plant. This is from a construction project on a university campus. Could be a portion of the plant. For instructional purposes."

"Not much sense in spending money for that, though," Dohan noted. "Might as well build the whole thing."

"That's what they did in Iran," Ginzburg added.

"And that's what India did," Goldstein nodded.

"Any reason why that crate is sitting out there?"

"I don't know," Goldstein replied. "Do we have pictures from other days at this site?"

"Yes," Dohan answered.

"Let's take a look at them. The crate might have been delivered to the site on the day this photograph was taken, then moved to storage after that. They wouldn't leave these components out in the weather. This site is in the early stages. It'll be a while before they need the parts in this crate."

"Why do you say that?"

Goldstein pointed to the photo. "You can see in between the slats at the top. Looks like tubing of some kind. And that right there is a pressure relief valve. This stuff would be installed much later in construction."

Using numbers from the crate, Goldstein determined that items in the shipping crate originated from CAC Motil, a French manufacturer of power plant components. A check of people captured in other photos from the site yielded close-up views of two men wearing ID tags bearing the CAC Motil logo. Personnel rosters acquired from earlier regulatory disclosure reports showed the two men were Motil employees in the company's nuclear power plant division.

Based on information from photographs of the crate and details gleaned from similar photos taken at the site, Neyman and his team prepared a report indicating that the construction site was most likely being developed as a nuclear reactor. Probably with the notion of using it to operate an electric power generating plant. When the team was satisfied with the wording, Neyman forwarded the report for the director's review.

NETANYAHU

IN IRAN, the Ayatollah Khomeini's taped addresses continued to circulate among university students, finding an enthusiastic reception most notably with those at the University of Tehran. As Harawi had hoped, it wasn't long before student enthusiasm boiled over onto the streets of Tehran. Daily protests, which varied in size from a few hundred to a thousand or more, soon became the norm.

The shah, physically weaker with more health issues than most people knew, relied heavily on SAVAK, the Iranian secret police and intelligence service, to keep demonstrators away from the palace and other government buildings, and to impose order in the streets. His heavy-handed approach kept the government and country functioning, but resulted in the arrest and imprisonment of thousands of political activists. The nation's political prisoner population swelled dramatically, all of which served to intensify student opposition to the shah's rule.

Video of the demonstrations was broadcast by PARS, the official government news agency, in heavily edited news reports. Broadcasts included voice-over commentary favorable to the shah and supportive of the actions his government took to quell the demonstrations, but everyone viewing the reports saw for themselves the brutality employed by police officers in their attempts to control the students.

Interviews of students prepared by reporters working with news agencies based in Qatar were much less favorable to the shah and his government. Those interviews were broadcast into Iran where—in spite of government attempts to block the transmissions—they were viewed by groups of Iranians who had satellite receivers and broadcast decoding equipment. They, in turn, recorded the reports and distributed them.

The reports produced sympathetic support for the student protesters. They also focused attention on the shah's ties with US government agencies, particularly the CIA, which served to broaden the students' base of support among older Iranians.

Demonstrators, buoyed by growing support from Iranian citizens who were not students, and energized by reports of CIA involvement, vilified the shah as an agent of American infidels and focused attention on the corruption of the royal family as proof of his inability to continue as the nation's leader. In response, still more students joined the crowds in the street, which grew larger every day.

With the protests in Iran seemingly unstoppable, Muslim students in countries throughout Europe, Asia, and parts of Africa took up the cause, either sending students to Tehran to lend their support or by launching their own demonstrations in the cities where they lived. As a result, student protests sprang up on the streets of many Middle Eastern cities.

At a pace alarming to the West, Muslim student protests quickly gave way to an Islamic revival that swept through the Middle East. With it came a rising tide of anti-American sentiment that found support throughout the region—with the singular exception of Israel.

✦ ✦ ✦

By 1976, numerous small cells of dissident Muslims were established in key countries around the world, including the US, France, the United Kingdom, Germany, and Canada. Those cells, dormant but tightly organized, had been established with cover from local mosques in major cities such as New York, Los Angeles, Paris, Berlin, and London. As protests in Iran gave way to open demonstrations, cells in the West became restless and eager to join the Islamic cause.

Unlike the students protesting in Islamabad, Karachi, and Tehran, members of the foreign cells operating under the cover of a local mosque received training in a radicalized version of Islam through weekly classes conducted by experienced clerics. Members of the cells who achieved high grades in class were sent abroad for sophisticated military training at bases located in Afghanistan and in remote portions of Pakistan. During that training, participants learned to combine their radical view of Islam with the use of military force to effect the spread of Islam. Comprised of men slightly older than the students, the groups tended to be settled, disciplined, and committed to a long-term plan.

Even more unlike the students in Tehran, these foreign cells were planning for aggressive, high-casualty action—truck bombs, car bombs, suicide bombs, and hijackings. That they were growing restless and eager to step into the fight posed a serious risk to the West, a risk that no one in the West fully understood.

One of those groups operating abroad was The Popular Front for the Liberation of Palestine (PFLP). Under the leadership of George Habash, PFLP established cells in East Jerusalem and Bethlehem that were obvious and active in Palestinian politics. Not so obviously, it established cells in Lebanon, Libya, Athens, and other locations outside of Palestine that operated out of the public eye.

Habash, a medical school graduate and practicing physician, founded PFLP as a leftwing political group through which he hoped to transform the Arab self-understanding from its backward perspective into one that reflected a twentieth century worldview. He attempted to do this primarily through political education and activism. His deputy, Wadie Haddad, however, was more interested in the use of force. Haddad, on his own, directed numerous PFLP attacks first on Israeli sites within Palestine and later on sites abroad that had an Israeli connection. Those attacks led to a fracturing of the relationship between Habash and Haddad.

By 1976, Haddad was openly recruiting PFLP members from the secretive cells abroad for use in his attacks outside of Palestine—a strategy that threatened to expose the cells to the public. To lend credence to those efforts and to deflect public attention away from the foreign cells, Haddad conducted his operations abroad under the name of the Popular Front for the Liberation of Palestine—External Operations (PFLP-EO).

On June 27, 1976, an Air France flight departed Tel Aviv bound for Paris. Not long after take-off, four passengers—two who were members of PFLP-EO and two who were members of a group known as German Revolution Cells—hijacked the flight. The plane landed at its scheduled first stop in Athens where it was joined by four additional hijackers. The plane then departed Athens for Benghazi, Libya, before continuing on to Entebbe, Uganda, where it was welcomed by Uganda's president, Idi Amin, who was accompanied by a detachment of troops from the Ugandan army.

After hours spent in the plane while it was parked on the tarmac in Entebbe, the hijackers moved passengers from the airplane into an old, unused terminal building. The hostages included eighty-four Israeli citizens. Once the hostages were inside the terminal building, the hijackers issued their demands—release pro-Palestinian prisoners being held in Israel in exchange for release of the hostages. They furnished a list of the specific prisoners they wanted set free.

Israel, under Prime Minister Yitzhak Rabin, established communications with the hijackers through Amin and attempted to gain the hostages' freedom through diplomatic negotiations. When that proved unsuccessful, a joint IDF-Mossad rescue operation was approved. Jonathan Netanyahu, then a Lt. Colonel, led the ground team tasked with the responsibility of entering the terminal building and freeing the hostages. July 4 was set as the date for that operation.

✦ ✦ ✦

By then, Benjamin had completed his master's degree at MIT and was working as an economic consultant with Boston Consulting Group. He was working there when news of the IDF raid at Entebbe reached US news outlets. Benjamin watched the television reports intently, wondering if Jonathan had been included in the rescue team. He wasn't worried. Jonathan was a highly skilled, expertly trained soldier and if he had the opportunity, Benjamin was certain he would have volunteered for the mission. But he wanted to know, one way or the other. As the day wore on and still there was no news about Jonathan, Benjamin made calls back to Israel contacting Oded Geller and other friends who might know more than was being reported on television.

Late that afternoon, Benjamin received a phone call from the Israeli embassy in Washington. The caller's voice was tense and formal and right away Benjamin knew the call was not good news. "I am Simcha Dinitz, at the Israeli Embassy in Washington, DC. I'm afraid I have some bad news for you, Benjamin."

"Yes, Mr. Ambassador?"

"As you've probably heard already, a special unit of our elite IDF forces conducted an operation at the Entebbe airport to rescue our citizens who were being held as hostages."

"Yes, sir."

"Your brother was the commander of that unit. And I am sad to inform you that during the course of that operation your brother was mortally wounded."

For a moment there was only silence on both ends of the conversation. "We are still gathering details about the matter, but I can tell you Jonathan was the only casualty of the operation. He was a brave man, Benjamin."

Benjamin was crushed by the news but as much as he wanted to sink into the depths of his own remorse, he thought immediately of his parents. "Have my parents been notified?"

"No. We called you first."

"Don't contact them. I'll visit them and tell them in person," Benjamin insisted.

"Okay. Let us know if we can help with arrangements."

"I will."

Having moved on from Dropsie, Benizon was teaching at Cornell University, located in Ithaca, New York, eight hours away from Boston. Determined that his parents should hear the news of Jonathan's death from a family member, he and Micki left that afternoon, drove straight through the night, and reached his parent's home early the next morning.

When they arrived, Benjamin peeked through the front window

and saw his father seated in front of the television in the living room. A remote in one hand, he switched between broadcast channels, shouting at the screen as he sorted through the morning news shows, no doubt looking for news of Jonathan.

From the look on his face, Benjamin knew what he was saying. "Come on. Why can't you report some real news?" Only he said it in Hebrew.

In the background, beyond the living room, his mother was seated at a table in the breakfast room. She had the morning paper folded and glanced at it as she ate. Benjamin watched them a moment, burning the image into his mind, fully aware that the moment he told them about Jonathan their lives would change forever.

Micki nudged his elbow. "Open the door. Let's go inside."

"Probably locked."

"Then ring the bell."

With a heavy sigh, Benjamin pressed the button on the doorframe, then waited. A moment later, his father's face appeared in the window above. At first Benzion had an expression of surprise, but that quickly faded as he saw the look on Benjamin's face. There was a rattle as he unlocked the door, then pulled it open.

"What happened?" he asked. "You didn't come out here on a whim."

By then, Celia was at the door, peering between the doorframe and Benzion's shoulder. "This is about Jonathan," she said, staring Benjamin in the eye. "Isn't it?"

"Yes, Mom."

"No!!" she shouted as she backed away, waving her hands in protest. "No! No! No!" She disappeared in the background and Micki pushed past them to follow her.

Benzion's hands shook and his voice trembled. "So, this is about Jonathan?"

"Yes, Dad. Jonathan is dead."

"I knew it!" Benzion shouted. "I knew it! I knew it! I knew it." He moved away from the door and collapsed into the chair by the television. Benjamin followed him and switched off the TV.

"He was in charge of the unit that made the raid at Entebbe," Benjamin explained. "They got everyone out safely. But he was killed."

"How many other men were killed?"

"He was the only one of ours. I don't know about the rest."

"When did it happen?"

"Yesterday, July 4."

"July 4," Benzion whispered. "A day for the Americans. And now a day for us." He looked away as tears filled his eyes. His lips trembled and he put his hand to his mouth, but the trembling became a sob and the tears that pooled in his eyes suddenly streamed down his cheeks. "So many plans... It was not supposed to end like this!"

As Benzion said those words his body began to shake, then went limp and he slid from the chair onto the floor where he landed on his knees and fell forward on his face, crying out in a groan that was both grievous and primordial. He struggled to make sense of what he'd just been told.

"Yoni! Yoni! Yoni!" he cried, using the name they'd first used when he was a baby. "You were my Yoni. You were the first. You were my best."

As Benzion lay face down on the floor, Benjamin sat by helplessly at first, then dropped to the floor beside his father and, for the first time since speaking with the embassy, allowed himself to dwell on the loss of Jonathan. Soon, he too, was overcome with emotion, joining his father in groans and sobs that went beyond words.

In the midst of their anguish, Iddo, a student at Cornell, came from his bedroom. By the tearful streaks down his cheeks, Benjamin knew he'd overheard enough to know that Jonathan was dead.

"Yoni is gone?" he asked.

"Yes," Benjamin replied. "He was commander of the team that raided Entebbe."

Tears returned to Iddo's eyes. "Yeah," he nodded. "Exactly what I expected." He wiped his eyes with the back of his hands. "Anyone else die?"

"None of ours."

Iddo shook his head. "I know I'm not supposed to, but I wish it was someone else." He collapsed against Benjamin's shoulder as sobs shook his body.

Sometime later that day, arrangements were made for the family to quickly return to Israel for Jonathan's funeral. They were joined there by Iddo.

Jonathan was eulogized by Shimon Peres, Israel's Defense Minister, in a military funeral attended by a large crowd with many dignitaries. Afterward, he was buried on Mount Herzl.

As the service came to a close, friends and relatives gathered around Benzion and Celia to express their condolences. Benjamin lingered with them until Oded Geller joined him. "Come with me," Geller urged. He grasped Benjamin's elbow and pulled him along. "We need to talk."

"Okay," Benjamin acquiesced. "But I don't have much time for—"

"You've got enough time for this."

Benjamin drew back from Geller's grasp but followed him a short distance away. Geller glanced over his shoulder, then leaned close and lowered his voice. "I have something for you."

Benjamin had a puzzled frown. "What is it?"

"It's from Jonathan."

Benjamin's look of surprise quickly faded to one of confusion. "What are you talking about?"

"I don't know."

"Oded, you aren't making any sense."

"Just come down to the car." Geller pointed down the hill. "I'll show you."

A white BMW was parked a short distance away. When they reached it, Oded gestured toward the passenger door. "Get in."

"I can't go anywhere," Benjamin protested. "I have to go with my family to my uncle's house." He glanced over his shoulder as if checking. "They're probably ready to go right now."

"We aren't going anywhere. And this won't take long. Just get in. I'll explain."

Benjamin opened the passenger door and waited while Oded made his way around to the opposite side of the car. "Okay," Benjamin said when they were seated inside. "What's this all about?"

"The day the story about the raid at the airport broke on the news, I found this on the dining room table at my apartment." Oded reached beneath the car seat and took out a large manila envelope. "No postage, no address, just my name on the front." He handed it to Benjamin.

"What makes you think it's for me?"

"Look inside."

One end of the envelope had been torn open. Benjamin glanced to see inside, then emptied the contents onto his lap. A note and a small, square package wrapped in brown paper tumbled out. He folded back the note and read. "Oded, I'm not sure what will happen in the next few days. If things work out, I'll be back to get this. If not, please deliver this to my brother Benjamin." Tears filled Benjamin's eyes. "He left this with you, for me?"

"Yeah, but here's the thing. It showed up the day the story of the raid appeared on the news. By then, Jonathan was already dead."

"So, any idea who brought it?"

"No. I asked around, you know. To see if anyone had seen anyone around the apartment that day, but they all said no." Geller pointed to the smaller package. "Do you know what that is?"

"Yeah." Benjamin held the package in his hands. "I think I know exactly what it is." After a moment he stuffed it into the pocket of his jacket and smiled over at Geller. "Thanks."

"You aren't going to open it?"

"Not now." Benjamin reached for the door handle. "I'll take care of it later."

"And you'll tell me what it is?"

"Maybe. One day." Benjamin opened the door. "But don't tell anyone about this, okay?"

✦ ✦ ✦

The loss of their oldest child was devastating to Benzion and Celia and while they were in Israel they discussed what to do next. Before returning to the US, they decided that Benzion would retire and they would return to Israel to live permanently, perhaps in a home near Tel Aviv.

For Benjamin, the loss of Jonathan was a turning point, too, but not in a good way. He and Jonathan had been close and his absence turned Benjamin's world upside down. As the older brother, Jonathan was the one who was expected to be the great achiever, the one with the notable career. Now, with him gone, that role fell to Benjamin. It was a role he had never seen himself fulfilling.

Adrift and aimless, Benjamin and Micki returned to Boston. Benjamin applied himself at work and spent time with Micki, trying to think of other things he could do besides the job at Boston Consulting Group. Something that might matter more than simply working in Boston and making money. During that time, Micki became pregnant. Benjamin was excited by the prospect of his first child, but was still adrift and searching for direction for his life.

At the office, Benjamin was placed in charge of a team working with a group of new clients. The assignment was a reward for his hard work and gave him a chance to significantly increase his income. One of the team members was a woman named Fleur Cates, an American whose father was Jewish. She and Benjamin spent long hours together, preparing complicated investment plans for their clients. Intelligent and witty, Benjamin enjoyed working with her and found their time together a relaxing escape from the tension he felt at home and from the emptiness he felt inside after the loss of Jonathan.

Over the next few months, Benjamin's hours at work grew longer and longer. He left the house early in the morning and came home late at night. He and Micki saw less and less of each other. Weekends, once reserved for family and friends, were now devoted to work. During the few hours that he *was* at home he was often tense and moody.

Finally, one evening, Micki told him she'd had enough. "I'm going back to Israel," she announced. Benjamin tried to persuade her to stay, but she said her mind was made up. She completed work on her degree, gave birth to their baby, then packed her belongings and moved back to Tel Aviv.

Still interested in repairing the relationship, Benjamin traveled back and forth between the US and Israel hoping to make things right with Micki. The distance, however, made regular travel difficult and as the year went by, he thought of returning to Israel, too, only this time as a permanent resident. Inside, he still hoped to reconcile with Micki, but he also thought of doing something to honor Jonathan. Something bigger than a plaque or scholarship. Perhaps a permanent organization to address the issues that gave rise to the trouble at Entebbe.

Using company resources, he searched for businesses in Israel where he might work. His attention soon focused on Rim Industries, a furniture manufacturer. He sent the company his resume and asked to discuss a position in marketing. After a series of interviews, he was offered a job, which he accepted.

A few weeks later, Benjamin resigned from the Boston Consulting Group, returned to Israel, and moved into a spare room at his parents' home. Not long after arriving, Benjamin talked to his parents about the mess he'd made of his marriage with Micki. "I would reconcile with her right now, but she isn't interested in that. Could you two talk to her? She might listen to you."

Benzion and Celia talked do Micki, but it did little good. "It's really over," Benzion reported. "She's filing for divorce." Benjamin felt guilty over the way things had turned out but there was little he could do to rectify the situation.

Several months after the divorce from Micki became final, a business trip took Benjamin to New York. Single and no longer constrained by marriage, he contacted Fleur, who was living in Manhattan. They had dinner together and spent the next few days roaming the city, enjoying each other's company.

Later, as Benjamin packed to return to Israel, he and Fleur made plans to continue their relationship even from a distance. "I'll come here," he said. "You can come there. We will visit. This will work out. I don't know how, but it will work out."

A whirlwind romance followed and during one of Benjamin's subsequent trips to New York they got married. Even then, Fleur still didn't want to live in Israel and he wouldn't move to New York. Instead, they were forced to continue living on separate continents, only now they did so as husband and wife.

38

NETANYAHU

IN IRAN, the shah's health continued to decline as unrest mounted in the streets of Tehran. Khomeini followers—many of them university students—organized themselves into a functioning group known as Muslim Student Followers of the Imam's Line. That September, the group called for a nationwide general strike which paralyzed the country.

All across the city, students attacked government buildings, foreign embassies, banks, and organizations viewed as a source of Western influence. Confrontations with the police grew more violent.

Finally, in November, after months of steadily rising tension, the shah announced he was leaving the country. The stated reason was his need to seek medical care for non-Hodgkin's lymphoma that could only be found abroad. Most people understood it as his abdication. From Paris, Khomeini instructed protestors to let the shah depart.

The day after the shah left Tehran, Khomeini returned. He was welcomed at the airport by an excited and overflowing crowd that ushered him down the street toward the center of the city.

Calm returned to the nation and within the following week Khomeini appointed a provisional government that quickly issued a call for a new constitution. Key clerics from across the country were summoned for a meeting in Tehran. There, the clerics developed plans for an Islamic regime, based on Sharia law, to rule Iran.

MIKE EVANS

While the clerics met, a group of students attacked the US embassy. At first their only intention seemed to be simply to make a point. They overwhelmed the guards and broke inside the compound. Police and embassy guards easily rounded them up and cleared the compound. That afternoon and evening, nonessential personnel were removed from the embassy and sent home.

Early in the morning two days later, another group of students gathered in front of the embassy. This time, the crowd was more militant than before and steadily grew in size. At midmorning, the students surged forward and swarmed over the gates in numbers too large for the guards to control.

The students easily took control of the grounds inside the compound and began moving from building to building, rounding up embassy employees and moving them to the consular affairs wing. This time, guards and embassy personnel were unable to dislodge them and by noon, fifty-two embassy employees had been seized as hostages.

Over the next few months, Khomeini and Iran's leading clerics successfully established the Islamic Republic of Iran, a nation ruled by a civilian government that included a popularly elected president and parliament. That civilian apparatus, however, was ultimately accountable to the nation's supreme leader, an Islamic cleric of the highest order, who was selected by a council of theological experts. The council's first official decision was to select the Ayatollah Ruhollah Khomeini as the nation's first supreme leader.

Though the government was nothing like what the West was used to, it was successful in restoring order. Except for those still holding hostages from the US embassy, the students who led the uprising returned to class and life in Iran soon returned to normal.

✦ ✦ ✦

With stability in Iran assured, and with the nation firmly under the control of Islamic theologians and clerics, the caliphs in Istanbul directed Harawi to transfer the nuclear scientists to Iran. Though unsettled at first by the move, the scientists found ready support and

348

quickly settled into place. Their work, largely limited thus far to papers and plans, received a similar greeting.

Though Iran had maintained a nuclear program under the shah, including several reactors and a modest stockpile of fuel, the program had fallen into disrepair during the later years of his rule as technicians loyal to the shah disappeared. At the same time Russia, one of the program's primary sponsors, secretly moved the nuclear fuel out of the country. By the time Khomeini returned to take control of the government, the existing reactors were inoperable and useless.

Rather than attempting to rejuvenate those existing and outdated facilities, the new effort concentrated on developing a new program. In the spirit of the Islamic Revolution, their program was touted as one that used uranium from indigenous Iranian sources to power reactors built solely by Iranians. A Muslim program, giving the world an all-Muslim nuclear reactor.

39

NETANYAHU

ONCE AGAIN living in Israel and working for Rim to strengthen and expand its marketing department, Benjamin began to develop plans for an institute to honor his brother, Jonathan. At first it was just an idea, then a collection of thoughts that he rolled around in his head as he went through the day. But over time, those ideas gave way to the notion of a permanent, lasting memorial.

An institution, he thought to himself as the concept became clearer. *One that will alert the world to the growing threat of global terrorism—the very thing that cost Jonathan his life. And not just a place for people to talk about it, but a place where they can come to work together in ways that move all of us toward eliminating the threat at the root.*

When he'd pushed the idea through several conceptual stages, Benjamin decided he'd gone as far as he could go without involving others and going public with the idea. But before he could do that, he needed to discuss the matter with his parents. Jonathan might have been his brother, but he was their son. He couldn't go forward with the idea without their support. After a moment to consider how best to do that, he decided to bring up the subject after dinner the following night.

"It would be an organization to promote the awareness of terror and the threat it poses to all of us," he explained, as he sat at the table and showed his parents the details he'd worked on thus far. "And it would work on a permanent basis to find solutions to the problem of global terrorism."

To Benjamin's great relief, his parents liked the idea and in the weeks that followed he began making concrete plans for the Jonathan Netanyahu Institute on Terrorism. The next year, the Institute was officially established and Benjamin was hard at work on the first of what he hoped would be the institute's many events.

✦ ✦ ✦

Later that year, as the third anniversary of Jonathan's death drew near, Benjamin wondered whether to mark the day with a strong publicity effort, foreshadowing the conference he was developing, or to observe it at home, alone with his parents. Both approaches had merit. Publicizing the terrorism conference would help drive up public awareness and interest. Spending the day, just the three of them, would keep it a personally private one, and would not subject his parents to any additional pressure from reporters.

In the end, Benjamin chose the latter—to spend the day at home, out of the public eye. He looked forward to devoting the time to reading, remembering, and thinking of what might have happened if Jonathan had lived.

Around one that afternoon there was a knock at the front door. Benjamin heard his father answer it and after a few minutes he walked into the living room to see who the caller might have been. Benzion was standing beside a rather tall man with dark hair, and a slender build. "Benjamin," Benzion said. "This is David Mickelson, a rabbi from New York."

"Good to meet you." Benjamin shook his hand and then glanced over at Benzion. "You two know each other?"

"Not at all," Mickelson answered. "I know this is the third anniversary of Jonathan's death. I read about it today in the Jerusalem Post, and that you would be remembering Jonathan at home with your father.

I just wanted to come by and let you know that I remembered him and his heroic actions, too. I know you are proud of him."

"Yes, we are."

Benzion gestured to the sofa. "Have a seat." He moved to a chair while Mickelson came around the end of the sofa. "Join us, Benjamin," Benzion added as he took a seat. "We can spare a little time for a visitor from New York." He looked over at Mickelson. "You know, I lived in New York once upon a time."

Mickelson nodded. "Yes, I read that somewhere. When you were working for Ze'ev Jabotinsky." They sat quietly a moment, then Mickelson said, "You both must have had dreams and plans for the future with Jonathan."

Benzion smiled. "Yes, I worked with him. He was a capable young man, and we expected a lot from him."

Mickelson looked over at Benjamin. "But *you* didn't expect anything, did you?"

Benjamin's eyes narrowed and a frown wrinkled his forehead. "I'm not sure what you mean by that."

"You simply enjoyed his presence," Mickelson elaborated. "And the way his presence insulated you from expectation."

"I don't think that's anything for you—"

"I know." Mickelson gestured apologetically with both hands. "It's rather abrupt for a stranger to come to your house and start talking about family matters, but it's true. As long as Jonathan was alive, you were protected. Now that he's gone, the expectations shift to you."

Benjamin stood. "I think it's time for you to leave now."

"Okay." Mickelson rose from his place on the sofa and turned toward Benjamin. "But before I go, I have a Word from the Lord for you."

Benjamin appeared indignant. "A word from the Lord?"

Mickelson placed his hands on Benjamin's shoulders. "This is what the Lord says to you. 'Jonathan loved his friend David; you loved your brother Jonathan. Out of the ashes of your despair will come strength from Me, and you will be the prime minister of Israel twice. The second time will be the most dangerous days of Israel's history.'

Before Benjamin could respond, Mickelson continued. "Benjamin, you are the Netanyahu. The one given by God. The one to whom the Promise of God has passed from previous generations and now finds its resting place in you. A promise given long ago will find its fulfillment in you and through you God will make Himself evident to the world."

Mickelson looked over at Benzion. "You have the ring?"

Benzion had a startled look. "What ring?"

"The Netanyahu ring," Mickelson explained.

"I gave..." Benzion stammered. "I gave it to Jonathan."

Mickelson had a kindly smile. "And now you think it is lost?"

Benzion sighed. "It was not among Jonathan's things."

"The ring is never lost," Mickelson explained. "It always follows the promise." He turned to Benjamin. "You know where it is, don't you?"

Benjamin nodded in Benzion's direction. "I know he gave it to Jonathan."

"Yes, and Jonathan gave it to you."

"I don't think—"

"Go get the ring," Mickelson urged in a friendly way. "Go get it and bring it out here."

Reluctantly, Benjamin retreated to the bedroom and a moment later returned with the small wooden box.

Mickelson's face brightened at the sight of it. "Open it."

Holding the box in the palm of his hand, Benjamin lifted the lid. The ring rested inside.

Benzion bristled at the sight of it. "How long have you had this?"

"Oded Geller gave it to me on the day of the funeral."

"Oded?" Benzion's voice was even sharper than before. "Why did he have it?"

"Jonathan sent it to him the day he left for Entebbe."

"Why didn't he send it to me?"

"I don't know." Benjamin shrugged. "I guess he didn't have time."

"I looked everywhere for it," Benzion continued. "Why didn't you tell me you had it?"

"Micki and I returned to Boston the day after the funeral. How was I supposed to know you were looking for it?"

"I didn't—"

Mickelson interrupted, "Regardless of how you came to have it, the ring follows the promise and it is here now. The ring of promise in the hands of the child of promise. The Netanyahu of this generation."

They talked a while longer, then Mickelson left. As they closed the door behind him, Benjamin looked over at Benzion. "What a moron," he chortled.

"Not an ordinary moron," Benzion noted. "But a genuine moron."

"How did he know about the ring?"

Benzion shook his head. "I don't know."

"Maybe there's more to this than either of us realizes."

"Perhaps." Benzion turned away. "I...I don't know. Look, I need a few minutes." He strode across the room and disappeared down the hallway.

Benjamin stood alone in the living room with the box in his hand as he tucked the lid beneath his arm and used his free hand to take out the ring. He'd studied it many times since Geller brought it to him, seeing it as an artifact from an ancient time in Jewish history. This time, however, he sensed something greater in it than merely an heirloom from three thousand years ago. This time, it seemed a thing of wonder. A thing of mystery. A thing of power.

Carefully, he slipped it onto the ring finger of his right hand. It slid over his knuckle and glided easily into place but was far too large. He twirled it around with his thumb once or twice, then slipped it off and dropped it into box. But as he replaced the lid, a second thought came to him and he lifted the ring from the box, then carefully placed it in his trouser pocket.

✦ ✦ ✦

The following day, at the invitation of Dan Ramon, a friend, Mickelson attended a Torah study at the home of Israeli Prime Minister, Menachem Begin. The study focused on verses from Deuteronomy and lasted several hours. When it was over, Ramon and Mickelson worked their way through the crowded room to Begin's side.

"Mr. Prime Minister," Ramon announced. "This is my friend, Rabbi David Mickelson. He's visiting here from New York."

"Mr. Prime Minister," Mickelson said. "It's good to see you."

"Yes, David," Begin replied. "What brings you all the way over here?"

"Business."

"To what do I owe this honor?"

"I went to the home of Benzion Netanyahu yesterday to comfort the family on the third anniversary of Yoni's death and while I was there I met the prime minister of Israel."

Begin frowned and shook his head. "No, I did not meet with you yesterday."

"It wasn't you, sir" Mickelson explained. "It was Benjamin Netanyahu."

"Who is he?" Begin asked. "I have never met him."

"He is the son of Benzion Netanyahu and the brother of Yoni Netanyahu."

"How do you know these things?"

"While I was there, the Word of The Lord came to me. And this is what the Lord said: 'Jonathan loved his friend David; Benjamin, you loved your brother Jonathan. Out of the ashes of your despair will come strength from Me, and you will be the prime minister of Israel twice. The second time will be the most dangerous days of Israel's history.'"

"And what does this have to do with me?"

"I think you should give him a job."

"To this Benjamin Netanyahu, whom I have never met? I don't know..." Begin's voice trailed off and he looked across the room. Reuben Hecht, his policy adviser was sitting nearby and listening closely to the conversation. "Reuben," Begin instructed. "*You* give him a job."

Hecht gave Mickelson a long, thoughtful expression. "We'll see what we can do."

Begin laughed out loud. "Reuben is my adviser." He reached over and patted Hecht on the shoulder. "He solves all my awkward problems."

✦ ✦ ✦

Using family connections and contacts developed while living in America, Benjamin attracted notable figures for the terrorism conference. Men like George Shultz and George H. W. Bush signed on as participants. He also included key people from within Israel, one of whom was Moshe Arens, a successful businessman and Knesset member.

Like most people in Israel, Benjamin knew of Arens through news reports and the occasional story about one of his business deals, but he and Arens were by no means close friends or associates. Still, he was a man of respect, and anyone attempting to discuss global terrorism from an Israeli perspective would have listed him as someone who ought to be included in the discussion.

Arens had been born in Lithuania where his father was an industrialist and his mother a dentist. The family moved to the United States in 1939, and settled in New York City. Moshe served in the US Army during World War II, then immigrated to Israel after the War of Independence. After serving as a professor at Technion, Israel's oldest university, he became a deputy director general at Israel Aircraft Industries.

Arens, always on the lookout for talented and capable people, was impressed by Benjamin's work at the Institute. He especially liked the manner in which Benjamin brought together so many credible experts from around the world for meaningful and significant discussion. And he made a mental note to keep track of Benjamin's career.

✦ ✦ ✦

As a result of Mossad's earlier intelligence on Iraq's nuclear program, some of it obtained by Benjamin's brother, Jonathan, Israel initiated regular surveillance of the suspected reactor construction site near Baghdad. Beginning with operatives on the ground and flyovers from reconnaissance aircraft, the surveillance program steadily grew into a sophisticated effort using satellite technology that provided a stream of daily images for review by Gideon Neyman and his sixth-floor analysts.

By early 1981, that stream of images indicated the reactor cooling tower was complete. "The reactor itself will be operational sometime in the latter half of the year," Moshe Goldstein commented as they reviewed the latest photographs from the site.

"Are you certain?" Neyman asked.

"As certain as one can be when reviewing only these images."

Neyman and his team prepared a report on the latest images and passed it up the chain of command to Baruch Gutmann, the director of Mossad. Gutmann reviewed the information and sent the report on to Menachem Begin, Israel's prime minister. Begin ordered Mossad and IDF to begin planning for an attack on the reactor. "We can't let it go active," he warned.

That summer, Israeli jets bombed the Iraqi reactor, completely destroying it. Iraq and other Arab nations denounced the attack, but none of them responded militarily.

Like most Israelis, news of the attack on the Iraqi reactor caught Benjamin off-guard. And, like everyone else, he was forced to watch television news programs to get the latest details on the matter. He was intrigued by the tactical approach and interested in how the attack would affect international opinion of Israel, but as he switched through the television channels, listening to the latest reports for details of the mission, he, for the first time, felt like an outsider looking in from the street.

When Jonathan was alive, he'd had someone on the inside who kept him informed of significant events. Not in a way that compromised the integrity of a mission, but one who might give him an occasional hint about when to pay attention to the news. More often, Jonathan would regale Benjamin with the details days after an operation was successfully completed, as they relaxed together sipping a beer or smoking a cigar.

Now, with Jonathan gone, Benjamin had none of that. None of the inside story. And none of the comradery he'd enjoyed with his older brother.

✦ ✦ ✦

The following fall, Ephraim Evron, Israel's ambassador to the United States, announced his retirement from politics and government service. After taking time to consider the position, Begin appointed Moshe Arens to fill the vacancy. Arens, looking for someone to serve as political attaché at the embassy in Washington, consulted with Reuben Hecht for people who might be capable of the job and acceptable to Begin.

Without hesitation, Hecht advised, "You should appoint Benjamin Netanyahu."

Arens remembered Benjamin, his organizational skills at the terrorism institute, and his success at Rim. He located Benjamin that afternoon and offered him the position of political attaché.

By then, Benjamin and Fleur's trans-Atlantic living arrangement—he in one place, her in another—was putting a strain on their marriage. With little hesitation, he accepted Arens' offer and moved to Washington. For five days each week, he worked at the embassy and lived in an apartment in Georgetown. On weekends, he made the short flight home to Fleur in New York City.

Work at the embassy proved helpful to both Benjamin and his mentor, Arens. For Arens, the successful discharge of his duties at the embassy led to his appointment the following year as Israel's Minister of Defense. For Benjamin, his work with Arens led to an appointment as chief of mission at the embassy in Washington. Not long after that, he was appointed as Israel's ambassador to the United Nations, a position that required his fulltime presence at UN headquarters in New York. For the first time, life with Fleur settled into an even rhythm.

✦ ✦ ✦

The Muslim world, though still bound by many of its ancient traditions, had changed by then. The Islamic Revolution that had first emerged in Iran was now global and largely powered by youth. Many of those young activists had visited other major countries beyond the Middle East, particularly countries in the West, and realized to their dismay just how far Muslim countries had fallen behind the major countries of the world.

They attributed that condition to exploitation by the West, primarily at the hands of the United States, a premise that most Muslims found readily credible and one that became the foundational truth of a message that had tremendous appeal to the masses.

Unlike days gone by, when Muslims were ruled by tribal elders, the current Islamic revolution was led by younger leaders who gained their credibility in the streets. Men like Osama bin Laden in South Central Asia, a fighter who gained notoriety with the Mujahedeen in Afghanistan. In the Gaza Strip, there were rumors of young men banding together to fight, and continuing reports of a more threatening organization in Lebanon. There were numerous smaller groups, but all of them were based upon a radicalized version of Islam.

Rather than relying on the armies of nations, as had been the historical westernized practice, these young leaders formed their followers into decentralized cells that were connected only by a loose arrangement of relationships. It was an arrangement that ignored the caliphs. Rather than fight that trend, the Five Caliphs decided to optimize their efforts by cooperating with it.

In many ways, the winds of change that swept over the Middle East were more refreshing for the caliphs than for anyone else. Beginning with World War I and accelerating during World War II, they had found themselves drawn further and further away from their original purpose—mediation between Muslim groups to settle differences in the understanding of the Koran and Islamic tradition. Instead, they were pushed toward political intervention in the affairs of neighboring states and peoples.

Now, with politics no longer an issue under their control, the caliphs were free to take a more strategic role in Islamic affairs. Instead of intervention in the affairs of state, they could take on roles uniquely suited to the age of information. In matters of religion, they could become the repository of strategic wisdom, scholarship, and theological understanding. And in the affairs of state, they could make themselves indispensable as the source of intelligence.

In conjunction with that new focus, Samad Harawi began recruiting contacts and sources in key countries around the world. He slowly built a network that supplied him with the latest information, often alerting him to coming events long before news of them became public. It was from that network of regional contacts that Harawi first learned of Benjamin Netanyahu's political interests. He passed the information on to Barakat who instructed him to develop a file on Benjamin.

NETANYAHU

BENJAMIN ENJOYED working at the UN but by 1987, he began to look ahead to what might be next in his life. As much as he understood and enjoyed life in America, Israel was his home and as the months went by he thought again and again of returning there to run for elected office. That dream, however, faced one major obstacle—Fleur.

An American to the core, Fleur steadfastly refused to move to Israel, insisting instead that they return to their previous arrangement with her in New York and him in Israel. That would not have posed a problem to a non-political career, but for Benjamin, having a wife on one continent while he sought election to office on another would never work. He would be branded by his political opponents as an American interloper and marginalized before the campaigning hardly began.

They needed to talk about it, to work their way through the idea, but Benjamin was certain they would be unable to do that without the discussion devolving into an argument. There was no one on his staff with whom he could talk about it, either. *And maybe no one in my life at all*, he thought. But then he remembered his father.

Since Jonathan's death, Benjamin and his father had begun to talk more than they had before, but the conversations never seemed to reach the intimacy his father had with Jonathan. Benjamin never doubted his father loved and cared for him; they just never communicated much and when Benjamin tried, it seemed as if his father defaulted to criticism rather than support. Still, with no one else with whom he could talk, and with a critical perspective not really a bad thing when it came to politics, he decided to talk to his father on his next trip to Israel and see what he had to offer on the topic.

The following month, Benjamin was in Israel to discuss deteriorating conditions between Israel, the Palestinian Liberation Organization, Fatah, and Yasser Arafat. Late one afternoon, he visited with his father at his home in Jerusalem.

Benzion listened as Benjamin told him of his political dreams. His eyes were fixed on his son and he had an expression that Benjamin had seen many times when his father talked about serious subjects.

When, at last, Benjamin paused, Benzion said, "Everyone has a purpose in life. Not like the way the religious will tell you, but simply because of whom they are. They have a purpose and they must follow that purpose. You have a purpose in life and you must follow that purpose."

"There's only one office that really means anything."

Benzion nodded. "In spite of what everyone says about the Knesset, the real power is with the prime minister."

"But that's a big step."

"Yes. It's a big step, but you don't have to take it all at once. In fact, you *can't* take it all at once."

"What do you mean?"

"The process. It's broken up so that you can't get to that office without building support in the party."

"So, where do I begin?"

"Your wife," Benzion replied.

Benjamin blushed and looked away. Benzion raised an eyebrow. "You haven't talked to her about this?"

Benjamin shook his head. "No."

"Worried about what she'll say?"

"I know what she'll say."

"She might surprise you. When she sees how much it means to you."

"She's been rather consistent about it so far."

"Well," Benzion sighed, "anyway, that's where you begin. After that, you know many people. You've organized many things in the past. A campaign is nothing more than an organization created for a single purpose. The key to that is in having a manager who knows you well enough to make decisions without having to ask you about everything all the time. Got anyone in mind?"

Benjamin nodded. "Oded Geller."

"Oded is a good man. His work in television and radio would be a big help. Can't do a campaign now without those two. In my day, you could just ride around shaking hands. Not now."

"Perhaps I should begin with Oded."

"No, son. Your wife first, then Oded. If your wife won't support you in this, maybe you should think about doing something else."

✦ ✦ ✦

Back in New York, Benjamin took Fleur out for dinner. Afterward, as they walked back to the apartment, he told her about his dream of returning to Israel and running for office.

"What office?" she asked, knowing full well Benjamin would never be satisfied with anything but Israel's top elective position.

"Ultimately, there is only one office that affects policy on an international level."

"Prime Minister," she replied knowingly.

"Yes."

"And you think that is possible?"

Benjamin looked over at her, his eyes suddenly alert. "Don't you?"

"Yes, and that's the part that worries me."

"Why?"

"We would be in the limelight. Constantly. Reporters, politicians—women chasing you. And not just for a while and then gone, but for the rest of our lives."

Benjamin frowned. "Women chasing me?"

"Success is a powerful aphrodisiac." Fleur smiled at him. "I should know."

He blushed. "Would you at least think about it?"

"Okay, I'll consider it."

"I can't do this without you," he added.

Later that month, Fleur reluctantly agreed to move to Israel. "I know this is what you want to do. And I realize you can't do it with you over there and me over here."

"But you don't like it."

"I was born and raised in the United States. It's as much my home as Israel is yours."

"I never really thought of it that way."

"Do you think I can find a marketing job there?"

"I suppose. But I'm not sure what there is in marketing right now. It won't be anything like what you would have in New York."

"What about your old job at Rim?"

"What about it?"

"Think they would consider me for it?"

"I don't know. But whether they would or not, they might be able to help you find something," Benjamin suggested. "I'll give them a call and find out."

With Fleur seemingly on board, Benjamin invited Oded Geller to come to New York for a visit. After a trip to an art museum and lunch in Central Park, Benjamin brought the conversation around to politics and carefully told Geller what he planned to do.

"Well it's about time," Geller enthused when Benjamin finished.

"What do you mean?"

"We've been waiting for you to do this and wondering when it would happen."

Benjamin had a puzzled frown. "We? Who's been waiting?"

"Everyone we know back in Israel."

"You've talked about me running for office?"

"Yes. Hasn't that been a foregone conclusion since...you know...since we were kids?"

Benjamin had a sheepish grin. "I didn't know it was that obvious."

"Good thing you don't play poker."

"Why?"

"You have no bluff. Whatever you do, you've always been all in, straight-forward, overwhelm them with size and strength. And if that's not enough, you'll work the opposition to death. But bluff and finesse aren't really your style." Geller smiled at him. "When I tell them we're doing this, they'll all want to quit their jobs and get started right away."

For the next several days, Benjamin and Geller talked about Israeli politics, issues that would be important, and a strategy that would make the most of Benjamin's strengths.

The plan was simple—return home, run for a seat in the Knesset, and use that position as leverage to obtain a ministerial appointment. Then build on that appointment and run for party leadership. After that, they would wait for the right opportunity and then run for prime minister. Both understood, without even discussing it, that he would run as a member of the Likud Party, Israel's largest conservative political party. After settling on a general strategy they divided it into individual steps and began sorting through the details of each one. "We need to identify people who can help us set up an office and get things ready," Benjamin suggested.

"Yes, I can find someone for that. We'll need a well-coordinated media campaign for your return. So that you arrive with a big splash."

Benjamin agreed. "But I think we should approach this as if we're the guys on the outside."

"Right," Geller nodded. "The others are entrenched party people. Likud princes."

"We'll need to hit them with a high-impact media campaign. Right from the beginning. Use it to create momentum in the press. Roll over them and never give them a chance."

Geller agreed. "Crowds everywhere you go. TV reporters, interviews. Reporters prepared in advance."

"Can you do it?"

"Do you really have to ask?"

"Not at all," Benjamin smiled. "I guess what I really want to know is, *will* you do it?"

"If you think I'm letting someone else do this, you're sorely mistaken, pal."

✦ ✦ ✦

Despite her earlier attempts to accommodate Benjamin's political ambitions, Fleur found she was unable to reconcile herself to the prospect of a very public life in Israel. As she'd suggested before, she was born an American and had lived there all her life. As Benjamin's commitment to return to Israel and run for elected office continued to grow, the meaning and significance of life in America grew more important to her.

Finally, after wrestling with her own mind and heart, she reluctantly, but without regret, told him she could not go with him. At first they attempted to work out an acceptable arrangement but in the end, they decided to divorce.

In 1988, after four years of service at the United Nation, Benjamin stepped down from his post as Israel's ambassador to the UN and returned to Israel. He arrived at the airport in Tel Aviv to exactly the kind of media frenzy he'd dreamed about. Crowds at the airport were jammed into the corridors, main lobby, and entrance outside at the curbside drop-off.

As he rode through the streets of Tel Aviv, crowds were gathered at every intersection and at outside coffee shops and restaurants along the route as they rode toward Jerusalem. And an hour later, when they reached the apartment building where he would live much larger and more enthusiastic crowds met them on the street. *I knew Geller was good,* Benjamin thought, *but I didn't know he was this good.* This was the kind of arrival they needed to get their campaign started with a bang. And if Geller's performance with other aspects of the campaign were anything like this, their work would be much easier than he at first imagined.

Benjamin settled into the apartment on the outskirts of Jerusalem. There he went to work building a campaign operation that could place him high enough in the Likud primary to be in line for a seat in the Knesset, should the party do well in the general election. With an organization more American than Israeli, he hoped to not only capture a victory in the coming election, but to develop an organization that could easily be adapted and changed to address his future interests.

A few days after his arrival, Benjamin met with Geller and a small group of politically minded people Geller had recruited. All of them were knowledgeable in their fields but they were young and none of them had a history of party involvement. Still, they were eager to get busy and began coordinating Benjamin's activities to coincide with the media schedule he and Geller created—all of it geared toward winning the current election to the Knesset, while simultaneously positioning him for the ultimate goal of winning a national election that would pave the way to the prime minister's office.

For those initial weeks, Geller had a media schedule that put Benjamin on all available Israeli and global TV and radio stations, seizing the moment to take advantage of news coverage of his return and his opinions about events in the Middle East. Though not overtly political in nature, the interviews put him before the people of Israel and the world as a knowledgable expert on Middle Eastern affairs. Having lived much of his life in the United States, he was particularly adept at couching his comments in the broader context of US-Israeli and US-Palestinian relations.

During those first weeks, Benjamin also received offers daily that presented employment opportunities with almost every major company in Israel. Many of those offers were attractive and he considered them all carefully. Finally, however, he decided to reject them all and concentrate on obtaining the job he really wanted—the position of prime minister of Israel. To reach that goal he would need total concentration on the plan he and Geller had formed. A long-range plan that, barring some new and unforeseen difficulty, would require at least three years to execute.

Instead of relying on a traditional job for financial support, Benjamin decided to fund his campaign through donations. He financed the effort by raising money from Israeli businessmen, some of whom had sent the many offers that he'd just rejected, and with contributions from American businessmen whom he'd come to know through his work at

Boston Consulting. To tap into those resources, he made frequent and repeated trips to New York, Boston, Miami, and other major US cities.

✦ ✦ ✦

A month or two later, during an interview on Israeli state television, Benjamin announced his intention to stand for election to the Knesset as a Likud member. The announcement set off arduous rounds of travel, this time keeping him on the run from place to place in Israel meeting with local Likud branches. He and members of his team visited large and small communities, many of whom had been neglected by past party leadership, who relied on reputation and position to keep them in power.

Leadership at the local level was awed by Benjamin's youthful charm, his articulate presentations on complex issues, and his winsome personality. So much so that they quickly came over to his side. That change of loyalty, largely unnoticed by traditional party leadership, marked a subtle but significant shift of power within the Likud Party.

Benjamin worked relentlessly, putting in long hours each day that kept him away from home until late at night. Most weeks found him working all seven days attending party meetings where he was the featured speaker and afterward attending receptions where he met party members and shook as many hands as possible.

On Primary Election Day, members of the Likud Party gathered at Herzliya Country Club to vote and to await the results. Likud princes, mostly second generation conservative politicians—David Levy, Roni Milo, Ehud Ulmert, and Dan Meridor—discounted Benjamin's chances for success. After all, members of their respective families had participated in Israel's affairs of state since before independence, many risking their lives and fortunes to do so. Benjamin Netanyahu—who was he and what had he done?

When the votes were counted that election evening, Benjamin sat in fifth place. Not as strong as he would have liked but still enough to hand the party princes a resounding defeat. The Likud Party elite, caught off-guard by the results, did little in the form of celebration. Instead they were surprised, shocked, dismayed, and infuriated. "He is an outsider," they said to news reporters and anyone else who would listen. "He's the son of an outsider. Young, brash, and newly arrived to this business. He understands nothing of what it takes to lead this country."

As the night wore on their remarks became more pointed. "Ask him about America," they chided. "He can tell you all about US politics, but when it comes to Likud Party affairs and to the matters of state that affect us all here in Israel, he is woefully ignorant."

Reporters on the scene and announcers in the studio, however, were careful to inform their listeners that Benjamin had not been hiding for the past ten years and had, in fact, served at both the Israeli embassy and as Israel's ambassador to the United Nations. The last position one that, by protocol, out-ranked any position his detractors had held.

The party elites, having little of substance to say in response, turned once again to their well-worn spin. "We earned our position in the party. And now this Netanyahu kid swoops in here in a storm and tries to steal the whole thing right out from under us. It'll never happen."

Rather than uniting behind the winners of that first electoral round, the respective personalities dug in for a fight. And very soon after that, the young and largely untried Netanyahu Camp found itself at war with other major political camps and cliques of the party.

NETANYAHU

IN THE GENERAL ELECTION held later that year, Benjamin was elected to the Knesset on the first ballot by an overwhelming majority. The Likud Party elite, once again caught off-guard, were infuriated, but there was nothing they could do to thwart the results. With Benjamin's victory, and with the victories of other candidates in positions further down the ticket, the Likud Party won a number of additional seats in the Knesset and Yitzhak Shamir, the party's leader, was elected prime minister.

During the transition, Shamir appointed Moshe Arens as foreign minister. Arens asked for Benjamin to serve as a deputy minister. Shamir agreed and Benjamin readily accepted.

✦ ✦ ✦

As deputy foreign minister, Benjamin was placed in charge of propaganda—crafting the Israeli government's image and presenting it to the nation and the world. In addition to providing access to every media outlet in the world, the position also gave him an opportunity to address policy while it was still in development. It was a job for which he was perfectly suited.

Benjamin was very camera-friendly and equally conversant with American culture. Those two advantages enabled him to communicate Israeli culture and perspective to Americans in a way that Americans could understand. It also allowed him to shape the news to favor Israel.

As a deputy minister, Benjamin received daily security and intelligence briefings. From those briefings and his own curiosity, he learned of Mossad's decades-long operations inside Iraq. For several years rumors had persisted about Israel's clandestine efforts to penetrate deep inside Iraq. After assuming office, Benjamin learned that not only were those rumors true, but his brother Jonathan had participated in that effort.

Armed with inside information and cloaked in the trappings of office and power, Benjamin talked to some of Jonathan's friends who confirmed what he'd already learned: Jonathan had been a member of the first special missions unit that went into Iraq with Mossad to gather on-sight intelligence.

One of those friends explained, "They went to a site on the campus at Baghdad University. I don't know what they wanted to find out there, but that was the point of the mission. To reach a building on the campus, report on activities inside the building, and take photographs of the construction area that was behind it."

"Any idea what they were looking for?"

"Not really. But if you're that interested in what they were doing, you should talk to Hoshea Malkin."

"Who is he?"

"He was the Mossad agent who coordinated the operation."

"Where is he now?

"He retired last year, I think. Lives in the outskirts of Jerusalem."

Benjamin located an address for Malkin and a few days later rode out to his house. Malkin confirmed much of what Benjamin already knew. "Jonathan's pictures gave our analysts their first glimpse of the site."

"What was so important about the site?"

"Iraq was constructing a nuclear reactor," Malkin explained. "The pictures your brother took provided the intelligence they needed to confirm that was what the Iraqis were doing. Building a reactor. He went to the site. Was supposed to observe it from a safe location. Mossad didn't want any of us to get captured. They were afraid it would turn into a big deal with the press. Cause a lot of problems for everybody. But you know Jonathan. He always had to do the brave thing."

Benjamin beamed with pride. "That's the way he was." He paused a moment, "So, was that all they did there? Take pictures?"

"Like I said, he watched from a safe distance at first but while he was doing that he studied the area and figured out how to get closer to the actual site. I'm not sure how he did it, but he wandered around that site as if he was supposed to be there. No one raised any questions. And the whole time he was snapping pictures just as fast as he could. Brought them back to headquarters. Allowed analysts to confirm that they really were building a nuclear reactor there. We also located a centrifuge farm on that mission."

Benjamin looked puzzled. "The reports mention only a reactor."

Malkin nodded. "I know. But there was a centrifuge operation there, too. I think it was in the building. The one right there by the site."

"Is it still there?"

Malkin shook his head. "Nah. They destroyed it during the bombing attack."

"Reports don't mention that either," Benjamin noted.

"I know," Malkin smiled. "The reports don't mention a lot of things."

That evening, Benjamin visited with his father and told him what he learned about Jonathan's involvement in the earliest efforts to gather intelligence about the Iraqi reactor site. "Pictures he took from the site were crucial in the determination by our analysts of what it really was."

Benzion nodded. "His work on that mission was the thing that got him noticed for the Entebbe hostage raid."

Benjamin looked surprised. "I didn't know that. How did you find out about it?"

"Someone told me. I can't remember who it was. That's the way he was, though. Always had to be in on the big things. Up front. Taking the lead."

"What's curious to me is that Iraq never responded to that attack.

They protested, but never took any action against us. At least as far as I know."

"You're right. And it's not just that they didn't react then. They had little involvement at all in *any* of the recent wars. They avoided our war of independence, and the 1967 war. And they didn't respond to this attack."

Benjamin frowned. "Why not?"

"Well," Benzion replied slowly, "I don't have access to the information available at your level, but I would want to know when their nuclear program began."

"You think that had something to do with their lack of involvement?"

Benzion shrugged. "I don't know, but if I were prime minister, that's a question I would want answered. Did they fail to respond because they didn't want to risk discovery or destruction of their nuclear program? A war with us would almost certainly have brought bombing attacks on Baghdad. Those attacks could easily have damaged their research facility without our knowing it was part of a nuclear program."

Benjamin nodded slowly. "Jonathan's name turns up in the most unexpected places."

They talked a while longer, then Benjamin stood to leave. Benzion said, "Jonathan told me some other things."

Benjamin arched an eyebrow. "Like what? Anything he was involved in was classified. I'm surprised he even told you as much as he did."

"He was reluctant to talk about his own involvement in things but he told me about other things."

"Like?"

"Mossad has information suggesting there is a group of men in Istanbul who control events and activities in the Muslim world."

"Dad, we've talked about this kind of thing a hundred times. There is—"

"I know we've talked about it," Benzion interrupted. "But Jonathan told me that this version is true. These five men are not well-known and I don't think there are any pictures of them anywhere, but those who know them refer to them as the Five Caliphs. An ancient self-perpetuating organization. Been in existence since the seventh century. Had more control in the past than they do now, but they are still an influential group. Jonathan wondered if Iraq could build a nuclear program without approval of the Five Caliphs."

"I don't know." Benjamin turned toward the door to leave. "I just thought it was interesting that Jonathan was involved in operations inside Iraq."

"Yes," Benzion walked with Benjamin to the door. "And what he told me about the Five Caliphs is equally as intriguing." He placed his hand on Benjamin's shoulder. "Keep your eyes and ears open. Perhaps you will find out what's really going on."

NETANYAHU

WHEN NOT ATTENDING to his official duties, Benjamin spent as much time as possible raising money to finance his political career. That work took him to locations throughout Israel and on a regular basis to places like New York, Washington, and Chicago. During a layover in Paris on one of those trips he wandered into an airport coffee shop and took a place in line to order.

Unnoticed, one of Harawi's agents followed Benjamin and took a place in line a few people behind him. The agent wore slacks, a dress shirt with no tie, and a natty brown jacket. Over his shoulder he carried a leather messenger bag with the strap twisted and crinkled at the buckle and at first glance he looked like any other traveler in the airport that day. But beneath his jacket, tucked snuggly into the waistband of his trousers, was a small cassette recorder with a thin black cord that ran to a tiny microphone that was pinned through the buttonhole on his lapel.

While standing in line to give his order, Netanyahu noticed the woman in front of him and found her very attractive. He struck up a conversation and learned she was an El Al flight attendant named Sara Ben-Arzi. They talked while they waited for their coffee and by the time their coffee was ready they were in a conversation too pleasant to end. They moved across the room to an open table along the wall and sat down to continue their conversation.

Harawi's agent ordered black coffee and moved quickly to a table near Benjamin and Sara and watched as they sat together most of the afternoon, talking, flirting, and enjoying each other's company. Preoccupied as they were, they never noticed the agent or his microphone, or the small camera he'd taken from the leather messenger bag and set atop the table.

Finally, Sara had to go and as she stood to leave Benjamin gave her one of his business cards. She scribbled her address and phone number on the back of a napkin. They kissed each other on the cheek, said goodbye and agreed to stay in touch. Benjamin watched as she walked across the café, and out the door. When she was out of sight he glanced down at the napkin, scanned the information, and chuckled. *I'll never hear from her again.* Then he stuffed the note in his pocket and took a last sip from his coffee cup.

Harawi's agent lingered in the airport watching Benjamin until he boarded the flight for Tel Aviv. When the plane backed away from the gate, the agent walked up the corridor to a restaurant where he took a seat at a table in back and wrote a summary of what he had just observed. While he worked, a man carrying an identical leather messenger bag took a seat at the table next to him.

When the first agent finished writing his report he placed it inside his leather bag along with the cassette from the recorder. Then he set the bag on the floor beside his chair.

The man at the next table ordered only hot tea and when he finished the cup, he picked up the first agent's messenger bag and walked away with it. The first agent waited until he was gone, then retrieved the remaining messenger bag and glanced inside to make sure it had what he needed for his next mission. Satisfied that it did, he finished his meal and walked up the corridor to the main terminal building. From there he boarded the Chunnel train to London where he was scheduled to pick up the trail of his next assignment.

Later that week, Sara phoned Benjamin from Paris and told him she had to work a flight to New York in a few hours and then would be off for a two-day break. "I have an apartment there," she said. "You should catch a flight and meet me." Benjamin agreed and departed that evening for New York.

When Benjamin arrived at New York's Kennedy Airport, one of Harawi's agents was there to observe him. The agent followed at a safe distance as Benjamin made his way through the concourse to a corridor and into the main terminal. Benjamin carried a small suitcase and walked past the luggage carousels to the taxi stand out front. Moments later, he entered a taxi and departed for Manhattan.

By then Harawi's agents had compiled a dossier on Sara that was almost as thorough as the one they had on Benjamin. Agents working in New York were ensconced in an apartment building that afforded a view of her apartment windows. From there they observed her activities day and night. They were waiting and ready when Benjamin arrived that evening. Using microphones and electronic listening devices placed inside the apartment, they recorded his conversation with Sara while their cameras snapped pictures of them as they embraced.

✦ ✦ ✦

After a year in office, Shamir moved Moshe Arens to Ministry of Defense and appointed David Levy as foreign minister. Despite the shuffling of officials at the top, Benjamin retained his position as deputy foreign minister. At first it seemed as though the arrangement would work, but rather quickly old animosity about the election became a problem, especially with Levy's staff, who seized every opportunity to cast Benjamin in a poor light. As a result, Benjamin was no longer informed of meetings, schedules, policy discussions, and the like, and his requests for information—information necessary for him to do his job as the public face of Israeli policy—were ignored to the point of impairing his ability to execute the responsibilities of his office.

Denied information from the Foreign Ministry, Benjamin went to the prime minister's office each day and read their memos and releases. He also was present for the prime minister's daily security brief from Mossad. It didn't take long for Shamir to notice Benjamin's constant presence in the office. After one of their meetings, he told Ania Givaty, his deputy chief of staff, to find out why Benjamin was always there.

It didn't take Givaty long to understand the problem. She reported back to Shamir in the afternoon of that same day. "You asked about Mr. Netanyahu."

"Yes," Shamir replied. "What did you find?"

"Apparently, the real problem is that Mr. Netanyahu won the election."

A frown wrinkled Shamir's brow. "That's a problem?"

Givaty smiled. "He didn't just win. He came in first in both votes."

"How well I remember. Totally surprised Levy."

"Yes, sir," Givaty replied. "I think Roni Milo, Ehud Ulmert, and Dan Meridor were unhappy about it, too."

Shamir shook his head. "Wouldn't it be nice if we could put aside our differences after the election and simply govern the country with integrity?"

"Yes, sir."

"Should I say something to Levy about this?"

"I don't know." Givaty had a troubled look. "Two or three of Levy's staff members are particularly dissatisfied. They've frozen Mr. Netanyahu out of briefings, removed his name from schedule distribution lists, directed memo traffic away from him, that sort of thing."

"They want him to fail at his job."

"Yes."

"Levy puts up with this?"

"They've managed to keep him angry enough at Mr. Netanyahu that he hasn't noticed what they are doing to him."

"I should fire them all."

"Wouldn't we have to form a new coalition to stay in office?"

"Yes," Shamir sighed. "And maybe I should. We could let Benjamin form a government in my place."

"Levy would probably get beyond all of this on his own, but with his staff prodding him at every turn..."

Shamir held up his hand to indicate he'd heard enough. "Okay, just tell Benjamin to move his office over here. Find some space for him somewhere and get him a secretary. Then prepare a memo moving his duties to us. He can handle publicity from here as an extension of my office. Should have done it that way in the first place."

✦ ✦ ✦

In 1991, Iraq, now under the leadership of Saddam Hussein, invaded Kuwait. The United States responded by assembling a large military force in the desert of Saudi Arabia, positioning it to the west of the Kuwaiti border. That military force consisted of men, equipment, and materiel from the United States, Great Britain, Saudi Arabia, Qatar, and other Arab states. While it assembled a military force, the US issued a demand that Iraq withdraw immediately or face the consequences of an invasion.

When Hussein did not withdraw his troops, the US-led coalition force entered Kuwait and, in spite of previous dire assessments to the contrary, swept in unimpeded, destroying Iraqi tanks and capturing Iraqi soldiers at will.

Facing defeat at the hands of the United States, Hussein ordered Scud missile attacks against Israel. Although many of the missiles failed to reach their intended target, a few caused significant property damage and were collaterally responsible for the deaths of seventy-five people. Regardless of their tactical ineffectiveness, worry spread throughout Israel that the missile strikes would escalate to a chemical attack. Rumors to that effect spread with each new attack.

Because his position now functioned as a part of the prime minister's office, Benjamin was present at most major policy deliberations.

When the missile attacks began, he did his best to argue for a response that went beyond the knee-jerk reaction that many sought.

"The Arabs are merely trying to provoke us into responding against them," he claimed, mirroring the pleas of US president George Bush who was on the phone almost constantly, urging Shamir to refrain from a military response.

"And why would they do that?" someone asked.

"As it stands right now," Benjamin explained, "this war has the United States on the side of the Arabs. Hussein knows he can't win that war. He will lose, as he already is doing. The only way he can win now is to divert Arab cooperation away from the United States. Even then, I'm not sure he can win, but that's his only hope."

Someone from the policy section spoke up. "And what do the attacks on us have to do with that?"

"If we respond," Benjamin continued, "Iraq will say that we have attacked them and they will call on all Arab countries to attack us. They want to make the war about Jews versus Arabs and use that to draw Arab support away from the US effort and focus everyone on us."

"And you think that's the only way they can win?"

"I know it's the only way they can win," Benjamin stated confidently. "Which is why we need to stay out of this fight."

"Rather difficult to do, when they're lobbing rockets at us."

Benjamin looked over at Shamir. "We want Saddam Hussein removed from power as much as anyone. The US has the best opportunity to do that. We should give them room to accomplish that."

After several more meetings, Shamir agreed to refrain from giving a military response, but worry still ran high in Israel. And as he issued the order delaying military operations, he called Benjamin aside. "I agree with you about what Iraq is trying to do. But I can't let these attacks continue much longer without a response from us. I understand what the United States is attempting to accomplish, but I am not prime minister of the United States. I am prime minister of Israel. The safety of Israeli citizens is my primary concern."

"Certainly, Mr. Prime Minister. But if we—"

Shamir cut him off. "I know all the arguments. I'm just telling you my thoughts so you can get yourself ready. If these attacks go on much longer, I'm going to order IDF to respond. They're ready to go. They've been practicing for several operations that will put an end to these attacks. If the attacks continue, I'm giving the order."

In spite of the seriousness of the situation, Benjamin saw a positive media side and in subsequent meetings suggested they distribute gas masks to everyone. "That will give some assurance to our citizens that we are aware of what they're facing and we're doing something about it. Then we play up the situation in the press, while playing it down everywhere else."

Shamir approved the concept. "But make certain we have enough masks for this to work."

When the meeting ended Benjamin assigned one of his assistants to determine the number of gas masks available for issuance to the public. After determining that enough were on hand, masks were issued along with instructions on how families could shelter in place in the event of a gas or chemical attack. Within hours of their issuance, pictures of families, including small children, wearing their masks appeared on newscasts.

That same day, Benjamin did an interview with CNN and appeared on camera with his gas mask and pack in hand. While he was on the air emergency sirens sounded, warning of an incoming missile attack. Still on camera, he calmly reached down to his pack, took out his mask, and put it on, then adjusted it for a correct fit. He finished the live interview while wearing the mask.

Almost immediately, the segment received widespread air play which was repeated the remainder of the evening and into the next day. Benjamin's office was flooded with requests for interviews which he readily granted. Those follow-up interviews received almost as much airplay as the original and pushed the story into a second news cycle, which meant four days of television exposure for Israel and for Benjamin. Once again, Levy's staff was furious and accused Benjamin of grandstanding for his own benefit.

✦ ✦ ✦

The war to liberate Kuwait from Iraqi occupation took much less time than anyone had expected. In that brief few days of combat, however, the world saw a real-time display of US military superiority. The resounding victory that followed gave new momentum to US efforts to bring peace to the Middle East.

In an effort to capitalize on that momentum, the US and Soviet Union co-sponsored a peace conference with the stated goal of restarting the stalled Arab-Israeli peace initiative. Formal sessions of the summit were held at the Royal Palace in Madrid, Spain, with delegations attending from Israel, Gaza, and the West Bank, along with those from the US, Soviet Union, Egypt, Jordan, Syria, and Lebanon.

The conference opened on October 30 and ran through November 1, with lengthier multilateral negotiations scheduled thereafter in Moscow and Washington, DC. Although President George H. W. Bush gave an opening speech, most countries sent their foreign ministers and staff to handle the daily sessions. Israel, however, was represented by Prime Minister Shamir. As a member of the prime minister's office, Benjamin was included in Shamir's traveling entourage, while Levy remained behind in Jerusalem.

During a recess on Thursday, Benjamin wandered outside the meeting hall and spotted David Mickelson standing in the corridor. Farouk al-Sharaa, the Syrian foreign minister, was a few feet away, talking with 'Amr Musa, the Egyptian foreign minister.

Michelson was dressed in a blue pinstripe suit with a small presidential library pin on his lapel. A lanyard hung around his neck and connected to it was a press credential that identified him as a journalist with *The New York Times*. He wore no yarmulke or other indication of his rabbinic standing and appeared to those who didn't know better as only a member of the press pool.

As they talked, al-Sharaa showed something to Musa and the expression on both their faces changed. That change caught Benjamin's attention and he wondered what they were discussing.

A few minutes later, the recess ended and everyone returned to the meeting hall to continue the negotiating session. Mickelson was seated with the press pool, listening to the proceedings, when someone handed him a cell phone. "This is for you," he was informed.

Mickelson responded with a perplexed look, then took the cell phone and brought it to his ear. "Yes? This is Rabbi Mickelson."

"Imagine my surprise at seeing you here," Benjamin said.

Mickelson recognized the voice immediately. "Yes," he whispered. "I thought you might be here."

"You just decided to show up?"

"Ahh...you know," Mickelson explained in a guarded tone. "Friends with friends."

"I see. Step out of the room so we can talk."

"Sure." Mickelson rose from his chair and stepped into the corridor. "Is something wrong?"

"You were in that corridor earlier today, standing near 'Amr Musa, during the break, I believe."

"Yes."

"He was talking to Farouk al-Sharaa."

"Right."

"They were looking at something. Could you hear what they said or see what they were doing?"

"Yes, al-Sharaa had a picture of Prime Minister Shamir. It was taken when Shamir was a young man in Lehi. Fighting the British before statehood."

"Why did he have that?"

"al-Sharaa intends to show it to the conference and accuse the prime minister of being a terrorist."

"Oh." Benjamin said. "What exactly did he say?"

Mickelson recited the conversation: "Tomorrow in the meeting, I am going to accuse Yitzhak Shamir of being a terrorist, before all the leaders of the world."

Late in the afternoon of the following day, which was Friday, al-Sharaa was scheduled to make a statement to the conference. President Bush was in attendance, as was Soviet Premier Gorbachev. About three that afternoon, Shamir got up from his seat and said, "I am an Orthodox Jew. This evening is Shabbat and I have to go to Jerusalem." And with that, the entire Israeli delegation departed from the conference.

A few minutes later, al-Sharaa rose to present the Syrian position on substantive negotiations. In the process, he offered the photograph of Shamir as an attempt to label Shamir a terrorist based on his actions against the British fifty years earlier. It was a heavily nuanced argument aimed at countering Shamir's earlier statements labeling the PLO and other Arab organizations as terrorists based on their *present* activity. However, having been forewarned by Benjamin, who relayed Mickelson's information, no one from the Israeli delegation was present, leaving al-Sharaa to make his accusation to a section of empty chairs.

News reporters, however, were very much in attendance and more than glad to provide the public with details of the incident. The details—the Syrian delegation's smiles and frowns that might have otherwise lent support to the growing worldwide impatience with Israeli intransigence—came across instead as mean-spirited pettiness. And against a backdrop of the seriousness of the issues at hand, the mood of the conference shifted in an instant against the Syrian delegation, in particular, and Arabs, in general. In that single moment they were transformed from victims to aggressors. Allegations against them that were earlier seen as evidence of Shamir's unreasonableness suddenly became quite the opposite.

Shamir wasn't the only one who received a boost in public opinion from al-Sharaa's failed stunt. As Shamir's adviser, Benjamin's name and presence already was associated with the conference.

When the incident with the Syrian delegation caught reporters' attention, they naturally turned to him for the Israeli reaction. And once more, he became the face of Israel's response—a response that now seemed perfectly reasonable and so obviously right.

NETANYAHU

AS ORIGINALLY CONCEIVED, the modern state of Israel followed a parliamentary system of government. The primary governing authority was vested in a one hundred-twenty member legislative body known as the Knesset. A prime minister served as head of government. Membership in the Knesset was proportional to the results of a state-wide election held every four years. The party with the most Knesset delegates generally determined who the prime minister would be.

But as Israel's 1992 legislative elections approached, a movement arose among delegates in the Knesset to switch the election of the prime minister from an indirect election—with the results determined by party leadership based on the results of legislative elections—to a direct one in which the people would cast a vote specifically for the candidate of their choice. It was a proposal that would allow the *people* to decide the matter, rather than party insiders.

Understandably, Yitzhak Shamir, the current prime minister, and all the Likud Party leaders were against it. Benjamin, however, was intrigued by the proposal and when a legislative bill was finally introduced, he reviewed it and sided with the people. It wasn't long before word of that got out.

Likud leadership responded by cajoling, arguing, and threatening Benjamin in an all-out effort to convince him that the measure should be defeated. Benjamin, however, thought the people favored direct elections. He also was certain they abhorred the potential for corruption and arrogance of the old system, which placed the final decision of who should or should not be named prime minister in the hands of the party's old guard. *And well they should,* he thought, *direct elections are fairer and certainly straight forward.*

Those considerations aside, there was one other very good reason for Benjamin to favor direct elections—they were much easier for him to win. The system was filled with bureaucratic loopholes and rampant with inefficiencies.

Not only that, Likud Party leadership was adamantly opposed to Benjamin attaining elected office. With elections to the Knesset, they had little option but to grant him a seat. Those elections were, after all, determined by the people. However, to advance under the old system Benjamin would need the consent and collusion of the party leadership. They were the ones who approved and announced the party's chosen candidate. That was an announcement and approval Benjamin knew would never come.

"He's just like his father," Benjamin heard them say on occasions when they thought he couldn't hear them talking. "Stubborn and opinionated."

"And a fanatic."

"A rightwing fanatic."

"I thought that's what *we* were," someone else added with a chuckle.

"No," another responded. "We're conservative. Not fanatics."

✦ ✦ ✦

Facing yet another dilemma, Benjamin paid a call on his father. Over tea at the kitchen table, he laid out the situation—details about the provisions of the pending legislation, Likud's official response, Shamir's reaction, Likud leadership's continued harassment of him.

"So," he said when finished, "if I vote for the measure I'll be in a good position with the voters, but the party leadership will marginalize me and I'll be pretty much ruined. If I vote with party leadership, I'll be on their side but the voters will hate me."

"You can't trust party leadership," Benzion instructed. "You've already made them angry. If you give in to them now, they'll still be mad at you. They'll still marginalize you. And they'll even find a way to use your vote against you."

"So, if I vote the way they want me to vote, it'll only get them off my back for right now?"

"Maybe. But if you do that, you'll still lose everything."

"What do you mean?"

"You'll lose your integrity with the party and with the voters," Benzion explained, "by voting for something you don't believe in and doing so just because of its benefit to you personally. You'll lose any sense of power or respect you might have with the party because you took an unpopular position on the matter and they had to resort to arm-twisting to get you to follow the party line. Giving in to that is a sign of weakness. Give in now and you'll lose both the voters and the party."

"So, giving them what they want now is not going to change my position."

"No. It won't. At least not for the good." Benzion looked at him a moment, as if deep in thought. "These things always seem big and complex. But they're really not. You should do what is right and not let others persuade you or force you to change your mind."

"Sounds profound when you say it. When I say it to myself it sounds too simple."

"I have found that these profoundly troubling decisions we face really are just that—profoundly simple."

Benzion stared at him a moment, twice opening his mouth as if to speak and twice pushing the moment aside. The look on his face did not escape Benjamin's notice. "What's the matter?"

"Nothing."

Benjamin smiled. "I think that *nothing* is more like something."

"It's...it's not time."

Again, Benzion seemed to have more to say and Benjamin tried to convince him to say it, but Benzion shook his head. "It's not time yet. We'll talk more, later."

Benjamin looked concerned. "Is everything okay?"

"Everything is fine," Benzion patted his son on the arm. "Everything is fine."

"Mom is okay?"

"Yes. Your mother is well," Benzion insisted. "It has nothing to do with her." He stood and placed his hand on Benjamin's shoulder. "Come now. You can't spend all day sitting here. You have things to do yet."

Reluctantly, Benjamin stood and gave his father a hug, then walked with him toward the front door. "You'll call me if you change your mind?"

A frown wrinkled Benzion's forehead. "Change my mind?"

"And decide to tell me what you wanted to say earlier."

"We'll talk about it, just not today."

Benjamin pulled him close once more, and kissed his father on top of his head. "Okay, I'll see you later." And with that, he stepped outside and was gone.

✦ ✦ ✦

Meanwhile, Benjamin continued to see Sara, sometimes meeting her at her apartment in New York and sometimes at his apartment in Tel Aviv. Geller and most of the others on his political staff realized he was seeing someone but did not know her name or anything else about her.

For most of them, this was not a problem, but for Geller it was a potential liability that needed to be addressed. After dodging the issue for several months, he finally brought the matter up with Benjamin as they concluded one of their regular weekly meetings.

"Look, there's one more thing we need to discuss."

"What's that?"

"You've been gone from the office on some routine basis or other, usually Friday and Monday. But sometimes other days."

"Has that been a problem?"

"Not in terms of events or the other things we're doing or votes in the Knesset or any of that. But in terms of the politics of the matter..."

Benjamin frowned. "What are you talking about?"

"It's rather obvious you are seeing someone. But it's equally obvious you haven't bothered to bring her around to meet any of us. None of the staff knows who she is."

"It's not the staff's business," Benjamin replied curtly.

"That's where you're wrong."

Benjamin's eyes held a hint of anger. "You're telling me my romantic life—assuming that is what this about—is the business of my political staff?"

"These aren't just staff members," Geller answered firmly. "These are people who have hitched their lives to your wagon. You can't do what you want to do without them. But if they come along with you on this venture, they put their futures on the line, too. This isn't just about you anymore." He gestured with a sweep of his arm, "The public at large out there, yeah, it's none of their business. But I'm not talking about the public at large. I'm talking about us. You. Me. The core of committed people who have been with us since the beginning."

Benjamin was on the defensive and his words came sharply. "And how is my personal life a risk to them?"

"I've already told you. This is no longer just about you. It's about all of us. And unanswered questions about your life leave you—and that includes all of us—open to attacks by Levy and all the others. The long-term plans we've discussed will be rough enough without them adding to it."

"So what are you saying?" Benjamin stood. "I don't—"

"Sit down." Geller tapped the tabletop with his index finger. "And tell me what's going on."

Benjamin gave a heavy sigh as he dropped onto a chair and explained his relationship with Sara.

✦ ✦ ✦

A few weeks later, Benjamin arrived for a political event at Haifa with Sara on his arm. He escorted her around the room, taking time to introduce her to each of the members of his staff. Geller was pleased and did his best to make the moment as light and enjoyable as possible.

In the weeks that followed, Sara regularly appeared with Benjamin in public, taking to the campaign trail like a seasoned political operative. Not only that, she also showed up for menial tasks like stuffing envelopes, addressing them, and handing out leaflets.

Several months later, Benjamin invited his political team to his parents' home in Jerusalem for a birthday party in honor of his father. When they arrived they found the house decorated with streamers and lights out front. Geller met them at the door and ushered them through the house to a door that led to a courtyard out back. The courtyard was lit with torches and there were chairs arranged in rows facing away from the house.

Shahar Ofer glanced around. "This doesn't look like a birthday party."

"No, it doesn't," Anna Arkin replied. "Looks more like a wedding."

Shahar turned in Geller's direction. "What is this?"

"A party," Geller grinned as he crossed the room toward them.

"You said it was a birthday party," Anna added.

"Well," Geller replied sheepishly. "We changed that."

"To what?"

"A wedding."

"A wedding?" Shahar blurted. "Whose wedding?"

"Mine," a voice said from behind them.

They wheeled in that direction to see Benjamin coming through the doorway with Sara at his side. "We thought we'd surprise you. Did it work?"

✦ ✦ ✦

Not long after Benjamin and Sara were married, the Knesset voted on the direct election bill. Against the Likud Party leadership's opinion and desire, Benjamin stuck to the dictates of his conscience and voted in favor of it. The measure passed and as soon as the results were made known, Shamir sent for Benjamin to join him in his office. Other Likud leaders were there and as Benjamin entered the room they all verbally assailed him.

"I did what my conscience told me I should do," Benjamin offered. "I did what I thought was best for the people."

"But it's not best for the party," Shamir railed.

"The Knesset wasn't created to serve the party. It was created to serve the people of Israel."

They shouted and screamed at him all the more, then Shamir said, "You are ruined with the party. You'll never get elected to anything, either." Benjamin tried to respond but Shamir cut him off with a wave of his hand. "That's all. I'm finished with you."

Benjamin turned to leave and someone opened the door for him. "You're out," he said curtly. "And good riddance."

That evening, Benjamin met with Geller and told him about the meeting with Shamir. "It doesn't matter."

"Why not?"

"They can't stop you from getting elected. Appointed, maybe. But not elected."

"They can keep me off the ballot."

"Not really."

"Of course they can," Benjamin argued, raising his voice. "They control all of that."

"First of all," Geller replied calmly, "you're already on the ballot for the general election. They can't change that. And you forget one other thing, my friend."

"Please," Benjamin groused. "Not the cheery pep talk. Not from you."

"All of the local party officials sided with us," Geller continued. "If party leadership tries to keep you off the ballot anyway, we'll rally the local leaders—leaders from all those local organizations that you visited and spoke with—and we'll get them to help keep you on."

Benjamin stared at the floor a moment, then looked over at Geller. "Why wait until then?"

Geller frowned. "What are you saying?"

"I'm saying, if we wait until Shamir and Levy and the others cause us trouble, they'll have the upper hand. Why not take the offensive? Why not use their threats to rally the local leaders now?"

"Brilliant," Geller shouted, his eyes bright and alive. "We'll overwhelm the leadership in the general and they won't be able to stop us next time around. I'll get everyone in here now." He turned to the phone and lifted the receiver. "We'll work all night. We'll work straight through to election day." He was chattering now. "No sleep. Drink coffee the whole time."

Benjamin reached over with a pat on the back. "We can start tomorrow. Tomorrow will be soon enough."

✦ ✦ ✦

Later that year, during the general elections, Benjamin won his seat in the Knesset with more votes than any other Likud Party candidate. Shamir, standing for re-election as prime minister, was defeated by Yitzhak Rabin. Shortly after the results were announced, Shamir resigned from the party. Moshe Arens, second in party rank, was expected to take up the post of party leadership, but after Shamir quit Arens resigned, too. "The party needs younger leadership if it is to thrive," he explained. And just like that, Likud Party leadership was in total disarray.

Once again, Benjamin met with Geller to talk about whether he should enter the race for party leader. "The field is wide open," Geller observed. "Only David Levy and Benny Begin have any realistic hope of preventing you from winning. But I don't think they can. I don't think the local party leaders will allow it."

"It's a little risky, though," Benjamin mused. "Stepping up to take control so soon after entering office."

"You're a two-term Knesset member. It's not like you just arrived. And," Geller added, "a win here would put you at the top of the Likud list for prime minister."

"Think we can win?"

"I know we can win it. Have you talked about this with Sara?

Benjamin nodded. "She's excited about it."

"Are you sure?"

"Yeah, why?"

"Well, this could get a little rough. Running for party leadership and then prime minister. Back to back. If she doesn't want you to run, it could be a problem."

Benjamin chuckled. "She's with me on it. Don't worry about it."

"Okay."

"First we have to win the party leadership race," Benjamin outlined. "Let's concentrate on that and take it one step at a time."

44

NETANYAHU

THE ENVELOPE THAT IRAN'S trade minister, Mostafa Najjar, gave to Ri Su Yong's handler when they met in Beijing contained a request to meet with Hwang Tu-Bong, head of North Korea's Strategic Rocket Forces.

Two weeks after returning from the Beijing meeting, Zhao Wei, an assistant in the business trade relations section of the Chinese embassy arrived unannounced at Najjar's office.

"This won't take long," he assured as Najjar ushered him to a chair on the far side of the room.

"Would you care for tea?"

Wei shook his head no.

"Coffee perhaps?"

"No. Really. As I said, this won't take long."

"Then, how may I help you?"

"I have been instructed to give this to you," Wei answered. He reached into the inside pocket of his jacket and took out an envelope which he handed to Najjar.

Najjar took the envelope from Wei and carefully lifted the flap. Inside he found a letter from Tu-Bong inviting him to come to Pyongyang, North Korea's capital, for a visit as a guest of the state.

"I am available to facilitate a response if one is required."

Najjar glanced up from reading the letter and turned toward the door. "Just one moment. I'll be right back."

Najjar stepped out to a secretary who sat at a desk near his office door. He handed her the letter from Tu-Bong and told her to prepare a response, then returned to his office and rejoined Wei. "I will have a response for you momentarily."

"Well then," Wei said. "Perhaps I shall have some of that coffee you mentioned earlier."

"Certainly," Najjar moved behind the desk. He placed a call to a steward, then hung up the phone and moved back to where Wei was seated.

Wei smiled up at Najjar. "Perhaps we do have one thing to discuss."

"And what might that be?"

"Oil."

Two months later, Najjar traveled to North Korea and met with Tu-Bong. He toured several North Korean rocket facilities and conducted a series of meetings with top North Korean officials including discussions with his peer, the minister of foreign trade.

Six weeks after Najjar returned from his trip, a container ship arrived at Iran's Kharg Island port facility. Cargo manifests and other documents indicated the ship was carrying clothing. Most of the containers were off-loaded and hauled away by truck to warehouses located in Iran's major cities where the contents were unloaded and routinely distributed to stores.

The remaining containers, fifteen in all, were taken to Iran's missile testing facility at Qom. Inside the containers, beneath a top layer of crates filled with cotton sweatshirts, were half a dozen propulsion systems for long-range missiles, an assortment of other critical parts, and three Rodong-1 Missiles having a range of 1,500 kilometers.

✦ ✦ ✦

Mossad operatives working in Iran heard nothing of the container ship or the missiles and parts delivered to Qom. However, they did hear rumors of a reactor planned for construction at Isfahan. Two Mossad operatives were sent there to see for themselves and discovered a construction site. Upon closer inspection they found evidence that the location was being prepared for a reactor. Probably one based on a French design. As if to emphasize the point, two French engineers were seen on the site.

Perhaps even more unsettling than the reactor was the fact that work on the site was being conducted in the open, as if the Iranians had no fear of being discovered. Not by anyone on the ground and not by anyone viewing the area with the aid of a satellite.

After viewing the site, the agents prepared a report of their findings which was to be forwarded to Mossad headquarters in Tel Aviv where it was reviewed by analysts. Mossad director Michael Eilon, having succeeded Baruch Gutmann, convened a meeting in his office to discuss the matter.

Ury Liebermann, head of Mossad's Interstellar Security group spoke up. "Is it possible this was not authorized by the French government? I mean, is it possible a French company is involved in this project without specific approval of the French government?"

"Not really," Gideon Neyman answered.

Amos Megged, supervisor of clandestine operations, elaborated. "I suppose it's possible. But I think what Gideon is saying is it's not very likely they acted without approval of their own government."

"Let's ask them," someone offered.

Eilon shook his head. "Can't ask them."

"Why not?"

"If we ask, we'll be disclosing that we know about the site," Neyman offered. "And if they find out we know about it, they would have no trouble at all working backwards to figure out how we know the things we know."

"And then," Kollek added, "hundreds of men and women who work for us in-country would suddenly be in great danger of being discovered."

"So what do we do?"

"Sit on the information," Megged said flatly.

Neyman commented, "No one in that office knows how to keep a secret."

Eilon summarily cut off the discussion. "I have no choice but to notify the prime minister. But let's look at this report again." He held the report from Isfahan. "These two agents point out something very interesting."

Neyman spoke up. "You mean the part about how the site is right out there in the open for anyone with a satellite to see?"

"Yes," Eilon replied. "What do you make of that?"

"The Russians and the Americans are the only ones with that kind of technology."

"You think the Iranians know exactly where the US satellites are located?" Eilon asked. "Do the Iranians have the ability to collect that kind of information about satellite activity?"

Neyman shook his head. "No, I don't think so."

"So," Eilon continued, "if they don't have the ability to get it for themselves, then someone had to provide the information to them."

"And there's only two possibilities for that," Neyman said.

"I think we could safely eliminate the Americans," Megged interjected. "Not much possibility the US would share that kind of intelligence with Iran."

"Which leaves only the Russians."

The discussion continued for another hour as they explored the possibilities presented by the notion that Russia and Iran had a cooperative relationship, and that Russia would share information about US satellites with them.

✦ ✦ ✦

Later that day, Eilon visited Prime Minister Rabin in his office and gave him an extensive briefing on Iran's nuclear program, the latest information collected by agents on the ground there, and the most recently discovered reactor construction site near Isfahan.

"Is this their only reactor construction site?" Rabin asked. He'd been standing the entire time and now wandered near the window, his arms behind his back.

"It's one of the few we know about," Eilon said. "Difficult to say if it's the only one, though."

"They inherited several reactors from the shah, didn't they?"

"Yes, sir. But most of those were in disrepair."

"I understand those sites are more extensive then we first assumed."

"Yes, sir. They are."

Rabin paused and looked out the window for what seemed to Eilon like a long time. Then he turned away and glanced down at his desk. "Very well. We need to prepare a response to this latest information."

"Not yet," Eilon replied.

"Why not?"

"None of the ministers know about this latest information. We need to brief them and get them all up to speed before we announce new policy."

"I'm not talking about announcing our response now or making a response. Not yet. But we need to get to work on deciding what an eventual response would be. I'm not going to wait for them to use a bomb against us."

"Yes, sir."

"Then we should meet with General Cohen and bring the IDF chief of staff up to date on what we've learned."

"Yes, sir."

"We'll need to discuss this with him in an open and frank conversation."

"Certainly." Eilon had an amused smile which Rabin noticed immediately.

"Something about our situation amuse you?"

"No, sir," Eilon answered quickly. "It's just...well...would you really attack Iran?"

Rabin's eyes were ablaze. "Wouldn't you?"

"I would have attacked them a long time ago," Eilon said. "But I'm not asking about me. I'm asking about you."

Rabin turned away once more and gazed out the window. "You should pray I never have to make that decision."

✦ ✦ ✦

That evening, Rabin and Eilon met with General Cohen. They discussed Iran's nuclear program including the reactor construction site and the possibility there might be others. Huddled over a map that lay across Rabin's desk, they studied known nuclear sites.

"We know for certain about these three," Cohen pointed to sites near Tehran.

"Those are facilities constructed during the shah's rule?"

"Yes," Cohen said.

"There's a test site over here, as well." Eilon indicated a location west of the city.

"And there's a storage facility down here." Cohen pointed to another spot on the map.

"Anything else we know for certain?"

"There's an abandoned reactor over here near Rasht," Eilon added.

"Abandoned?"

"During the first years of the Islamic Revolution they didn't have technicians who could operate it so they simply withdrew the fuel and shut it down."

"How many more sites like that do they have?"

"Just three," Eilon again pointed to the map.

They discussed options, arguing about what to do. Finally, Rabin ordered Cohen to prepare plans to address the sites that posed the most immediate risk to Israel's security. "We'll meet again when you have those plans ready."

When they were gone, Rabin stood at the window and stared out at the approaching darkness and found it appropriately metaphoric of the situation he faced. "Darkness," he muttered. "Nuclear weapons bring mankind nothing but darkness."

45

NETANYAHU

IN THE UNITED STATES, Bill Clinton was in his first term as president. Young and untried in international affairs, he'd spent the first two years stumbling from one incident to the next as he learned the role of his office in foreign policy. Now, a new crisis loomed as rumors of Iran's reactor construction slowly leaked out. That's when the CIA picked up on the activity, alerted its operatives in the region, and requested details from anyone with information about the matter. Two agents already in Iran were sent to the site to see for themselves whether the rumors were true.

At the same time, NSA re-tasked one of its satellites to pass over the suspected area. It didn't take long for analysts to confirm what others had suggested—Iran was constructing a reactor at Isfahan.

Armed with that information, Paul Biggs, the NSA director, prepared a full briefing for the president which Biggs presented himself. When he concluded, the president called a meeting of his national security team to review the situation and discuss their options. They met in the Oval Office.

Biggs brought the team up to speed on the latest satellite images and other information they'd collected about Iran's reactor. "The one thing we don't know yet," he added as he concluded his presentation, "is whether and to what extent Israel will react to this project. Thus far, they've made no public announcements about it."

Gil Martin from the CIA commented first. "That's probably because they don't know about it." He spoke with a condescending sense of superiority. "They don't have that kind of capability."

Kurt McKinney, an assistant to the president, shook his head. "Mr. President, I think it's highly likely they *do* know. They keep a very close watch over this sort of thing."

Lloyd White, secretary of defense, agreed with Martin. "I'm with Gil, Mr. President. I don't think the Israelis know about this project. Otherwise, they would have spoken out about it."

Mike Yeager, the state department's undersecretary for arms control and international security, joined the discussion. "I think they know. They just don't want to reveal how they know it."

"That seems improbable to me," Martin countered.

President Clinton, his reading glasses perched halfway down his nose, looked over at Martin. "I think we both know that anything is possible."

"We can always ask them," McKinney suggested.

Stokely Raskin, Clinton's chief of staff, shook his head. "Mr. President, I don't think we should do that."

McKinney glanced in his direction. "Why not?"

"If we ask them about it," Raskin explained, "they'll be forced to either disclose or lie."

President Clinton nodded. "And why treat a friend that way?"

Martin nodded as well. "What do you suggest, Mr. President?"

Clinton glanced around the room. "Why not simply act on our own information? Everyone knows we have the best satellite capability in the world. I think we should act on our own information and save Israel from having to be involved."

Yeager shook his head. "I think we at least have to tell them what we're doing. Maybe it shouldn't come from you, but we have to tell them at some level."

"Perhaps," Clinton decided. "But not to elicit their help or participation." He scooted forward in his chair and took off his glasses. "If we respond alone, it's just the US against a Middle Eastern country. Everyone's familiar with that scenario. Other countries will complain about it but no one will take any action against us. But if we act jointly with the Israelis it becomes a Jewish attack supported by the US. We do that and everyone will line up against Israel *and* us."

McKinney spoke up, "Very well, Mr. President. How are we going to respond?"

"We use the best tool we have," Clinton grinned. "We go public with the truth."

"That's it?"

"If the last fifty years have taught us anything, it's that the information age offers us responsive measures that are far more powerful than armed conflict. We don't always have to resort to war to manage regional threats."

"Mr. President," Yeager attempted to press his earlier point. "We have many—"

Raskin cut him off with a wave of his hand. "You've heard the president's decision on the matter." He looked over at McKinney. "Alert Andrew at the UN and tell him to prepare a request for a Security Council meeting. I'll notify the press secretary's office and alert the speech writers to get ready with a statement."

✦ ✦ ✦

In Israel the following day, Ariel Yosef tapped lightly on the prime minister's office door, then pushed it open. Rabin looked up. "You need to see me?"

Yosef came through the doorway and stood near Rabin's desk. "As you know, I often have lunch with a contact at the US embassy."

"That's what you've told me."

"I just talked to him a few minutes ago." Yosef glanced nervously over his shoulder, as if checking the door, then lowered his voice. "He says US satellites have discovered a nuclear reactor construction site in Iran."

Rabin looked up. "Where?"

"Isfahan."

"He told you this?"

"Yes."

"You didn't ask him?"

"No, sir. He called and invited me to lunch. That's when he told me."

"Did he tell you what they plan to do about it?"

"They plan to demand a Security Council meeting at the UN."

Rabin looked pleased. "They're going public with the information?"

"Yes, sir."

Rabin leaned back in his chair, his eyes focused on a point in the distance, deep in thought. Yosef looked bewildered. "Did we know this already?"

"Don't worry about it." Rabin had a satisfied smile.

✦ ✦ ✦

The following day, Andrew Chapman, the US ambassador to the UN, announced that the United States had conclusive proof that Iran was constructing a reactor at Isfahan. He demanded an emergency session of the Security Council and requested an order requiring Iran to immediately cease all work at the site pending a full review by UN inspectors.

In a statement presented to the general session, Iran's ambassador, Hasan Maleki, admitted Iran was constructing a reactor, but insisted it was only for peaceful purposes. "It will power an electric generation facility. Our country needs electrical power."

When the session went into recess, Maleki hurried to his office and contacted Iranian president Akbar Rafsanjani. He outlined the accusations made by the United States and the evidence that supported those charges.

After the call, Rafsanjani telephoned the office of Sayyed Ali Hosseini Khamenei, Iran's current Supreme Leader, and scheduled a time to meet with him to discuss the information relayed by Maleki.

Khamenei and Rafsanjani met that afternoon at Khamenei's official residence in the Sadabad complex, a collection of palaces created by Shah Pahlavi and his predecessors. An assistant ushered Rafsanjani to a parlor where he was seated on a comfortable sofa. Twenty minutes later, Khamenei entered the room and took a seat in a chair across from him. "You have heard from Maleki?"

"The security council has agreed to hear the United States' petition," Rafsanjani answered. "There will be a call for sanctions against us, I'm sure."

"Will the UN pass such a measure?"

"Yes, but China would be willing to veto it, if we ask."

Khamenei nodded his head thoughtfully. "And their veto will come with conditions."

"Probably something to do with oil."

Khamenei stroked his beard slowly. "What about negotiating directly with the United States?"

Rafsanjani shook his head. "The US is leading the fight on this issue. I don't think they want to negotiate privately with us."

Khamenei's face was expressionless. "Bill Clinton is a smart man."

"He's also an ambitious man," Rafsanjani added. "And full of self-confidence."

"But he might be inclined toward negotiations just because he thinks he can out-negotiate us."

"You may be correct."

Khamenei sighed. "Then perhaps you should contact the Americans first and if that does not prove fruitful, ask the Chinese for a veto."

"I think Bill Clinton is a dangerous man. Raising the issue of private negotiations with them will make us appear weak."

"Then raise it with the public first."

"You mean, now?"

"If the US refuses to meet with us, then announce that we offered to meet, but they declined."

"Yes," Rafsanjani bowed. "As you wish."

✦ ✦ ✦

After meeting with Khamenei, Rafsanjani contacted Seyed Ansari, the head of Iran's Atomic Energy Organization which oversaw the country's nuclear program. They arranged to meet in the parking lot of Azadi Stadium, a soccer facility on the north side of Tehran, not far from Khamenei's residence.

Ansari's car was already there when Rafsanjani arrived. Rafsanjani's driver parked beside it and opened the door for him. As Rafsanjani stepped out, Ansari joined him and they strolled slowly across the lot together.

"You are aware of the trouble awaiting us at the UN?" Rafsanjani began.

"Yes," Ansari replied.

"Can we secure our existing material?"

"That would take months. Perhaps even longer."

"What about just the best of it?" Rafsanjani asked. "The most enriched."

"Even securing *only* the best would take weeks."

"You have a safe place to put it?"

"Yes."

"A place where no one else can find it?"

"Yes."

"Then I suggest you get busy doing so immediately," Rafsanjani ordered.

✦ ✦ ✦

Before the UN Security Council convened to take up the US petition against Iran, Maleki proposed a round of unilateral discussions directly with the US over the question of Iran's desire for a nuclear program and the US desire to limit nuclear proliferation in the Middle East region. Chapman, on behalf of the US, agreed to meet with Maleki for nonbinding discussions. The two parties held their initial meeting late that afternoon in a conference room across the corridor from the Secretary-General's office. As they gathered around the conference table, Maleki suggested they begin by setting the parameters of their talks.

Chapman appeared dismayed. "I thought we made that clear already. Halt construction on the nuclear reactor at Isfahan, cease work on any other reactors you might have in development, and allow inspectors to confirm that construction at those sites has been halted."

"And if we suspend construction at Isfahan now, the United States will agree to forgo any unilateral action against us while we talk?"

"No," Chapman argued, "that's not what we said."

"But for now," Maleki responded. "If we suspend for now, you will agree for now?"

"At *all* of your nuclear reactor sites."

"At Isfahan," Maleki smiled. "For now."

Chapman sighed. "And you will allow inspectors to confirm construction has been halted?"

"Yes. At Isfahan."

"Very well," Chapman answered with resignation. "If you halt construction at Isfahan immediately and allow inspectors to confirm you've stopped, we will take no military action against Iran for now. But any ultimate settlement must include disclosure and inspection at all other nuclear reactor sites in Iran."

"Very well. I must discuss this matter further with authorities in Tehran. Perhaps we should meet again tomorrow. So that you have an opportunity to confirm our intentions."

Chapman wearily nodded his head. "We should talk again tomorrow."

The following day, Chapman and Maleki returned to the conference room. Maleki greeted him with a smile. "I assume you have viewed the Isfahan site with one of your satellites."

"Yes," Chapman said.

"And you are satisfied we have ceased construction at the site?"

For a moment, Chapman thought of leaving the room altogether. *This is going nowhere*, he thought. But still, work at the reactor site *was* stopped. So, once again he put aside his personal feelings. "Right. Now, let's discuss the inspectors. They will need unlimited access to your reactor site."

"They can have unlimited access to the construction site at Isfahan," Maleki stressed.

"The inspectors," Chapman continued, "will be from the UN's International Atomic Energy Agency Commission."

"We agree. However we must choose half and you must choose half."

"I don't think that will be a problem." Chapman glanced through his papers. "They will need to begin work as soon as we finish with our agreement and the Security Council approves it."

"I do not foresee that as problematic."

46

NETANYAHU

MEANWHILE, as instructed by Seyed Ansari, workers at Iran's centrifuge sites were busy preparing all uranium purified above twenty percent for immediate shipment to undisclosed locations outside the expected purview of UN inspectors. In Hamadan—a city of half a million people located about four hundred kilometers west of Tehran—Farzan Ameri, an Iranian born CIA operative, sat in a car parked outside a warehouse that was located across the road from one of those centrifuge facilities.

Ameri watched as a truck pulling a flatbed trailer drove from the site. A nuclear material transportation container was perched on the trailer and the truck's engine seemed to labor under the weight of its load. The truck was accompanied by military vehicles carrying armed soldiers.

When the truck and its accompanying convoy was a safe distance ahead, Ameri started the car, steered it away from the warehouse, and made his way to the road, reaching the pavement just as the convoy disappeared over the crest of a low rise. He turned the car onto the road, pressed his foot down on the accelerator, and followed after them.

Four hours later, the convoy arrived at a secure but unmarked facility near Pishva, about seventy meters south of Tehran. As the truck turned from the highway to the facility's entrance, Ameri passed it by and turned the car into a warehouse section situated just past the facility and on the same side of the road. He brought the car to a stop at the first building and glanced out the window.

From his position, Ameri had a clear view of the facility next door. He watched as the truck and trailer sat at a security checkpoint. After only a cursory review by the guards, the truck moved past the checkpoint and disappeared behind a building.

With the truck now out of sight, Ameri put the car in gear and drove toward the back of the warehouse section, passing rows and rows of single-story industrial buildings, until he reached the last building.

A moment later, the truck with the transportation flask still on its trailer, came into sight as it rounded the corner on the far side of a building next door. It rumbled past the building to a point midway between its corners, then slowed even more and gently swung in an arc until the truck and trailer were perpendicular to the building. There the truck came to a stop and the driver slowly backed the trailer up to one of the building's large rollup doors. Ameri watched a moment longer, then put car in gear and drove back toward the road. When he reached the pavement, he turned and sped away.

An hour later, Ameri reached Tehran and made his way to Gole Rezaeeieh, a café located on Gavam Saltane Street not far from Martyr's Square, a site dedicated to the shooting deaths of young protesters during the Islamic Revolution. Ameri parked the car in an alley nearby and walked up the street to the café.

At the café, Ameri took a seat at a table in back, ordered a cup of coffee, and drank it while watching the front door. In a few minutes, the door opened and Akbar Bijani, also a CIA operative, entered the room. He slowly made his way to the back and took a seat at the table with Ameri.

"This place is not good," Bijani muttered. "Too many people listening. Too many watching."

Ameri dismissed his concerns with a wave of the hand. "They're mostly tourists today. I wouldn't worry about it."

"I'm not worried," Bijani replied coldly. "I just notice that kind of stuff. People listening. Eyes watching. That sort of thing."

"Then let's go someplace where we can talk," Ameri suggested with a broad smile.

✦ ✦ ✦

From the coffee shop near the center of Tehran, Ameri and Bijani traveled to a farm house located about four kilometers from town. The house served as a safe house and was maintained by the CIA.

While they sat at a table in the kitchen drinking coffee, Bijani talked about meeting someone who worked at the site in Pishva. "We've met several times. Usually at a coffee shop on the west side of the city. According to him, entry to the facility in Pishva is tightly controlled. The usual ID badge, of course, but in addition they use fingerprint and retina scanners even for typical workers. If they suspect something is amiss, they sometimes check DNA."

"That's some serious stuff," Ameri observed. "Especially for Iran."

Bijani nodded. "So is this." He drew an automatic pistol from inside his jacket. Without so much as a blink of an eye, he pointed the pistol at Ameri.

"Hey!" Ameri exclaimed. "What are you doing?"

Without a moment's hesitation, Bijani squeezed the trigger and shot Ameri twice in the head. Ameri flopped against the back of the chair, his mouth open, eyes wide as if staring up at the ceiling.

✦ ✦ ✦

Uziel Gantz and Elazar Menacham Shach, both Mossad operatives, watched from a hilltop behind the house. Using a telescope, they periodically scanned the windows, hoping to catch a glimpse of what might be happening inside. They were watching when Ameri appeared in the frame, slumped in his chair.

A moment later, Bijani came into view as he checked Ameri's pockets and removed the contents. He disappeared from view while he shoved the items into his own pockets, then reappeared briefly through a window to the left as he moved toward the door.

Seconds later, Bijani came from the house, walked to the car, and got in behind the steering wheel and drove away.

Gantz looked over at Shach. "Did you expect that?"

Shach shook his head. "No, but I have always wondered if they could really do it."

"Do what?"

"Spy for the US," Shach said. "Both of them are Persian by birth."

"But they were raised from childhood in the US," Gantz countered. "They don't know anything else but American culture."

"Not exactly," Shach said dryly.

"What do you mean?"

"They were raised in the US but as Muslim," Shach explained. "Not as Caucasians of European descent. Their childhood had a distinct emphasis on everything *Iranian*, not American."

"We should follow him and find out where he's going."

"No," Shach responded. "We should report what we saw and stick to our job. The container on that truck they were following is only used for one thing—hauling enriched uranium."

"Or plutonium," Gantz corrected.

"All the more reason to pass this information on to Tel Aviv and let the CIA handle their own problems."

NETANYAHU

CONVINCED THE US was taking the lead against Iran and its nuclear program, Yitzhak Rabin, Israel's prime minister, met with Micheal Eilon, Mossad director, and General Yehuda Cohen, the IDF chief of staff. Together, they reviewed written response plans designed to neutralize or destroy as many of Iran's nuclear reactors as possible.

Rabin pointed to a list of sites. "You are certain all of these sites are nuclear reactors?"

"Yes," Eilon responded.

"I see six on here," Rabin noted.

"Yes."

"I thought they were only Building One."

"Plus the one we discovered in Rasht," General Cohen responded.

Rabin looked over at Eilon. "Have we told the Americans about it?"

"I think someone leaked it to them."

"But nothing about these other sites," Rabin pointed to a page from the plans.

"No, we didn't want them to find out how we obtained the information."

Rabin nodded his head slowly. "I understand." He glanced through the pages, then laid them aside and sat up straight in his chair. "Well," he summarized, "I think we have created a good response plan. It does all that we wanted and perhaps a little more." He lifted his head to look them in the eye. "But I have decided to wait and monitor further developments. The United States has put its integrity on the line. I suspect they will not back down until they have reached an acceptable result."

"Very well, Mr. Prime Minister," Eilon stood to leave. General Cohen stood also and started toward the door.

"General," Rabin called. Cohen paused and turned to face him. "I expect you to follow my decision."

"Certainly, Mr. Prime Minister," the general replied. "That is my duty."

✦ ✦ ✦

While Eilon met with Rabin, the report from Gantz and Shach—the Mossad agents in Iran—arrived in Tel Aviv. That report included details about the movement of product from a centrifuge facility at Hamedan using a specialized transportation container, a description of its destination at the facility in Pishva, and photographs. It also included information about the two men, apparently CIA operatives, working the same transfer. Analysts examined the photographs and determined that the device on the truck was a transportation container for radioactive materials.

When he returned to his office, Eilon found Amos Megged, supervisor of clandestine operations, and Gideon Neyman waiting for him with Amon Podell from the lab, and Omri Peretz, supervisor of the photography and images section.

"We received a report from our agents in Iran," Megged handed him the report.

Eilon looked over at Neyman. "Your section has reviewed it?"

"Yes, sir," Neyman replied.

Eilon took a seat at his desk and scanned the report. As he reached the end of the first page he glanced up at Omri Peretz, supervisor of the photography. "You've analyzed the photographs?"

"Yes, sir."

"And you are certain the truck was carrying a radioactive transportation flask?"

"Not one that is currently approved," Peretz replied, "but it would have been fifteen years ago."

"What's it approved for?

"Transporting enriched uranium and plutonium."

"So, if there was uranium in that container," Eilon asked, "it would be twenty percent pure?"

"Or higher," Peretz responded. "Or it could contain plutonium."

"If they are using it for its designed purpose," Eilon added.

"Yes," Peretz conceded. "That would be correct."

"What about your meeting with the prime minister?" Neyman asked. "Is the response plan approved?"

"He decided to put it off."

"Perhaps you should go back to him and show him this report."

"No, I don't think so."

"Why not?" Neyman insisted.

"We don't want this to be made public. It would expose our agents."

"It doesn't have to be made public," Podell suggested. "We simply tell him this changes things. That he has to strike now, before it's too late."

"It's already too late," Eilon sighed.

Neyman looked puzzled. "What do you mean?"

"If they moved the enriched uranium from this site," Eilon indicated on the report, "then don't you think they moved it from the others, too?"

"Yes," Neyman said with a note of resignation. "I suppose so."

"And do we know where they put the uranium from the other sites?"

"No, sir. Not all of it and certainly not from the other sites. We don't even know for certain the movement of the uranium had anything to do with developments at the UN."

Eilon looked at Neyman. "Is that what your gut tells you? That this move was unrelated to events at the UN?"

"My gut tells me the movement of the uranium is directly linked to events at the UN. They've been stalling to give themselves more time to get the higher enriched uranium to a safer location. One that would be difficult for inspectors to locate."

Eilon laid aside the report and turned to Megged. "Tell our people in Iran to get busy locating all sites for enriched uranium."

"That'll be like starting over."

"Not exactly. They know where all of the production facilities are located. Mining through the first stage of refining."

"Yes."

"And they know where the unenriched uranium is kept."

"Right."

"So, they know where to begin now looking for activity."

"Still," Megged ventured, "it will be a monumental task, locating the enriched stockpiles."

"Which means you should stop talking and get busy."

Eilon turned in Neyman's direction. "And you, get your analysts busy sorting through what we know and see if we can help them figure this out."

48

NET*A*NYA*H*U

AS BENJAMIN AND HIS STAFF continued to work toward taking control of the Likud Party, they became concerned about the overall image of the campaign. To address that, Geller hired Pnina Brosh, a media consultant who lived in Haifa. In the weeks that followed, Benjamin and Pnina worked closely together, often at late hours. One thing led to another and they began seeing each other romantically.

Unbeknownst to Benjamin, agents working for Samad Harawi's intelligence network—the same intelligence network that photographed him with Sara in the Paris airport—continued to tail Benjamin, as they had done since his entry into politics. And not merely tail him, they collected hours of video and hundreds of photographs in the process. All of it duly and regularly forwarded to Harawi's office in Istanbul where it was logged and filed away.

As Benjamin's affair with Pnina Brosh heated up, Harawi's agents collected hours of video of the two together, some of it showing them in compromising positions. Agents were assigned to cover Pnina separately, even when Benjamin was not with her, and operatives in Istanbul began compiling a dossier on her.

Not far into the campaign effort, Harawi and his team of analysts became convinced that Benjamin would win the election for chairmanship of the Likud Party. "There's something different about this one,"

Harawi cautioned anyone who listened. "He comes from a long line of determined, rightwing advocates. If he gets established, he might just do what his political ancestors wanted. He might take control of the entire region, including parts on the east side of the Jordan River."

In an effort to prevent Benjamin from winning the chairmanship election—a victory that would go a long way toward establishing him as a political force to be reckoned with—Harawi ordered the release of surveillance video showing Benjamin with Pnina in an obviously romantic moment, along with a written summary providing details about their relationship. A few days later, a copy of the video and background information made its way to an agent in Tel Aviv with directions to pass it on to Saleh Hazan in Jerusalem.

✦ ✦ ✦

Though not as extensive or as ruthless as Harawi's, the Likud Party maintained its own intelligence network that collected data on everyone and everything—rumors, hard facts, photographs, video and the like—pertaining to their own party members and to the opposition as well. Key operatives in the network were full-time employees of the party but below them were various part-time contributors and paid informants who supplied the network with raw information and in many cases gave them the first indication of where trouble might lie. Saleh Hazan was one of those lowest-level contacts in the network.

Though Muslim by faith, Hazan had forgone any outward display of religious belief in order to infiltrate the Likud network. Bolstered by information supplied by Harawi's agents, he established himself as a reliable source of particularly incriminating evidence. The kind that no political operative could ignore or resist.

One of those to whom Hazan reported was Ehud Deri, a man who was part of the Likud network but who secretly worked for David Levy, passing new information to Levy before sending it on to party head-quarters. When Hazan received the video and report on Benjamin and Pnina, he passed it to Deri.

✦ ✦ ✦

Being thoroughly enamored of American culture—and of Bill Clinton in particular—Benjamin modeled his approach to the campaign after that of Clinton. Sara modeled her approach on that of Hillary Clinton. Pnina Brosh managed their effort very well and to the public Benjamin and Sara appeared as a perfect, young family. Photo opportunities of the couple with their youngest children in tow were provided for the press on a frequent and liberal basis. Campaign advertisements reiterated the message and interviews were staged to create the same positive, energetic impression.

In the midst of that, however, Geller began hearing rumors that Benjamin had been seeing another woman. He suspected the rumors were true, having already figured it out from things he'd seen and heard for himself.

That Benjamin was having an affair wasn't a problem in and of itself. For Israelis, questions of adultery and infidelity were private matters best left to the couple's discretion. But that's where the problem lay for Benjamin and for Geller. Sara was not someone who would tolerate an open view of marriage, which made an affair a serious threat to Benjamin's campaign and to his future in politics.

This was not an issue they could ignore but before confronting Benjamin on the matter, Geller needed to find out if the rumors really were true and, if so, whether anyone had any evidence of the affair. And, he needed to do that without raising anyone's suspicion. For that kind of information, he had little choice but to turn to the party's own intelligence network.

The Likud Party intelligence network was spread far and wide and was managed at the top by Daniel Geffen who, oddly enough given his position, was a man with a reputation for honesty and discretion. Geller arranged to meet him in a secluded courtyard at the Tel Aviv Museum of Art.

"Things are heating up with the campaign," Geller commented.

"So I noticed. But your guy seems to be handling himself in a good way."

"That's what I wanted to talk to you about."

"That's why most people want to talk to me." Geffen smiled in Geller's direction. "Has someone made an accusation?"

"No," Geller replied. "But that's what I was going to ask you. Have you heard anything?"

"Like what?"

"Like...the usual. You know. Sex. Drugs. Acts of indiscretion." Geller gave a frustrated sigh. "I don't know what I'm supposed to say. I just don't want to get surprised. So, I guess what I want to know is whether you've heard anything that sounds like trouble headed our way."

"Nothing. Not a word. And I assume from your level of frustration you haven't heard anything either."

"Not a word."

"It's good for you to be worried. Part of your job. You worry so the candidate doesn't have to."

Geller nodded. "I suppose you're right. It's just too quiet, though. Too calm, too...nice."

"Would you like for me to check around?"

"I would love for you to check around."

"I'll see what I can find out."

"Good. Just make sure you keep it quiet. I don't want to cause a problem where there isn't one to begin with."

"I understand," Geffen replied.

Two days later, Geffen reported back with information that confirmed the affair. "Our sources tell me he's been seeing a woman named Pnina Brosh. She lives in Haifa."

"Does anyone have any evidence?"

"Lots of rumors about someone following him. Plenty—"

"Our people following him? Geller asked, cutting him off. "From Likud?"

"No. We don't have anyone on him. But there are plenty of stories about video and photographs of your guy. No one has seen them, but there are plenty of people out there who say they exist."

"You'll let me know if you see any of it."

"You'll be my first call."

✦ ✦ ✦

A few days later, Benjamin returned home from an extended speaking schedule to find Sara waiting for him in the living room. From the look on her face he could tell she was upset. "Someone called the house this morning," she began. He leaned over to kiss her but she turned away before their lips touched.

"What does that mean? Someone called here. I imagine you get lots of calls."

"Not like this one."

He took a seat across from her. "What is it, Sara, what's wrong?"

"They said you were having an affair," she blurted, no longer able to contain her emotions. "They said they have video! That if you drop out, they'll forget all about it. If you don't, they're going public with it."

Benjamin reached out to take her in his arms. "Sara, I promise, this—"

"Video, Benjamin!" Her voice was loud and angry. "They have video of you and a woman. Together. Doing...whatever it is men and women do when they cheat on their spouses."

Benjamin tried once more to calm her down. "Sara, I promise, this supposed affair never happened."

"They have video, Benjamin," she repeated for the third time. "Why would they tell me that if it never happened."

"I...don't know." Benjamin's eyes darted away from her and his cheeks blushed a bright pink. Sara lunged toward him. "Don't lie to me!" she shouted. He wrapped his arms around her in a hug but she wriggled free. "How could you?" she said, her voice growing louder. "Why did you do this? And why did you do it in the midst of this campaign?"

"This is David Levy," Benjamin huffed. "Or someone who works for him."

Sara paused long enough for a deep frown to appear on her forehead. "David Levy is having an affair?"

"No," Benjamin answered. "He's the one behind the call and the threat."

"I don't care about who's behind the call," Sara shouted. "You betrayed me! You betrayed us. You betrayed your family. Your campaign."

Benjamin, unable to do anything to stop her, simply stood by and listened.

"What's her name?" Sara asked.

"I think you'd be better off not knowing that."

"I want to know," she demanded. "I have a right to know."

"Well, I'm not telling you."

"Why not?'

"Because I don't want you tracking her down and confronting her."

"Oh," Sara ridiculed in a mocking tone. "Now you're going to protect her."

Benjamin shook his head. "No! I'm going to protect *us*. We don't need any more bad publicity than what these accusations will bring."

"Ha," she laughed angrily, "You should have thought about that before you took up with that woman."

✦ ✦ ✦

The next day, Benjamin went to his workplace and walked straight into Geller's office. "There's something I have to tell you," he said as he closed the door behind him.

"Okay," Geller replied. "Tell me."

For the next fifteen minutes, Benjamin told Geller about the affair and about the phone call Sara received. "So, we have to decide what to do about this. If they've called her and made a threat like that it won't be long before this gets in the news."

"Well, one thing's for certain. We're not dropping out. I don't care if they do go public. We aren't quitting. If you do that, you'll be finished in Israeli politics and the party will be forever in the hands of the people we distrust the most." He looked Benjamin in the eye. "We aren't dropping out."

"Okay, I agree. Quitting is not an option."

"And I don't know yet what to do about the campaign and the media," Geller continued. "But you have to tell the staff about this and you have to do it sooner rather than later."

Benjamin agreed. "Bring them all in here. I'll tell them now."

Geller walked from behind his desk, stepped to the door, and moved down the hallway. A few moments later, he returned with the permanent staff trailing behind him. Very quickly, the room filled to capacity with campaign workers seated in the chairs, on the corners of the desk, and leaning against the wall.

When they were all in place, Benjamin stood and, in a serious tone, told them what happened. "So," he added when he'd finished explaining the situation, "I apologize for putting you in this position. I know the commitment and sacrifices you have made to work here. To help us do something that is real and vital and has the power to transform our country. You've put a lot of trust and faith in me and I apologize for treating you and your trust in such a disgraceful manner."

Benjamin paused a moment and glanced around the room. "But as difficult as the moment is, we have to go on. I'm not going to quit, but we have to decide what to do next." He slipped his hand into his pocket and his finger touched the Netanyahu ring. "I mean, I'm not running as Husband of The Year. If America can re-elect Bill Clinton, Israel can elect me."

As he spoke, Benjamin thought of David and Bathsheba and how God had mercy on them. His sense of confidence, which had been shaken badly at first, now returned. This time with a knowing sense of who was attempting to blackmail him.

Geller spoke up. "What do you want to do?"

"I want to go public with it," Benjamin specified.

Heads nodded as others in the room agreed. Then someone in the corner spoke up. "I think that's the wrong thing to do."

"Why?" Benjamin asked.

"The public won't care about the affair. The only people who care about it are you and Sara."

"Unless she's unattractive," someone interjected in a half-hearted attempt at humor. "Then the public will think you have bad taste and you'll lose in a landslide."

Laughter tittered across the room, then someone else added in a serious tone, "If you wait until they publicize it, they'll be seen as the bad guy. They'll be the ones who dredged up your private life. If you speak up now, it'll make people wonder what else you're covering up."

Benjamin looked puzzled. "How so?"

"You'd be disclosing an affair as the basis of blackmail, when the public won't see it as blackmail level trouble. Especially since whoever's behind this talked to your wife first."

Benjamin's puzzled look became a frown. "I'm afraid I still don't understand."

"If someone wanted to do this sort of thing the right way, they would have talked to you without telling her. They would have threatened to tell her about the affair if you didn't drop out. That's the only way disclosure by them that could hurt you. At home. With your wife. Not with the general public."

Benjamin looked over at Geller. "What do you think?"

"I think these are good points to consider, but waiting puts the other side in the driver's seat. If we wait, they will control the story. If we go public first, *we* will control it."

"What's the downside to going public?"

Geller thought for a moment. "There's not really any big downside with the public."

"When could we do it?"

"Tonight." Geller checked his wristwatch, "We can do it during the news broadcast tonight."

Benjamin looked surprised. "Are you sure you can arrange it that quickly?"

"Yes," Geller replied. "If we're going to be first with the story, we can't wait around."

Benjamin grimaced. "Okay. Tonight it is."

"But," Geller cautioned, "you have to tell Sara immediately. She has to know this is coming, before she sees it on television."

"Right," Benjamin agreed. "You can set it up with the stations?"

"Yes."

"Okay. Call them. Make the arrangements." Benjamin started toward the door. "I'm going home now, but I'll be back in an hour."

✦ ✦ ✦

That evening, Benjamin appeared on the state television news broadcast. He told about the affair and the phone call to his wife in an attempt to coerce him into quitting the campaign for party chairmanship. When he finished, the interviewer asked, "Who do you think is behind all this?"

"Someone high up in the Likud leadership," Benjamin replied. "I don't think I have to name names. Everyone knows who they are. They're a clubby group."

"Why would they even attempt something like this?"

"First of all, I've never been the Likud Party leadership's candidate for anything. But beyond that, the Likud Party executive committee has been deciding on candidates in a collective manner since the beginning. That puts the selection process ultimately in the hands of a few who feel they are entitled by birthright or political ties to make those choices for the people. We are gradually changing that and I have been at the forefront of those changes. Putting the party back in the hands of party members. Many at the top do not like that and have adamantly opposed me in that effort. Now, they've sunk to a new low, trying to blackmail me and coerce me into dropping out of the race, just because they think I might win."

"Do you think you can win?"

"Yes, I do." Benjamin's eyes were bright with excitement for the first time that evening. "Our campaign is talking about issues that matter, not running around peeking in bedroom windows and making videos of private lives. Terrorism is the number one threat to our future. That's the issue we're focused on."

As he came from the television studio, a Likud member met him in the hall. "That was a brave tactic, going on the air like that."

"Thanks," Benjamin grinned.

"Not much to thank me about. What you did was brave, but you're ruined with the party."

"Why do you say that?"

"You've called them out. You've talked publicly about the dirty secret that leadership of both parties want never to be revealed. You've done that now. You've revealed it and they won't let you get away with it."

Benjamin gave him a friendly pat on the shoulder. "We'll see about that. We'll just see about that."

NET∧NYAHU

SELECTING INSPECTORS for review of Iran's nuclear sites turned into a three-week ordeal but finally, almost a month after the Council ruled on the petition and more than three months after the original petition had been filed, inspectors were on their way to Isfahan. They arrived in Iran on a Sunday with work scheduled to begin on Monday.

Known officially as the United Nations Special Commission for Inspection and Deterrence (UNSCOM-ID), the delegation of inspectors and support staff set up temporary offices on the campus of Isfahan University in a building that afforded a clear view of the reactor construction site. John Adler, a nuclear physicist from the University of Chicago, chaired the delegation.

Inspections at Isfahan went smoothly and the delegation confirmed that no further construction had occurred there since cessation was first indicated by Hasan Maleki. Not long after that, Adler reported that his inspectors visited two Iranian centrifuge sites and a storage facility in Hamadan. Evidence found at the storage facility suggested highly enriched uranium had been recently removed from it. Neither the centrifuge sites nor the storage facility in Hamadan were within the team's mandate and no mention was made of how the inspectors gained access to either location.

Iranian officials in Tehran appeared to have been caught off-guard by news that the inspection team had visited Hamadan and for several days issued no official response. Finally, however, Seyed Ansari, head of Iran's Atomic Energy Organization, issued an official statement in which he denied that Iran had any uranium that was enriched beyond twenty percent and denied that uranium of any kind or sort had been removed from the Hamadan location.

Because of suspicions raised by review of the Hamadan storage facility, Adler asked for the locations to which the removed material had been taken. Two weeks later, Seyed Ansari responded to the request by announcing Iran's refusal to disclose the location of any further sites associated with its nuclear program, declared the presence of UN inspectors a violation of Iranian sovereignty, and ordered them to leave at once.

When news of Ansari's announcement reached the United States, Andrew Chapman introduced an enforcement petition before the Security Council calling for sanctions against Iran for non-compliance with the UN Security Council's resolution regarding Iran's consent to inspections. Delegates to the council debated the matter, with ambassadors from China and Russia employing a broad range of parliamentary tactics and procedures to delay the matter. Their attempts to frustrate the council's work only served to make the need for sanctions more obvious and when the demand for sanctions finally came to a vote, it passed with only China and Russia voting against. No one attempted a veto.

With further work no longer possible, Adler and his inspectors returned to Isfahan and gathered essential documents and data collected from their work at the reactor site and departed Iran for the United States. The moment they cleared Iranian airspace, the Security Council issued an order freezing all Iranian bank accounts, prohibiting the export or import of Iranian oil and petroleum products, and prohibiting banks in member states from handling Iranian financial transactions.

50

NETANYAHU

ON ELECTION DAY in Israel, members of the Likud Party gathered in the clubhouse at Herzliya Country Club, located about twenty kilometers north of Tel Aviv, to cast their vote for party chairman and to watch as results arrived from local party organizations scattered across the country. Party regulars and elites were out in full force, clustered around the cash bar and huddled in the corners. They talked among themselves reassuring each other that events of the preceding weeks would be enough to turn back Benjamin's challenge and keep the party securely under their control.

Benjamin's campaign staff was out in full force, too, but they weren't spending their time talking or visiting with one another. Instead, they worked the entrance, greeting supporters at the door and escorting them to vote first before they enjoyed the evening.

Campaign staff was also evident in the villages and towns where Benjamin and his team had worked so hard to establish new local party organizations. Enthusiasm at the local level ran high that year with many members participating in a party election for the first time. Benjamin and his staff hoped that enthusiasm would translate into enough votes to overcome those generated by traditional party regulars.

Benjamin's election night operation was coordinated by Geller who monitored the evening's events from an RV that sat on the parking lot behind the clubhouse. Telephones installed inside kept him in constant contact with a network of well-trained operatives working the local party organizations. All through the evening, he worked the phones, answering questions and solving problems—getting a ride to the poll for a supporter, cajoling a reluctant member, assuring another of Benjamin's support for their cause.

With Geller handling election night details, Benjamin spent the evening with Sara, schmoozing party members, visiting with friends, and generally having a good time. Campaign staff who saw them noted how happy and relaxed they seemed together.

About eight that evening, as polling places at the local organizations began to close, party workers set about the task of counting the ballots. At each of the polling places, someone from Benjamin's campaign staff watched carefully to make certain results were properly tabulated. When the results were finally known, those operatives telephoned them to Geller in the RV.

Normally, the official vote count for each candidate would be tabulated in a clubhouse room down the hall from the ballroom, then posted on a board in the ballroom with updates made throughout the evening. That night, however, the numbers on the board showed only the earliest results and went without update well past nine o'clock.

When Geller realized the official results were delayed, he left the RV and made his way down the hall to the tabulating room. The door slammed closed behind him and a moment later the muffled sound of angry voices drifted from the room. The voices grew louder as anger turned to frustration. Shouts were heard and several members gathered in the hallway, trying to hear what was being said behind the door.

Benjamin noticed the group in the hall and started in that direction. Sara, who remained at his side, tugged on his arm. "Benjamin. Stay out here."

"I'm going to find out what's going on in there," he pointed toward the door.

"I don't think you should," Sara insisted.

"Why not?"

Shahar Ofer, one of Benjamin's speechwriters and closest advisers, stepped up. "Geller's in there. He will take care of it."

"What are they doing?"

"Arguing over the results."

"What's there to argue about?" Benjamin wondered. "Count the votes, post the results."

Anna Arkin, who stood nearby, spoke up. "I think that's where the problem lies."

"What problem?"

"The count didn't turn out the way they wanted."

"They're in there now looking for a way to fix it," Shahar added.

"You mean, they're trying to steal the election."

"I mean, Geller will handle it. He's had experienced with..."

Just then, the door opened and Hoshea Karpin, Likud Party's secretary, emerged from the room. He was followed by half a dozen party regulars and Geller. Benjamin caught Geller's eye. "What was that about?"

"They were trying to steer things in a different direction." Geller held up a sheaf of papers. "But I already knew the results. They couldn't do much against this."

Benjamin smiled. "Our people reported it in to us?"

"Yes, Mr. Chairman," Geller grinned. "Our people called in the results. The insiders couldn't argue with the numbers."

"We won?" Sara asked.

"Yes," Geller's eyes grew misty as he looked over at Benjamin. "You are now chairman of the party." He gestured toward the hallway. "We should go to the ballroom and make sure the results are reported on the board."

Those standing in the hall began to clap. Benjamin put an arm across Geller's shoulder and gave him a friendly hug. "Thank you. I couldn't have done this without you."

"Thank you for giving me the chance," Geller responded.

Shahar moved closer. "We should all go down to the ballroom."

"Yes," Sara took Benjamin's arm. "Come on." She tugged a little harder. "Let's go see what they show for a count."

Geller took the lead as they trooped down the hall to the ballroom doorway, then stepped aside to let Benjamin and Sara enter the room first. As they entered, the room erupted in applause. David Levy, Roni Milo, Ehud Ulmert, and Dan Meridor, who were standing near the leader board, had no choice but to acknowledge Benjamin's win.

✦ ✦ ✦

Early the next morning, Benjamin and Geller went to Likud Party headquarters. What they found—furniture broken and outdated equipment in disrepair—left them shaking their heads. "How did they let it get this way?"

"Most of this will have to be replaced," Geller observed.

"Do you have the financial records?"

"They were supposed to leave the books in the safe."

"Let's have a look," Benjamin coaxed.

Geller led the way down the hall to an office. The safe was located behind a picture that hung on the wall opposite the door. Geller set the picture aside, spun the dial, then twisted the handle and opened the safe door. The financial ledger was there along with assorted records and other documents. He took out the book, closed the safe door, and placed the book on a nearby desk.

Benjamin pulled up a chair to the front side of the desk and gestured to the empty chair on the opposite side. "This will be your office. Which makes this your desk." He smiled up at Geller. "So have a seat."

Geller sat behind the desk and looked over at Benjamin. "You realize, we're in party headquarters. And you're party chairman."

"Believe me," Benjamin leafed through the ledger. "I thought about it all night."

"Once we were kids, playing on the street," Geller continued. "And now we're here."

"Yeah," Benjamin grinned. "I don't think anyone who knew us then thought we'd get this far."

Geller looked over at him. "Still a ways to go."

"But to get there, we have to do this right." Benjamin tapped the desk for emphasis. "We have to make Likud the envy of everyone."

"Then let's get started." Geller reached across the desk and gently turned the ledger around so he could see.

They both huddled over the book a moment, then finally Benjamin asked, "Does this mean what I think it means?"

"Yeah," Geller groaned. "We're broke."

Benjamin slid back in his chair. "I don't know the breakdown on it, but the figures in there for salaries look rather high."

"The staff rolls are bloated," Geller agreed, still scanning the pages in the ledger.

"You looked at them already?"

"Yeah. Bart Strauss brought me over here last night and gave the staff rolls to me."

"Think we can cut any of the positions?"

"We'll have to," Geller replied. "But before we do that, we need an organizational chart. That will help us determine the personnel we need."

"So, that's where we should begin. Create a chart that reflects what we want the party to be. Then we'll determine the staff we need for those positions, and build the budget from there."

They spent the remainder of the day working on party leadership organization and staff selection. As the afternoon gave way to evening, Benjamin leaned back in the chair and raised his arms over his head, stretching. After a pause, he looked over at Geller. "I am announcing this afternoon that you have accepted the position of party secretary general."

Geller smiled. "You're funny."

"No, I am serious." Benjamin checked his wristwatch yet again. "Anna was supposed to give a statement to the press an hour ago."

"You didn't."

"Yes," Benjamin nodded. "I did. If you don't like the title, we'll change it in a few months. But you are in charge of the day-to-day operation of the party. I have no one else who can handle it."

"Okay," Geller said. "And what about salary?"

"We'll talk about it when you send me a draft of the budget."

"And the personnel questions?"

"We've been talking about personnel all day. You know me better than anyone else. You know the kind of people I can work with and the kind I can't. You've been running this campaign since we began." Benjamin stood and gestured to the books and papers on Geller's desk. "Straighten it all out. Make it work."

"Okay, what are you going to do?"

Benjamin turned toward the door. "I'll be out raising money. I've seen enough today to know that we can't fix the party with personnel cuts alone. Or with budget tightening alone. We need more money."

"Do you want to review the personnel cuts before I announce them?"

"No. Just make it work."

Over the next ten days, Geller cut the employee roster, reducing fulltime Party staff to only the essential positions. He filled many of those positions with people he brought over from the campaign. The remaining campaign staff not given Party positions were retained with the campaign. Even so, the employee cuts were steep with entire sections of the old campaign structure eliminated. The old guard of the party was not happy with the decision.

✦ ✦ ✦

While Geller grappled with staff and budget issues, Benjamin went to work raising money, first among donors in Israel, then in the US. To American audiences, he stressed the importance of Israel as an ally against the growing terrorist threat.

Before the election, when he worked as a member of the Prime Minister's staff, Benjamin had been privy to the Prime Minister's daily security briefings and knew most of the details about attempts by Iraq and Iran to develop full-scale nuclear weapons programs. That information—along with the special briefing he now received as party chairman—carried Israel's most secretive designation and he was careful not to touch upon anything in his speeches that even hinted at the content of those briefings.

But that did not keep him from pointing out items already reported in the news—Iran's obstructive conduct during recent UN negotiations and statements about Iran's nuclear program made by Iran's UN ambassador during open sessions of the UN Security Council and the UN General Assembly. He cited those as tacit admissions by Iran of the magnitude of its program, then also noted them as examples of why negotiations would never work with predominantly Muslim countries. "Instead," he noted, "the world needs a strong Israel as the first line of defense. The frontline of deterrence, against an Arab world that hates us both."

With an eye always on expenses, Benjamin kept the trips short and the accommodations simple, but they proved to be quite fruitful as a source of funding for Likud. And for most of those trips, Sara was at his side, ever the supportive wife. Always conscious of the American obsession with appearance, she worked hard to keep Benjamin focused, poised, and friendly with the media.

✦ ✦ ✦

With the budget in better shape and the employee rolls trimmed for a lean and efficient staff, Benjamin met with Geller to discuss political strategy.

"We need to break up Rabin's coalition," Geller observed.

Benjamin glanced away. "You mean bring down Rabin's government?"

"Yes. We need to push them into early elections."

"I don't know..." Benjamin looked toward the windows, obviously wrestling with Geller's suggestion. "I'll have to think about that."

"We have the momentum," Geller continued, ignoring Benjamin's reluctance. "Everyone knows who you are. Your name recognition is higher than it has ever been. You're seen as the young, capable, rising star. Ready to replace the old leadership. We need to capitalize on that and keep going, right to the top."

Benjamin did not respond immediately and they both sat quietly staring blankly into space. "How would we do that?" Benjamin asked, finally.

"National security was a key issue with our supporters," Geller outlined. "I think we should keep stressing it. Do as many national security speeches in as many places as you can handle."

"That might work," Benjamin slowly nodded his head, as if conceding the notion. "Terrorism might be a point of difference for us, also," he offered. "That's what we need—issues we can support, but on which we differ from Rabin. Use the speeches to address the underlying substantive issues but also stress our differences."

Geller understood Benjamin's hesitance to attack Rabin. Still, business was business. If they waited for Rabin to set the next election, he would delay as long as possible and by then, Benjamin would have faded from the public's attention into the morass of inner-party squabbles. The former insiders would see to that. For Benjamin to win an election as prime minister, he had to continue the fight now. Both of them knew he was right, but for Benjamin it was an uncomfortable choice.

Not long after their discussion, two Palestinians detonated suicide bombs in Jerusalem, one in a crowded night club, the other in a popular coffee shop. Geller, ever the political operative, seized the moment sending messages to all Israeli television stations and American networks letting their schedulers know that Benjamin was available for interviews. All of them pounced on the opportunity and booked him for immediate appearances.

Benjamin spent that first evening, just hours after the explosions, making the rounds among television studios and remote interview locations. At each he stressed the issue of security, the threat posed locally, and the global threat posed by terrorist interest in nuclear arms, an Iraq or Iran armed with nuclear weapons, and the need to guard against government sponsorship of terrorist groups.

In extended interviews he also talked about Iran's obstructing tactics at the UN and its expulsion of UN inspectors. "That is proof in and of itself that Iran's nuclear program is far more advanced than they are willing to admit," he related, being careful to avoid mention of classified information. "Security ought to be the top priority on any prime minister's list," he added, deftly bringing the international discussion back to local politics. "But it seems to have slipped from the attention of the current government."

Geller and others who knew him could see the last line was difficult for him to deliver. But in the world of Israeli politics it was a necessity. And if the situation were reversed, with Benjamin as the sitting prime minister, a rising candidate would deliver even harsher words against Benjamin.

As happened before when Benjamin appeared on television during times of crisis, his interviews received airplay around the world. Sound bites were used in newscasts the following day and beyond, taking his exposure from the first news cycle to the second and beyond.

But just as Benjamin's message gained traction with the public, Rabin announced that he and Yasser Arafat, Chairman of the Palestinian Liberation Organization, had conducted secret peace negotiations, sponsored by US President Bill Clinton, to end the decades-long conflict between Israel and the Palestinians now living in the West Bank and Gaza strip. Those talks produced a series of agreements known as the Oslo Accords which provided a framework for peace.

Seemingly in an instant, Israel erupted in shouts of joy, alive with optimism and hopeful for the future. Ivry Bronfman, a member of the Knesset from the Labor Party, expressed that feeling in a quote that was repeated almost as often as any other. "This might finally be the end of prevailing Arab violence."

And overnight, Likud was behind the times. Interview opportunities for Benjamin evaporated. No one now wanted to hear his point of view on questions of terrorism and national security. Instead, guests appeared on television announcing the end of Likud. "The Likud Party is finished as a viable party in the selection of prime minister," one suggested. Another went even further. "Labor will be the permanent majority party into the foreseeable future. Perhaps even a permanent, overwhelming majority that all other parties are incapable of challenging."

51

NETANYAHU

AT LIKUD HEADQUARTERS, Benjamin refused to give in to what others were saying. Instead of joining them in pronouncing the end of Likud Party viability, he reminded his staff about coming municipal elections. "We have a strong slate of candidates. Let's get to work. We can win those elections and build our strength with the local Party organizations. Most of them have been overlooked in the past and left to fend for themselves. We have resources they can't reach and if we bring them to bear on these elections, we can make a big difference."

"That's all well and good," someone said, "but our national approach is dead in the water."

"No it's not," Benjamin countered. "Does anyone really think that Labor will create a permanent majority?" He glanced around the room as if seriously awaiting a response. When no one spoke up, he continued. "I don't think they can, or will, do that. And neither do you. Likud is Israel's leading party of opposition. We stand first and foremost for security of our nation. That is our government's primary responsibility. We've stood for that since the Party was founded and we stand for it now." He scanned the room once more. "If we continue to proclaim our message, I am confident we will find the way forward."

Not content to leave the elections to his staff, Benjamin traveled the length of Israel time and time again, appearing with municipal candidates and giving speeches to all groups, large or small. When not doing that, he was busy raising money for the Party and its candidates.

The Party staff, inspired and challenged by Benjamin's enthusiasm, applied itself with renewed courage. They worked to support every Party municipal candidate by offering not just money but polling data, assistance in preparing effective printed pieces, mailing coordination in dispersing those pieces to likely voters, and campaign workers to take the candidates' message house-to-house. They promoted, facilitated, and coordinated press coverage, finding newsworthy stories for each of the candidates, assuring coverage in both print and television outlets.

When the election was over, Likud candidates held a majority of the municipal positions. Party staff made certain Benjamin appeared on the nightly newscasts to discuss the election outcomes. They watched him from Party headquarters and as election night drew to a close, Likud had begun to slowly inch its way back to a national audience.

In the midst of the municipal election cycle, Jewish settlers in the West Bank digested the Oslo Accords and realized that peace under the Oslo process would require Israel to cede control of land they occupied. Unless they gave up, abandoned their property, and relocated to homes within the boundaries of Israel proper, they would become subject to the Palestinian Authority. Unwilling to do that, they staged protests that attracted large numbers of participants. Large numbers caught the eye of the news media and broadcast teams were sent to cover them for the nightly televised newscasts.

On a rare evening at the Party office, Benjamin saw a report of the protests on television. As he watched, he shouted for Geller to join him. As Geller entered the room, Benjamin pointed to the TV monitor in his office. "This is our opportunity."

Geller frowned. "For what?"

Benjamin had a boyish grin. "To win back the momentum lost to Rabin."

"How?"

Benjamin pointed to the TV monitor again. "We will join them," he revealed enthusiastically. "Lend our voice to their efforts. Get our message out with theirs. Just like we did with the municipal elections."

"And become the party of the opposition," Geller added slowly.

"Exactly. They may be in the West Bank, but they are Israeli settlers, sent there with the government's encouragement and support. The government owes them the same consideration it gives to those living within our accepted borders."

"Including a duty not to negotiate a deal with Arafat that hands them over to his control."

"Yes," Benjamin turned again to the TV. "This is the opportunity we've been looking for. An incident we can use to press our point."

In the weeks that followed, Benjamin traveled with staff members throughout the West Bank, returning to the strategy they had employed when he first returned from America—going settlement to settlement, giving speeches, and forming new Likud branches—only this time they did it in the West Bank.

Establishing West Bank Likud branches incorporated Jewish activists there into the party. This bolstered the Party's efforts and opened up a new constituency, but it pushed Benjamin's rhetoric further to the right. The change was slight at first but as his popularity among settlers increased, the rhetoric grew even more conservative in tone and Benjamin's delivery became more strident.

With his message once again finding reception, Benjamin turned to Israel's orthodox rabbis. They were intrigued by the things he said in his speeches, but inclusion of the orthodox rabbis pushed the message still further to the right.

Geller was concerned about the shift in the nature and tone of the message but Benjamin saw the message connecting with settler and orthodox anger. "This is the only way to win," he insisted. "We have to come at Rabin from the right. He sold out large portions of our citizens and our land. Men fought and died for that land. Now they propose to hand it over to Arafat's control. And in exchange for what? Peace? No. The *illusion* of peace."

Geller heard lines and phrases from Benjamin's stump speech and for the first time considered the notion that he just might believe what he was saying. *The speeches are not just speeches*, he thought. *They're ideas deep in his heart.*

Some of the West Bank leaders took Benjamin's message even further, into hate speeches against Rabin and his government. Repeating Benjamin's suggestion that Rabin sold them out to Arabs for the illusion of peace. Only now the statements delivered by Benjamin as a suggestion were transformed by Jewish activists into an accusation. "Rabin is a traitor," they shouted. "And he deserves to die." Rather than shrinking from the extreme rhetoric, crowds whipped themselves into a frenzy. Only this time it was a frenzy of anger, all of it directed toward Rabin.

When Benjamin spoke, the crowds responded with chants of their slogans—"Rabin must go!"

"Rabin is a traitor!"

"Death to Rabin!"

Geller, once again concerned about the message and the crowd's response, took Benjamin aside. "We are on the verge of losing control of the crowds. I think you should consider softening your message a little. Not much, just enough to tone it down."

Benjamin shook his head. "Why should I? We're only pointing out what Rabin has done and is doing. We're not making this stuff up."

"Yes, but the crowds are getting out of hand."

"I think they understand it's just politics."

"I think *you* see it that way, but this isn't America. This is Israel. Our crowds are filled with people from the far right. People who do not know the limits you and I know. Their ancestors blew up the King David Hotel in an effort to force the British out. These are the children of the men who assassinated the UN negotiator during the War of Independence over virtually the same issues as you raise today."

Benjamin smiled. "Relax." He patted Geller on the shoulder. "It'll never come to that."

✦ ✦ ✦

A few weeks later, Benjamin and Sara were enjoying dinner at home when a newscaster appeared on television with a report that Rabin had been the victim of an attempted assassination. "Rabin was gunned down following the conclusion of a mass rally at Kings of Israel Square in Tel Aviv." Images from the scene showed the steps of city hall where he'd been shot. Blood-soaked bandages and packaging littered the area near the base of city hall steps.

"I can't believe someone would do this!" Benjamin shouted.

"Is this related to the agreement he signed with Arafat?"

"I don't know."

"Are you going to the office?"

He looked over at Sara. "I think I should. Do you mind?"

"Not at all. You'll have to prepare a statement for the press."

"I'm not capitalizing on this for political gain. Besides, we don't yet know the full extent of his injuries."

"I know that. But you're a leading Israeli politician. Head of the Likud Party. I think at least one reporter will ask you for your comments."

"Yeah," Benjamin sighed. "I suppose you're right."

Benjamin arose from the dinner table and telephoned Geller at home. When he got no answer he phoned the office. Geller answered the call. "Are you coming in?"

"Yes," Benjamin said. "Better round up the staff."

"Most of them are already here."

Thirty minutes later, Benjamin pushed open the door to Likud's office suite and stepped inside. Anna glanced up from her desk as he appeared. "What's the latest?" Benjamin asked.

"Well," she began with a cautious tone, "unofficial reports indicate Rabin has died. Supposedly an official announcement will come later today. And, rumor on the street is that Rabin's widow blames us for Rabin's death."

"Nonsense," Benjamin asserted. "Everyone knows I had nothing to do with it."

"She says it was your speeches that excited the West Bank crowds. That you saw what was happening and encouraged them."

"Leah Rabin wouldn't say something like that. No one will believe it if she did."

Geller came from his office and appeared in the hallway. "We may just find out about that."

"How?"

"Sources at the TV stations say she's going public with her opinion tonight."

"She's issuing a statement?"

"Issuing a statement and appearing on television to deliver it."

Benjamin looked concerned. "Have you confirmed this?"

"She'll be on after the evening news."

"Anything we can do about it?"

Geller shook his head. "Just sit tight and take it. Anything we might say in response will only make the situation worse."

Official news of Rabin's death came later in the afternoon. As rumors suggested, Leah Rabin appeared that evening and made her assertions. "There definitely was incitement which was strongly absorbed and found itself a murderer, who did this because he felt he had the broad support with an extremist public." But she stopped short of blaming anyone by name.

Many Labor Party members and those who supported the peace process with Arafat were not so careful. They laid the blame for Rabin's death squarely at the feet of Benjamin, the strident tone and energy of his speeches, and a failure to calm the crowds when they began chanting hate speech directed at Rabin.

Benjamin followed Geller's advice—for a while—and remained quiet regarding Mrs. Rabin's statement. But when the politicians began their attacks on him, he could take it no more. Geller arranged for television interviews and Benjamin appeared for live broadcasts.

"These attempts now to make political hay out of this," he told the interviewer, "to try to say it's the responsibility of the Likud, are like asking whether Lee Harvey Oswald was a Republican or a Democrat and then blaming the Party."

Repeated media appearances helped fend off other politicians, but members of the news media already had turned against him and Likud. For the next week, nightly newscasts showed politician after politician repeating what they'd said after the Oslo Accords became public. "Likud is dead. Labor has become the overwhelming majority, so strong that no other party can challenge it."

✦ ✦ ✦

As attacks in the media continued, Benjamin went to see his father to find out his opinion on the assassination and the suggestion that his speeches incited right wing zealots to kill Rabin.

Benzion dismissed his concerns with a wave of his hand. "Most of the people speaking against you are Labor Party executives and television reporters trying to make a name for themselves so they can gain a reputation or attract more viewers. I'm not even sure why you pay them any attention at all."

"Voters watch them," Benjamin replied.

"The masses watch them," Benzion countered. "But they have a way of making up their own minds. They enjoy the entertainment factor of watching someone squirm, but when Election Day arrives they will think only of the candidates and the issues that affect their lives. Do you know what those issues are?"

"National security, the economy, education, peace."

"Yes," Benzion agreed, "but which of those ranks foremost in their minds?"

"National security."

"Right. Because without that, none of the others are possible."

Benjamin eyes darted away and his voice took a solemn tone. "That news from Oslo was a big surprise." He looked over at his father. "Did you know anything about it?"

"No. Did you?"

"Not a thing."

"When the people read the accords and digest their content, they will not be nearly so enthusiastic. We would have to cede the West Bank to the Palestinian Authority in order to have peace." Benzion's voice was louder and his eyes flashed. "Never. You must never surrender land for peace. And in this case, the illusion of peace."

✦ ✦ ✦

Over the next several days, Benjamin and Geller crafted a response to questions about whether his speeches contributed to Rabin's death that carefully turned the issue in their direction. Then they accepted interviews in which they were sure he would be asked about the issue. When the question came, Benjamin was ready.

"No one could deny that many who attend our political rallies are enthusiastic for change. These are people who live under the same threatening menace as the prime minister. But I did not incite them or encourage them in any manner. They were not and are not a part of our campaign or political apparatus. But I will say this—and I say it only because others have made these baseless accusations against me and against Likud—and I say this with all due respect to the late prime minister—the people you see at our rallies have read the Oslo Accords and understand that it means they must give up their homes and property for the sake of a peace they know will never come. They've seen it before. They've lived it before. We concede to Palestinian demands, and they demand more. In this case, the concession would involve the property of Israeli citizens, and those citizens do not want to do that. And when you see them at our rallies, they are there because of the Oslo Accords. Others in our nation may be in favor of the Accords but they are not being asked to surrender anything to obtain it. People who attend our rallies know this. They know that others are willing to force them to leave *their* homes, so others may obtain a so-called political victory."

Invariably, the news reporter asked the obvious. "So, you're saying the Oslo Accords are as responsible for the assassination as your speeches."

"Yes," Benjamin replied. "I'm saying if my speeches incited the crowd to acts of violence, then announcement of the Accords and the contents of those Accords did also, and at an equal or greater level."

And slowly, the media discussion shifted from the role of Benjamin's speeches in Rabin's death to the role of the Oslo Accords. And then the discussion moved on from Rabin's death to focus solely on the Oslo Accords themselves.

NETANYAHU

WITH THE TRAGIC DEATH of Rabin, the composition of the Knesset did not change. Labor Party still held the same majority that got Rabin elected to office as prime minister. His death, however, left the prime minister's position unfilled. Because Labor held a majority of the Knesset and because Rabin had been elected as a Labor Party candidate, Ezer Weizman, the President of Israel, asked the Labor Party to elect a successor to complete Rabin's term. The Labor Party selected Shimon Peres to fill the term as Acting Prime Minister, but he was in a weak position right from the beginning.

As soon as the selection of Peres was announced, many Knesset members from minor parties, who had previously voted with Labor, abandoned the coalition. Peres had to work hard to attract the necessary support to remain in office.

Benjamin recognized the vulnerability of Peres' situation immediately. He, Geller, and a few others met at Likud Party headquarters to discuss a strategy for taking advantage of that weakness.

"With Rabin out and Peres in office as his replacement, he's sure to be the Labor candidate for prime minister in upcoming elections," Benjamin announced. "We need to take advantage of the situation he's in right now and force him into early elections."

"Even so, that election is still more than a year away," someone noted.

"Anything can happen between now and then," Geller responded.

"But that can cut both ways. It can work against us just the same as it can work for us."

"Peres will want to press for prompt implementation of the Oslo Accords," Geller noted, moving the conversation back to more practical ground, "before Arafat finds an excuse to back out. He doesn't want to wait to do that until after the next regular election. He wants to move now. But to do that, he needs an electoral mandate. He needs to work from a position of strength. Rabin had a mandate. Peres does not."

"So what are you saying?" Benjamin asked.

"I think Peres will call for early elections."

"What would that mean for us?"

Geller smiled, "It means we will win."

✦ ✦ ✦

As Geller suggested, Peres did indeed call for early elections. And, as expected, Peres was confirmed as the Labor candidate for prime minister. Benjamin won Likud's nomination for the position.

Campaigning for the post was intense. With the Oslo Accords still registering high among voter incentive, both men sought to use it to their advantage. Peres held the lead in most opinion polls, which seemed to confirm the support for implementation of the Accords, but as Election Day approached Benjamin closed the gap, though he still trailed Peres in all opinion polls, some by a considerable margin. As a consequence, Benjamin and the Likud Party found it difficult to get bookings for television interviews beyond those that talked about the fall of the Likud Party and the end of terrorism as a political tool.

Then, a week before the election, Palestinian suicide bombers struck Israel in five separate incidents. Most of the bombs had been aimed at Jerusalem businesses but two of them were against targets near Tel Aviv and appeared to have been coordinated with the others.

Suddenly, national security and international terrorism were back on the minds of Israelis. Benjamin and Likud, with their consistent message on both, were relevant again. Requests for media interviews poured in to Likud headquarters. Benjamin took them all.

At those interviews, he talked about Hamas and the Arab nations that surround Israel, the threat from Iran's nuclear program, and the need to take action beyond implementation of mere sanctions. "We need to do this now," he underlined. "Not three months from now."

In the final days of campaigning, Benjamin's rallies were packed, and not just with rightwing zealots. Serious politicians, political operatives, and key influencers now gave him a closer look.

On election night, May 29, 1996, Benjamin gathered with supporters in a ballroom at the Sheraton Hotel Tel Aviv, where they watched as results were announced on television. Late that evening—in spite of the affair and the accusations that he had incited a level of opposition that resulted in Rabin's death—Benjamin was declared the winner, overcoming Shimon Peres, the Labor Party's candidate, by 32,000 votes. The ballroom erupted in cheers. A few moments later, Benjamin gave a speech thanking them all for their hard work and urging a spirit of cooperation across party lines to work in Israel's best interests.

Later, as Benjamin and Sara came from the building to return home, they were confronted by a crowd that carried signs and chanted loudly, "King Bibi! King Bibi! King Bibi!" The poignancy of the moment was not lost on Benjamin and as the crowd continued to shout and call his name, he felt inside his pocket for the Netanyahu ring. *King Bibi*, he thought—Bibi being the diminutive form of his proper name—*perhaps now is the time.*

✦ ✦ ✦

On his first day in office as prime minister, Benjamin remembered the Netanyahu ring and all that he'd overheard his father say about it. He also remembered that day in Jonathan's bedroom after his father gave the ring to Jonathan, and how misty Jonathan's eyes became as they talked about it. Now, Jonathan was gone and he was the one elected to office.

So, when he left the house that morning he took the ring, still in its box, and brought it with him to the office. He'd intended to set the box on a shelf with the lid propped open so visitors could see the ring inside. But as he stood there in his office, he imagined a conversation with someone who saw it and asked about it. Explaining the ring and how he was a direct descendant of David seemed too...creepy.

Instead of wearing the ring, he left the lid in place and glanced around for somewhere to set it. An open spot on a shelf behind his desk caught his eye and he placed the box there, then took a seat at his desk and went to work.

✦ ✦ ✦

Although Likud won the 1996 general election for prime minister with Benjamin as its standard bearer, Labor won a majority of seats in the Knesset. In order to govern, Benjamin was forced to form a coalition that would support his initiatives in the Knesset. Rather than forming that coalition with Labor, which would have required moderating concessions, he turned to Shas and United Torah, two small, far-right, orthodox Jewish political parties that favored Judaism's core beliefs without European liberalizing influences.

Although neither of these parties ever held more than a handful of seats in the Knesset, Israel's parliamentary form of government often placed them in the deciding position when either of Israel's larger parties attempted to form a government. It was a position both had come to enjoy and one that limited Benjamin's power from the beginning.

When Benjamin took office, he inherited the Oslo Accords which Yitzhak Rabin negotiated on behalf of Israel, but which Benjamin opposed both in his heart and in his official position as a candidate for office. Israel's conservative parties opposed the agreements as well.

Still, the task of fulfilling Israel's obligations under the Accords, which had been duly approved before Rabin's death, fell to Benjamin and his administration. With more than half of Israel's citizens supporting the measure and with the Knesset having approved and adopted them as law, he couldn't simply denounce the agreements and declare them null and void. Not surprisingly, however, Benjamin delayed implementation as long as possible. Yasser Arafat, for all his supposed enthusiasm about the agreements, delayed implementation of the Palestinian Authority's obligations, too.

Soon, peace activists in Israel and around the world noticed the inaction and called for full and complete compliance with the Oslo expectations. When that failed to bring a response, they organized marches and demonstrations at numerous locations outside the Middle East, demanding implementation of the Accords. News networks picked up the story and soon world leaders were forced to take up the cause.

Bill Clinton, now in his final term as US president, and thinking of his legacy, discussed the issue with his staff and cabinet. After mulling the idea over for a few days, Clinton decided to intervene.

In a public statement issued from the White House he announced the initiation of an effort to get the peace process moving forward. Justifying a US role in it, he said, "We sponsored the meetings that led to the Oslo Accords, and although in the agreements that resulted from those meetings the US undertook no substantive obligations, the spirit of those agreements seems to lay on us a continuing duty to do our best to see that the goals and aims of the agreements are met. And that we intend to do."

Martin Walker, US Ambassador to Israel, was alerted and participated in discussions by secure video link with the State Department in anticipation of the renewed effort. Not long after that, a steady stream of envoys and political insiders descended upon Israel in an attempt to convince Benjamin to participate in an additional round of discussions with Arafat.

In response, Benjamin assembled his own advisors to discuss the matter. "You have no choice," Anna Arkin advised. "You have to meet with Arafat and discuss the matter."

"Why?"

"Why not?"

"Arafat is a terrorist," Benjamin blurted. "Why should I meet with him face-to-face and elevate him to the status and stature of a statesman?"

Shahar Ofer spoke up. "He acknowledged our right to exist in the discussions and agreements with Rabin. What more can he do? What more does he *have* to do?"

"And, on a practical level," Anna added, "America is our primary ally. They want this Agreement. They want the Oslo process and want to see it followed. We need to cooperate with them as much as possible. We can't go it alone."

"But the Arabs don't want peace," Benjamin argued. "You notice, they have dragged their feet on this from the day they signed the Accords. And they aren't the ones calling for implementation. People who don't even live here are stirring this up. The Palestinians aren't demonstrating in the streets. And that's because they don't want the Accords."

"We don't know that," Anna cautioned. "Not for a certainty."

"Yes we do," Benjamin argued. "They want what they've always wanted. They want it all. When they negotiate and make an offer, they aren't really making an offer they want to see accepted as a final conclusion of the matter. They're making an offer to see how far we will go to agree with them. If we accept their offer, they'll view it as a sign of weakness and find a way to demand more. American liberals don't understand the Arab mind. We aren't in a peace negotiation. We're in a war. When Arabs fight, they fight to avenge something—family, country, or, most often, their religion. Victory comes when their enemy and everyone associated with their enemy is dead. And if they can't do that in a single generation, the generation that follows will take up the cause and fight on."

Benjamin's staff listened in stunned silence until finally he paused and took a deep breath. "So," he smiled, "I guess you sensed my frustration in dealing with Arafat."

A collective sigh went up from the room. "We sort of picked up on that," Geller commented.

✦ ✦ ✦

That weekend, Benjamin and Sara were at his parent's home in Jerusalem. Benjamin, still wrestling with how to respond to the international pressure being placed on him to move forward with Arafat, was withdrawn, brooding, and preoccupied.

Benzion took him aside to the study. "What's bothering you? You're not yourself today."

"The Oslo Accords," Benjamin answered flatly. "That's what's bothering me."

"Do you mean the Accords, or the way the whole world seems to be lining up against us?"

"In the last ten days I've received calls from every country we might consider our friend," Benjamin related. "All of them telling me I have an obligation to move forward with implementation of the Accords."

"What about the Americans?"

"They're leading the pack. The US ambassador's been to see me so many times I think he has an office in the building. Bill Clinton's called two or three times. Labor Party members called."

"This is how it is once you're in office," Benzion advised. "Everyone wants a piece of you. Everyone wants to advise you and be in the know. But you have to resist them and remain true to the calling on your life."

Benjamin looked away. "What does that mean?"

"For you, it means restore, protect, defend, and expand the Davidic Kingdom."

"But for what purpose?"

"To restore Israel," Benzion's replied sharply. "To re-establish us as a people, as a nation with a collective identity. A collective future. Taking control of the land secured by our ancestors. Extending Israel's reach to both sides of the Jordan River."

"I'm not so sure about that," Benjamin sighed. "I don't think the world will allow us to drive out all the Arabs."

"I don't know why not," Benzion's voice became even more strident as he talked. "They sit around and listen while Arabs articulate their evil messages of annihilation for the Jews. And then say nothing in our defense. But when someone complains about how terrible the Arabs are being treated, they all come after us with knives drawn." Benzion lowered his voice. "You can't give in to these people, Benjamin. You can't! Israel extends to both sides of the Jordan River. There will be no peace for us until we control the entire region."

"I'm just not sure Jabotinsky's views are going to be workable today," Benjamin responded. "Not from a practical perspective."

"No," Benzion insisted. "That's the talk of appeasement. You can't give in to it. Rabin's Oslo agreement is a land for peace agreement. That's the central premise of the whole thing. We give the Arabs land in the West Bank, they leave us alone. It will never be enough. Which is why you can't let the Arabs get away with bombings and mortar attacks, either. You have to hit. Every time they hit us, we hit back. That's all they understand. We learned that in Russia during the pogroms."

Benjamin looked over at him and for the first time that day a genuine smile spread over his face. "Pops, you were just a boy then. You were never in a pogrom."

"But I know what happened," Benzion insisted. "I heard the stories. And I know that when we fought back, they left us alone."

"Well," Benjamin sighed, "my problem right now isn't about responding to mortar attacks or suicide bombers. My problem is with settlers in the West Bank who have made their homes there and who want to remain there, and a Knesset approved agreement with the Palestinians that requires them to move."

"That's not your problem," Benzion responded. "Your problem is, you want Bill Clinton to like you *and* you want to remain Israel's prime minister at the same time."

✦ ✦ ✦

In the days that followed, more US envoys, mostly international security experts from influential colleges and universities, continued to make the rounds in the Middle East, repeatedly meeting with leaders on both sides of the Arab-Israeli conflict. They went out for dinner with political leaders of all types and posed for pictures with anyone who asked, but when the smiles were exhausted and the friendliness faded away, all of them had but one purpose—to convince Benjamin to talk with Arafat as a means of continuing the viability of the Oslo Accords.

President Clinton called Benjamin regularly, too. They got along well and shared mutual respect for each other. And, Benzion was right—Clinton's opinions and friendship had a significant influence on Benjamin.

But for Benjamin, the strategic importance of the Oslo agreement—an importance he could not ignore, no matter who appealed to him—lay in domestic politics. The people who supported him—West Bank settlers and conservative rabbis—were opposed to the Accords, both in their specific terms and in their central premise. Land for peace was not an option for them and so it could not, in the final analysis, ever be an option for Benjamin.

✦ ✦ ✦

With the Arab-Israeli peace process in tatters, Bill Clinton had no choice but to ramp up the pressure on Benjamin to participate. Clinton, after all, had staked much of his legacy on finding a solution to this ancient problem. To do that, he invited Benjamin to the White House for a series of talks. The stated purpose was simply to convince Benjamin to meet with Arafat and talk. "It just means talking in person," he stressed. "That's all. No predetermined terms. No anticipated outcomes."

After prevaricating to the last moment, Benjamin gave in and agreed to come to the White House to discuss the potential for a meeting with Arafat. "That's all." Benjamin insisted. "To discuss the *possibility* of meeting with him. I don't want to get up there and find him waiting to join us or stepping out of a closet somewhere by surprise."

"Just you and me," Clinton assured, but both men knew things were not as simple as that.

"He intends to pressure me into surrendering land for peace," Benjamin lamented in a meeting with Geller. "That is something I cannot do."

"Then we really do have a problem," Geller replied.

"We've always had that problem," Benjamin added.

"But this one is more troublesome than most."

"How so?"

"President Clinton sees an Israeli-Arab agreement as a centerpiece of his legacy."

Benjamin frowned. "Why do they worry so much about that?"

"Well, in his case, he's served two terms. Their constitution won't allow him to serve more. If he operated under our rules, he could very easily win a third term. Perhaps even eclipse Roosevelt."

"Maybe so, but we need to find a way to back him off. I don't like being bullied into *anything*."

"There's always our natural ally," Geller suggested.

"Who is that?"

"The American Christian Right."

Benjamin turned his chair away from the desk for a glimpse through the office window. "Perhaps you should call our friend Jerry Falwell and see what he thinks of this situation."

"I think that would be an excellent place to start."

Two days later, Geller told Benjamin that Falwell was willing to arrange an event. "If we will give him the date. A longer lead time would be better but shorter works well, too. Creates a sense of urgency. Always helpful to get the people out to a meeting. So, when are we going?"

"We've agreed to meet with President Clinton on January 22. If this is to work, we have to meet with Falwell before then. So, January 21?"

"The day before?"

"Yes."

"That's close."

"Close is good for us. Forces the other side to act with urgency. That always helps with negotiations."

"What are we negotiating?"

"The future of the Zionist dreams for a safe and secure state."

"You'd give that away?"

"Hardly." Benjamin was still seated with his chair turned to one side. "Exactly the opposite." His eyes were focused on something seemingly visible through the window, but his mind was far away and when he spoke there was a sense of distraction in his voice. "Have we heard from Rabbi Mickelson lately?"

"No, were you expecting to?"

"See if you can get in touch with him."

"What should I say is the reason for the phone call?"

"Ask him if he has a word for us."

Geller frowned. "A word?"

"Yes. A word from the Lord."

"Okay."

There was a hint of reluctance in Geller's voice which Benjamin caught immediately. "That makes you uncomfortable?" he asked.

"No. It's just that, a Jewish prime minister calling a rabbi in New York and asking for a word from the Lord sounds a lot like evangelical Christianity."

Benjamin glanced back at Geller with a grin. "Then I'll fit right in with Falwell's group."

✦ ✦ ✦

As planned, Benjamin traveled to the United States well ahead of his meeting with President Clinton and spent the time calling on Jewish groups in New York. His advance party, headed by David bar Ilan, a senior policy advisor, went on to Washington, DC and set up their operations in the Mayflower Hotel.

On the morning of January 21, Benjamin and Geller traveled to Virginia where they spent the day with Jerry Falwell and a handful of key Christian leaders, discussing the situation in the Middle East and the role the US government might play in bringing about a peaceful resolution to conflict there.

That evening, Benjamin spoke to a group of one-thousand conservative evangelical Christian supporters. Some of his address covered topics he'd mentioned earlier in the day, but as he came to the end of his speech he turned to the Zionist dream and the history of working with Arabs in Palestine. "We want peace. Israel has existed as a sovereign state for fifty years and each of those years has been marked by armed conflict. Israel wants peace. I want peace. But in order to achieve peace between Israel and the Palestinians, there must be a mutual desire for peace on the other side. Arabs don't want peace. They want total control and they want us dead."

He paused for effect, then added with a wisp of a smile, "Or gone. Some of them would be satisfied if we simply moved away to live somewhere else." Laughter rippled through the audience. "Those are the ones your politicians refer to as moderate Arabs." The crowd roared with laughter that turned to applause.

"Tomorrow I will meet your president," he continued. "I like President Clinton. He was a friend to us during his first term and has carried that friendship into his second term. But when I see him tomorrow he will summon all of his political bluster and hand-wringing and body language and whatever other powers of persuasion he may have in an effort to convince me to accept the basic premise of the Oslo Accords. But that, my friends, I cannot and will not do. Those agreements were predicated on the false doctrine of land for peace. The badly mistaken notion that if we surrender land in the West Bank to complete Arab control—to bring about Arab sovereignty—the Arabs will go away satisfied and live with us in peace.

"The Arabs were offered that on at least six different occasions going all the way back to the Sultans, and they refused the offer each time, choosing instead to fight for total control of the entire region.

"They were offered what they wanted under your president Jimmy Carter and they turned it down. They were offered what they wanted under your president George Bush, and they turned it down. We agreed to an implementation of the Oslo Accords, but after taking steps on our part toward implementation of those agreements, we found no response from them toward fulfillment of *their* duties."

After the address, Netanyahu and Geller returned to Washington and Blair House, the president's official facility for guests located across the street from the White House, where they would stay for the remainder of their visit. As they parted company in the hall outside the head-of-state suite, Netanyahu asked, "Did you ever get in touch with Rabbi Mickelson?"

"Yes," Geller replied. "He said he thought he had a Word for you but needed to make certain." He shrugged his shoulders. "Something like that."

"Call him again. I want to know what he heard. I need to hear from him before we meet with President Clinton tomorrow."

The following morning, Netanyahu and Geller met in the sitting room downstairs for coffee before walking across Pennsylvania Avenue to the White House. As they talked and sipped coffee, Benjamin asked Geller if Rabbi Mickelson had called him back.

"I talked to him last night," Geller explained. "Turns out, he's here in town right now. Staying over at the Mayflower Hotel. I asked David bar Ilan to meet with him." He glanced at his watch. "They should be talking right now."

✦ ✦ ✦

While Benjamin and Geller relaxed at Blair House, David bar Ilan met with Rabbi Mickelson in the sitting area of bar Ilan's room.

"The prime minister is not able to meet with you," bar Ilan began. "He asked me to convey his regards. He is at Blair House, but wanted me to ask you a question."

"Okay. What's the question?"

"It feels strange to ask, but here it is. 'Has God told you anything?' I don't know what he meant by that. Is it a private joke between the two of you?"

"No, it's not a joke," Mickelson replied. "Tell him not to give up on Hebron. God is going to judge Bill Clinton today. There will be a major distraction during the meeting."

"What kind of distraction?"

"I don't know, but before the meeting is over there will be a major disruption that will take the president from the meeting and occupy his time for the remainder of the day. By then, the status will have changed and he will no longer be in a position as strong as he once was."

"I'm not sure I understand this."

"Just please," Mickelson urged. "Tell him what I said. Don't give up Hebron and don't worry about the meeting. There will be a major distraction that will take President Clinton from the meeting and occupy his attention the remainder of the day."

✦ ✦ ✦

A little before nine that morning, Benjamin and Geller came from Blair House and, flanked by their security detail, walked the short distance over to the White House. As they reached the driveway that led to the West Wing, Geller's cell phone rang. The call was from David bar Ilan, who conveyed the Word Mickelson had given him.

By the time Geller ended the call, Benjamin was already inside the White House. Geller rushed through the entrance and found him waiting at the building's security checkpoint. Once past the security screening, they were led by an intern to the Mural Room.

When they were alone, Benjamin asked, "Was that Rabbi Mickelson on the phone?"

"David bar Ilan," Geller answered.

"Did he meet with Mickelson?"

"Yes."

"What did he say?"

"That you should not give up Hebron and that you should be bold and courageous. That before the meeting is over, the president will encounter a major disruption. One that will take him from the meeting and occupy his attention for the remainder of the day."

Benjamin's forehead wrinkled in a thoughtful frown. "I wonder what he could be talking about."

"I have no idea. Something's going to happen that will take the pressure off of us, I suppose."

"Okay. So we should string this out until help arrives?"

"I suppose."

"Hope he's right," Benjamin said.

"Me, too."

A few minutes later, the door opened with unusual force and President Clinton entered the room already tense and angry. "Of all the people you could meet with," Clinton railed. "You had to pick Jerry Falwell?"

Geller glanced around for a way out of the room but when Clinton took a seat opposite Benjamin, he was trapped.

"Reverend Falwell has been a longtime supporter of Israel," Benjamin countered.

"Jerry Falwell has spent the last two years making my life miserable. Claiming I was involved in drug deals. Claiming I followed a political strategy that included murder to gain elected office. And all of it based on a single discredited video recording. He's a disgrace to everything the Gospel stands for. I've got no use for him at all."

"There were many people at the event aside from him," Benjamin offered. Then remembering Rabbi Mickelson's word he added, "But that's not why we're here today, either."

"No, it's not—I mean," Clinton muttered, "It's just that I'll have to spend the next week talking about how tense the US—Israeli relationship has become...when I need to be sitting with you and Arafat talking about the peace process."

"Mr. President, as I have said before, the Oslo Accords rest upon the premise of exchanging land for peace. I will never agree to that."

"Israel's already signed and approved the Accords. You have no choice but to implement them."

"We started to do that, but they made no move toward fulfilling their duties."

"You were supposed to go first."

"And that is not right, either," Benjamin countered.

"You're dealing with Arafat," Clinton questioned. "And you expect everything to be perfect?"

"No, but I would expect a show of good faith. Beginning with a call for reduced terrorist attacks inside Israel. That would be a good place to start."

"Like I said, don't start lecturing me. Not this morning."

"I'm not lecturing you, Mr. President. I'm telling you what you need to get from them. That's what you should concentrate on. How can the US get the Palestinians to implement their part of the agreement? They've made no effort to curb terrorist attacks from there or the Gaza Strip. This is just more of the same thing we've heard since the first Zionists returned."

"I know what your country has faced. But if you think Falwell and John Hagee and the others can support you in a way that's better than the protection of the US military, or the extension of aid and credit by the federal government, go right ahead and rely on them."

"Wait, Mr. President." Netanyahu motioned with his hands. "You aren't now suggesting that our entire relationship turns on whether we give in to these excessive and unreasonable Arab demands are you? That unless we give in we risk receiving further aid and cooperation from the US? Is that what you're saying?"

"I'm saying, if this continues we are no longer going to—"

Just then, there was a tap at the door as it opened and an assistant entered the room. He handed Clinton a note and waited for a response. The president blushed as he read the note. Then all the color drained from his face. "I...I have something I must take care of," Clinton said. "We can't complete the meeting." He pushed back from the table and stood. Benjamin did likewise. "We'll have to meet later."

"Certainly Mr. President," Benjamin replied.

Clinton gestured with the note. "This thing may take all day. Can you hang out here a little longer until I see?"

"Certainly, Mr. President."

When Clinton had gone and the door to the Mural Room closed, Benjamin looked over at Geller. "What just happened?"

"I think we just had Rabbi Mickelson's big interruption."

Twenty minutes later, Stokely Raskin, the president's chief of staff, came to the Mural Room and informed Benjamin and Geller that Clinton would be busy for the remainder of the day.

"What happened?" Benjamin asked.

"The special prosecutor investigating the White Water development in Arkansas delivered a round of new subpoenas opening a separate investigation of an alleged affair involving President Clinton and a young intern named Monica Lewinsky. It's about to break on television."

Raskin escorted them through the first floor to the building entrance on the west side. As they walked up the driveway toward Pennsylvania Avenue, Benjamin said, "Get bar Ilan on the phone." Geller placed the call and handed his cell phone to Benjamin.

A moment later, bar Ilan as on the phone. "Hey, David, the Rabbi was right."

"That was one of the strangest conversations I've had in a long time. What happened?"

"There was a major distraction. Something about Clinton having an affair with an intern named Monica Lewinsky."

"Hey," bar Ilan said. "I'm watching that right now on a noon news show. Sam Donaldson is breaking the story at this very moment."

"Well, tell Rabbi Mickelson next time I will need more information from God."

"Sounds like he gave you just what you needed."

"I just hope Bill Clinton doesn't think that young intern was a Mossad plant," Benjamin laughed."

✦ ✦ ✦

The Monica Lewinsky story diverted Clinton's attention for the next several months, but he continued to telephone Benjamin and the two had lengthy discussions through the spring and summer about moving forward with the implementation of the Oslo Accords. After holding out at first, and then further quibbling to the last moment, Benjamin eventually gave in and asked Clinton to arrange the meeting with Arafat. "If he says he will meet, I will agree also."

That fall, Benjamin and Arafat met for face-to-face talks at Aspen Institute's Wye River Conference Center in Maryland. Their meeting was moderated by US Secretary of State Madeleine Albright and, after eight days of discussion, produced the Wye River Accord, which provided steps and timetables for implementation of the Accords.

News of that agreement was received favorably by many in Israel, but not by the conservative groups on whom Benjamin relied for political support. When he returned to Israel, representatives from West Bank settlers and orthodox rabbis were waiting to meet with him to register their complaints.

53

NETANYAHU

EVEN WITH THE Wye River agreement in place, Clinton and members of his administration continued to press Benjamin for greater concessions. "You have to learn to work together, Israelis and Palestinians," Clinton said. "That's the only way to get past this. Agreements between heads of state can help. They can provide a framework. But real cooperation can only occur when the people join each other in the marketplace—the marketplace of goods and services and the marketplace of ideas. That's when the trouble will disappear."

"Mr. President," Benjamin replied, "Arab leaders don't want to cooperate with us. And they don't want their people to cooperate. They don't know about marketplaces of any kind. Certainly not a marketplace of ideas. They solve their problems by conquering, subduing, and annihilating not just anyone who opposes them, but anyone who isn't an Arab. And that, Mr. President, includes you and every American citizen of non-Arab descent."

"They wanted that in the past," Clinton said dismissively, "but this generation is different. This generation realizes its limitations and simply wants to live in peace."

Benjamin shook his head. "That's not really the situation we face. And America is as much an enemy to them as we are. But I will talk with

Arafat further. I'm not saying ahead of time that I will agree with him, but I'll talk to him and treat what he says in a serious manner."

✦ ✦ ✦

The following July, Benjamin met with Arafat to begin discussions on the final status of Gaza and the West Bank. A series of meetings followed, some taking place in Jerusalem and some in Washington, DC. The following January, they met again, this time at the White House under the supervision of US Secretary of State Albright.

In only a matter of days, the two sides reached agreement on the basic status of Hebron, which included a large part of the West Bank that gave the Palestinian Authority control over eighty percent of the Hebron area. Before signing the agreement, however, Benjamin returned to Israel and met with his advisors to discuss the matter.

After listening intently while he explained the agreement's terms, Shahar Ofer said, "Well it's about time we did something."

Benjamin smiled. "You think we should have done this before now?"

"I think the agreement is a good thing."

"We need to do this," Anna inserted.

"Our troops in Gaza are nothing but targets," Shahar added. "They serve no useful purpose in changing the status quo there."

"And as to the West Bank?" Benjamin asked.

"The West Bank is far more stable than Gaza," Geller offered. "We need to encourage development in the West Bank as a way of bringing about change in Gaza. Cooperate in the West Bank, produce real change, show the people of Gaza what we can do together. Give them a reason to want the same."

Benjamin was intrigued by the notion, especially its synergy, but as he looked around the room he realized his father was right. Except for Geller, they were all quite young. Few of them had a context older than the past ten years. Still, the points they made left him wanting to try.

✦ ✦ ✦

In spite of his success as a politician, Benjamin still felt the need to discuss major events and decisions with his father. So, the night before the Hebron agreement was announced, he stopped by to see him. Benjamin found him in a poor mood.

"I don't like it," Benzion groused as he held the door to let Benjamin enter.

"What's the matter, Pop?" Benjamin asked, as if he didn't already know.

"There will be trouble ahead for you." Benzion pushed the door closed and locked it. "Perhaps the end of your government."

"Will I have to go back to selling furniture?" Benjamin quipped.

"Laugh all you want," Benzion replied as he led the way to the living room. "Right wing factions were already upset by the Wye River agreement. This will push them over the edge." He reached a chair and eased down. "It's not a good idea practically speaking, and it's not a good idea from a political perspective. And from a long view of the situation, it's even worse."

Benjamin took a seat on the sofa. "How so?"

"You are surrendering a portion of land rightfully part of Israel for the illusion of peace." Benzion sat up straight and slid forward in his chair. "As I've insisted before, we must never do that. And to make things even worse, you get nothing from them in return."

It must have sounded good sixty years earlier, Benjamin thought, *but even then, few were accepting the idea of holding out for control of all of Palestine.* Now, the shortcomings of that approach seemed all too clear. "We can't police the entire region. Not while surrounded by people with capable armies who really hate us. We need to limit our exposure to war."

"If Ben-Gurion had listened to us," Benzion said, "all this would have been avoided."

"I'm not sure it was Ben-Gurion's fault. He had to work within his limitations. If he hadn't found a way forward with that, most of us would still be living in Europe and this area would be controlled by Arab gunmen."

Benzion seemed not to hear him. "I'm serious. For you to continue in office with this agreement with Arafat, this approach, this land for peace strategy, you'd have to share the convictions of your heart with your constituency and show them how this peace fits into a concept of what will make their lives better. But for that, you'd need a broad strategy for Israel's future and you don't have one. Your only vision of the future is to remain in office. That's it."

The words stung, but Benjamin stuffed down the emotion and looked away. "I'm doing the best I can," he sighed.

"But you're focused on pleasing the wrong people. Bill Clinton. American liberals. That's who you're trying to please. You spend your time listening to them and to advisers who don't understand the broad sweep of history."

Benjamin smiled. How many times had he heard his father say those things about his staff? "The people around me are the ones who got me to where I am. I can't ignore them."

"That's what I mean," Benzion said, his voice rising in intensity and volume. "Think about what you just said and who you're trying to please when you talk like that."

"I'm into it now, Dad," Benjamin said finally. "There's nothing to do but work our way through it."

Benzion settled back in his chair. "Well, it's going to get rough. You're about to feel all alone."

✦ ✦ ✦

The agreement regarding Hebron—officially known as The Protocol Concerning the Redeployment in Hebron—was announced the following day. Dissent from the political Right, barely contained before, erupted with ferocity. West Bank Israeli settlers took to the streets of their settlements to protest the agreement's terms. Others appeared in large numbers on the streets of Jerusalem and Tel Aviv. Orthodox rabbis also made their complaints known, as did members of the Knesset from the far right, some of whom called for early elections.

Though the agreement marked a step forward for the Oslo peace process—and for the relationship between Benjamin and Arafat, too—it did little to silence critics outside Israel, who seemed only to want more from this tiny country. Some went so far as to accuse Israel of promoting a policy of apartheid.

Beyond street demonstrations and remarks to reporters, dissatisfaction among far right political groups led to a realignment among minor parties. Two of them—Shas and United Torah—who had been part of Benjamin's governing coalition, withdrew their support. Benjamin quickly cobbled together a new majority that allowed him to remain in office until the next scheduled general election, but for the remainder of his term he was weakened considerably and lost in the general election.

NETANYAHU

NO LONGER PRIME MINISTER, Benjamin maintained a business office, using core personnel from his political team as the staff for a consulting firm. They worked with communications companies regarding internal structure and efficiency, and lobbied the Knesset for favorable telecommunications regulations. Benjamin continued to speak out at every opportunity about the need to fight global terrorism, but he did not immediately seek elected office, either in Likud or in the Israeli government.

Then, late one afternoon in September 2001, Benjamin was in a coffee shop in Jerusalem with Geller when a television monitor near the front counter showed video of an airliner crashing into an office building.

"Where's that?" He pointed over Geller's shoulder to the screen behind him.

Geller craned to see. "Looks like New York."

"It *is* New York," he said, his eyes wide. "That's one of the office towers at the World Trade Center."

"Yeah, and that plane flew right into it."

"Is that happening now?"

"I don't know." Geller glanced at his watch. "It's nearly five here, and nearly nine in the morning there."

While they talked, another plane slammed into the second Trade Center tower.

MIKE EVANS

"This is horrible," Benjamin whispered.

"Hey," Geller called to the clerk. "Turn that up so we can hear what's going on."

They listened with others in the shop as reporters on television tried to make sense of events, but before they'd plumbed the depths of the story from New York, a report appeared showing flames and smoke rising from the Pentagon in Washington, DC.

"This is really serious!"

"But who would do such a thing?"

Benjamin looked over at him. "I think we both know many who would do it. The real question is who would have access to the people *and* the money to actually make it happen."

They watched the monitor a moment longer, then Benjamin turned toward the door. "Come on. This changes everything. We need to get back to the office."

"Everything?" Geller trailed after him. "What are you talking about?"

"No one will want to hear Labor's overly optimistic visions of an idyllic future. Not after this."

"National security," Geller said as they reached Benjamin's car.

"Exactly," Benjamin replied. "And we'll have the perfect answer for them."

With Benjamin in the driver's seat, he and Geller raced back to the office. They found everyone crowded around the television near Benjamin's desk, watching scenes from New York as the story there continued to unfold. Moments later, the first Trade Center tower collapsed to the ground, followed minutes later by the disintegration of the second tower.

Benjamin looked over at Geller. "We need to get on television."

"I don't think that will be a problem. They'll be talking about this in the US all day and they'll run out of fresh faces and perspectives very quickly."

"What should I say?"

Before Geller could answer, Anna supplied, "We're sorry."

"That all Israelis stand with America," someone offered.

"That we have been warning the West of the dangers posed by radical Islam," Geller added. "Now, sadly and tragically, perhaps we can do something about it."

"Stay away from that," Shahar warned.

"Why?"

"Sounds like you're glad for the attacks."

"And no one has said Muslims had anything to do with it."

"They haven't said that yet," another corrected. "But they will soon enough."

"Sounds like we're trying to politicize the death of several thousand people."

"It *is* political."

"Maybe so, but we don't want to be the first to frame it that way."

"Good point."

Geller turned to an assistant. "Call the networks in New York. See if anyone wants to interview Benjamin Netanyahu."

Within the hour, Benjamin was in a studio, staring at a camera, listening to a producer in New York as he prepared to appear live on CNN. By then, news reports had caught up with Washington's focus on a radical Islamic group known as Al Qaeda, operating in Afghanistan.

"Al Qaeda is just the tip of the spear," Benjamin intoned. "Al Qaeda, Hamas here in the Middle East. They all have state sponsorship. Places like Iraq with its longstanding desire for nuclear weapons. Iran with its growing nuclear capability. They provide safe haven, financing, personnel, equipment, and supplies that allow these groups to operate."

"We've heard mention of North Korea from some White House sources," the newscaster enjoined. "Have you seen any connection between radical Islam and North Korea?"

"North Korea is a threat," Benjamin replied, "but not in terms of a direct military threat. They don't have the capacity to project military power very far beyond the Korean Peninsula. The chief threat they pose is in the export of technology and the specialized production processes necessary to create precision parts required by modern-era nuclear weapons."

"And you think these Islamic groups are in the market for those items?"

"I think radical Islamic groups all over this region are in the market for anything they can get that helps them maximize their ability to kill, maim, and destroy all who stand in their way."

"And by this region you mean the Middle East?"

"Islam has a grip on the region from Syria all the way to Indonesia and beyond. Most Muslims in that region are peaceful people who simply want to live their lives. But, radical elements within their religion are working day and night to turn that region into their domain for waging war on the rest of the world. What we've seen today in New York and Washington is but the most recent salvo in that war."

✦ ✦ ✦

As Benjamin noted, after the events of September 11, the global conversation changed as, for the next eight years, the US and other countries in the West concentrated on fighting terrorism and on the discovery of potential trouble before it occurred. America, with George W. Bush as president, invaded first Afghanistan, then Iraq, and while doing that, sent military special missions units, and individual assassins the world over searching for terrorists to capture or kill.

During that time, Benjamin was a frequent participant in the global conversation on terror and the appropriate responses to it, speaking on every occasion about the need to root out terrorism in all its forms. His background in the study of terrorism—going back to the time of his brother Jonathan's death and the conferences on terrorism that he organized and conducted—made him a favorite dinner speaker, talk show guest, and college lecturer. As the US debated its options against Iraq, Benjamin testified before congress regarding the threat posed to Israel and the US by Iraq's desire for nuclear weapons—and by Iran's even more sophisticated nuclear weapons program—which threatened the stability of the entire region.

"Iraq is intent on developing a nuclear program," Benjamin enlightened, "but Iran already has such a program and it is well along toward producing a nuclear weapon from it. Not a dirty bomb, though they could do that now, but a nuclear bomb. And while everyone is focused on Al Qaeda, the Taliban, and the like, the main threat we face in the long term is from a nuclear Iran. We cannot stand by and watch while Iran or Iraq obtain the ability to deliver a nuclear bomb on their neighbors. If they ever reach a point where they are producing nuclear weapons, every country in the region will become their hostage. And if they develop long-range missile capability, every nation in the world will be at their beck and call."

With his basic political team still intact from the 1996 and 1999 campaigns, Benjamin once again built a grassroots organization and shored up his relationships with local Likud branch leaders, in anticipation of entering the election of 2003. He was set to enter the general election that year but in an unexpected move, he was offered the post of finance minister in the government of Ariel Sharon, a position which he accepted and held until 2005.

In 2005, he announced as a candidate from the Likud Party in that year's legislative election, stating, "This is the key to everything. Knesset elections are where Party candidates separate themselves from mere Party members." He won a seat in the Knesset that year and then took the chairmanship of the Likud Party.

55

NETANYAHU

IN 2009, Benjamin again entered the race for prime minister and was elected to the office for a second time. The day after the election Benjamin visited his father. Benzion was now living alone, Celia having died nine years earlier. Still, his mind was sharp and he was just as quick with his critique of Likud politics, including the choices and decisions made by his son.

They sat in the living room and drank coffee while they talked. "I didn't listen to you the first time," Benjamin admitted. "I should have done that. If I had, things would have turned out very differently."

"You made too many concessions. It cost you the support of your coalition."

"What do you think we'll face now?"

Benzion pondered for a moment, "The world has changed. I know that sounds like a cliché, but it's true. Things are different now. And not just with President Obama in office." He paused to take a sip of coffee before continuing. "America has spent eight years fighting multiple wars. Iraq, Afghanistan, their global war on terror. All of it financed with debt. Too much debt. The financial debacle of 2008 was one of the results."

"There was plenty of blame to go around on that one," Benjamin added.

Benzion took another sip. "But when it comes to terrorism and global war to defeat it, the American people have moved on. Europeans have, too. The machinery of government—the permanent part that remains from president to president, prime minister to prime minister—is still stuck in the mire of national security, passenger screening, suspicious packages, and reading everyone's email. But the people—the typical man or woman in the street in New York or London—see it for what it is—the frantic over-reaction of government officials. The campaign of Barack Obama and his election to the presidency was as much about the American people moving on from the terrorist attacks and the wars as it was about electing the first African American president."

Benjamin grinned. "You're on a roll today, Dad."

"What do you mean?"

"I haven't heard you lecture like this in a long time."

"Well, don't discount what I say."

Benjamin held up a hand in protest. "I wouldn't think of it."

Benzion took another sip of coffee and gazed down at the floor a moment, as if his mind had suddenly taken him to a different place. But a moment later he looked over at Benjamin. "This is a good day."

"Something happen?"

"I remembered Rabbi Mickelson."

"Mickelson?" Benjamin chuckled. "What about him?"

"When he was here that day. In the summer."

"Right," Benjamin nodded. "The summer of 1979. The third anniversary of Entebbe."

"When he was here that day, he prophesied over you and said you would be elected prime minister twice."

Benjamin's eyes opened in a look of surprise. "He did, didn't he?"

"Yes. And it's come true. That has always been the test of whether someone really was a prophet."

Benjamin had a puzzled frown. "What was?"

"Whether their words came true."

"Maybe I should give him a call."

"Maybe so."

✦ ✦ ✦

At the time Benjamin took office, Barack Obama was already well into his initial term as president of the United States. During his first year in office, Obama focused on shoring up the US financial system, reworking the domestic healthcare policy, and developing better relationships with leaders in the Middle East. After eight years of war, he suggested, the US needed to mend its relationships with Arab countries not directly implicated in the attacks on New York and Washington.

In speeches at home he announced that a two-state solution for the Palestinian question was the only choice available. Privately, he was very suspicious of Benjamin and the effect the revisionist perspective might have on him. "Benjamin is seriously out of touch with the world," he commented on numerous occasions.

To get diplomatic efforts moving, Obama appointed George Mitchell, a retired US Senator from Maine, as his Middle East envoy. Mitchell was sent to find out from firsthand experience where Benjamin stood on the region's key issues. "See if he is supportive of a two-state solution and whether he's willing to negotiate with the Palestinians," Obama directed.

"It might be good if the two of you sat down together," Mitchell suggested. "I met him years ago, while I was in the senate. He's one way at a distance and quite another in a one-on-one setting."

"I'm willing to talk if he wants to. But find out what he has to say first. Then you can suggest a visit to the White House if you need to. We could see him in the spring."

Four days after his appointment, Mitchell traveled to Israel and met with Benjamin to press the Obama perspective.

"I am not opposed to negotiation," Benjamin told him, "but any negotiation with Palestinian leaders depends on the Palestinians formally recognizing Israel's right to exist."

"I thought they had done that already," Mitchell replied.

"Maybe they did, but I want Arafat to say it again."

"I'm not sure that's a good negotiating strategy. Better to just hold him to his prior statements than to attempt to force him to say it again."

"I'll meet with Arafat." Benjamin leaned back in his chair. "He and I have talked numerous times over the Oslo Accords and the Hebron agreement. But they'll have to acknowledge our right to exist before I sign anything."

"Okay."

"Tell me something, George."

"Certainly, if I can."

"Does President Obama know what he's doing?"

"Well," Mitchell began slowly, "In general I think he's in pretty good shape."

"Dealing with the Palestinians is not like dealing with Europeans. Europeans have a thousand-year history of diplomacy and a shared meaning with their neighbors. Palestinians come from a *six* thousand-year tribal tradition where every weakness is exploited, every strength pressed to the limit. A tradition in which disagreements are not worked out through understanding and treaty but through use of the blade. Where shared understanding includes vendetta, torture, and humiliation."

"I'm sure President Obama knows the situation is different here."

"I think he's going to need some help," Benjamin warned. "Otherwise, he's going to stumble into trouble. Hamas, leaders in Iraq and Iran. Saudi Arabia. They may use familiar words when dealing with him, but, as you know, they mean something totally different."

"I think if we stick to the topic of peace we'll be okay," Mitchell said.

"That's just it," Benjamin allowed a hint of frustration to show. "They do not want peace with us. Or with you, for that matter. They want to eliminate us. That is what they mean when they use the term peace. Peace will come for them when all Israelis are dead."

"I think you and President Obama need to spend some time together."

"I'll be glad to talk to him. But I'm serious, George. I don't think he knows as much about this part of the world as he thinks he knows."

✦ ✦ ✦

In May, Benjamin traveled to the United States and met with

President Obama in the White House library. Both men were suspicious of each other and had difficulty avoiding curt, argumentative exchanges.

When the topic turned to the proposed two-state solution for the Arab-Israeli conflict, Benjamin reiterated his position that a two-state solution would never work. "We have attempted that solution since before the days of the British Mandate and the Palestinians have refused to accept it. We are not the ones who cause the problem. They are the ones who rejected the solution."

"We'll make it clear," Obama stressed, "that we're not authorizing any additional territory or condoning additional attacks."

"But they know you will do nothing against them if they *do* attack us."

"We have many measures at our disposal."

"Oh?" Benjamin said with mock surprise. "You're going to send a carrier task force to the region and bomb Palestinian rocket and mortar positions?"

Obama looked perturbed. "I don't think—"

Benjamin cut him off. "You're going to put US troops on the ground in Gaza to make them comply?"

Obama looked away.

"That is what I mean." Benjamin lowered his voice. "They know you won't take military action against them to make them comply." He looked Obama in the eye. "They know that, Mr. President. Nothing you say will ever be backed up by the use of military force against them."

"It doesn't have to come to that."

"It wouldn't come to that if we were European countries negotiating the terms of a European peace," Benjamin argued. "But we're not. We're two Middle Eastern peoples. This is the world of tribal traditions. A world where meaning comes from the sharp edge of a sword."

"You've had some success working with Arafat on the West Bank."

"Yes." Benjamin nodded. "We have."

"So why not extend that same cooperation to Gaza?"

"With the West Bank, we really only have to deal with Arafat and Fatah. In Gaza, we have many smaller factions to address. They understand even less about Western diplomacy and negotiation. If we agree to their demands, they'll refuse to accept it and demand more."

"How can you say that?"

"Because that is the history of the Arabs in Palestine. They want it all. The entire region. They've been saying that for a hundred years and more and doing everything in their power to make it a reality. Ask Bill Clinton about dealing with Arafat. He convinced Ehud Barak to give Arafat everything Arafat demanded and every time Ehud agreed, Arafat wanted something more. And when he ran out of demands and would have been forced to concede, he walked away—even though he would have been given everything he wanted."

✦ ✦ ✦

When Benjamin returned from Washington, he went to see his father. This time, they stood by the kitchen counter and talked over a cup of coffee.

"That's what I told you before," Benzion reminded when Benjamin told him about the conversation with President Obama. "He just doesn't understand. The Arabs have been offered a state in Palestine four or five times over the past sixty years and each time, they refused it because the offer didn't include the entire region"

"And they fought instead."

"Yes. And every time they fought against us they lost control of more and more area."

"I don't think President Obama knows or understands much about that."

"I know," Benzion sighed. "He's sold out to the liberals. And I don't mean liberal politicians, but the liberal mindset. They know most of the facts, they just don't always draw the correct conclusions."

"They seem to think an Arab state would solve the entire problem."

"An Arab state—a true state with an army of its own—would systematically eliminate all of us."

"I've tried to tell Obama this but he doesn't accept it."

Benzion had a knowing look. "I told you when we first talked about him, back when he was campaigning for office—he's a smart guy and he wants everyone to know he's the smartest guy in the room, which means he is unteachable."

Benjamin was perplexed. "So, how do we handle this? Israel cannot survive without the US as our primary ally."

"I'm not sure how to address all of the details," Benzion admitted. "But I know you must hold fast to the original dream. A dream of a Jewish state in our native land of Israel. One in which we occupy all the original territory on both sides of the Jordan."

"You've reminded me of that." Benjamin drained the last of the coffee from his cup. "But it's also what the Arabs want. They want a state that controls the entire region." He set his cup on the counter. "We can't both have the entirety of the same region."

"Well, I have no answer other than the one I've been giving most of my life. We aren't merely building a state in Palestine. We are restoring Israel to the time of David."

"I'm not sure I can say that." Benjamin looked down at the floor. "Not sure I can fail to say it, either."

Benzion was frustrated. "Look, son, you can decide for yourself. I can't tell you what to do. No one can."

"Jonathan could."

"Yes." Benzion nodded his head. "I'm sure your brother could have told us exactly what to do. But he's not here, so, we'll have to work with what we have."

"Back then. When we were kids. You didn't think I would get this far, did you?"

"I thought you would have gone the way you were going when Micki left."

"Business."

"Yes." Benzion looked away. "You were good at it. You had a mind for numbers and ideas. I assumed you would follow that. Politics is a messy business."

"And now?"

Benzion turned to look at him. "Now, my son is prime minister of the nation of Israel. Not just once, but twice so far." He looked away once more and cleared his throat. "Deal with the Palestinians, the Americans, and anyone else. Deal with them the way you think best. Just *do it*. Assert your authority as head of state. Everyone else will support you. Just stand up and be heard."

✦ ✦ ✦

Back at the office, Benjamin sat at his desk and stared out the window, lost in thought about the conversation with his father and the question of how to deal with the Palestinians. A knock at the door brought him back to the moment and he turned to see Geller standing in the doorway. "You wanted to talk?" Geller asked.

"Yeah. Close the door and have a seat."

"Has something happened that I don't know about?"

"We need to figure out our position on the Palestinians."

"Okay." Geller took a seat. "I thought we had a position on them already."

"I don't think so."

"We're opposed to a Palestinian state because of Hamas' control in Gaza."

"We should turn that around. Make it a positive expression of the same ideas."

"Maybe you have something in mind?"

Benjamin opened the top drawer of his desk and took out a notepad and tossed it to Geller. "Something like this."

Geller caught the pad and glanced at the top sheet. "Recognition of Israel's right to exist." He read aloud. "Demilitarized state. Jerusalem as our capital." Geller looked up from the page. "I think we should go back to Arafat's acceptance of the Oslo Accords—the first round. He signed a document that indicated their acceptance of us."

"I know," Benjamin replied. "But I think they have recanted on that. And even if they haven't, I want that in the language of any agreement we sign with them."

"You think this speech will move them that far?"

"You don't?"

Geller shrugged his shoulders. "I don't know. What you've written sounds a lot like what we've been saying all the time. And I don't think they'll agree to a demilitarized state."

"Maybe not, but I'm saying this is where I am. They can be anywhere they want. *This* is where I am."

Geller nodded. "Fair enough."

"They can't reasonably expect us to abandon Jerusalem." Benjamin smiled. "I don't think the Knesset would ever agree to it."

"I guess the question then is, would they agree to share use of it?"

"I would let them use it," Benjamin replied. "But I'm not agreeing to shared control. Not now."

"Maybe later?"

"Maybe later, when someone else is prime minister, or in a different time...after a long history of cooperation and peace...maybe. But I'm not doing it. Not now."

"Okay, I'll get this information to the speech writers. Tell them to build a speech around it."

"Good," Benjamin nodded. "Now. Where should I deliver that speech?"

Geller glanced down at a datebook that rested on his lap. "You're scheduled to speak at Bar-Ilan University. What about that?"

"I think it's a good idea."

"Then I'll put the writers to work and get in touch with the university to work out the details."

Geller's speechwriters crafted a brilliant first draft, to which Benjamin added his own touches. He rehearsed it several times and had key lines tested by a media group, just to make sure they would go over well.

The version of the speech that Benjamin delivered indicated his willingness to accept a two-state solution to the Palestinian issue, but only if that proposed Palestinian state had no military, if Jerusalem remained Israel's unified capital, and there was no right of Arabs to return to Palestine. The speech was crafted to perfection and Benjamin gave it an inspired delivery, hoping to impress upon Palestinians just how much he wanted peace and cooperation between the two groups. The Palestinians did not see it that way.

By then, Arafat had died and Mahmoud Abbas, who had been elected president of the Palestinian National Authority (PA), was serving in multiple positions as prime minister of the PNA and the first president of the Palestinian State. In reality, however, he exercised effective control over only the West Bank, Hamas having seized power in Gaza.

Asked about the speech, Abbas dismissed the question with a smirk, "It marks the end of peace negotiations." And as quickly as the peace process had arisen, it faded from the public agenda.

56

NETANYAHU

WHILE BENJAMIN STRUGGLED to find a way forward with the Palestinian peace process, the nations of Western Europe experienced a rise in immigrants from the Middle East. Spurred on by violence in Iraq, Syria, and Gaza, they steadily made their way westward eventually settling principally in the United Kingdom, Germany, and France. As Europe's Muslim population rose, so also did acts of violence by Muslims against European citizens.

Seemingly overnight, European governments that previously had ignored threats from the Middle East gave it their full attention. It wasn't long before that new-found interest settled on Iran as key to resolving the region's troubles and an Iran free of sanctions as key to any meaningful solution.

With the United States having led the effort to impose sanctions on Iran, European leaders concluded that the US should lead the way toward restarting negotiations with Iran about its nuclear program. Consequently, they began lobbying President Obama and influential American liberals to lead the diplomatic effort.

President Obama expressed an immediate interest in the suggestion and directed his secretary of state, John Kerry, to explore the possibility of American involvement. It was a decision that would profoundly influence Benjamin's relationship with the new American president and US-Israeli diplomatic relations at every level.

✦ ✦ ✦

Throughout his previous term as prime minister—and even before then when serving in Shamir's government—Benjamin had been kept abreast of the latest developments in Iran, much of it based on information that was far better than anything the United States or other Western nations possessed. Most of it came from Mossad operatives working in Iran as part of a long-term intelligence network, operatives who spent their adult lives as Iranian citizens. The information they provided led to an assessment of Iran's nuclear program that was quite different from that of the United States.

In his ongoing discussions with President Obama, Benjamin found himself facing a dilemma. He could have offered the intelligence information and underlying photographs and other evidence in an attempt to persuade Obama of the accuracy of Mossad's assessment of the situation. Or, he could keep silent, assert his position without substantiation, and appear to President Obama and his advisers as a stubborn politician with an outdated worldview, unwilling to embrace the times, and failing to trust his country's most important ally.

Inwardly, Benjamin longed to be personally understood, not just by President Obama but by all who knew him. That was the internal angst with which he'd wrestled all of his life. This, however, was bigger than him. This was about the protection of an intelligence operation the likes of which the West would never conceive and never attempt. An intelligence operation that rested on the backs of men and women who undertook to live and work in Iran as Iranians. Mossad operatives who, if discovered, would most certainly lose their lives. Perhaps even on the spot. And so the question of whether to reveal his sources to President Obama came down to one question: Could he trust Barack Obama?

As he wrestled with that question he realized that whether Barack Obama was trustworthy or not, as President of the United States he would be obligated to share the information with his own intelligence community—the CIA, the NSA, and others. Enough information to convince the President to abandon the talks with Iran that would be more than enough for US intelligence agencies to figure out what Mossad had been doing. And that was more than Benjamin could set in motion, trust Obama or not.

So, throughout his meetings at the White House, Benjamin kept quiet about what he knew. Instead of making the bold, but unsubstantiated, assertion that Iran would probably develop a nuclear bomb in a matter of months, not years, and that it already had the ability to deliver a nuclear bomb to its neighbors with its current, conventional rockets.

As Benjamin had expected, President Obama found his position unverifiable and assessed Benjamin as one who was seriously out of step with current developments in the Middle East and even within Israel itself. Seeing him as an ideologue who was mired in an historic context that spoke to a different time and different conditions.

That assessment put an edge to President Obama's voice and a frown on his brow, which Benjamin found personally condescending and off-putting. A man of Obama's intellect, Benjamin assumed, ought to be able to disagree with him and still accept him as a peer. That Obama could not, strained their relationship nearly to the breaking point.

✦ ✦ ✦

Forced to look for alternative ways to convince the US not to proceed toward an agreement with Iran, Benjamin cast about for other means to reveal Mossad's information on Iran without revealing how it was discovered.

In the midst of that effort, a manila envelope arrived at Benjamin's office. He opened it to find a copy of the most recent proposed agreement with Iran. He read it quickly, then convened a meeting of his closest advisers—those who came with him from the campaign staff to the prime minister's office, people who had been with him the longest. He had a pretty good idea how Mossad analysts would view the document, and the IDF general staff had already made a risk assessment of Iran's program. The views he needed were of a different sort. Not the technical perspective of the permanent government. What he needed right then was something more personal. Something tailored to his views. What he needed was a view of his own perspective.

"I only have this single copy," Benjamin told the group crowded around a table in his private study. "And I think once you've read it you'll agree with my decision not to make more." He handed the document to Shahar. "Scan it quickly. Don't try to read every word. Then pass the pages on as you finish them. We need to discuss this now."

"Well," Shahar said as she passed along the first page. "They're giving Iran everything and getting nothing in return."

Anna Arkin took the first page from Shahar, scanned it, then looked up to take the next page. "This agreement only extends for five years."

Benjamin waited patiently as the pages circulated the room, listening and watching as others shared their observations.

A moment later, Gad Naharin, one of youngest in the group but who had proved himself indispensable in analyzing delicate situations, spoke up. "One thing I've noticed, neither the US nor any of the European nations negotiating this so-called deal with Iran are in danger of attack from Iran." He glanced around the room as if waiting for someone to agree with him. When no one picked up on his cues he looked down at the page in his hand.

"Exactly," Benjamin said. "*We* are the ones who will be attacked. *We're* the ones who would be threatened by a nuclear Iran."

"Us and every other country in the Middle East," Geller added.

"And if Iran gets away with this," Naharin opined, "every nation in the Middle East will start its own nuclear program."

"As an initial matter," Geller offered, "I think the agreement must acknowledge our right to exist."

"Absolutely," someone answered.

"I'm not so sure that's appropriate," Naharin countered.

Benjamin was startled. "Not appropriate?"

"We are not a party to these talks or to any proposed agreement," Naharin pointed out. "Seems a little strange suggesting to the United States that it demand that Iran acknowledge our right to exist."

Benjamin had a pained expression. "I can't believe I'm hearing this from you."

"It would be a demand that would almost assuredly scuttle the talks," Naharin explained. "Iran would never accept it and I think most of the others would see past it to its real purpose."

"Which would be?" Anna asked.

Naharin smiled, "To scuttle the talks."

Benjamin laughed out loud and everyone in the room seemed to relax. They continued to discuss the proposals that appeared overtly in the document and the hidden assumptions that lay behind them, each one giving their analysis and opinion in a lively discussion of terms and conditions, anticipated outcomes, and the effect an agreement with Iran might have on Israel's long-term relationship with the US.

When they concluded, Benjamin met alone with Geller. "We need to schedule as many meetings as possible where I can talk about Iran and the threat posed to the Middle East by the Iranians' nuclear program."

"Okay," Geller ventured cautiously. "You have a speech on this prepared already?"

"No. Not yet. We'll need to get some people to work on one."

Geller had an amused look. "Not the usual writers?"

"No. Put Shahar on it. And Anna." He glanced up at Geller. "And add Gad Naharin to it."

"He's never worked on a speech before."

"I know. But I like his attitude."

"Okay. Any places in mind that you particularly wanted to go with this message?"

Benjamin looked over at him once more. "As many places as possible. Large or small. Just like the campaign. Only this time, we aren't running for office. We're running to stop the greatest diplomatic blunder since Chamberlain and the Munich Agreement."

"Then why are we talking to groups here in Israel? Most of them would agree with you."

"Who said we're just talking to them?" Benjamin grinned. "Get me out beyond our borders. Out where the message will stir up discussion.

Where reporters will be glad for a different story to report. You set up the meetings. I'll take them all."

✦ ✦ ✦

The following month, Iran held its presidential election. Hassan Rouhani was elected to office. President Obama, White House advisers, and almost every European leader saw Rouhani as a moderate. Someone whose term in office might offer the best opportunity of obtaining a reasonable agreement regarding Iran's nuclear program. That assessment of the election was the primary force behind Obama's decision to move quickly toward an agreement. Before Ali Khamenei, Iran's Supreme Commander, had time to move Rouhani and his cabinet in a different direction.

Not long after the election, representatives from the United States, United Kingdom, Russia, France, China, Germany, and the European Union met in Geneva for formal discussions about the terms and conditions necessary for an acceptable agreement with Iran. After several vigorous, and sometimes heated, rounds revising drafts of a proposed basic agreement, Iran was invited to participate.

Much to everyone's relief, Rouhani, with Khamenei's approval, accepted the offer. Iranian representatives arrived in Geneva the following day and joined the substantive discussions at once.

✦ ✦ ✦

While talks continued in Geneva, Benjamin embarked on a series of speaking engagements that took him to half a dozen events in Israel and Europe. The series had been designed to educate and motivate leaders of the world to adopt his position regarding an agreement with Iran. Buoyed by his staff's assessment, he had begun that first campaign with high expectations.

Audiences in Israel, some quite large, gave him a warm reception. But beyond Israel's borders, he had little success in convincing others to join him in opposing the Iran talks. After a week of meetings, he returned to Jerusalem tired and dejected.

The morning after his return, Benjamin came to the office with coffee cup in hand and a contentious scowl on his face. Just as he dropped onto the chair at his desk his father entered the room. Benzion grabbed a chair near the doorway, pulled it over in front of the desk, and sat down.

Almost immediately, their conversation turned to Benjamin's recent trip, the threat of a nuclear Iran, and the absurdity of trying to obtain an agreement with anyone from Tehran.

"I've been speaking out." Benjamin's voice had an unusually sharp edge. "I'm doing what you suggested. Taking positions I really believe instead of trying to create answers that will please someone else."

"That's good," Benzion assured. "You'll never please everyone anyway, which is why I tell you to focus instead on the calling of your life."

Benjamin sighed. "I don't think I know much about that part."

Benzion had a puzzled frown. "What do you mean?"

"I've been trying to find that *calling*. To see how things are opening up in my life. That's why I've been out there trying to convince the world that Iran is a problem for everyone." Benjamin scooted his chair up to the desk and cradled the coffee cup with both hands. "That seems to be my role right now. But I have little to show for the effort."

"I know it seems that way, but...." Benzion fell silent when he realized Benjamin had stopped listening and was staring at a document that lay on the desktop. Instead of continuing, he let his gaze wander over the room until his eyes came to the Netanyahu ring box sitting on a shelf behind Benjamin's desk. He glanced down at Benjamin's hands and saw his fingers were bare. "You aren't wearing the ring."

"No," Benjamin replied, glancing in his father's direction. "It's too big for my finger. I was...you know...worried about losing it."

Benzion gave him a knowing look. "Worried? Or embarrassed?"

Benjamin set the coffee cup on the desktop and leaned back in his chair. "I'm not embarrassed to be a descendant of David, if that's what you mean."

"But you are embarrassed to assert your birthright as ruler of the Davidic Kingdom."

"That seems rather...presumptive right now, don't you think?"

"It's not presumptive to accept the role God has given you."

"Come on, Dad," Benjamin said in a frustrated tone. "The world would never stand for an announcement about the return of the kingdom, and you know it."

"The world won't stand for a lot of things," Benzion responded sharply. "Look, I realize we live in a world of political realities that sometimes limit the ideal and force it to yield to the practical, at least for the moment. But think about this." He paused as a smile crept over his face. "All of mandatory Palestine except Transjordan is under our control."

Benjamin placed his hands on the armrests of the chair. "Not completely."

"No," Benzion admitted. "Not completely. But I don't think David had absolute control during his time, either. And his kingdom was not always the same size."

Benjamin had a curious look. "What do you mean?"

"I mean, it expanded and contracted with the reality of the day. But it was always the Davidic Kingdom and they never stopped working to expand and develop it in a way that favored the kingdom."

"So, what is my role?"

"Your role is the same now as it's always been—to be faithful to the calling upon your life."

"And after that? Then what?"

"Hold onto as much of the kingdom as possible, and expand it when you can."

There was a knock at the door, then it opened a little and a secretary peered through the crack. "They need to talk to you."

"Okay, I'm on my way." Benjamin looked over at his father. "I have to step across the hall. I'll be back in a minute."

"Okay. Take all the time you need."

"I'll be back, Dad." Benjamin insisted. "I just have to see about this."

While Benjamin was gone, Benzion stood and moved behind the desk. He took the ring box from the shelf and looked inside. *This should have been Jonathan's,* he thought to himself. *He would have been proud to be a descendant of David and proud to wear the Netanyahu ring.* He took the ring from its place and held it up admiringly. *It should have never gone to Benjamin. Jonathan had no right to give it to him.*

After a moment, Benzion slipped the ring into his pocket and returned the box to its place on the shelf, then turned toward the door and made his way out. As he passed a secretary's desk he said to her, "Tell my son I'll see him later."

✦ ✦ ✦

As the Obama administration continued to push for a nuclear deal with Iran, news of various drafts and positions on the issues continued to leak to the press. Along with those leaks came persistent rumors that the parties were closer than they'd ever been to reaching an agreement.

The US Congress, controlled by conservative Republicans, pushed back, threatening to cut off funding for further negotiating sessions. In the event the administration reached a deal of the kind being currently discussed, conservatives vied to pass legislation making the deal of no force and effect under US law.

Questioned about whether an obstructionist strategy might be successful, John Muhlenberg, Speaker of the House, answered, "I think we might have the votes already to defund any agreement the Obama administration makes with Iran. We might pass that legislation anyway, regardless of whether the president reaches a deal. We can't have the president going off on his own, negotiating with just *anyone.*"

Despite fears that President Obama was pushing negotiations with Iran in a pell-mell dash toward *any* agreement, talks in Geneva slowed. As spring gave way to summer, progress seemed more elusive than ever. But as fall approached signs seemed to indicate the parties might be close once again.

Finally, in late November, the parties reached a deal limiting Iran's nuclear development program to continued work only with stockpiles of uranium enriched no higher than five percent. Uranium already enriched to higher levels was to be transferred out of the country to designated repositories, or converted to uranium oxide. In addition, the agreement imposed limitations on development and use of new centrifuge sites. Once Iran showed evidence of compliance with those measures, existing economic and financial sanctions would be lifted. Terms of the agreement extended over a fifteen year period.

Mossad operatives, who'd been in Geneva since talks began, obtained a copy of the agreement before news of it became public. Within hours, a copy was placed on Benjamin's desk. He read it quickly, then called Geller to his office.

"They've reached an agreement in Geneva." Benjamin handed the document to Geller.

"They're actually going to sign this one?"

"Yes."

"How bad is it?"

"Not quite as terrible as earlier drafts."

Geller nodded as he skimmed the pages. "They must have worked hard to get this much."

"I'm sure they did," Benjamin agreed. "But it does nothing to remove or eliminate the potential for obtaining nuclear weapons. And they seem to be totally unaware of what Iran is actually doing on the ground."

"Well," Geller said slowly, "they could only go as far as the parties were willing to agree." He looked over at Benjamin. "They have no way to force Iran to agree to anything."

"I know," Benjamin sighed. "But it only goes out to fifteen years. And even with that, the limitations are slowly lifted on most aspects."

"But it will allow inspectors to build a database of information on the program. Having people on the ground, in-country, with access to the sites is nothing to scoff at. At least not in the world of diplomacy."

"But we know what they're doing. They're hiding uranium that's enriched far beyond what this agreement addresses." Benjamin pointed toward the papers in Geller's hands. "Which means their breakout period is only a matter of months, not years as Kerry and Obama believe. They could develop a bomb and test it within months of signing this agreement."

"I know," Geller admitted. "But at least it's a start."

"It's nothing."

"It's the direction the United States wants to take," Geller insisted. "We've had our say. Maybe it's time for us to move a little closer to their position and find something good to say about it. Instead of constantly detracting from it."

"Do you think the CIA knows how much highly enriched uranium Iran has hidden?"

"I don't know," Geller admitted. "Most of their agents are in and out on short-term assignments."

"Every morning, someone from Mossad gives me a security briefing. They update me regularly about the location of those stockpiles. And the attempts they've interdicted. Just the other day they stopped an attempt to transfer some of it to Hezbollah."

Geller was appalled. "I didn't hear about that. Mossad really did that? How did they stop them?"

"Drone strike on the truck."

"And no one noticed the radiation dispersal at the blast site?"

"We didn't hit the transportation canister. Just the cab of the truck." Benjamin paused a moment, then continued, "You know, the thing that bothers me even more is the US knows what Iran is doing, and doesn't care. Or worse, is helping them do it."

"That's not likely. If they knew, they couldn't possibly ignore it. The results of ignoring it would jeopardize everything they've tried to accomplish in the Middle East. And conspiring with Iran does the same thing. I mean, if the US was ignoring Iran or helping them, they would be putting Iran in the regional driver's seat. They couldn't possibly want that."

Benjamin glared at him. "I don't intend to wait around while Iran develops weapons that can obliterate our people."

"I think Iran knows what would happen if they tried," Geller responded. "And right now, we need to walk our public rhetoric back from the brink."

"What do you mean by that?"

"I mean, conspiracy theories are fine for people in the US but for a head of government from the State of Israel, it does us no good. We must find a way to hold our own coalition together and avoid alienating members of America's Democratic Party. For most of the twentieth century they formed the core of our US constituency. We don't want to destroy that completely."

Both men were silent a moment as Geller finished reading the agreement and tossed it on Benjamin's desk. "It's a start. I think that was all it was supposed to be. And it will provide building blocks that can lead to a more permanent solution. But at least it's a start. I'll have some of the writers work on remarks and maybe a draft of a speech for you."

NETANYAHU

AS NEWS of the agreement with Iran broke to the public, politicians and statesmen around the world seemed to accept it favorably. In the US, however, Republican members of Congress once again expressed their displeasure and renewed vows to make certain it never became law in the United States. Rather than cower in the face of that threat, members of President Obama's administration went to work, lobbying for congressional approval of the measure. Both sides seemed bent on having their way. Nothing in their past working relationship suggested anything but a hard-fought intergovernmental battle.

In the midst of that, Geller received an email from Wesley Orr, an oilman and industrialist from Houston, Texas. Together with his younger brother Frank, he owned the family business, Orr Petroleum, a professional football team, two pro basketball teams, and a collection of automobile dealerships. Worth billions, the Orr brothers were longtime Republican Party donors.

Geller had met both of the Orrs years earlier, when they decided to expand their sphere of influence by funding candidates in select political races outside the United States. Israel was of particular interest to them and Benjamin had benefited from their largesse on several occasions.

"Heathrow," the message read. "Tuesday at Noon. Terminal Five.

On the benches across from Carluccio's." Geller knew the location well. They'd met there before.

The next day, Geller flew to Paris and on the following Tuesday took a short flight to London's Heathrow Airport. As instructed, he took a seat near Carluccio's coffee shop and waited. Forty-five minutes later, Wesley Orr appeared in the distance as he made his way through the terminal. A tall, lanky American, he sauntered up to the bench where Geller was waiting and took a seat next to him.

"What was so secretive we had to meet here?" Geller asked.

Wesley ignored the question. "Would your boss be interested in talking to Congress?"

"He talks to Congressmen all the time," Geller responded.

"No," Wesley wagged his finger to make a point. "Not Congressmen—Congress."

"You mean, appear and give a formal address to Congress?"

"A joint session," Wesley said. "Would he be interested?"

"Certainly, but I would have to discuss it with him."

"Let me know as soon as you can."

"How long do I have?"

"I need your answer by next Thursday."

"Okay. Are you spending the night?"

Wesley pushed himself up from the bench. He paused and glanced at his wristwatch. "No. Got just enough time to make my connection."

Geller called after. "Thanks, Wes."

Wesley glanced over his shoulder with a smile. "My pleasure."

✦ ✦ ✦

Geller arrived back in Tel Aviv the next day and went straight to Benjamin's office where he found the prime minister hunched over a file that lay open on his desktop. Geller closed the door behind him and started across the room.

"I have a meeting in a few minutes," Benjamin commented without looking up. "So whatever you have, make it quick."

Geller flopped onto a chair near the desk. "You know how you told me to set you up with as many speeches as possible?"

"Yes."

"And you wanted to get outside of Israel as much as possible?"

"Yes." Benjamin looked over at Geller, suddenly giving him his undivided attention. "What have you done now?"

"Would you like to appear before a joint session of Congress and deliver your speech to them?"

Benjamin looked intrigued. "Is this a real offer? I mean, I wouldn't want word to get out about it from us and then find out next week that there never was anything to the offer in the first place."

"I would never allow you to get into a situation like that."

"When do they want me to do it?"

"I don't know the date yet, but we have to let them know by Thursday if we agree to do it." Benjamin leaned back in his chair. When he didn't respond immediately, Geller added, "It wouldn't hurt to be the prime minister who addressed the US Congress."

"You mean in our next election?"

"It's only a few months away."

"What will the White House say about it?"

"I don't know," Geller shrugged. "Don't tell them."

Benjamin frowned. "Don't tell them?"

"Yeah."

"I am a head of state. They are the US Congress. From a protocol standpoint, I outrank them. The Speaker of the House and I are not peers."

"Does that matter?" Geller smiled. "I'm just asking."

"It does to most heads of state. As a matter of courtesy, if nothing else, invitations of this nature usually come from the White House. Are you suggesting this invitation won't come from them?"

"I don't see how it could."

"How so?"

"Republican Congress. Democratic White House." Geller ticked off all the reasons on his fingers. "You, an outspoken critic and opponent of policy Obama has staked a lot of his credibility on. Congress threatening to block it with their own legislation."

"Fair point," Benjamin conceded. "Still, these things are always cleared through heads of state."

"If you ask Obama," Geller insisted, "he'll just say no."

"Then how are you suggesting we proceed?"

"You give me the go ahead and I'll report back that you will agree to do it," Geller explained. "Then we'll work out the details."

"Who contacted you about this?"

"I'm not sure you should know that."

"I don't think I can decide if I don't," Benjamin replied.

"Wesley Orr."

"Okay. That makes things a little more certain. He's been a friend of ours for a long time."

"And whatever he arranges tends to work out right."

"Okay."

Geller scooted up straight in the chair. "You'll do it?"

Benjamin nodded and once more bent over the file on his desk. "Tell Wes I'll do it and that I appreciate the invitation."

Geller left Benjamin's office and walked down the hall to his own where he took a seat at his desk and sent an email to Wesley Orr indicating that Benjamin would be delighted to accept an invitation to address the Congress of the United States.

Two days later, John Muhlenberg, the Speaker of the House, announced his intention to invite Benjamin to address a session of the House of Representatives. Later that same week, a spokesman for the Obama administration issued a tersely worded statement indicating they had not approved the invitation and that if Benjamin accepted, he would not be welcome at the White House during his visit. No mention was made of whether the administration would formally block Benjamin's attempt to enter the country.

Beyond the White House, the invitation sparked controversy in the US, with prominent politicians and Middle East experts arguing that as a matter of courtesy and protocol Benjamin should not address Congress without White House cooperation. Members of Congress, always sensitive when it came to questions of House independence and its power to manage its own affairs, were generally supportive of the invitation but cautious about whether Benjamin should accept. Some Democrats, however, seeing it as an attempt to undercut President Obama's efforts to gain approval of the deal with Iran, announced they would not attend Benjamin's speech.

Nongovernmental Jewish agencies were divided over the issue. Those traditionally aligned with the World Zionist Organization issued a statement against the address. Those traditionally aligned with the Revisionist position urged Benjamin to accept.

✦ ✦ ✦

Benjamin met with Geller once more to consider what to do. They discussed the arguments for accepting the invitation and those for declining it. "And," Geller added, "we need to consider how the agreement with Iran changes the complexity of the issue."

"What do you mean?"

"Are you going there to lobby the House against the deal?"

"I've been lobbying everyone against the deal," Benjamin responded.

"Yes, but now there's an actual agreement on the table."

"To which we are opposed."

"Declining, as a matter of courtesy to President Obama, would score points with the White House," Geller observed.

"Yes, but didn't we already indicate we would give the speech?"

"That was a preliminary yes, given to a friend. Our friends would understand if we now had to back out."

Benjamin grinned. "We still have friends?"

"That reminds me. It's time to make the rounds with the local Likud chapters. At least with the leadership."

"Maybe that's why I like the House of Representatives," Benjamin quipped with a smile. "We both are always running for office."

"We should do something different with the local leadership. More than just showing up at the chapter meetings."

"Like what?"

"Maybe sponsor a dinner to honor them."

"If we do, just make sure we do that for all of them. If we leave out even one, it will look like we're slighting him."

"Okay, but back to the speech. There's really no way to accept that offer and not look like you're lobbying Congress against the Iran agreement."

"Unless I don't."

Geller looked perplexed. "Don't give it?"

"No. What if I give the speech, but don't lobby Congress."

"Okay," Geller nodded. "Then what will you say in the speech?"

"Same thing I've been saying. Only, I won't take private meetings with individual Congressmen."

"We could soften your language a little, too."

Benjamin tapped his finger on the desktop for emphasis. "I'm going to speak against the agreement. An agreement with Iran under the terms they've reached poses a terrible risk to us. But you can soften the language a little. Just a little," he added, gesturing to show the amount with his thumb and index finger.

"Congress must know your position by now anyway," Geller suggested.

"Yes. And I'm sure they will introduce legislation to block the agreement at every turn. And my going there gives the appearance I am supporting their legislative efforts. But we need the public forum Washington provides." Benjamin looked over at Geller. "We need the world to see that Israel once again is on the brink of disaster, only this time clearly and unequivocally opposing the forces that come against her."

"Bold move, speaking against a president's policy initiative on his own turf."

"I'm not opposed to an initiative. We need an agreement with Iran," Benjamin insisted. "I'm just opposed to *this* agreement." The telephone on his desk buzzed, and Benjamin stood. "I have a meeting. Tell them I'll be glad to address the US Congress."

✦ ✦ ✦

When Geller was gone, Benjamin turned to the shelf that held the Netanyahu ring box. He lifted the box from its place and set it on the desktop, then raised the lid and glanced inside, expecting to see the ring. Instead, he saw only the fabric that lined the box's interior. The ring was gone.

A sinking feeling jabbed Benjamin in the stomach followed by a sense of despair at the sudden realization he would have to explain the ring's loss to his father. Already his mind raced ahead to that moment and the things his father might say to him.

"But I have to talk to him," Benjamin muttered to himself. "There's just no other choice."

The phone on his desk buzzed again, reminding him of the meeting he was supposed to attend. *I'll do that,* he told himself. *I'll go to the meeting, then I'll go to my father's house and tell him the ring is gone. And then he can berate me for losing it and I can tell him maybe it left because I am not worthy of its blessing.*

✦ ✦ ✦

Later that afternoon, Benjamin rode across town to see his father. At one hundred two years of age and suffering from several physical ailments, Benzion was now confined to his bed. His mind, however, was as sharp as ever and he smiled as Benjamin appeared at the doorway. "I was hoping you would stop by today."

Benjamin paused to let Benzion's nurse slip by.

"Something on your mind?" Benjamin asked when they were alone.

"No, I just wanted to see you." He studied Benjamin a moment. "But from the look on your face I think you might have something on *your* mind."

Benjamin moved a chair closer to the bed and took a seat. He crossed his legs and straightened the cuff of his pants with a flick of his hand. "Yeah," he said finally. "There's something on my mind."

"What is it?"

Benjamin hesitated a moment longer. "Dad," he began finally, "I've lost the ring." He sat with his eyes focused on the floor, expecting to hear the grating sound of his father's angry response. When nothing happened, he glanced up. "Did you hear me, Dad? I lost the Netanyahu ring."

"Look in the drawer," Benzion replied. "The top drawer."

A puzzled frown wrinkled Benjamin's forehead.

"Look in the top drawer of the dresser," Benzion repeated.

Benjamin stood and moved across the room to the dresser, then opened the top drawer. "Feel all the way to the back," Benzion directed. "Near the corner."

Benjamin placed his hand inside the drawer, worked it beneath the socks near the front, and pushed it all the way to the back. As his fingers reached the back of the drawer, he felt them brush against an envelope. He drew it out and held it up to see. The envelope was smooth with the flap sealed flat against the back, but an object inside formed a bulge at one end.

"Open it," Benzion directed.

Benjamin tore off the end of the envelope and the Netanyahu ring tumbled into his hand. He looked over at Benzion. "How did it get in here?"

Benzion turned his head away. "I took it," he admitted sheepishly.

"Why?"

"I was angry," Benzion explained. "I saw you weren't wearing it and I was mad. You stepped out of the office for a minute and while you were gone, I took it." He looked at Benjamin. "I'm sorry."

Tears filled Benjamin's eyes at the sound of those words. In all his life he'd never heard his father apologize to anyone for anything—certainly not to him—and for a moment he was tempted to open up about how he knew Jonathan was the family favorite and he was sorry he couldn't live up to the example his older brother had set. But the anguished look on his father's face made him stop short.

They both knew the things that had been said that never should have been spoken, and the things unsaid that most surely should have been addressed. They knew all of that and knowing it, there was no longer a need to hear it. Instead, Benjamin smiled, "That's okay." He gestured with the ring. "I have it now."

"Slip it on," Benzion urged.

"It doesn't fit," Benjamin replied. "Remember? It's too big."

"Maybe your finger was just too small before." Benzion urged once more. "Try it now."

Benjamin grasped the ring and studied it a moment, thinking about all the generations that followed from David to him. Hundreds of generations had longed for the day when the Davidic kingdom might be restored but they never saw it. Now, at last, the ring had come to him—and at a time when Israel's hold on Palestine, at least the part of it between the Mediterranean Sea and the Jordan River, might yet be fulfilled.

"Put it on," Benzion repeated. "Let's see what it looks like."

Benjamin slipped the ring onto the fourth finger of his right hand and felt it slide snuggly into place. "Hey!" he exclaimed, his eyes wide with surprise. "It fits!" He held his hand for Benzion to see. "It was too big before, but now it's just right."

"You are a Netanyahu," Benzion whispered. "Given by God to bless His people. This is the purpose for which you were elected to office. This is the purpose for which you were born."

"I thought you didn't believe in stuff like that."

"I didn't before."

"What happened?"

"You changed my mind."

"I did?"

"Seeing you in office. How you've grown and changed. The circumstances have come together in your day." Benzion paused to wipe his eyes. "The way the ring found its way to you even though I tried to give it to Jonathan."

Tears filled both their eyes and there was an awkwardness about them that they would have found distasteful and neither of them would have endured. But now, they seemed to relish it. And Benjamin wondered to himself why that was so—but he kept those thoughts to himself and dared not raise them. Not now, that he finally had the intimacy with Benzion that Jonathan had known and enjoyed.

They talked a while longer, neither wanting the visit to end, but the momentum of the day finally caught up with them and Benjamin had to go. They said their goodbyes, with Benjamin leaning over to give his father a hug and Benzion wrapping his arms tightly around Benjamin's back. They lingered a moment, then finally parted company.

As he walked from the house, Benjamin glanced down at the ring, now in its place on his finger, and thought, *I am a Netanyahu. Son of a Netanyahu. Grandson, though many generations removed, of King David. And whether I prevail or perish, I shall go down fighting for Israel. Not the Israel of the West. And not the Israel of Herzl or Jabotinsky. But the Israel of the Netanyahus. The Israel given to us by God.*

58

NETANYAHU

WHILE THE DEBATE about Benjamin's address to the US congress raged on, an Israeli Ofek-10 satellite, stationed in a geosynchronous orbit high above the Middle East, peered down on the Iranian landscape. Since coming online the year before, the satellite had provided Mossad a steady stream of images and data from Iran, but nothing that indicated an immediate threat. Shortly before midnight, however, the satellite's onboard early warning sensors detected an unusual and anomalous burst of energy from the surface below.

Instantly, the Ofek's high-resolution radar located the burst at a spot near Qom, Iran. At the same time, its antennas locked onto multiple streams of telemetry emanating from the site. An onboard computer captured those transmissions and relayed the information to a Mossad ground station located atop Mount Meron in northern Galilee.

As the satellite went active an alarm sounded on a control panel inside the Mount Meron station. Yigal Kishon, one of the technicians who manned the station, pressed a reset switch to silence the alarm, then checked a nearby screen.

Nisim Rovina called to him from the opposite side of the room. "What do we have this time, Yigal?"

"Missile launch," Yigal replied.

"Where?"

"Iran."

"Target acquired?"

"None."

"Just another test?"

"Maybe."

Reacting to the tone of Kishon's voice, Rovina came to his side and leaned in close for a view of the panel's instruments. "Something different about this one?"

"Yeah. We've had other launches from that site, but never one big enough to trigger the satellite's sensors at the alert level."

"Better notify the base."

"Right," Kishon reached for a phone.

✦ ✦ ✦

A report of Iran's missile launch, along with accompanying information regarding the telemetry transmissions, was forwarded to Mossad headquarters in Tel Aviv. Gideon Neyman's analysts reviewed it and determined that Iran had conducted tests of a missile much larger than any they previously were known to possess.

Neyman delivered the report to Michael Eilon, the director of Mossad. Gutmann read the report and supporting information, then called Amos Megged to his office.

Gutmann tossed the report across the desk to Megged. "Take a look at this."

Megged glanced through the report, then looked up at Gutmann. "This presents a serious problem."

"I know."

"If this report is correct," Megged said, "Iran has developed a missile capable of reaching targets anywhere in the region."

"Any suggestions on how we could find out if that's really what they have?"

Megged leaned back in his chair. "We could put some men in there to have a look."

"We already have agents in-country."

Megged shook his head. "Not for this."

"Why not?"

"We've spent too much time, money, and effort getting them established and positioned to provide inside information about Iran's nuclear program. I don't want to jeopardize that long-term operation over this," he added, pointing to the report that lay on the desk.

"You think *any* agents we task with an assignment like this will be caught?"

"I think that's a definite possibility."

"I don't think we have any choice," Gutmann related. "We need to know what Iran is doing. And with the US negotiating deals with them and lifting sanctions, I don't think we can rely on them for support."

Megged smiled. "You sound like the prime minister."

"Yeah," Gutmann acknowledged. "That's because he's right. With the uranium we've already verified, Iran could build a bomb in less than two months. And I'll guarantee you," he tapped his index finger for emphasis, "that missile we detected was designed to carry a nuclear bomb."

"Okay." Megged nodded. "But don't verify that threat with the agents already there."

"Then what do you suggest?"

"Use a special team. A team that can get in and out quickly."

"An expendable team."

"A team whose capture won't destroy a network we've spent years building for other purposes."

"How many would you need?"

"Five."

"Okay. Select five agents, have them report to you, and get moving."

"Have you notified the prime minister and asked him about sending in a team?"

"That's next on my list."

"Think he'll go for it?"

"I think we may have the opposite problem."

"Holding him back?"

"Yes. But get moving with your team and have them ready to go as soon as he approves. We don't have much time to spare."

✦ ✦ ✦

That afternoon, Gutmann met with Benjamin in the prime minister's office where he laid out the images and data from the satellite indicating a missile launch from inside Iran. By the time of their meeting, analysts had decrypted key portions of the telemetry transmitted from that missile, which further supported the original conclusion—that Iran had modified one of its satellite launch vehicles to increase its range and payload capacity.

"And you think this missile launch was a test of those modifications?"

Gutmann addressed the prime minister's question, "We're certain of it. This was a version of their Simorgh satellite missile."

"Which you suggest has been further modified for use in delivering a warhead."

"Yes, Mr. Prime Minister. That appears to be what they are working toward."

"And you think that warhead might be a nuclear warhead. But you have no hard evidence to prove it."

"No, sir," Gutmann admitted. "We don't have hard evidence."

"What would it take to get that evidence?"

"We would need to place agents on the ground at the facility in Qom."

Benjamin looked up from Gutmann's written report. "You do realize how absurd that sounds?"

"I wouldn't call it absurd."

"No? What would you call it?"

"Risky."

"Extremely."

"Yes, Mr. Prime Minister. Extremely risky."

Benjamin leaned back from his desk. "Mossad already has a network of operatives working inside Iran."

"Yes."

"Why not use them?"

"Megged doesn't want to risk them. They've been a source of highly reliable information and he'd like for them to remain that way."

"Do you think we could do this? Could we put agents inside the facility and determine what the Iranians are doing?"

"We can get them into the country. And they could reasonably be expected to gain access to the facility. But there is some question about whether they could get out."

Benjamin looked perplexed. "If they can't get out with that information what good does it do us? And if they're discovered we would face an international incident. One that could easily jeopardize the recent agreement over Iran's nuclear program."

"We weren't thinking of the potential for an international incident."

"Then what were you thinking of?"

"The safety of Israel."

The comment caught Benjamin off-guard, but before he could reply Gutmann added, "We'll give them a means to send their information to us."

Benjamin looked away. "I don't know...Still a lot of risk." His voice trailed off as he stared out the window, his hands folded in his lap, his mind mulling over the options.

Without consciously thinking of it, he traced a finger over the Netanyahu ring, around and around the setting—the seal at the top—the ancient seal... And then he remembered the ring and looked down at it. "I am a Netanyahu," he whispered softly. "Son of a Netanyahu. Grandson, though many generations removed, of King David. And whether I prevail or perish, I shall go down fighting for Israel."

Gutmann had a puzzled expression. "I'm sorry, Mr. Prime Minister. I couldn't quite hear what you were saying."

Benjamin turned away from the window and looked over at him, "We have a list of the sites where Iran is hiding its highly enriched uranium?"

"Yes. We have information on the sites they disclosed to the UN and the sites they still hold in secret."

"And we have the same information for their centrifuges?"

"Yes, sir. The ones they've disclosed and the ones they have not revealed."

"And in my briefings you have told me from time to time about Iran's interest in moving some of that uranium into Lebanon, distributing it to Hezbollah."

"Yes, sir. We've heard chatter about it and we've intercepted one or two of their actual attempts."

"Any indication they've tried to use this against the US?"

"They would like to, but right now I think their primary goal is obtaining relief from the sanctions. Those sanctions have had a serious effect on their economy and on the sustainability of their military forces."

Benjamin's eyes widened in a look of realization as the situation appeared to him more clearly than ever before.

No matter what Israel did, Iran would never walk away from its agreement with the West. Iran needed that agreement. It was their way to freedom from the sanctions. Limits on uranium and centrifuges were the West's idea. Iran's goal was to obtain relief from the sanctions and now that they had it, they weren't about to let a spat with Israel over a Mossad team get in their way.

"Have you discussed this proposed operation with anyone at IDF?"

"No, sir. Not yet. I was waiting to see if—"

Benjamin cut him off with a wave of his hand. "Don't talk to them."

Gutmann frowned. "Don't tell them?"

"Get your men into the facility at Qom, get them out, and do it as quietly as possible."

"Yes, sir. But I'll have to tell IDF something. We're thinking of using one of their teams."

"Then tell them something else, but not about this."

"Yes, sir."

"And I need you to prepare a report about the sites they've disclosed and the ones they haven't. Include a few photographs of one or two of the secret sites. And include details about Iran's attempts to transfer some of the uranium to Hezbollah and the potential threats to the US."

"When do you need it?"

"Have it ready for me immediately, but don't send it until I ask for it." Benjamin stood, "Get that team in there right away."

✦ ✦ ✦

The following afternoon, Omer Weinberg, Asaf Springer, Matti Halfin, Harel Shapira, and Yishai Shorr—members of an elite IDF Hostage Response Team trained in fast, high-risk, in-and-out rescue operations—reported to Megged in a briefing room at Palmachim Air Base. In twenty minutes, he gave them a thumbnail sketch of the operation, outlining the objectives in short sentences. "Get in. Examine their test facility. Find out what they've been working on with this last missile they tested."

"Any theory about what that might be?" Weinberg asked.

"We think they've modified an existing aerospace launcher for longer, heavier service." Megged took a deep breath. "We need you in and out in a matter of days. This is an attempt to confirm or dismiss critical information. That's all. You're not conducting a long-term surveillance program."

"How many days do we have in-country?" Halfin asked.

"Not more than three."

"How much time do we have to prepare for this before we embark?" Shorr asked.

"None. You'll leave tonight. When you're on the ground, you'll proceed to a rendezvous point. Someone will meet you there and show you where to go." Gutmann glanced around the room again. "If anyone wants out, now is the time to say so. When we walk out that door, there'll be no turning back." He waited a moment longer and when still no one responded, he continued, "Very well. Weinberg, you're senior man on the team. You're in charge. Come with me for a moment. The rest of you, get your gear and gather in the day room."

✦ ✦ ✦

After a two-hour flight, Weinberg and the team landed on the desert floor east of Qom and made their way to the rendezvous point just to the east of Highway Seven. They were met there by Moshik Amdursky who arrived in a truck. He collected them and their gear, then drove them to a safe house not far from the rocket testing facility.

They were joined at the safe house by Yehoram Hendel, an agent already working in-country, who gave them information about the test site, the terrain, and a brief sketch of what they'd gleaned from the site thus far.

Using Hendel's information, Weinberg's team spent the next day observing the site from atop a hill to the east of the launch pads. That afternoon, they gathered around a table in the safe house.

Weinberg unfolded a sketch. "Okay. This is where we are right now." He pointed to a spot on the page. "Based on information passed to Mossad earlier, this is where we need to go." He tapped a square on the paper with his index finger.

"What is that?"

"The rocket assembly building."

"That's pretty far from the front gate," Shorr noted.

"We're not going through the front gate."

"Then how are we getting in there?"

Weinberg pointed to another spot on the page. "We're going through here." He traced his finger along a dark line. "Through the perimeter fence."

✦ ✦ ✦

Weinberg and his team spent the following day reviewing their assignments, preparing their gear, and napping. As darkness approached they cooked a meal and sat at a table to eat. No one talked much and as time passed they drifted off one by one to be alone.

Hendel, who'd tried to make conversation but with no success, looked over at Weinberg. "Did something happen? Did I miss something?"

Weinberg frowned. "About what?"

"Everyone seems tense. Moody. Like they're getting ready to fight."

Weinberg smiled at him. "You're very perceptive."

A frown wrinkled Hendel's forehead. "What's going on?" He stared at Weinberg a moment, then his eyes brightened in a look of realization. "You're doing it tonight?"

"As soon as the truck gets here."

"You've been here less than a week," Hendel protested. "Do you really think you're ready?"

"We're trained for this sort of thing. Get in. Learn what we need to know. Get out."

"One of the extraction teams we used to hear about? Well, just don't leave without me."

Weinberg looked surprised. "What are you talking about?"

"I'm leaving with you," Hendel said flatly.

"They didn't tell us that."

"I don't know what they told you. But I can't stay here now," Hendel explained. "If Iranian authorities noticed anything about this operation, and saw me with you, and knew that I was still here after you're gone, they would find me. And then a large portion of the permanent team would be in jeopardy. I'm leaving when you leave."

✦ ✦ ✦

That night, Weinberg's team dressed and equipped themselves as Iranian soldiers—complete with special issue Melli combat boots and Heckler & Koch G3 battle rifles—then departed from the safe house in Amdursky's truck. Half an hour later, Amdursky dropped them behind a hill that shielded them from view of anyone at the testing site.

Moving quietly and in an unhurried manner, they climbed from the truck, unloaded their gear, and stepped out of sight behind a clump of overgrown bushes. There, they wired up their personal communications equipment, tested to make certain it worked properly, then lifted their packs to their shoulders and strapped them in place.

While Weinberg led the others on foot to the east, Springer moved straight up the hill to a position along the crest—a point below the ridgeline offering the best view of the terrain below while exposing the least possible view of his body.

Lying there, out of sight of guards at the test facility, Springer shrugged his shoulders free of the backpack and took out a laptop. He rested it on the ground beside him, pressed the power button, and waited as it came to life. When the operating software was booted into place, he scanned the airways for an active network. In a matter of seconds, he located one operated by the military unit guarding the test facility. With little effort, he hacked his way into the network and wormed inside the test site's security system. Moments later, he took control of the security cameras positioned along the fence at the east side of the property.

Using security cameras on that side of the facility and a video program on his laptop, Springer recorded images from along the fence, located the affected monitors in the front gate guardhouse, and placed them on a continuous video playback loop showing the video he'd just created. Anyone checking the monitor would see only images from the video loop, not actual images from the fence. When Springer finished, he closed the laptop lid to hide the screen, and shifted his position to lie on his stomach near the crest of the ridge.

A few minutes later, Springer caught sight of Weinberg and the others as they approached, moving toward the perimeter fence on that side. Not long after that, Weinberg's voice came from the earbud in Springer's ear. "How are we doing?"

"The fence is ours." Springer answered.

"Roger," Weinberg replied.

Working with speed and precision, Weinberg and the men with him cut through the fence, crossed to the other side, and then secured the severed ends to make the hole less obvious.

"Which way?" Weinberg asked.

From his position atop the hill to the south, Springer directed, "To your right."

Weinberg and his team made their way in that direction, moving along the lee of an electrical substation to the corner opposite a single-story building. They paused there, checking to make certain they had not been spotted.

"Okay," Weinberg radioed. "Help me out."

"The building should be in front of you," Springer replied.

The space between the electrical substation and the building was open and unprotected, offering Weinberg and his men an option. They could crouch low and cross the open space like intruders attempting to infiltrate a secure facility, or they could walk in standing fully upright, heads high, as if they were supposed to be there. Weinberg chose the latter and led the team toward the single-story building with a patient and deliberate gait.

Entrance to the building was guarded by a steel door that was locked securely. A placard affixed to the door identified it as Building One Three Eight and there was a keypad mounted to the right of the door facing.

Weinberg studied the keypad a moment, then said, "Talk to me."

"That's the one you want," Springer replied.

"Get me inside."

Springer hunched over the laptop and checked to make certain he was still connected to the front gate's wireless network and that no one had discovered his presence. Satisfied that everything was in order, he scrolled through a directory file in the perimeter security program, then located a list of buildings. The list included corresponding entry codes for each building and he scrolled down to the one for Building One Three Eight.

"Five, three, eight, nine," Springer transmitted.

Weinberg entered the numbers on the keypad and waited. The delay was longer than he expected but finally the lock clicked. He pulled open the door and led the way inside.

A hall led toward the center of the building with offices opening from it. Near the center they found an elevator and next to it was a doorway to a stairwell that led beneath the ground floor.

"Should be an elevator near you," Springer prodded.

Weinberg adjusted the earbud in his ear. "Right," he stepped into the elevator and motioned for the others to follow.

Inside the elevator, a panel indicated there were four levels beneath the ground floor. Weinberg checked to make sure everyone was onboard, then pressed the button for the next floor below them and they slowly descended one level.

When they reached the next floor, the elevator's doors opened to a large, immaculately clean room with high ceilings and starkly bright florescent lighting. In the center of the room were three Rodong missiles, each positioned atop individual carriage chassis designed to make movement of the missiles an easy and quiet task.

Weinberg glanced around, then led the way from the elevator for a closer inspection of the room. His men spread out around the missiles, examining each one.

About fifteen meters long and one meter wide, the missiles were each powered by a single engine. The engine compartment, however, was empty on each one, as was the payload compartment in the nose cone.

After a cursory check of the room, Weinberg indicated by hand signals for Halfin and Shapira to remain there while he and Shorr continued down to the next floor below. Shapira and Halfin nodded and waited while Weinberg and Shorr made their way toward the elevator.

When Weinberg and Shorr were gone, Halfin removed a camera from the side pocket of his pack and began taking pictures of the missiles, being careful to include multiple images of the empty compartments. Shapira took a measuring tape and small notepad from the utility pocket of his pants and began measuring the missiles' dimensions.

Although the size of the room and its location underground was overwhelming, nothing seemed particularly alarming about the situation until Halfin noticed a doorway beyond the third missile. He tapped Shapira on the shoulder and pointed toward it, signaling by hand that they should check it out. Shapira considered the idea a moment, then shrugged his shoulders and agreed.

Ignoring the missiles for a moment, they made their way over to the door and cautiously turned the knob, then eased it open. Both men stood motionless at what they saw.

Beyond the door was a room even larger than the first and in it was a Qoqnoos SLV satellite launcher—one of the missiles used by the Iranian Space Agency to place its satellites into orbit. The missile lay on a transporter that would take it to the launch pad and like the missiles in the other room, the payload compartment of the Qoqnoos was open and empty.

While they stood there, gawking at the missile's size, Weinberg and Shorr approached behind them. Weinberg watched a moment from over Halfin's shoulder, then nudged him forward. Shapira and Shorr followed and all four men circled the missile in silence, taking pictures as they went.

Suddenly, the silence of the room was broken by the sound of an electric motor as it whirred to full speed. For an instant, the men froze in place. Then Shorr leaned close to Weinberg and gestured toward the doorway that led back to the room from which they'd come.

"Elevator," Shorr whispered.

Weinberg looked in that direction. Through the doorway, the elevator located on the opposite side of the first room was plainly visible. Above the elevator doors was a series of numbers from one to four. By then, the others had noticed the elevator, too, and they all watched together as the elevator car passed the first level and continued to the bottom.

When the moment passed, Weinberg waved for them to follow and started toward the door. Moving hurriedly, he led them back the way they'd come. Past the Qoqnoos, across to the door, and into the first room.

As they reached the three Rodong rockets the elevator motor came to life again, this time lifting the elevator car a single level from fourth to third.

"What do we do now?" Halfin asked, no longer whispering.

Next to the elevator was a door. A sign on it indicated it led to a stairwell. Shorr pointed to it. "I vote for the stairs."

"Too obvious," Weinberg warned. "That would be the first place they'd look for us."

"Hey, speaking of which," Shapira said. "Anybody notice there's no one down here?"

"Must be someone or the—"

The sound of voices coming from the other room interrupted them and seconds later three men came into view near the Qoqnoos.

"We gotta get out of here," Weinberg whispered.

In two strides he reached the stairwell door and pulled it open. The others followed him inside and started up the stairs toward the top. But as they moved toward the first landing, the door at the top opened and in the light that streamed through the doorway they saw armed Iranian soldiers. Weinberg hesitated with his next step. *Too late to shoot,* he thought. *And retreating would make us look guilty. No way forward but to go deeper in.*

"All clear," Weinberg spoke out in Persian. "We've come up from four and haven't seen a thing."

Just then, the door below on the first level opened and additional soldiers entered the stairwell. Someone called out, "Take them alive! We want them alive and able to talk."

59

NETANYAHU

TWO WEEKS LATER, accompanied by his wife, Sara, and members of his staff, Benjamin traveled to New York where he met with key Jewish organizations in an attempt to defuse the argument over his decision to accept Congress' invitation. From there, he traveled to Chicago, then on to Los Angeles, and back through Dallas before finally arriving in Washington, DC.

As he suggested to Geller, Benjamin kept lobbying to a minimum, meeting only with Muhlenberg and Arthur Tilson, the Republican whip. Instead of working Capitol Hill, he spent two days in the presidential suite at the Mayflower Hotel working on his speech, emerging only for dinner at a restaurant in Georgetown.

In the afternoon before his speech, Benjamin took a nap, ate a light meal, and read through his speech one last time. By then it was all but committed to memory and the thought briefly fluttered through his mind of delivering it without reference to the prepared text. Then, just as quickly, he dismissed the idea. This was the Congress of the United States, not a social club, and he was a head of state, not an entertainer. The text of the speech needed to be tight, clear, and concise, which it was, and his delivery needed to be formal, but not stiff. The text would provide the formality. He would make sure it wasn't stiff.

As afternoon gave way to evening, Benjamin showered, then dressed in a business suit and prepared for the ride over to Capitol Hill. Sara, who'd been getting ready in an adjoining room, joined him in the sitting area of their suite. With time to spare, they sat together on a sofa and savored their cups of coffee.

Thirty minutes later, Geller arrived to review the evening's events and then the three of them, accompanied by a security detail, rode in the elevator downstairs to the lobby. A black Cadillac limousine awaited them and soon they were on their way.

When they arrived at the Capitol, they were greeted by John Muhlenberg and the Senate Majority Leader. They ushered Benjamin and Sara inside the building and down a broad corridor to a bank of elevators. Doors for the one in the center were open and a guard was stationed inside. The Netanyahus entered with their detail and a moment later, the elevator ascended to the floors above.

Muhlenberg led Benjamin to an office suite located just off the House chamber. An aide showed Sara to her seat in the gallery.

A few minutes later, the Sergeant at Arms of the House collected Benjamin and escorted him to the entrance of the House Chamber. As the Speaker gaveled the Congress into a joint session, assistants pushed open the doors and Benjamin entered, making his way down the aisle to the right of the House well. He was greeted by thunderous applause and forced to move slowly as members reached out to shake hands, to share a word with him, and to make certain their faces appeared in photographs and videos of his arrival.

When he finally reached the well he made his way around to the rostrum where he greeted the Speaker and the Senate Minority Leader who were seated behind him. Applause continued a while longer as Benjamin turned to face the audience, waving to those whom he knew. Then, as the applause began to fade, he turned to the speech at hand.

"My friends," he began, his voice strong and full, "I'm deeply humbled by the opportunity to speak for a third time before the most important legislative body in the world, the United States Congress."

"I want to thank you all for being here today," he continued. "I know that my speech has been the subject of much controversy. I deeply regret that some perceive my being here as political. That was never my intention. I want to thank you, Democrats and Republicans alike, for your common support for Israel, year after year, decade after decade."

For the next forty-five minutes, Benjamin delivered a speech that was devoted to denouncing the agreement with Iran, a view that knowingly placed him in disagreement with President Obama and members of his administration, but which did so in a manner that seemed more like the complaint of one friend to another. Clearly, he wanted it to seem that way for, indeed, Israel was very dependent on the United States, particularly for military assistance. No one in Israel wanted to damage that arrangement.

Nor did he, as some had worried, disclose routine classified information shared with him by US intelligence agencies, some of which bore directly on the points he attempted to make regarding Iran's nuclear program. He also refrained from sharing similar information about Iran's missile program which had been supplied to him by Mossad and regarding which he'd sent the Mossad team to Iran's missile facility at Qom—a team that now was long overdue.

And he avoided confronting Jewish advocacy groups over their failure to stress Palestinian disregard for Israeli human rights, even while denouncing those Israelis for protecting their homes in the West Bank.

In fact, a listener who heard the speech without preconception might easily ask, "What was all the ruckus about?" And, indeed, that might be just the question that needed answering most, but one which politicians hoped to avoid. They needed the apparent polarity the "ruckus" had presented as a campaign tool—for House seats in the US and Knesset seats in Israel. And by that analysis, the speech was a roaring success, giving everyone precisely what they needed.

✦ ✦ ✦

After delivering the speech, Benjamin and Sara made their way down to the lower level of the capitol building and out to the limousine. An assistant held the door as they slid into the rear seat of the car, glad for a moment to relax before a round of social engagements later that evening.

Just before the motorcade departed, the car door opened once more and Geller appeared. Sara frowned at the disruption but Geller ignored her and turned to Benjamin.

"Sorry to interrupt, Mr. Prime Minister."

"What is it?"

"We have to stop at the embassy."

"It wasn't on the schedule," Benjamin replied.

"No, sir. It wasn't."

"Has something happened?"

Geller glanced first to Sara then back to Benjamin with a knowing look. "We have a problem."

"What kind of problem?"

"We can talk about it at the embassy."

"Why the embassy?"

"They have a SCIF," Geller answered.

Benjamin turned to Sara. "Someone can take you to the hotel."

"Will it take long?" she asked.

"I don't know." He leaned over and gave her a kiss. "I'll get there as soon as I can."

Geller escorted Sara to a second limo, then returned to Benjamin's side.

✦ ✦ ✦

Ten minutes later, the prime minister's motorcade reached the Israeli embassy. Benjamin and Geller exited the car and hurried inside. The ambassador was waiting and led them downstairs. "We're ready for you down here."

"Good," Benjamin replied. "Sorry to drop in like this."

At the bottom of the steps a corridor led to the left and at the end was the door to the SCIF—the Sensitive Compartmented Information Facility—capable of handling intelligence information at the highest level.

Halfway down the corridor Geller grabbed Benjamin and pulled him into the men's room. "What are you doing?" Benjamin protested.

"We have reports Iran is holding five men they claim were part of a Mossad team captured at a missile test site."

Benjamin's eyes darted away. "Mossad?"

"Yes."

"What missile site?"

"A rocket development center near Qom. They say—" A look of realization came over Geller. "What were they doing there?"

Benjamin avoided his gaze. "Why are you asking me?"

"Because I can tell—you already knew about this."

Benjamin stepped back and straightened his jacket. "Believe it or not, there are some things I can't tell even you."

Geller frowned. "You really knew about this mission?"

"Do you think," Benjamin began in an exasperated tone, "that I would come to the US to speak to Congress, in opposition to a policy their president supports while, at the same time, sending a Mossad team into Iran?"

Geller smiled. "I think that's *exactly* what you would do if you thought you could get away with it."

Benjamin patted Geller on the shoulder. "Yes. You would think that. But you know me better than most." He reached for the door. "Now come on, before my security detail comes in here looking for us."

✦ ✦ ✦

Thirty minutes later, Benjamin walked to the top of the steps on the first floor. He held a manila envelope. Geller was seated nearby and stood as Benjamin approached.

"Tell me something," Benjamin began with a twinkle in his eye. "Why do the heathen rage and the people imagine a vain thing?"

"Psalms?" Geller rolled his eyes. "We're quoting from the Psalms now?"

Benjamin began again, this time in a serious voice. "Why do the heathen rage and the people imagine a vain thing? The kings of the earth set themselves and the rulers take counsel together against the Lord, and against his anointed, saying, 'Let us break their bands asunder and cast away their cords from us. He that sits in the heavens shall laugh: the Lord shall have them in derision. Then shall he speak to them in his wrath and vex them with sore displeasure. Yet have I set my king upon my holy hill of Zion."

Geller smiled. "What kind of meeting did you have down there? I know it wasn't one of Begin's Torah classes."

"It was a government meeting. Just a government meeting."

"And how much do we know about the situation now?"

"About as much as we knew before."

Geller followed him out to the car and they both got in back. As they departed the embassy compound, Geller looked over at Benjamin. "Okay, are you going to tell me what happened back there?"

"Not much to tell," Benjamin replied. "We sent a Mossad team into a missile test site at Qom. They were discovered and captured."

"Are they still alive?"

"Yes." Benjamin gazed out the window. "They are for now."

"You seem remarkably untroubled," Geller noted.

"Iran is threatening to walk away from the agreement."

"Over this? Over our team that they captured?"

"Yes."

"Why?" Geller asked. "We are not a party to the agreement."

"That's exactly what I told President Obama."

Geller looked confused. "President Obama?"

"I talked to him a few minutes ago."

"What did he say?"

"He's angry."

"Over what?"

"He thinks I staged the speech tonight and the Mossad team in Iran as a desperate attempt to derail the agreement."

"And what did you tell him?"

"That we had proof Iran was cheating, right from the beginning."

"We have that proof?"

Benjamin held up the envelope. "Right here in my hands."

"Will he take a look at our information?"

"We're on our way over there now." Benjamin looked at Geller with a mischievous smile. "The Americans are now talking about walking away from the agreement."

"But I thought they were in *favor* of the agreement."

"They were, until I told him about the evidence we had."

"And now?"

"Now they're not so sure." Benjamin gestured again with the envelope. "We have pictures of Iran cheating. Moving their twenty percent uranium to undisclosed sites. Information about their missile tests. And information about their attempts to transfer some of it to Lebanon. I think America will have a change of mind."

"Lebanon?" Geller had a troubled look. "I didn't know about that."

"I know."

"And this will work, just like that?"

"America is big, but America can be moved by a single well-placed lever."

"And the contents of that envelope are the lever?"

"Yes, the things in this envelope, along with information from the missile test. That will just about do it."

Geller looked confused again. "What missile test?"

"Don't worry about it," Benjamin said with a dismissive gesture of his hand.

"And what if it doesn't work? What if the information we have doesn't provide the leverage we need? What if Iran comes after us and the US won't help?"

Benjamin ran his finger over the Netanyahu ring and smiled at Geller. "Relax. Iran isn't going to walk away from the agreement. They need it too much. And the US isn't going to let them kill our men, because if they do, we'll start blowing things up."

"Then why send those men in there at all?"

"Because we are Israelis," Benjamin answered. "Our enemies are not from another continent, separated from us by a wide ocean. They live right next door and we must never let them forget that we are bolder, more courageous, more resourceful than they."

"So this was just about a show of strength?"

"It's always about a show of strength."

"You risked them for that?"

Before Benjamin could answer, the car turned into the driveway at the White House. A guard waved them past the gate and they rolled quietly around to the West Wing entrance. When they came to a stop, a doorman opened the car door and Benjamin stepped out. As he started toward the building's entrance he turned the ring with his fingers so that he could feel the seal against his thumb.

"I am Benjamin Netanyahu," he whispered in a voice audible only to himself. "Brother of Jonathan and son of Benzion Netanyahu. Grandson of Nathan Mileikowsky and, though many generations removed, a son of David. And whether I prevail or perish, I shall go down fighting for Israel. Not the Israel of the West. And not the Israel of Herzl or Jabotinsky. But the Israel of the Netanyahus. The Israel given to us by God."

ACKNOWLEDGMENT

My deepest gratitude and sincere thanks to my writing partner, Joe Hilley, and to my executive assistant, Lanelle Shaw-Young, both of whom work diligently to assist me with turning my story ideas into great books. And to Arlen Young and Peter Glöege for making the finished product look and read its best. And to my wife, Carolyn, whose presence always makes everything better.

MICHAEL DAVID EVANS, the #1 *New York Times* bestselling author, is an award-winning journalist/Middle East analyst. Dr. Evans has appeared on hundreds of network television and radio shows including *Good Morning America, Crossfire* and *Nightline*, and *The Rush Limbaugh Show*, and on Fox Network, *CNN World News*, NBC, ABC, and CBS. His articles have been published in the *Wall Street Journal, USA Today, Washington Times, Jerusalem Post* and newspapers worldwide. More than twenty-five million copies of his books are in print, and he is the award-winning producer of nine documentaries based on his books.

Dr. Evans is considered one of the world's leading experts on Israel and the Middle East, and is one of the most sought-after speakers on that subject. He is the chairman of the board of the Ten Boom Holocaust Museum in Haarlem, Holland, and is the founder of Israel's first Christian museum—Friends of Zion: Heroes and History—in Jerusalem.

Dr. Evans has authored a number of books including: *History of Christian Zionism, Showdown with Nuclear Iran, Atomic Iran, The Next Move Beyond Iraq, The Final Move Beyond Iraq*, and *Countdown*. His body of work also includes the novels *Seven Days, GameChanger, The Samson Option, The Four Horsemen, The Locket, Born Again: 1967,* and *The Columbus Code.*

✦ ✦ ✦

Michael David Evans is available to speak or for interviews. Contact: EVENTS@drmichaeldevans.com.

BOOKS BY: MIKE EVANS

Israel: America's Key to Survival

Save Jerusalem

The Return

Jerusalem D.C.

Purity and Peace of Mind

Who Cries for the Hurting?

Living Fear Free

I Shall Not Want

Let My People Go

Jerusalem Betrayed

Seven Years of Shaking: A Vision

The Nuclear Bomb of Islam

Jerusalem Prophecies

Pray For Peace of Jerusalem

America's War:
The Beginning of the End

The Jerusalem Scroll

The Prayer of David

The Unanswered Prayers of Jesus

God Wrestling

The American Prophecies

Beyond Iraq: The Next Move

The Final Move beyond Iraq

Showdown with Nuclear Iran

Jimmy Carter: The Liberal Left
and World Chaos

Atomic Iran

Cursed

Betrayed

The Light

Corrie's Reflections & Meditations

The Revolution

The Final Generation

Seven Days

The Locket

Persia: The Final Jihad

GAMECHANGER SERIES:

GameChanger

Samson Option

The Four Horsemen

THE PROTOCOLS SERIES:

The Protocols

The Candidate

Jerusalem

The History of Christian Zionism

Countdown

Ten Boom: Betsie, Promise of God

Commanded Blessing

Born Again: 1948

Born Again: 1967

Presidents in Prophecy

Stand with Israel

Prayer, Power and Purpose

Turning Your Pain Into Gain

Christopher Columbus, Secret Jew

Living in the F.O.G.

Finding Favor with God

Finding Favor with Man

Unleashing God's Favor

The Jewish State: The Volunteers

See You in New York

Friends of Zion: Patterson & Wingate

The Columbus Code

The Temple

Satan, You Can't Have My Country!

Satan, You Can't Have Israel!

Lights in the Darkness

The Seven Feasts of Israel

Netanyahu

TO PURCHASE, CONTACT: orders@timeworthybooks.
com P. O. BOX 30000, PHOENIX, AZ 85046